THE MAN WHO RODE MIDNIGHT

The Man Who Rode Midnight

ELMER KELTON

DOUBLEDAY & COMPANY, INC.
GARDEN CITY, NEW YORK
1987

Library of Congress Cataloging-in-Publication Data

Kelton, Elmer.
The man who rode midnight.

I. Title.
PS3563.A2932M3   1987   813'.54   87-528
ISBN 0-385-24020-1

To my mother, Bea Kelton . . .

who has lived on ranches for eighty-odd years,
and made every one of them a better place.

THE MAN WHO RODE MIDNIGHT

Chapter 1

As the long asphalt miles rumbled monotonously beneath the wheels of the bus, Jim Ed Hendrix watched the green, rolling contours of the Dallas suburbs surrender gradually to the sparser, browner vegetation of Central Texas and finally to the ragged gray limestone outcrops of the western hill country. The engine labored noisily to climb, then the gears groaned as they struggled to hold against the long, steep descents that followed. Jim Ed frowned at the faint odor of diesel smoke. The hamburger he had grabbed while the bus idled briefly at noonday lay heavy and cold on his stomach, like one of those broken white stones lying in random profusion at the foot of each deep, scarred slash where hungry jaws of highway builders' machinery had gnawed passageway through a challenging hill.

About now, he thought glumly, *Jack and David are starting their walking tour of Europe. I ought to be with them.*

In the seat beside him, a pudgy, red-faced little man in his sixties slipped a pint bottle from the pocket of a frayed and rumpled business coat, ducked his head and took a nip. His sharp grimace suggested that the whisky brought enough pain to compensate any Puritan conscience that might find moral fault in pleasure. He looked up quickly to see if the driver's mirror might have betrayed the transgression. Jim Ed had declined an earlier offer of the bottle. He had no prejudice against whisky, but he had some reservations about secondhand spittle.

The little man said, "It shortens the miles."

Jim Ed frowned at the window and the blue-shadowed hills which stretched endlessly, one and then another, into the afternoon sun. "*Nothing* shortens the miles out here." With his pocketknife he cleaned his fingernails for the tenth time.

The man, who had said he was retired after forty-some years of breaking his back in the oil fields to enrich a few Houston millionaires, patted the bottle affectionately as he might a favored dog. Jim Ed wished he had chosen another seat, but the oil fielder had frowned upon the several Mexicans and a tired old black man who held the others, and upon a heavy set white woman whose challenging glare would wilt Johnsongrass. He had plumped himself down beside Jim Ed as the least objectionable of the available choices.

The whisky smell strong on his breath, he turned for a long look at Jim Ed's rock-music T-shirt, a sick-purple color with a garish decal extolling heavy metal. He asked, "Are you a yippie or a yuppie or a preppie, or what?"

Jim Ed did not feel like smiling but let a small one escape in spite of himself. He doubted the oil fielder knew one of the terms from another. "None of the above. I'm a brain surgeon."

The little man sniffed. "Whatever you are, you don't look like somebody that goes to a jerkwater town like Big River."

"It's not my town," Jim Ed declared defensively. "It's my grandfather's."

"You come out of Houston, I'll bet."

"Dallas."

"Same thing. They're all a trap for the workin' man. You're on vacation from college for the summer, I'd guess, or just out of a job." His tone implied a right to know.

"A little of both," Jim Ed acknowledged, torn between his relief at soon getting away from his talkative companion and his reluctance over facing that faded town for which his few visits over the years had never developed any affection. The oil fielder rattled on in exhaustive particulars about his trip to the veterans' hospital and the operation he had enjoyed there. When he wore out that subject, he proceeded into similar detail about the greatest event of an otherwise colorless life, his participation in World

War II. Staring wearily out the window at the passing miles of cedar and liveoak trees, grazing cattle, sheep and silver-fleeced Angora goats, Jim Ed nodded noncommittally from time to time. That was the only response necessary to encourage the monologue's happy flow. World War II had ended most of twenty years before Jim Ed was born. His interest in history was but little stronger than his interest in this pensioner's gallstones.

The veteran told of roughnecking on a wildcat drilling crew around Big River after the war. "We punched holes all over, and we got nothin' but dust in our eyes. Except for the scenery, there ain't nothin' but rocks and goats and rattlesnakes. This country could *use* some oil wells."

He reached for the bottle but changed his mind. He would probably wait until the driver was out of the bus. He warned, "Any lease hound ever tries to sell you an oil interest around this place, you run like hell."

Jim Ed shook his head. He was unlikely ever to be in the market for an oil lease, at Big River or anywhere else. The money in his pocket would hardly buy him a change of clothes.

The oil fielder pointed. "This hill country's a feast for the eyes even if it's a famine for the pocket. I wisht you'd look at that high bluff yonder. Ain't many places in Texas can show you a dropoff as wild as that. But you can't eat scenery."

Jim Ed gave only a grunt for a reply. His late Grandmother Maudie had told him once that the high brooding cliff was called Lover's Leap. Several similar places were scattered across Texas, each bearing its own localized story about a star crossed Indian boy and girl of opposite warring tribes who joined hands and leaped to their deaths in the cold, deep river below. He doubted that Indians had ever passed on such a legend to the white settlers who were driving them out of their homeland; they had been too busy shooting at each other to swap sentimental stories of blighted romance. The yarn probably owed more to Romeo and Juliet than to Comanche or Apache. But a spectacular landmark deserved a spectacular legend. That was what chambers of commerce were invented for.

The bus slowed, black diesel smoke thickening in its wake. He read the freshly painted billboard welcoming travelers to Big

River, Texas, SOON TO BE YOUR HEADQUARTERS FOR LONE STAR LAKE, THE FISHERMAN'S PARADISE. It further declared:
IF YOU LIVED HERE, YOU WOULD BE HOME NOW!

His garrulous companion said, "Well, then, I reckon you're home."

Jim Ed grimaced, thinking of Jack and David backpacking somewhere in France. He would have been with them if things hadn't come unraveled during what was to have been his final semester at the university. Now he was stuck with *this* place, and a grandfather who was almost a stranger to him.

The first houses at the edge of the town had the appearance of having outlived their time and any owner interest in maintenance. One roof sagged in the center, and an old washing machine shared its badly weathered front porch with a ruined couch, its cotton stuffing showing through bleached-out upholstery.

Traffic was modest except near a set of steel and wooden corrals and a long cement-tile building whose plain front bore a sign: BIG RIVER LIVESTOCK AUCTION. CATTLE, SHEEP, GOATS AND HORSES EVERY FRIDAY.

This was Friday. Jim Ed observed without relish a conglomeration of pickups, trailers, automobiles and trucks parked haphazardly all over a large open lot. The weekly auction in rural towns was a social event for ranchers and farmers. Over the roar of the engine he heard cattle bawling. Jim Ed rubbed his nose as he fancied the smell of dust, of drying manure, of ammonia-laden urine steaming in the sun. The bus driver braked suddenly to avoid collision with a dented pickup ponderously making a left-hand turn into a line of vehicles waiting to unload trailers of livestock. The driver declared impatiently that what this town needed more than a new lake was a hard-nosed highway patrolman who would make these farmers learn to drive or stay the hell off the road.

Big River's passenger and freight load did not justify a regular bus station. The driver pulled in front of the Levitt drugstore and parallel-parked in a yellow-painted space. He called, "Big River!" The wide front door opened with a hiss.

The oil fielder stood up to free Jim Ed from imprisonment in the window seat. Jim Ed reached overhead for a small canvas bag and a tiny hat that sported a small tuft of green feathers. Its brim was smaller even than the kind worn by Dallas Cowboys coach Tom Landry. Its urban conservatism—yuppie, he would call it—was in violent contradiction to his T-shirt and his rubber-soled running shoes.

The little man warned, "You better watch out for them Big River goat herders and cedar choppers. They may make you eat that jellybean hat."

Jim Ed said, "I'm a survivor." The contrast between his hat and the rest of his clothing had occasioned comment even on a campus accustomed to student eccentricity. That was the way he wanted it; just *let* them try to figure him out. The hat and T-shirt combination was a statement, a proclamation to whomever it might concern that he danced to his own music.

Ahead of him in the aisle a well-fleshed Mexican woman of middle age carried a suitcase she had not trusted attendants to check for her. She stepped down to an animated reunion with three nearly grown children and a short, dark man Jim Ed took to be her husband. All tried to hug her at once and flung a dozen questions without granting time for an answer. It struck Jim Ed odd that they all spoke English to her, not Spanish. The times were changing.

He stood in the open door, waiting for the family to clear the way. His glance cut to a tall, broad-shouldered man on whose shirt a tiny silver badge flashed a quick reflection of sunlight. The man was watching the family.

Sourly Jim Ed thought, *It'd be like some redneck country sheriff to roust the whole bunch just for being Mexicans.*

But the sheriff touched his fingers to the broad brim of a Western hat. "Welcome home, Serafina. How's the new grandbaby?"

This was the eighties, and times *were* changing, Jim Ed decided. Or perhaps it was just the vote. The man's smile appeared to be forced.

The woman gave the lawman a full and eager description, probably much more than he cared to know. The sheriff's gaze fastened suspiciously upon Jim Ed. It was a look Jim Ed had encountered before, usually preceding an unpleasant introduction to some officer who regarded youth as an automatic violation of one statute or another. He nervously flexed his fingers while the driver opened the baggage compartment low on the side of the bus. Jim Ed's skin prickled as he waited to retrieve his suitcase. He looked impatiently up and down the street. His grandfather was purposely letting him sweat a little, he thought.

Some wines mellowed with age. Others soured to vinegar. Wes Hendrix had always been contrary.

The sheriff moved close enough that he could have taken Jim Ed by the arm, looking at him as if he suspected he might be a pimp or a dope pusher. "Your bus'll be leavin' in a minute."

Jim Ed's stomach drew into a knot. He wished he had left that hamburger in the steamy little bus-station café where he had found it. "My grandfather's supposed to meet me here."

The sheriff frowned. "You don't look like anybody I know. Who's your granddaddy?"

Jim Ed saw a mud-streaked green pickup pull in against the curb across the street. Of a venerable age itself, it drew a four-wheel gooseneck livestock trailer from which much of the original paint had weathered away to leave the dull brown color of rust. A thin, angular old man in faded blue shirt and khaki pants stepped stiffly down into the street. He squinted against the sun and flipped away what was left of a cigarette. His gaze searched the front of the drugstore twice before it settled on Jim Ed with evident reluctance. The old man seemed to consider a moment before he hobbled across the street with a stubborn dignity that did not permit his yielding to the traffic.

Feeling a measure of relief, Jim Ed nodded in the old man's direction. "That's him."

The sheriff seemed displeased. "Wes Hendrix? You don't much favor *that* old reprobate. You must be Truman's boy." He started to turn away but paused. "Them clothes are apt to get you into a fight around here. Especially that hat. I don't like fightin' in my town." He gave Wes Hendrix a cool look, then moved on without speaking to him. The old man returned the look in kind, watching the sheriff walk into the brick-fronted drugstore. Jim Ed wondered what his grandfather had done to put himself crossways with the local constabulary.

Wes Hendrix took off a stained, misshapen rancher hat and rubbed a sleeve across his sweaty forehead. Jim Ed tensed under the pressure of unyielding gray eyes that appraised him like an unbroken colt and seemed to find him wanting. He had never been able to please his grandfather much; he had never discerned Wes's standards of excellence.

"Howdy, Tater," the old man said, finally.

Jim Ed waited in vain for Wes to offer him a hug, or even a handshake. He did not want to make the first move, so no move was made. He said, "They call me Jim Ed now."

"You used to answer to *Tater.* Was you havin' words with Wally Vincent?"

"Who?"

"The sheriff."

"He just welcomed me to town, is all."

The old man grunted, his expression saying he knew better.

Jim Ed remarked, "He didn't seem to like *your* looks any better."

"His wife inherited the ranch next to mine on the upriver side. He ain't been happy with me lately." Wes pointed his chin disapprovingly at Jim Ed's canvas bag. "Is that all the suitcase you got?"

The driver had finally set the other on the sidewalk. Jim Ed retrieved it.

Wes Hendrix continued to study him critically, from the hat to the T-shirt and down to the running shoes. "Reason I'm late, I had to drop a couple of calves off at the auction. I can spare the time if you want to buy yourself a decent hat."

Jim Ed's face warmed. "This one will do."

The old man frowned. "I hope you didn't pay much for it."

Jim Ed felt a rising disappointment and sense of pity. As a boy, on the rare occasions when he had seen his grandfather, he had thought him a strange, overpowering figure seven feet tall, a personification of the cowboy heroes on television. This Wes Hendrix was a wizened old man, half a head shorter than his grandson. His shoulders were bent, and his stubbled face looked more like Gabby Hayes than John Wayne. He had whisky on his breath, like the oil fielder on the bus.

Jim Ed had been given scant opportunity ever to become well acquainted with his grandfather. The few times he had visited his grandparents' little ranch during his boyhood had been largely his mother's doing, her sense of family duty and propriety overcoming the fact that an antagonism more formidable than a stone wall stood between Wes Hendrix and son Truman, Jim Ed's father. Grandmother Maudie used to visit Dallas a couple of times a year, but Wes had seldom come with her. When he did, he had paced the floor like a caged cat and always left earlier than intended. On the rare occasions when Jim Ed's father had reluctantly accompanied his family to his boyhood home, he had seemed likely to break out with hives and was grateful to see the place in his rearview mirror.

As Jim Ed studied this somber face, sun-punished and leathered and creased, he knew he had little in common with Wes Hendrix except the blood and the name.

Damn Jack and David, he thought.

From the direction of the bank across the street, Jim Ed recognized the druggist, Orville Levitt, striding briskly toward them, a small canvas cash bag in his hand. His quick step belied the fact that he was as old as Wes Hendrix. He had given Jim Ed an ice cream cone fifteen years ago when Wes had gone into his store to buy liniment. He had been mayor of this dubious metropolis then, and probably still was. Jim Ed thought he recalled his grandfather saying they had punched cattle together a long time ago. The friendship must have gone sour, because Levitt managed only a civil and distant "Wes," and nodded a small acknowledgment.

Wes Hendrix nodded back. "Orv." His eyes softened with a transient sadness, then cut away as the druggist entered the store. The old man started into the street. A car's brakes groaned, but Wes continued his slow and methodical pace. Jim Ed waited for the car to move on, then proceeded around his grandfather's pickup.

He could only guess how long ago Wes had bought the vehicle, probably the last year cattle had paid a decent profit to the men who raised them. That had been a long time. The front was battered more than a little, the bumper scarred by brush and rocks and God knew what else that got in the way of a driver seventy-seven years old. Jim Ed placed the suitcase and the canvas bag in the pickup bed on top of several empty tow-sacks to which green crumbs of cottonseed feed still clung amid a settling of dust and dried, curled leaves garnered as Wes had driven across his pastures, making his own road wherever he went. Jim Ed gripped the door handle and pondered the prudence of offering to drive.

His grandfather started the engine, as if he had read the thought and rejected it. Jim Ed shoved aside a coiled rope and a bridle to make room on the seat. He had to move an assortment of stock medicine, wire pinchers and general working tools to make footroom on the floor. He bumped his head on a rifle racked against the rear window.

"What's that for?" he asked.

His grandfather replied in a gravelly voice, "You never know when you may run into a son of a bitch that needs shootin'." Wes reached down protectively to retrieve a bottle, around which a brown paper sack was tightly twisted. Jim Ed slammed the door twice before it caught; it had been sprung by some mischance suffered in the line of duty.

Wes started to pull out into the street, stopping only after an insistent honking he could not ignore. A livestock truck roared around him, trailing smoke and dust. "I'll drive," he said. "You city boys spook me."

The window was streaked where a recent light shower had tracked through the heavy layer of old dust. Jim Ed rolled it down so he could see out. He saw little that had changed since he had come for his grandmother's funeral two years ago. Like most small towns too far from the city to profit from urban employment, this one looked like last year's vine dying on the trellis. Ranches and farms were no longer enough to keep a rural town's blood pumping. There might be a couple more vacated buildings on the courthouse square; he was sure he remembered a small grocery store in a stone structure now boarded up by weathered plywood sheets. An abandoned theater's marquee threatened to slump onto the sidewalk. Ironically, a sign in the adjoining window advertised video cassettes for rent.

"Wonder the place hasn't *all* died," he commented, feeling no particular sense of loss. His few visits to the town had been mercifully short.

Wes Hendrix grunted and thrust out his left arm to signal a turn; he never had converted to directional lights. "A lot of them are holdin' on, hopin' the lake'll make them rich." He said *lake* like a cussword.

Wes Hendrix had been spare of flesh all his life, but now he looked even thinner than Jim Ed had remembered him. Like many old cowboys living in a batch camp, he probably subsisted more on black coffee than on solid food since the death of his wife. And maybe whisky, judging by his breath. The best thing that could happen to him, Jim Ed reasoned, was that he move to town and settle into a steady diet of somebody else's cooking. That was one thing about which Jim Ed's father was right.

Jim Ed said, "Dad believes they're going to condemn your ranch for the lake. He wishes you'd quit fighting and sell them the land."

His grandfather's hard knuckles bulged on the steering wheel. "When cows climb trees!"

From farther back than Jim Ed could remember, his grandfather had been missing the first joint on his right index finger. That was one mark of a roper, for many a finger had been ground off between a rope and a saddlehorn. He pointed the stub at Jim Ed. "I *knowed* your daddy didn't send you here just because he thought I needed help. He always hated that ranch, from the time he was a button. He sent you to try and talk me into givin' up."

The subject had indeed arisen. Jim Ed regarded Wes Hendrix as being much like that oil fielder on the bus, still trying to live in a time buried and gone. Wes probably had little conception of life beyond the outside fences of that wornout, shirttail ranch to which he had devoted more than forty years of his life. The few times Grandmother Maudie had forced him into visiting the city, he had been like a child lost and bewildered.

Jim Ed said, "You could take the money and go anywhere you want to."

"I'm *already* where I want to be. I spent the first thirty years of my life huntin' that place. I ain't got thirty left to find me another one like it. If your daddy sent you here to lecture me, I'd just as well put you back on the bus."

That would have suited Jim Ed except that at the moment he had nowhere to go. He lacked the money to follow Jack and David on that promised trip to Europe. He could not return to Dallas for a while, not after the blowup that had resulted from his final-semester failure. The row had culminated in an ultimatum from his father. He lowered his voice. "I haven't said a word."

Wes grunted, glancing uneasily at him. "I tried to tell your daddy I'm no invalid. I don't need your help."

Jim Ed thought he wouldn't *be* much help.

Wes said, "Time you've dug a hundred postholes and put horsetracks all over the pastures, you'll wisht you was back in Dallas."

Jim Ed already wished he were.

Wes asked, "How's your mama?"

Jim Ed shrugged. "Just fine." Mama was always just fine. She never moved out of Truman Hendrix's shadow long enough for any life of her own.

"Good woman. I felt guilty about not warnin' her before she married your hardheaded daddy."

Wes lapsed into silence, turning loose of the wheel to fish in his shirt pocket. The pickup angled toward the ditch while Wes tried to worry one cigarette out of a pack. Jim Ed had to muster a strong will not to take hold of the steering wheel. That would have been surrender, of a sort. Wes corrected the course and struck a kitchen match against the dashboard, scarred by a thousand or two similar strikes.

The old man stared at Jim Ed, ignoring the road. "I wisht I'd had you with me twenty years ago. Now your city raisin' has probably put you beyond salvation."

Jim Ed was too tired from the trip to give his grandfather the satisfaction of baiting him into an argument. "Probably."

The Hendrix ranch lay nine miles east of town. A state farm-to-market asphalt pavement labored over, through and around the cedar-fringed hills, spending three miles to gain two. Now and again Jim Ed glimpsed the sparkling river, born of a thousand tiny springs that seeped and trickled and bubbled between flat seams of gray limestone layers deposited in the beds of ancient seas, later ripped and torn asunder by rumblings and spasms and upheavals in the earth's restless crust. The river's gift of life had drawn wild animals of infinite variety, making it a hunting ground for uncountable generations of warrior tribes who had battled to gain supremacy, mixing their blood with its clear cold waters. One after another had held dominance for a time, then was forced to yield to someone stronger in a long succession of violent displacements. The white man had come, finally, driving away the last of the bronzed warriors, then fighting one another for the right to this river and the bounties of the land around it. Sheepman had fought cattleman, and both had resisted the farmer. The faces changed, the voices changed, but always there was the river, and the struggle to own it.

Along the road, especially near to town, Jim Ed saw perhaps twenty fancy gateways of stone and steel and brick, bearing names like Angora Acres and Rancho Restful and The Poor Farm. He looked twice at a sign that declared Heavenly Days Ranch. These were the harbingers of an urban invasion, ten- and twenty- and fifty-acre *ranchettes*, homesites for city folk who wanted to play at the rustic life without suffering its discomforts. Most seemed to have a horse or two, and dogs of every size and hue that stood at the roadside, challenging the passing traffic.

He said, "The rancher who owned that land probably made more profit cutting it up than he ever saw from livestock."

Wes sniffed. "It's ruined forever. It'll never go back into production."

"How much did it ever produce in the first place?"

"It made meat for people's bellies, and fiber to put clothes on their backs. Now all it raises is taxes and dogs."

Wes Hendrix's gateway was plain, no sign to mark it, nothing bearing his name except a mailbox mounted on a cedar post at the edge of the road. He stopped the pickup and waited for the dust to pass. "Tater, I wisht you'd see if I got any mail."

Jim Ed knew it was useless to tell him he had disliked the nickname *Tater* even as a boy. Stepping out of the pickup, he was a little shaken by the mailbox. Though it still bore a shiny silver newness, it was punctured by perhaps a dozen bulletholes. Inside, he found a couple of newspapers, a bill and a handful of junk mail. He closed the box, scratching his finger on a sharp edge left by a lead slug passing through.

Climbing back into the pickup, he dropped the mail on the seat and sucked the little ruby of blood which formed atop the scratch. His concern was genuine. "They may shoot at *you* next, and not just your mailbox."

Wes shook his head and set the pickup bumping across the cattleguard onto a ranch road packed hard with that ubiquitous Texas surfacing material, caliche, which seemed to underlie much of the state's topsoil. "Kids, is all. Their folks cuss old Wes Hendrix, so the kids think it's all right. I don't get my innards into an uproar over somethin' as triflin' as a mailbox."

A quarter mile from the pavement, Wes turned off to the left, onto a twin-rut road worn into the turf by years of driving over the same tracks. Jim Ed had to grip the inside door handle to avoid being bounced out of his seat. He grabbed the mail as it pitched toward the floorboard. Wes bullied the vehicle up a steep grade and stopped on a barren limestone slab atop a rocky hill.

"Git out, Tater." The voice was too stern for Jim Ed to question why. Wes pushed his door open and hobbled stiff-legged beside him to the rimrock. He pointed. "Looky yonder. I want you to see why I'm not lettin' them take this place without they put up a fight. Ever see such a pretty sight in your life?"

Jim Ed blinked. All he could see was the side of the hill, layer stacked upon layer of limestone, steeper even than the side by which they had climbed. A remnant of spring bluebonnets still showed in spots where the sheep or goats had not yet found them, and the faded red and yellow of Indian paintbrushes was scattered like the liver splotches on Wes's hands. Cedar trees had invaded most of the way to the top of the hill. Down below, liveoaks grew in dark green mottes, almost black, and beyond them a line of towering native pecan trees marked the river's course. Heavy foliage hid the water from view. As scenery, he considered it a long way from the Alps. He refrained from giving voice to the thought. "Nice," he said, wanting to be kind. He knew instantly that it was not enough.

Wes gave him a glance that spoke both of anger and despair, then hobbled back toward the pickup. He peeled the paper sack down from the neck of the bottle and took a drink, then kept his silence as he drove.

The mile-and-a-half of graded road from the front gate to the house was maintained by county equipment when the precinct commissioner was on friendly terms with Wes but neglected when he was not. Lately it had deteriorated into ruts. Sharp rock outcrops would soon lacerate a standard highway tire. Wes used heavy-duties on his pickup; they looked as if they had been borrowed from a tractor. They rode that way, too, for Jim Ed felt that his teeth were rattling loose.

Wes's moody silence stirred Jim Ed to a little of guilt, and a need for at least an effort at communication. He had always heard that nothing set a rancher or farmer to talking quite so easily as bringing the topic around to rainfall, or the lack of it. "Looks like you've had moisture this spring."

The times he had visited here as a boy, the land had looked as if it hadn't felt the kiss of a raindrop in six months. This time he saw grass, green by hill-country standards. People out here didn't expect much, so they were not easily disappointed.

Wes acknowledged, "Had a couple inches last week. We just need one more."

Jim Ed judged that this country had needed *just one more* since the receding of Noah's flood.

Wes said nothing else. So much for conversation about the weather. Jim Ed tried but could not think of another topic in which they might share an interest.

The road labored over a steep hill before pitching down toward the little headquarters. Jim Ed saw the old frame house dwarfed among a dozen or so big liveoak trees. The dark, crooked branches and their heavy year-around foliage shielded the structure from much of summer's hot afternoon sunshine and screened out some of winter's cold north wind. The house was probably as old as Wes himself, its roof divided into four equal quarters that came to a peak at the center. The windows were tall so summer's southern breezes could dispel heat otherwise trapped beneath the high ceilings. It had been seventy years since people had quit building houses in that style. Most ranches which had not torn them down by now were delegating them to transient help, mostly illegal Mexican aliens who paused to earn traveling money before moving northward in the hope of higher-paying big-city employment.

Beyond the house lay Wes's livestock-working corrals, a few of steel but most of aging lumber and cedar pickets, sadly showing their years. One, most ancient of all, was built of stones, stacked without mortar, a legacy from the hard labor of ambitious German immigrants who had braved their way into these resisting hills when this had still been Indian country. Almost everything he could see looked old. An exception was a steel barn Wes had put up after a high wind took part of the roof from his old one and set the rest of the tired structure to leaning eastward. Jim Ed remembered his father's anger. Truman Hendrix declared that Wes had let Grandmother Maudie live in that drafty old house for forty-odd years, but he had built a new barn for himself. The priorities of an old-fashioned, tight-twisted rancher were not easy to understand.

A black-and-white Border Collie raced out to greet the pickup. Tail wagging furiously, the dog whipped back around and kept pace the last fifty yards.

A blue pickup of recent vintage stood in front of the barn. A man sat on the concrete step, whittling. A large boy whistled the dog to come to him, away from the pickup's path. As Wes pulled to a stop, the man closed the pocketknife blade with the heel of his hand and stood up. He had a smile big enough for somebody to fall into, Jim Ed thought. Except for the Mexican family at the bus, this was the first genuine smile he had seen since he had arrived in Big River.

It was also the first time he heard cheer in his grandfather's voice. "That's Bill Roper. He's foreman of the C Bars."

"C Bars? What's that?"

"The Chatfield-Dawson ranch. It surrounds us, pretty near, except upriver where Wally Vincent's ranch lays . . . his wife's, I mean. Bill's a throwback to the oldtime cowboys like I used to know. You got to hunt a long ways to find his caliber anymore." The old man seemed to shed ten years. He alighted from the pickup with spring in his step. He shook hands with the visitor, a grinning bear of a man who appeared to be edging into middle age. The look of him said *cowboy* . . . not the kind who slouched around Dallas country-Western honkytonks in tall-crowned hats and high-heeled boots never scarred by spurs, but the kind who knew which end of the cow got up first and could read a horse's mind by the way it twitched its ears.

Roper said, "Wes, when you goin' to sell me and Johnny that dog?"

"I couldn't do that. Ol' Pepper's the only one here who always knows what he's doin'." Wes gripped the boy's heavy shoulder and gave him a gentle shake. "I swear, Johnny, you ought to make fullback on the varsity this fall."

The boy said eagerly, "I just wish I could."

As Jim Ed walked around the pickup, the collie backed away skeptically, trying to manuever downwind and sample the scent without moving near enough to be touched. The dog was putting him on probation.

Roper looked at Jim Ed with curiosity, but he asked no questions. Wes seemed hesitant for a moment, then said, "That's my grandson, Tater, come out to show me how the city folks do things."

Ashamed of me, Jim Ed thought, surprised he was not resentful. Allowances had to be made for an old man's ways. "Jim Ed Hendrix," he said, hopeful of correcting the *Tater.*

Roper reached out with a hand big and calloused and strong enough to have crushed Jim Ed's into splinters, but the shake was gentle. It was also tentative, as if Roper agreed with the dog that an early judgment was not in order. "Pleased to meet you, Tater. I don't know what you can show your old granddaddy. He's already forgot more than most of us'll ever know."

Jim Ed's answer was a simple nod, ambiguous enough to be whatever the man expected.

Roper tried to hold the smile, but it faded after the first moments of greeting and shared friendship. Roper's eyes held a haunted look that betrayed uneasiness, perhaps even fear.

Roper's son appeared to be about twelve or fourteen, built to follow in his father's big footsteps. He stared at Jim Ed with open and honest curiosity, his gaze roving from the narrow-brimmed hat to the running shoes.

Wes said, "I'm fixin' to find out tomorrow what Tater knows about diggin' postholes. We'll be workin' on that new fence."

"New fence?" For an unguarded moment Roper showed surprise. "I thought you'd be holdin' off on that until the lake thing is settled." He seemed to catch himself.

Wes did not acknowledge the comment about the lake. "I can rotate the grazin' better if I split up that north pasture."

Now Jim Ed was surprised. Rotation grazing was a fairly modern concept, taught in all the best agricultural schools. He had taken for granted that his grandfather had not embraced a new idea in forty years.

Wes said, "You-all come on up to the house. Won't take long to fix a fresh pot of coffee."

Most things about the house spoke of age, but Jim Ed was intrigued to find the kitchen stove fired by butane gas. It looked some years from being new, so he must have seen it on an earlier visit; his memory had simply played him false. He had expected an obsolete wood-burning range. Over the years, when Jim Ed had complained about some inconvenience, his father would tell him at length about chopping a boxcar load of wood each year to keep that hungry range burning. The woodstove's heat had made the kitchen insufferable in summer. In winter it scorched the side nearest the fire while the other extremity froze.

Well, it was gone. Grandmother Maudie had probably put her foot down.

Wes carefully drained off the cold morning coffee into the sink while holding back some of the wet grounds with his hand. He added fresh coffee to the leavings and filled the pot with water, then set it on a burner and turned up the flame. Jim Ed had not believed civilized people boiled coffee anymore. Perhaps *civilized* people didn't.

Wes turned to the boy. "Sorry I ain't got no soda pop. But you'll find ice cream in the freezer."

Bill Roper snapped his finger. "That reminds me. Johnny, I wisht you'd run out to the pickup and fetch that sack your mama sent for Wes."

The boy had continued his guileless staring at Jim Ed. He seemed not to want to back away, but he said, "Yes sir."

They still raise them to snap to out here, Jim Ed thought.

The boy went out the door, the dog following with tail in high gear. Roper's face went serious. "I hate to come and dump my troubles on you, Wes. You got enough of your own."

Wes motioned for Roper to seat himself at the table. "What's botherin' you, Bill?"

"Had company over at the C Bars today. Real estate agent out of San Angelo."

"Not the first one of *them* you ever seen, was it?"

"No, but they never stayed long before. Most of the time Miz Livvy never let them get past her front porch. This one went plumb into the parlor. Then she asked me to take him in the pickup and give him a look-see over the place."

Wes stared a moment without blinking. "That don't mean she really figures on sellin'."

"It means she's thinkin' about it. The ranch has lost so much money the last few years . . ." Roper shook his head. "For the first time in my life, I'm scared. I've put twenty years into that job. I don't know what me and Hallie'll do if I lose it."

Wes's eyes were sad. "There's somethin' way out of balance in the world. People over in Africa are starvin' because they can't buy food. People here are starvin' because they can't sell it."

"At least you own this place, Wes. You've got grounds to fight them when they come to move you. I'm just a hired hand. I've got no right to even speak my mind."

Wes stared out the door at the boy, coming up the porch steps with a brown-paper grocery sack in his hand. "It's hard times for a lot of us. I just never believed it'd happen to anybody as big as the C Bars."

Bill Roper grimaced. "Maybe if Carr Dawson hadn't died so young . . . His mother tries, but Miz Livvy's gettin' old."

"Ain't we all?" Wes commented. He glanced impatiently toward the coffee. "*Some* people are lookin' for better times. Wally Vincent greeted Tater to town. Showed him his sheriff's badge. He figures they'll build the dam on his wife's land and back the water over mine, and the new lake'll make him rich. Me and my little old ranch stand in the way."

Roper nodded. "Some people'll let you mess with their wife, and some'll even let you ride their horse. But get between them and money, and the friendship's over."

The boy set the sack on the table. Roper said, "Hallie sent you some of her cookin', Wes. There's pie, amongst other things."

Wes's eyes gleamed in pleasure as he fumbled a foil wrapping from a package. "Apple. Tell her she oughtn't to've done it, but I'm much obliged. We'll cut that pie soon's the coffee's done."

Some of the trouble left Roper's eyes. He rubbed his stomach that pushed against a well-worn silver beltbuckle bearing the figure of a steer wrestler and the words *San Angelo, 1967.* "Hallie's been naggin' me to watch my girlish figure." But he made no move to leave. "If you'd like some more of her cookin', you come over to Liveoak Camp tomorrow. We'd be tickled to have the use of your ropin' arm in the brandin' pen."

The light flickered again in Wes's eyes. "Liveoak Camp," he said, savoring the words. Then he looked at Jim Ed, and the light faded. "I reckon not, Bill. Tater's just got here . . ."

"Bring him. He'd be welcome."

Wes said with a measure of doubt, "He's a city boy. He's apt to be standin' in the gate when you bring the cattle in."

Roper studied Jim Ed, but if he came to an opinion he kept it to himself. "Looks like a college boy to me. College boys can learn *anything.*" He leaned over the stove and lifted the lid from the coffeepot. "I believe it's about ready to pour," he said, indicating that the question was settled.

Jim Ed and Wes stood on the porch, watching the dog trail Roper's pickup the first fifty yards and then stand in the thin curtain of dust it raised climbing the hill. Jim Ed said, "Well, it looks like *everybody* around here's not mad at you."

Wes grunted. *"Everybody* ain't hopin' to make somethin' off of the land that belongs to *me."*

That pie was probably more than Wes normally ate for supper, Jim Ed judged by the thin look of him. But Wes said, "We'll tend to the stock first, then fix supper. I reckon a growin' boy needs his nourishment."

"I'm not a boy," Jim Ed said, "and I'm done growing."

"Your Uncle James Edward never could seem to get enough to eat. He was always lookin' ahead to supper." An old pain came into Wes's eyes. His gaze went to the mantle, to a studio portrait of a young cowboy who had some of Wes Hendrix's features.

James Edward Hendrix. He had died before Jim Ed was born. Jim Ed had inherited his name.

Wes hobbled to the mantle and reached toward the photo but stopped short of touching it. "Everything I ever wanted was for James Edward and your daddy. All the time they was growin' up, I was gettin' this ranch ready for them. Your daddy never liked it, but James Edward did. Wasn't nothin' he couldn't do a-horse-back. He could tell what a cow was fixin' to think before she thought it. Loved this place, that boy did."

He was silent a moment, then cleared his throat. "When you come along and they gave you his name, I sort of hoped that in a way you *were* him, come back to me. Remember when you was little? I let you ride in front of me on a horse."

Jim Ed remembered all too well. He had wet his britches out of fear that his grandfather would let him fall and the fool horse would step on him.

Wes went on, "You couldn't say *Granddad*, so you called me *Daddoo*. I kept hopin' your daddy might get tired of the city and move back to Big River. Then I could raise you to be the image of your uncle.

"But that's the way with dreams: the bad ones just haunt you, and the good ones never come true. People moved *away* from the country in them days; they didn't move *to* it."

When he turned from the picture, his eyes were more angry than sad. "Now it's in style for people to quit the city and move to the country, only they want to bring the city with them. Time they get through changin' it into everything they come here to run away from, there won't be nothin' left of the country."

Jim Ed said, "They'll pay you three times what this place is worth."

Wes's eyes crackled. "How do *you* know what it's worth? How do *you* put a price on forty-odd years? You ain't *lived* half that long." He stalked into the kitchen, where Jim Ed heard him running water into a tin bucket, rinsing it for the milking.

Jim Ed walked to the mantle and studied the picture of the uncle he knew only from a handful of old photographs. James Edward Hendrix could as well have lived a hundred years ago for all the closeness Jim Ed could feel toward him.

His attention shifted to another photograph, one much older and turning brown. It showed a slender young man on a pitching black horse, a rodeo crowd in the background. In fading ink near the bottom of the picture, he recognized his grandmother's hand: *Wes Hendrix, on Midnight.*

It seemed unreal, somehow, that Wes Hendrix had ever been that young. Had it not been for the writing, Jim Ed would not have recognized him.

Wes said gruffly, "You better change into some old clothes, then meet me out at the barn. Even a city dude ought to learn how to feed stock and handle a milk cow. They'll pave over the last blade of grass someday, and drown the last tree in an artificial lake so some damnfool from town can race a motorboat. You ought to at least remember what it used to be like."

Little had changed in his uncle's room in almost thirty years. Schoolbooks and a dozen Luke Short paperback Western novels still sat on a bookshelf, along with a silver trophy for exhibiting the county livestock show's grand champion steer in 1956, the last year of James Edward's life. Above the bookshelf hung a guitar probably not dusted since Maudie Hendrix died. Jim Ed examined a set of 45-rpm records in a box beside a big-spindle player. They carried such names as Hank Williams and Eddy Arnold, Gene Autry and Tex Ritter. Finding not even an Elvis Presley, he closed the box and went out into the living room. His grandfather was slumped in a reclining chair that looked twice too large for him, reading the San Angelo *Standard-Times.*

Jim Ed asked, "What do you do around here for entertainment?"

Wes lowered the newspaper. "Entertainment?" It was as if he did not understand the word. "There's a whole shelf of good books yonder."

Jim Ed had already looked them over. A couple dealt with livestock health and nutrition. Most were on Texas and Western history, particularly about lawmen and outlaws and the ranching industry. Not one was on any subject Jim Ed considered relevant to the real world.

Wes said, "There's always the television."

It was a color set, probably Grandmother Maudie's choosing. Jim Ed turned it on but found only two stations. One resembled a January snowstorm. The other was showing an old movie he had already seen and didn't like.

Wes said, "Maudie always watched the soap operas. Them people was like old friends to her."

Jim Ed turned off the television. "How do you keep from going crazy out here all by yourself with nothing to do?"

Wes pondered. "A man can do worse than be by himself. He can read. He can think. He can sit on the porch and listen to the sounds of life out yonder."

Jim Ed argued, "There's nothing out there for miles."

"You just got to learn how to listen. It's all around you, like music."

Jim Ed frowned. His father was right. Wes Hendrix had been on this place too long for his own good.

Wes said, "James Edward knew. He was tuned to this place. He could tell you the name of everything that sang in the dark."

Jim Ed stood in the open front door, listening. He heard only the high-pitched noise of crickets, the chatter of birds, the croaking of a frog down at a water tank, a cow bawling somewhere, the distant bleating of a lamb. He heard no music.

"We can't be somebody else," he commented. "I'm not James."

Wes's voice was so low Jim Ed barely heard it. "No, you sure as hell ain't." Wes got up and hunched out into the kitchen. He poured leftover coffee into a cup and fetched a bottle of bourbon out of the pantry. He poured a liberal amount of whisky into the coffee and extended the bottle toward Jim Ed. "You don't drink this stuff, do you?"

Before Jim Ed could say he did, Wes said he didn't. "You're too young. It can be balm to an *old* man, but it's a curse to a young one." He drank some of the coffee and refilled with pure whisky. Carrying the cup, he touched the wall switch and left the kitchen dark.

"Good night, Tater."

Jim Ed had trouble going to sleep. He dozed off, then awakened, momentarily disoriented. A gentle breeze from the south lifted the curtains around the open window. It was the noise that bothered him, or rather the lack of it. He heard no rumble of traffic, no horns, no television played too loudly.

Or perhaps he did. There *was* a sound of some kind, distant music that reached him in fragments torn by the breeze. He thought for a moment it was imagination, but he heard it again. He wondered if Wes might have left his bedroom radio playing softly when he went to sleep. Then he decided the sound came from outside. He slid out of bed and went to the window. He heard it more clearly, though it came from the other side of the house. He walked through the living room and out onto the porch.

He saw his grandfather's slight figure silhouetted against the moonlit barn, the dog beside him. Wes Hendrix sat on a bench under one of the huge liveoak trees, fiddle beneath his chin. He played a slow, melancholy melody, vaguely familiar though Jim Ed did not know its name.

He had not seen his grandfather weep at the funeral of Maudie Hendrix, and he had wondered how the old man could maintain such unyielding self-control. He sensed that Wes was weeping now, through the music he drew from that old fiddle.

Jim Ed listened until he began to feel uneasily that he was intruding on private grief. He quietly retreated into the house and returned to his bed. The last he knew as he dropped off to sleep, that music still reached him through the open window like a faraway cry for help that he did not know how to answer.

Chapter 2

At the Chatfield-Dawson C Bar Ranch headquarters, fifteen miles from Wes Hendrix's place, Bill Roper turned over slowly in bed for the twentieth time to look at the lighted face of a digital clock on the nightstand. It said a quarter past four, three minutes later than the last time he had looked. He swore beneath his breath, then reached out to turn off the alarm, set for four-thirty.

His wife's voice startled him. She said, "We'd just as well get up. It's almost time anyway."

"I didn't go to wake you," he said apologetically. "I've been lyin' here with my eyes open for an hour."

"Longer than that," Hallie replied, switching on the bedlamp. "I heard you go to the bathroom at two-thirty. Didn't you sleep at all?"

"Not much," he admitted. He looked at her, lying there facing him with her nightgown hanging loosely off one shoulder, a long strand of dark brown hair dangling in front of a face that to him was still the high-school cheerleader he had known twenty years ago. He was compelled to reach out and touch her with a hand large and strong and gentle. Her warm hand came up to close over his fingers and bring them down to press firmly against her soft bosom.

"Still thinking about Wes," she asked, "or about *us?*"

"Both. In a way, we're in the same fix. We don't want to leave where we're at, but other people make the decisions."

"You're a good man, Bill. A good man will always find something."

"Ranch jobs like mine don't hang off of the trees. This has been the best one a man could ever hope for."

"We'll be all right, Bill."

Roper frowned. That was Hallie's response to every challenge that arose. He envied her quiet faith and acceptance of whatever came, but it placed all the more burden on him to try to control those challenges. He said, "I've kept thinkin' about Wes's grandson."

"Don't tell me *he* kept you awake."

"I've been comparin' him and Johnny. I'm glad we've been able to bring Johnny up here instead of in some town. That Tater . . . I don't know how to figure city boys like him. It's like tryin' to read a book in another language."

"If he's kin to Wes, he has good stuff in him. Give him a chance."

"Johnny was real taken by him. I don't guess he ever saw anybody quite like him before. If we have to leave this place and move to a city, Johnny could wind up bein' like that Tater."

"You worry too much. You've got Johnny off to a strong start. He won't make a wrong turn now. Give yourself more credit, Bill. Give *us* more credit, and Johnny too."

He pulled himself up to a sitting position and slid his legs from beneath the cotton sheet that had been his only cover. Hallie reached to touch his arm, and he warmed to her. Even after sharing a bed with her all these years, he was still easily aroused when she touched him unexpectedly.

She said, "Worrying over this ranch will just make an old man of you for nothing, because there's precious little you can do about it. You can't make the cattle market better. You can't make the cows have twins." Her fingers tightened on his arm. "Maybe it's time you went on your own anyway. That's what you've wanted for years. And this is the time to buy in, isn't it, when everything seems to be at the bottom?"

"It's what we've been savin' for. But we haven't saved enough yet. We don't have the money to buy livestock and pay for a land lease too, even if we could find a good place available. I need to hold on to this job for a few more years."

He pushed to a stand, bringing his hand to his hip where an old twinge seemed to be worsening, a legacy of bad horses long dead but well remembered. The follies of youthful cowboy exuberance were coming home to roost in his middle age. He walked to the window. Somewhere a calf bawled, and a cow answered. He looked up at stars sharp and crystalline in a black sky. Not a sign of sunup showed yet. "It's fixin' to be a pretty day for workin' cattle at Liveoak Camp."

He pulled on his trousers first. He had never gotten over an old shyness about exposing his bare legs to Hallie any longer than necessary. He could not believe there was anything attractive about a man from the waist down, even to a loving and generously tolerant woman like Hallie. "I wish you'd've let me hire Serafina Sanchez to help you with the cookin' over there today. It'll be a heavy load for you."

"You've been carrying a heavy load for this ranch yourself. If Miz Livvy has to sell the place, maybe at least it'll go to somebody who has the money to do things properly for a change, and not have to scrimp and make do on nothing, and work double to keep from hiring more help."

"Chances are that anybody who buys this place will already have his own crew. He'll want to start fresh and not have a holdover like me always tellin' him how we *used* to do things." He reached down to pick up a high-heeled boot that had a spur buckled on it. The spur jingled softly. "You know what that real estate salesman told me yesterday? Said he's got a client out of Houston lookin' for a hill country ranch he can turn into a year-around huntin' preserve. Wants to stock it with exotic game animals and build a huntin' lodge. A glorified dude ranch . . . Even if they was to make me an offer, I couldn't stay here for that. Old Major Chatfield would turn over in his grave."

"There's always my brother John. He's been after you for years to move to San Angelo and join him in the grocery business."

Roper tugged on his boot. "What could I do in a store, sack groceries? I know about raisin' beef and mutton. I'm too far along in life to go back to school, or to change directions." His voice was somewhere between anger and hurt.

Hallie slipped her arms around him from behind. He felt the warmth of her breasts against his back, and her comforting lips pressed against his shoulder. "We'll do all right," she said. "We've always done all right."

As long as he had known her, he had never seen anything shake her much. She had always been able to walk through shambles and find a four-leaf clover. He turned into her arms and held her, and an old wanting kindled quickly. His gaze drifted again to the clock. "Damn!" he whispered. "If we just had another twenty minutes."

She kissed his cheek and made a soft giggle that he never heard anywhere except the bedroom. "We don't, but it'll be night again bye and bye."

Jim Ed awoke with a start as Wes Hendrix's knuckles rapped fiercely against his door. The voice was equally jarring. "Rouse up, Tater. Daylight's wastin'!"

Jim Ed reluctantly opened his eyes. He saw only blackness. "Daylight?" He felt as if he had just crawled back into bed after watching his grandfather draw music out of the fiddle beneath the liveoaks. He closed his eyes, but Wes would not let him return to sleep. The old man fumbled inside the door and found the wall switch. Even behind closed lids, the bright light brought pain to Jim Ed's eyes.

Wes said, "I've put the coffee on. You fix some bacon and eggs while I go out and milk Ol' Red." Allowing no time for questions or objections, he left with the milk bucket in hand. If Wes had not awakened Jim Ed already, the slamming of the screen door would have done it. Jim Ed listened to his grandfather's boots tromping heavily across the porch and down the wooden steps into the yard. The old man was humming a tune, at this ungodly time of the morning.

A rooster crowed. Wes had probably waked him up.

Grumbling, Jim Ed found the floor with his feet and stumbled to the closet where he had hung his clothes. It took him a minute to remember he and Wes were going to work cattle today. He shuddered and looked at the clock beside his bed. Four-thirty. He could not remember when he had been up this early, except a few times he had been up this late. No wonder Wes was drawn up thin as a whipporwill. He didn't get enough sleep.

Yawning, Jim Ed pulled the rock-music T-shirt over his head. Instead of the running shoes, he put on a pair of cowboy boots Grandmother Maudie had given him once for Christmas. They had been designed to fit into a set of leather-covered stirrups and rub against a horse, but Jim Ed had restricted their service mostly to cement and asphalt. If bootmakers still depended upon working cowboys for their trade, theirs would have become a vanished art.

He found eggs and bacon in the refrigerator and poked around in the lower cabinets for a skillet. He fried the bacon first, four strips apiece, and poured off the excess grease into a coffee can that showed prior use for the purpose. What Wes would do with the collected grease Jim Ed had no idea. He was not sure he wanted to know, because it was probable he would eventually eat it in some concoction of the old man's. He started the eggs, buttered four slices of lightbread and shoved them into an electric toaster like the one he used at home. Wes's kitchen had most of the standard conveniences. Grandmother Maudie's doing, Jim Ed surmised. Left to his own devices, Wes would probably still be cooking outdoors over a shallow pit.

He heard his grandfather's boots on the porch, and the door slammed. The dog Pepper stood just outside the screen, tail wagging vigorously. Wes said, "He loves milkin' time. I always pour him a little warm milk right out of the bucket."

Jim Ed frowned, turning the eggs. "Do you milk this early every morning?"

"No, I ordinarily don't get up till five-thirty. But today we got a ways to travel."

Jim Ed grunted. "It doesn't take long to spend the night around this place. Especially for fiddle players."

Wes strained the fresh milk into a crock jar. "Sorry if I woke you up. Sometimes when I can't sleep, makin' a little music helps. I'll try not to disturb you again."

Jim Ed shrugged. "It's your place. You do whatever you feel like."

The old man's face went somber. "I'd always kind of hoped it might be *your* place someday."

"I'm a city boy. What would I know about operating a place like this?"

"A man can learn anything he sets his mind to, if he wants it bad enough. That's the hitch, I suppose: *wantin'* to."

Jim Ed plopped the eggs onto two plates alongside the bacon. He removed the bread from the toaster and found it had stayed half a minute too long. It was edible enough but blackened on the edges.

Wes eyed it warily. "You know how to make biscuits?"

Jim Ed shook his head. "I'm afraid not."

"I'll teach you, first chance we get. A ranch had just as well have all hands afoot as to not have any biscuits." The old man spent a moment frowning at the T-shirt but said nothing about it. He did not tarry long at the table. He looked at the kitchen clock and declared that they had better get a move on; he did not like to keep a working crew waiting.

Jim Ed thought that if this working crew depended upon a seventy-seven-year-old man and a dude from Dallas, it was in trouble before it started.

Wes detoured by the chicken pen to open the gate so his hens could move out into the barnyard and scratch for food. He had penned them at nightfall behind a high net fence to protect them from the many predators which roamed these hills, alert for plunder.

The old man had left two horses in a small foot-trap the evening before. Shaking a steel bucket that contained a little feed, he coaxed them into a cedar-picket corral. He said over his shoulder, "I take it for granted that you know how to ride."

Jim Ed said, "Some friends of mine have a horse farm near Denton. I go there with them sometimes."

"The C Bars ain't no horse farm. But maybe you won't be too much in the way."

Jim Ed sensed a loss of the jovial mood that had set his grandfather to humming when he first went out to milk. The T-shirt, or burned toast instead of biscuits, perhaps. Either would have reminded Wes that Jim Ed was a fish floundering on dry land.

It isn't my fault I don't belong here, he thought. Nobody had asked him if he had *wanted* to come.

Wes talked softly to one of the horses, and it accepted the bridle. Jim Ed could not tell the horse's color; the morning was still too dark. Wes pointed. "You can use that saddle."

The horse made a rolling sound in its nose when Jim Ed approached him with the blanket. Wes said, "He don't know you. Just keep talkin' and let him know you won't hurt him."

"How do I know he won't hurt *me?*"

"Faith, boy. Faith can shake a mountain down."

Wes's horse trailer was plain, not one of those factory-fancy covered jobs that Jim Ed had seen the horse-show and rodeo people pulling up and down the highways. This one did not even have a top; it was open to the sky and whatever might fall from it. Swinging the tailgate, Wes motioned for Jim Ed to walk around the outside and lead his horse up into the trailer. The horse went, though he seemed still shy. When Jim Ed started to tie the reins on the trailer's left side, the old man said, "Tie him on the right. That way he's angled toward the bar ditch instead of lookin' at the middle of the road and all the traffic comin' at him. Nobody but sheepherders tie horses on the left."

"This ranch has sheep," Jim Ed pointed out.

"But it don't have no sheep*herders*." Wes paused. "At least, it *didn't* have." He put his own horse into the trailer at an angle just behind Jim Ed's, tied the reins and latched the tailgate. His gaze went to Jim Ed's tiny-brimmed hat. "That dinky thing won't keep the sun out of your eyes."

"It's the only one I have."

"You can wear a straw hat of mine."

Jim Ed would have accepted the offer if his grandfather had not made a challenge of it. "I don't mind a little sun."

"Git in the pickup, then. Daylight's wastin'."

Jim Ed saw not even a *promise* of daylight. Any early color that might be emerging low against the dark sky was blocked off by a rugged line of rough mountains to the east. At least, Jim Ed would call them mountains. Wes said they were just hills, but he had not lived his life in Dallas. Jim Ed climbed into the vehicle and slammed the door twice before it latched. His father might be wrong about many things, he thought, but he was right about this ranch and the lifestyle it demanded. Old Wes had lived with it so long that he did not realize there was any other way.

The dog Pepper jumped eagerly against Wes's door, but Wes told him he had to stay home. The dog drew back in disappointment. Wes said, "It's bred into him to want to work. He ain't like a lot of *people,* lookin' for a cool shade and a soft chair."

The pickup, its engine cold, struggled to pull the heavy trailer up the long hill toward the farm-to-market highway. A dozen Angora goats decided they had to hurry across the road at the last moment, their silky fleeces flouncing with each jump they made. They forced Wes to brake down and lose his momentum. The headlights reflected brightly against road dust that swirled in the animals' wake.

"Why do you keep goats?" Jim Ed asked.

"For the mohair. I shear them twice a year, and there's a steady market for it. Better than there is for calves."

"They just don't fit the old-cowboy image."

"This country's natural for goats. They do good on liveoak and brush that'd starve a cow. And what the goats won't eat, the sheep will. A man's got to go with the country and raise whatever fits it. He can't change the country to suit himself."

"When they show Texas ranches on television it's never sheep and goats. It's always horses and cattle and cowboys."

"When they talk about Texas oil they don't show some poor old boy out yonder diggin' a ditch with a dull shovel. But he's part of it too. Without him, there wouldn't be no rich fellers in tall glass towers."

In the darkness Jim Ed had only a vague idea about the country they drove through. He simply had a sense that they were moving farther and farther from town, deeper into an alien land.

He had visited no ranches other than his grandfather's, and a couple of horse outfits north of Dallas. He did not know what to expect of the Chatfield-Dawson except that as a major operation it should probably have a showy entrance gate and a mansion house. That was the big-ranch image he had cultivated from magazines and movies. He was disappointed when Wes turned off the pavement and crossed an open cattleguard little better than his own. A small board sign was attached to a post beside it, but the pickup's lights touched it so briefly that Jim Ed could not read what it said.

Darkness was just beginning to lift when a bend in the rough road revealed two steel-towered windmills, a set of cedar-picket and wooden corrals, a small frame house and a steel barn not unlike Wes Hendrix's. Jim Ed declared, "This is all there is to it? Not much to show for the reputation."

"This ain't the headquarters," Wes said. "This is Liveoak Camp." He spoke the name almost with reverence. "Best part of the whole outfit, I always thought. Small but fine. Like a real fine woman."

Jim Ed saw no comparison. In fact, he saw nothing to indicate the place had even felt a woman's touch. It had the Spartan look of a bachelor camp, and the same sense of age and fatigue as his grandfather's. Several pickups and trailers were parked between the house and the barn. Horses still stood in a couple of trailers, others tied to fences. Jim Ed saw three school-age boys hunched beside the barn step. One was Bill Roper's son Johnny. Johnny pointed, and the other two boys stood up to stare at Jim Ed. One chuckled, but Johnny Roper did not. Jim Ed's stomach drew into a knot, for new situations and strange people had always made him uneasy. He had no shared experience with hill-country smalltowners and ranch folk. He could argue with some validity that they did not even share a language.

Two men leaned against a fence, talking. Rather, one was talking and the other was listening with the desperate air of hope for an outside interruption. Wes and Jim Ed provided that opportunity. Stocky Bill Roper stepped away from the fence and walked to meet Wes's pickup. The other man followed, still talking and gesturing, his thin face dark and serious. Roper said, "Git out and come in." His broad smile lighted up the morning. "Savin' coffee for you in the kitchen, Wes." He gave Jim Ed a tentative nod that could be taken for a greeting without committing himself.

Wes got out and shook hands. He introduced Jim Ed to Fuller Gibson, who ranched on the far side of Liveoak. Gibson, fiftyish, had the leathered face of an outdoor man, and a hand that felt as rough as it looked. He acknowledged Jim Ed with reservation, studying him up and down. Jim Ed mustered a stern determination and stared into those critical eyes like an Aggie freshman bulling his way through a line of upperclassmen.

Fuller picked up his monologue where the interruption had left it. "Wes, I was tellin' Bill, this cattle market is as sick as ever I seen it. I just don't know how they expect a man to stay. It's them Chicago traders manipulatin' the futures market. They're fixin' to ruin us all."

Wes sympathized, "I've been sayin' the same thing for years." Jim Ed suspected his grandfather wouldn't know the futures market from a flea market. Wes turned to Jim Ed. "Let's unload the horses before we go to the house. They like solid ground under their feet."

In the dawn's light Jim Ed saw that the horse Wes had assigned him was a bay. Wes's was a dun. In the dark he could not have told them apart. He wondered how Wes did.

Wes said, "Come on, Yellowhammer," and led the dun to a fence to tie him. Jim Ed followed suit with the suspicious bay. Roper escorted the newcomers to the house. Gibson walked along, shifting his condemnation from the Chicago traders to the U.S. Department of Agriculture and its lack of concern for what was happening to the producer. Wes stomped his feet on a floor-mat before entering. Jim Ed thought it prudent to follow form though he doubted that anything on his boots would be detrimental to this venerable structure. It was every bit as old as the one Wes lived in. From the look of it, no one stayed here permanently; it was used as a camp for working days like this one, and probably for city hunters who came in the fall to terrorize the deer herd.

Three or four more men stood in the kitchen, coffee cups in their hands. They had a few words for Wes, and all spoke civilly to Jim Ed once they realized he belonged with the old man. He was aware that most stared at him, especially the T-shirt and his small hat. Some showed amusement, some disapproval. *Well,* he thought defensively, *they can't accuse me of trying to look like something I'm not.*

Bill Roper poured Jim Ed a cup of black coffee from a big pot on the stove. He pointed to the table. "There's a doughnut or two left yonder. Sugar and cream if you need them, Tater."

Jim Ed supposed the *Tater* name was going to haunt him like a pregnant girlfriend, however hard he might try to shed it. He bit into the last fried doughnut and knew it had not come out of a grocery sack; it had the rich flavor of homemade. He scooped a spoonful of sugar into the black coffee and looked for the cream. It was in a small can, condensed milk already congealed around two holes punched in its top. He decided to drink his coffee black.

He noticed a girl standing in a doorway that led to a dark back room. At first glance he had mistaken her for a boy. She wore a boy's loose workclothes, an old blue shirt and jeans faded almost to the color of a summer sky. They gave her about as much shape as a sack of feed. A cowboy hat, set squarely and firmly on her head, looked as battered as if horses tromped on it every morning but Sunday. What he noticed most about her were her large and expressive eyes, brown almost to the point of being black, like those of some pretty Mexican girls he had seen. She returned his stare without blink or blush.

He judged her to be twenty, give or take a couple of years. Having seen no other women, he assumed she was responsible for the doughnuts. He held up the bit left of his. "This is good. I wish you'd made a dozen more."

Those dark eyes turned to ice. "I can cook, but I am not *a* cook. Hallie Roper made those."

Her manner took him across the grain. "Well, then, if you don't cook, what *do* you do around here?"

The ice thickened. "Hell, pilgrim, I supervise this operation."

Jim Ed dipped a finger into the sugar where the doughnuts had been. *"Pilgrim?* You've seen too many John Wayne movies."

"Maybe you haven't seen enough of them. You sure don't look like Wes Hendrix."

Under other circumstances he might have regarded that as a compliment, but he knew she did not mean it as one. She gave him a long, hard study, head to foot. Her voice carried sarcasm as sour as horse sweat. "In fact, you don't look like *anything,* except maybe a breakout from the San Antonio zoo. I doubt you'll do enough work even to earn that doughnut you just put away."

"I'll earn my keep," he said stiffly.

"Maybe. Let's just see what the day brings, pilgrim. I'll bet you'll be hunting water and shade before ten o'clock."

"Bet you."

Fuller Gibson's line of criticism had changed again. He was talking about the aimless younger generation and how they were dragging the country down the road to ruin.

Bill Roper gave Jim Ed an uncomfortable glance and looked out the window. "I believe everybody's come, and it's daylight. We'd just as well go amongst them." Spurs jingled as men and high-school boys walked across the linoleum-covered floor. It creaked and groaned under their weight. Wes and Jim Ed were among the last ones out. Jim Ed looked around for the girl, but she had gone on ahead. He saw her walking toward the horses with a big-shouldered young man who looked as if he might play for the Dallas Cowboys, or at least the Houston Oilers.

Pilgrim. He smarted over that. He might be from the city, but he wasn't some Yankee snowbird come down from the North to enjoy Texas's advantages and then complain because it was not like the place he had escaped from.

He untied the bay horse and lifted his foot toward the stirrup. Wes said, "Hold on, Tater. You better lead Ol' Rowdy around and work the kinks out before you mount him. He's been known to hump up a little."

Jim Ed blinked in surprise. "*You* ride him, don't you?"

"Well, yes, but I didn't just come here yesterday. I been ridin' horses like him all my life."

Jim Ed wondered how his grandfather had lived to be seventy-seven. Wes fell in beside his grandson, leading his own dun horse. Jim Ed had to assume he did so for the same reason. He said, "It seems to me you've reached an age that you ought to ride gentle horses."

"Beans ain't beans without a little chili powder in them."

He watched his grandfather speak quietly to the dun horse and pat it on the neck, then grasp the reins and a bit of the mane in his left hand, the saddlehorn in his right. He swung up with the ease of a young man just eligible to vote.

Jim Ed tried to emulate him, but the grace was lacking. So was the horse's patience. Rowdy never let Jim Ed's right boot find the stirrup. He took a long jump that bounced Jim Ed almost high enough for his foot to hit the cantle. The second jump divorced Jim Ed entirely from the saddle. For a second or two he seemed suspended in midair, then the ground came rushing up to knock half the breath out of him. His belly took the first impact, his jaw the second, making his teeth hurt all the way out to his ears. He pushed up on his hands, coughing dust.

Looking down from the saddle, Wes said, "You better get up and climb back on him. Else he'll think he's got away with it."

Jim Ed pushed slowly to his feet, fighting for breath. He expected to see the horse running away, but Rowdy stood there calmly watching him. "I thought he *did* . . . get away with it."

Wes said, "Only if you don't get back on him. You always got to watch Ol' Rowdy first thing of a mornin'. He's playful."

Jim Ed heard several men and boys chuckling. What cut worst of all, however, was a high-pitched giggle that he knew came from the girl. He made a point of not looking at her. He reached reluctantly for the reins, afraid the horse would pitch again before he could even get back into the saddle.

Wes said, "He's had his fun for the mornin'. He ain't greedy. Get back aboard before you spoil him."

Dryly Jim Ed said, "I wouldn't want to do *that.*" His glance caught the girl's brown eyes, still laughing silently. His face warmed. He hoped to see her do something clumsy, but she boarded her blue roan horse with a flash and a flare that he suspected were for his benefit. Jim Ed took a tight grip on the saddlehorn and swung up. The horse stood still this time.

Bill Roper smiled. "You done good, Tater. A lot of town boys never would've gotten back on." Jim Ed nodded a grateful acknowledgment for even a small compliment.

A black horse crowhopped a little with the brawny young man he had seen walking with the girl. He heard her shout, "Way to go, Shorty!"

For somebody else, she hollered. At least the action drew attention away from Jim Ed.

"Who *is* that girl?" he quietly asked his grandfather.

Wes narrowed his eyes, covering a smile. "Already stuck a burr under your blanket, ain't she?"

"I get a pain from women in hobnailed boots who bust their butts trying to prove they can do anything a man can."

Amusement tugged at Wes's mouth. "She's already proved it to just about everybody around here. I expect she wants to be sure *you* know."

"Know what?"

"That she's a Dawson. She was a cowgirl before she was old enough to be a *school*girl. Try to get the best of Glory B. and you'll look like you fell through an outdoor toilet."

"Glory B.?" Jim Ed had to laugh in spite of himself. "Sounds like some tabernacle evangelist."

"Maybe so. She's made more than one smart-aleck old boy ask his Maker for mercy. Her mama named her Gloria Beth, but she's the only one who calls her that. Don't you be tryin' any big-city tricks on Glory B. She's been there."

Jim Ed expected more treachery from the bay, but the horse seemed gentle as a dog. The riders moved single-file through a plank gate held open by Johnny Roper. The boy took his time closing the gate, then spurred the horse into a lope to catch up. Jim Ed suspected he had opened the gate for a chance to enjoy the run afterward, for he had the look of a cat that had just whipped the dog. Bill Roper looked back disapprovingly but said nothing. The boy made a studious effort not to see.

Jim Ed had heard the word *roundup* as long as he could remember, but he had no idea how one was conducted, nor had he felt any particular desire to learn. He sensed a contagious excitement in the riders around him, including his grandfather. He discerned that most did not live on ranches; they came from town. Though livelihood might be derived from office or store, from selling insurance or making sick motors run again, family roots were sunk firmly in the shallow, black, flint-laced soil of this challenging land. Wes pointed to first one, then another, telling Jim Ed that "his daddy used to have a little ranch down the river from the

Indian bluffs till the fifties drouth broke him," or "the old homeplace wasn't big enough for all the boys to stay, so he let his brother have it and taken up the study of law." About a considerably overweight man whose light complexion bespoke little time spent in the sunshine, Wes said, "It was a damned shame about Rupert. The country lost a fine cowpuncher when he taken up schoolteachin'."

Jim Ed asked, "What're they all doing here, then? They can't earn much from a day's work on horseback."

"They ain't gettin' paid, no more than me and you are. They just come out for the chance to ride a horse and chouse a few cattle. That's why Bill sets his cow works for a Saturday."

Jim Ed frowned. "The unions had better never hear about this. The Chatfield-Dawson ranch is getting a lot of labor without paying for it."

"There's people penned up in your cities that'd pay a hundred dollars to do what we're doin' today and be tickled at the price. We're gettin' it free."

Jim Ed shrugged. Big deal. His bay horse snorted and jumped to one side as an armadillo broke from beneath a clump of shinnery oak and scurried to sanctuary in a hole under an upturned, rotting liveoak tree. Jim Ed gripped the saddlehorn to keep his seat. He saw a quiet reproach in his grandfather's eyes. An experienced cowboy would not have to grab leather.

Wes continued, "There was a time when Bill Roper would've driven to San Angelo and hired him a first-rate crew. Used to be some good cowpunchers hung around the Naylor Hotel and Donaho's saddle shop, waitin' for day work. But them old boys've died out or got stove-up or found better pay doin' somethin' else. So Bill makes do with kids and neighbor help and people he can coax out from town. Things ain't like they used to be." Regret came into his voice. "Times, I wonder if they ever was."

The riders, strung out in twos and threes, held their horses to an easy trot and followed a netwire fence. The schoolboys clustered together, chattering and laughing and dropping their voices to tell jokes they would not want the Dawson girl to hear. Jim Ed thought that was a wasted effort. She probably knew worse stories than they did. She rode beside the big athlete on the black horse. Jim Ed wondered idly if that was her idea or his. Not that he gave a damn one way or the other.

Fuller Gibson was talking about how the Big River country's livestock-carrying capacity had declined in the years he had known it. "The way taxes keep goin' up and the production keeps goin' down, I don't see how we can stay much longer."

Already sore from the fall, Jim Ed would have bet a six-pack of longneck beer that the riders had traveled five miles before they reached the pasture's far side. Wes told him it was more like two. "First full-time cowboy job I ever had was on the C Bars," Wes said. "Them days, it was ten miles to the back side in most of their pastures. But the country's been whittled down. Nowadays you can spit from one fence to another."

"And you don't approve?"

"It was necessary. Approvin' and likin' ain't the same."

Jim Ed pondered the difference as Bill Roper led the procession along the fence. After a couple of hundred yards he looked back. "Wes, if you and Tater wouldn't mind, I'll drop you-all off here. You'll probably want to give us a while to get on across." It was stated more as suggestion than instruction.

Wes nodded. "Best offer we've had since the coffee."

Jim Ed watched while the rest of the horsebackers went on. His gaze followed the Dawson girl until she and the big bruiser named Shorty were lost to him in the cedars. So far as he had noticed, she had not looked at Jim Ed once since they had left camp, and she did not look back at him now.

He watched his grandfather fish a cigarette out of a pack. The stub finger was an inconvenience but not a real handicap.

Wes said, "Bill'll drop the rest off one at a time till he gets to the other side. Then we'll form a line and push the cattle back the way we come. Bill gave me and you the shortest and easiest way to go, right down the fence."

"That's all there is to a roundup? Seems kind of tame."

"It wouldn't've been, in the old days. But now they've bred these cattle for gentle. A few may snort a little and try to cut back, but it's all bluff. Like most people. Call their hand and they'll turn around."

"Like you're calling the bluff on those lake people?"

Wes took a long drag on the cigarette and gazed off across the hills, across massive distant liveoak trees that were green but looked blue in morning's light. He did not reply. Jim Ed turned his head to one side but cautiously cut a glance at his grandfather. He saw pain in those pale gray eyes.

This, perhaps, might be Wes Hendrix's last roundup, save for the one that would gather the livestock from his little ranch for a final time. This one, at least, he could enjoy. Jim Ed resolved to say no more about the lake and spare the old man that provocation.

Bill Roper dropped Fuller Gibson out of the group and left him to wait a couple of hundred yards away. Jim Ed smiled, thinking how relieved Roper must be not to have to listen to Gibson for a while. He said, "There's a man who could lay a chill over a Fourth of July barbecue."

Wes nodded. "He was just a workin' cowboy till he married a ranch. Used to cuss the rich. Used to argue that they ought to take up all the money in the country, put it in one pot and let everybody draw out equal. Now he plays the stock market and cusses the government. There ain't no better cure for a socialist than a little dose of capital."

Gibson dismounted and walked a few steps, stretching his legs, draining off some of the morning coffee. Jim Ed thought of the time lost waiting in the camphouse for daylight, and waiting now for the rest of the riders to reach the far side of the pasture. He could have spent that time in bed. "The old army game," he commented, fidgeting with impatience. "Hurry up and wait."

Wes seemed totally relaxed in the saddle. "There's an old sayin' they used to throw at me when I was a button. *I know you're hungry, and I know you're tired, but if you didn't want to work, you oughtn't to've hired.*"

"I didn't hire," Jim Ed said. "I got sent." He realized he had said too much.

Wes's face furrowed. "By your daddy, to try and talk me into sellin' out and hangin' up my saddle."

Jim Ed had already denied that once. "He wouldn't have sent *me* on that errand."

"He must've said *somethin'*."

"He said the more somebody tried to argue with you, the stronger you set your mind."

Wes nodded. "You've probably noticed your daddy inherited the same trait."

"It's been hard to overlook."

"I may not've given Truman much else, but I gave him a double dose of stubbornness. Ain't nobody goin' to run over your daddy without he has a hell of a fight."

Jim Ed remembered the long, awkward silences between his father and his grandfather, the rare times he had seen them together. Once they progressed beyond the weather and perhaps a few words on state and national politics, they seemed to have exhausted the extent of their common ground. Father and son remained forever strangers.

In recent years Jim Ed's relationship to his father had become no better than his father's to Wes.

Fuller Gibson remounted, after a while, and began walking his horse forward. Wes said, "Let him move on a little ways before we start, so any cattle he pushes in our direction won't cut behind us."

By the time Wes's spurs jingled softly against the dun horse's ribs, Jim Ed could hear the bawling of cattle disturbed by other riders. Calves and their anxious mothers were becoming separated in the drive. He found himself somehow drawn to the distant sound, as he had at times been drawn to the distant moaning of a train in the night, a train going somewhere far away.

The first animals he and Wes encountered were sheep, ewes with big early-spring lambs already well along toward the size of their mothers. A ewe stamped her foot, and the animals broke into a run. They fanned apart at first, then drew back together. Wes said, "Let's skirt around and leave them be. No use throwin' sheep into the cattle drive."

For a while it seemed the sheep *wanted* to join the drive, for they kept moving ahead of the horsemen. But after a time they came upon the fence and stopped to look back. Satisfied that Wes and Jim Ed were passing them by, they stayed. A couple of ewes bleated. Lambs dropped to their knees and began to punch at their mothers' udders. Jim Ed smiled, for the size of the lambs made it a ridiculous sight.

Wes said, "Most of the milk is probably dried up already. Them lambs ain't gettin' much from their mamas but companionship. Which ain't no small thing, I guess. Everybody needs companionship sometimes. I suppose you've found that out for yourself by now, ain't you, Tater?"

"I do all right."

"You got a girl?"

"No steady one right now. I just play the field."

"Nothin' wrong with that, I suppose, long's a young feller don't get careless and have to pay the fiddler for the dance."

"I've never been *that* careless. I learned about the birds and the bees a long time ago."

"I hope so, because some of them birds can sting worse than a bee." Wes frowned. "It wasn't some such of a girl trouble that brought you out here, was it?"

"No," Jim Ed said sharply, surprised that a man so far over the hill would even harbor thoughts on such a subject.

"Just wondered. Nowadays it seems like all the kids've taken free samples before they're your age. Not like *my* time. Them days, we had respect."

Jim Ed said, "I don't suppose *you* ever took any samples."

Wes grunted and turned his head toward a clatter in the cedar brush. "Watch, now. Fuller's pushin' some cattle towards us."

Chapter 3

Glory B. Dawson was in her natural element, working cattle on horseback, especially on her blue roan. The animal had an easy-flowing saddlegait she had always cherished, for it could carry her miles across the constant challenge of the Chatfield-Dawson ranch's broken terrain without overly tiring her. As far back as she could remember, she had always felt most free in the saddle, under the big, open, pale-blue sky with the muted pastel colors of the hill country spread around her. It was a view that seemed different with each passing hour, the changing sunlight, the shifting shadows altering color and form. She listened to the strike of horses' hoofs and glanced around as Shorty Bigham's black mount stumbled, then caught itself.

She demanded, "When're you going to swap that horse for a good one? He'll fall over his own shadow one of these days and flatten your face up against a rock."

Shorty grinned. Since they had been children in the second grade she had been able to say outrageous things to him without drawing a spark of resentment. "Him and me are a pretty good match. We're both a little klutzy."

If anyone else said that, she would take offense in Shorty's behalf. She had done so, many times. True, he could be a little awkward, a big blundering mule of a man who did not fully realize the extent of his own strength. But he harbored no pretensions, no illusions. He took life head-on, the way it came at him, and did not ask for favor or allowances. Since they had been schoolchildren together, he had stood between her and anyone who would dare to make light of the fact that she wore her clothes like a boy and would rather ride in a horse show than dance at a school prom. And she had challenged more than one who had disparaged Shorty Bigham as nothing more than a big dumb football player whose father owned a trucking company.

Off to her left she could see Bill Roper's son Johnny, and beyond him Bill himself, taking the outside of the drive, the longest and most difficult ride. Johnny was slapping a coiled rope against his leg, trying to scare along a young calf that did not understand what the strange creature wanted of it. The calf's mother, ambling a little ahead, kept turning and bawling for her offspring to follow.

"That's a pretty sight," Glory B. said. "I missed it when I was away in school."

"I don't know what you wanted to keep goin' to school for anyway," Shorty commented. "You already know more than you'll likely ever use. How much college does it take to teach you how to follow a cow and calf?"

"There's a lot more to it than just following. There's genetics and range management and marketing. You can't learn it all on horseback, sad to say."

Shorty had seldom been reticent about what was turning in his mind, even when reticence would have been a virtue. "What good'll all that do you if you have to sell out?"

She gave him a sharp look that was as near reproach as she ever got with Shorty. "Who told you we're selling out?"

He shrugged. "I hear talk. They say your grandmother's gone just about to the end of her string. They say she's tryin' to run the place like her daddy did, and your granddaddy did, and it just won't cut the mustard anymore."

"My great-grandfather Chatfield started putting this place together when he came home from the Spanish-American war. There are three generations of us still living here, and there'll be hell among the yearlings before this family sells out."

"There's been other ranches have to sell, older'n this one. Even these old rocky hills'll wear down with time."

"These old rocky hills'll wear down a lot more before we give them up. If anybody tells you different, you send him to me. I'll straighten him out."

Shorty shrugged again, his defenses raised. "Just tellin' you what I've heard." He moved off to the right to restart a cow that had stopped to grab a few mouthfuls of grass. He hollered at her in a falsetto voice that set her to moving, but not at a very lively gait. He pulled the black horse back beside Glory B.'s roan, his face apprehensive. "I wouldn't want to stay in Big River if you had to leave here."

She reached out and placed an affectionate hand on his arm. "Don't you be listening to any more talk like that. I was raised on this ranch. I intend to raise my kids here."

He managed a tentative little smile that she knew masked a nervous doubt. "Yours and who else's? It takes two for that."

"There'll be time enough."

"I'm ready to start whenever you are."

"I'm surprised at you," she scolded mildly, "letting your mind dwell on such things."

"I can't help it. My mind naturally runs thataway, watchin' how a horse bounces you up and down."

Involuntarily she brought a hand up to her bosom. A flash of warmth came to her face. It was not an unpleasant sensation. Glory B. smiled. "I suppose that's as close as you'll come to asking me to marry you."

His face had also reddened. "I never was very good with words."

She touched his arm again. "We'll see, Shorty. We'll see." That was as near as she was going to come to giving him a definite *maybe*.

They pushed the cattle through scattered cedar and a broad stretch of knee-high shinoak growth toward a high, flat-topped hill which lay beyond the camp corrals. As the drive narrowed down and the riders began closing with each other, the cattle converged into a sizable, noisy herd. Every animal seemed to be bawling at once. Through the dust Glory B. could see Wes Hendrix on the far side against the fence, with his grandson from Dallas.

Shorty commented, "I see the city boy didn't get lost."

"He had his grandfather watching out for him. Wes knows Liveoak Camp like he knows his own bedroom. They tell me he batched here once, a long time ago. He cowboyed for my great-grandfather, he and Orville Levitt both."

"Old Orville, that runs the drugstore? Hard to picture him as a cowboy."

"Well, he was. I've heard my grandmother talk about them."

Shorty mused, "You don't find many like Wes still around."

"And when he's gone, who'll take his place? Not that rock-and-roll grandson, that's for damned sure."

Shorty's eyes narrowed. "You ever see him before?"

"Not that I remember. Why?"

"You jumped on him awful hard this mornin', is all. I thought maybe you already knew him."

"As far as I know, this is the first time I ever laid eyes on him. If I'm lucky, it'll be the last."

"Just struck me funny that you got on his case so quick. Maybe he reminds you of somebody."

Glory B. gave Shorty a surprised study, wondering how he could know, wondering if he could read something in her face. "He reminds me of a *type* I ran into when I first went off to school. Know-it-all big-city boys who think it's their God-given mission to deliver the gospel to us poor beknighted colonials from way out here in the boonies." She realized her voice went bitter, and she tried to take the sting from it. "He just seems to fit the pattern."

Shorty's frown deepened. "That first Christmas you came home from school, I knew you'd changed. I figured somebody must've hurt you pretty bad."

She could not bring herself to look him squarely in the eyes. *Damn*, but he could be perceptive sometimes for a big dumb football player.

He said, "Anybody ever treats you like that, you send him to me. I'll clean his plow for him."

She felt the color rise again, and this time it *was* an unpleasant sensation. "There's a cow and calf yonder," she said, pointing. "They're fixing to try and cut back on you."

Jim Ed had grimly set his mind to endure the roundup with the straightest face he could muster, like a midterm examination for which he had not cracked a book. However, the sight of a dozen red-and-white Hereford cows and their calves stirred the bay horse to excitement, and Jim Ed found himself caught up to some degree in the contagion. The cattle's only evident purpose was to get away as they trotted at an angle fifty yards beyond Jim Ed and Wes. One cow jerked up her head in surprise. She evidently had regarded herself as having escaped from other horsemen who had disturbed her early-morning grazing. Jim Ed was intrigued by the way the horse Rowdy followed the cattle with its alert ears and seemed to want to close with them.

Wes said, "He's like Pepper; he wants to work."

"Likes to pitch, too," Jim Ed observed.

"He just don't like your hat."

The cattle confronted the netwire fence and stopped. The dominant cow of the bunch raised her head high and looked back. Seeing that the horsemen moved toward her, she struck a long trot down the fence. Jim Ed caught a whiff of dust raised by the hoofs as the others followed her. He surmised by the satisfaction in his grandfather's face that all was progressing as it should.

Wes Hendrix's shoulders had squared, and his back was straight as a hoe handle. Sitting on a horse seemed to wipe years from the etched scoreboard of his face. As he watched those cattle and listened to others bawling in the distance, his eyes lighted with the fires of remembrance. Jim Ed looked down the fence again and said, "I must be missing something."

"What?" Wes asked.

"You're seeing something I don't. Your eyes must be different."

Wes shrugged. "It's all this." He made a sweeping motion. "The country, the cattle, the mornin' cool . . . all of it. Hell, boy, you've got nothin' like this in the city."

"These ranches all look the same to me, nothing but limestone hills and liveoak trees and cedar brush."

"It all goes to what you've taught your eyes to see. To me, one city house appears the same as any other. But on my place or here on Liveoak you could lead me anywhere blindfolded and I could tell you where I'm at."

"It still all looks the same to me."

Wes stared at something in the distance. "Best job I ever had was here on Liveoak Camp. Just a button of twenty when I come . . . younger than you are now. Sometimes I've wished I'd never left."

"Why *did* you?"

Regret came over Wes's face like a shadow. "Because I *was* a button. A button's always got an itch to travel, lookin' for somethin' better down the road. It ain't there, usually, but he has to go and see for himself.

"I growed up on the plains, on a little old starveout ranch so flat you could see into the middle of next week. I'd always wanted to live where they had hills, so I come south huntin' for work. They was needin' a hand on the old Chatfield outfit—that was before it was the Chatfield-Dawson. Old Major Chatfield—he'd been with Teddy Roosevelt's Rough Riders—he sent me over here to Liveoak. I come to love this place."

"But you left it."

"There was reasons." He grimaced. "I taken it in my head I wanted to rodeo. I broke broncs for the Chatfields, and I was a middlin' good hand with a loop. But the major had a rule against ropin' stock without good cause. One day I was practicin' on some calves when I seen the old major himself, a-watchin' me. He didn't talk, just rode off lookin' grieved and waited for me at the house. We ate dinner without hardly a word. Finally he says, 'I hate to let you go, Wes. Would you promise me you won't ever rope any more stock?' He wasn't a man I could lie to. I says, 'I wouldn't want to make you a promise I couldn't keep.' So I rolled up my beddin' and taken off down the road.

"But I never could get this place out of my mind. When I was older and finally able to buy a little acreage of my own, I wanted it close to Liveoak. Everything I ever done, I patterned after the ways the major taught me. A cowman, he was, and a gentleman. No better man ever lived."

Blinking, Wes looked toward the distant bawling of cattle.

"Them was good times, good people. Ain't many things still like they was then. Liveoak Camp comes as close as anything."

Jim Ed thought, *Not much has changed at your ranch, either, except that you've gotten older.* But on reflection he knew that was not true. The old man had not stood still. He had electricity instead of coal-oil lamps. He had a pickup so he didn't need as many horses, and a trailer so the horses didn't have to walk so far. He had a steel barn. He even had television. But one thing would never change: a mind-set that went back to Teddy Roosevelt, and probably farther.

A sobering question came to him. *When I'm his age, will I be telling everybody that the good old days ended when I stopped being young?*

The bawling of cattle became louder and closer. Dust arose from the stirring of all those hoofs, though recent rains had greened the grass. He reflected that the only thing about this country which could bring a tear to *his* eye was the dust.

Two steel windmills stood outlined against a big flat-topped hill stair-stepped by alternating layers of limestone, like a massive birthday cake. Jim Ed realized he was almost back to the corrals. The scattered riders were moving together again, pushing what seemed a tremendous herd of cattle. "Must be five or six hundred," he commented.

Wes snorted. "How do you expect to get along in the world if you don't know how to count?" He made several fast motions with his right hand, the fingers spread apart. "About a hundred cows, maybe a couple more, with late calves at their sides. That many all bawlin' for one another, the noise'll make you think there's a thousand of them. It's like coyotes. Two of them boogers at night'll make you imagine there's a dozen."

Several Angora goats had become mixed up in the drive, though the horsemen had managed to leave the sheep behind. Wes said dryly, "Wherever you don't want a goat to be, that's the first place to go and look for him."

A slim rider on a blue roan horse rode slowly among the cattle and worked the goats to the outside. Jim Ed was impressed by the easy skill that manuevered the animals without stirring them to fright. The dust cleared a little, and he realized he was watching the Dawson girl. He said sourly, "I guess they put up with her because she's the boss's daughter."

Wes shook his head. "The boss's *grand*daughter. Her daddy got killed in a car wreck a couple of years ago. They put up with her because she's the best cowboy here, barrin' Bill Roper . . . and maybe me. If I was you, I'd watch Glory B. and learn."

"No sunburned country girl has got anything to teach me."

Wes grunted and studiously lighted another cigarette.

As Glory B. pushed the goats to the outside, Bill Roper cut in behind them and hazed them away from the cattle. He shouted something to his husky son, who drifted the goats out a hundred yards or so. The boy did not turn his back on them until he was satisfied they would keep going.

The girl opened a plank gate and led her horse into a corral, then remounted. A few cows warily followed her, and the rest fell in behind. When it appeared they might start running, she rode in closer and slowed them. Wes said letting cattle run spoiled them and tended to make them wild. Besides, there was always a risk of trampling calves. He added, "I wish I'd had the chance to train you when you was the age of Bill Roper's boy."

"But he'll probably be a cowboy the rest of his life. I won't."

"Johnny's got a sharp mind and a set of hands that can do anything he takes a notion to. It don't matter what trade he goes into; he'll be a better man because he learned to be a good cowboy." His voice sharpened. "I don't remember hearin' what kind of trade *you're* figurin' on."

"I've been majoring in business administration. Dad always badgered me to be an accountant, like he is. It's safe and sure, he says. But the longer I went, the less I liked the idea of being chained to ledgers and accounts and a computer terminal all my life." He did not tell Wes that he had sloughed off and flunked the final semester of his senior year. "I don't know what I want."

Wes grumbled, "If you don't know what it is, you'll never get it."

Jim Ed followed his grandfather and the cattle into the pen, where dust arose windmill high, burning his eyes, making him cough. Roper's son closed the plank gate behind them. The other riders led their horses into an adjacent empty pen. Jim Ed swung down from the saddle and was immediately dismayed, for his tired legs tried to buckle. Swaying, he grasped the saddle for support. The ground seemed only inches from his face, and it was moving.

Wes said, "You ain't used to this. You been sittin' high up on that horse all mornin', and now all of a sudden you can't tell how far it is to your feet. Be careful how you step away. You're liable to eat a mouthful of dirt. Or somethin'."

The girl walked by, leading her roan horse. "Hang in there, pilgrim. We'll make a man out of you yet."

He retorted, "You're trying to make a man out of *yourself*. I don't think you've got the materials."

She grinned. "Majoring in anatomy are you, pilgrim?"

Hers didn't look like much, hidden beneath a dusty, slouchy old shirt and faded jeans. He supposed it must suit that big old boy who looked like a football player, though, because he was walking fast to catch up with Glory B.

Jim Ed glanced at Wes. "Is it lunchtime?" He was not hungry, but he wished he could lie down somewhere and rest, even if on the hard ground.

"We got time to scout that pasture before dinner and pick up any cattle we missed. Unless your butt's too sore to ride."

"Is *she* goin'?"

"I expect she will."

"Then my butt can stand it. Maybe I'll get lucky and see her fall on *hers*."

The ride gave him ample time for regret. He could feel grimy sweat between his rump and the saddle, and on the insides of his legs where the leather rubbed. The salt from perspiration set up a burning that persisted no matter how he shifted his weight. He stood in the stirrups at intervals, hoping for relief, but his aching knees made him sit again. The torment was always there.

Wes seemed aware of his discomfort, if not particularly sympathetic. "You'll toughen up. You can't appreciate heaven till you've been through hell."

Unwilling to acknowledge any problem, Jim Ed gritted his teeth and kept his gaze set straight ahead.

The scouting seemed to take longer than the first drive, but Jim

Ed realized that the galling of his rump and the insides of his legs made two hours stretch like four. The riders' sweep picked up only six cows and their calves. It hardly seemed worth the effort, he thought. The clanking of the two windmills was as welcome as the ringing of the bell at the end of Friday classes. Inside the corral, Jim Ed dismounted with care and deliberation. He walked stiff-legged, trying to find some manner of moving that would not aggravate the searing heat between his buttocks. Each step made the jeans rub fire against his thighs.

He heard a metallic clanging from the direction of the house. Wes said, "Dinnertime. Tie your horse, Tater."

Jim Ed might have shown more interest in death than in food. He wondered where he would find strength to endure the second half of this interminable day. He stole a glance at the Dawson girl. She betrayed no evidence of discomfort or fatigue. He watched enviously as Bill Roper lifted one foot at a time to the second plank on a fence and unsnapped his leather chaps. It was all Jim Ed could do to drag one foot ahead of the other. He tried to keep up with his grandfather as the crew walked toward the old camp house, a dozen pairs of spurs jingling, but the pain held him to short steps, and he fell behind. Bill Roper waited at the door while the others went in.

"Tater," he said, "the first couple of days after I got home from the army, I thought the chappin'd kill me. Wait here a minute." He was back shortly with an old towel and a can of talcum powder. His smile spoke more of sympathy than of amusement. "Slip off out yonder behind the windmill. Wash yourself good, then use plenty of this powder where you hurt the most. It won't cure you, but it'll raise your odds for survival."

Jim Ed knew no way to express the depth of his gratitude. Taking short steps, he made his way to one of the windmills where an old shed shielded him from view. He found a spigot in the pipe a couple of feet above the ground. He lowered his jeans and his drawers, wet half of the towel and touched it to his fiery skin. The cold water made him stiffen with shock, but it eased the burning. He washed away the salty sweat and dried himself with the other end of the towel. He applied the talcum in a profligate manner, spilling much of it. He pulled up the jeans and brushed away as much of the telltale powder as he could. He washed his hands under the spigot again, spread the towel on a bottom brace to dry in the sun and returned to the house, trying to carry the talcum can inconspicuously. Walking with less pain, he began to entertain serious hope of eventual recovery.

He met the men and boys coming outside with filled plates, carrying iced tea in big fruit cans or hot coffee in crock mugs large enough to drown a small cat. Wes was among them. "Better hurry in there, Tater. A man won't get rich cowboyin' for this outfit, or any other, but he'll eat good."

He found fragrant steam rising from a kitchen table laden with pan-fried steaks, big brown-topped biscuits, thick-cut fried potatoes, red beans and an assortment of vegetables. A friendly, pretty-eyed woman younger than his mother stood beside the stove, wiping her hands on a flour-spotted apron, prompting each passing man and boy to take more. When one of them called her Hallie, he knew she was Bill Roper's wife. She said sternly to her son, "You, Johnny, you skimped on everything but the butter and biscuits. You go back and put some more meat on that plate, and some *frijoli* beans."

The boy reddened, looking uneasily at his school friends, but he complied. The woman's attention went to Jim Ed. She gave him a quick appraisal, her gaze touching but a moment on his hat. He thought her handsome, considering that she was probably on the downhill side of her thirties. She said, "You'd be Wes's grandson."

"I'm Jim Ed Hendrix, from Dallas."

Glory B. Dawson stood at the kitchen cabinet with the big football player. She was eating from her plate beside the sink. Her smile was wicked. "This pilgrim moves like a turtle with rheumatism. But since the *working* crew has been fed, I guess we can let him have some leftovers."

Hallie gave Jim Ed an easy smile that took ten years off of her age. "They call you Tater, I believe." Before he could correct her, she said, "Tater, I can't say you look much like Wes, except that neither one of you has enough flesh on your bones to stand up against a March wind. You fill that plate good now, do you hear? I won't let you away from this house till I see you loosen that belt."

Few things made Jim Ed more uncomfortable than women who wanted to baby him. His mother's sisters had always made a big to-do, leaving him feeling like some helpless child. Even his own mother aroused more discomfort than appreciation on those rare occasions when she came at him with a protective air. He tried to make allowances, telling himself they all meant well. But his embarrassment was the worse because the Dawson girl took it in with an air of faint derision. He gave her a challenging glance and made his way to the door with a full plate and a can of iced tea that tried to slip from his grasp because it was slick with condensation.

He found a place in the dense shade of an ancient liveoak tree, near Wes. Several young cowboys squatted on their heels. Jim Ed tried but was too sore. He sat flat on the ground like most of the older men whose knees no longer tolerated abuse. The first bite told him his grandfather had not exaggerated Hallie's cooking. The solid food soon made him forget at least some of his soreness.

Jim Ed assumed the men would rush through the meal and go directly back to work, but they stretched on the grass in the shade of the trees. Fuller Gibson started a monologue about the evils of the Federal Reserve system. Wes lay on the hard wooden porch and dropped off to sleep. Some of the younger boys went to a large round concrete water tank and found a cane pole with a line and a fishhook on it. They scratched around and came up with a couple of bugs, which they impaled on the hook and cast into the water. They fished with considerable determination but without any luck.

Jim Ed had noticed young Johnny Roper observing him with the same open curiosity as yesterday. *I must look to him like I've just climbed out of a tree—or a flying saucer,* he thought. He asked the boy, "Are there any fish in that tank?"

Johnny had helped bait the hook and watched while one of the other boys patiently dragged the line back and forth across the water. "We've never caught any. But it beats takin' a nap."

After about an hour Bill Roper quietly got up from the porch and sauntered casually toward the corrals. The others took his silent cue and followed. The boys reluctantly put the cane pole back where they had found it, the bugs drowned but otherwise intact.

Roper and one of the cowboys lifted a cylindrical steel contraption from the back of a pickup and carried it through the gate into a cedar-picket pen where the calves waited, cut off from their mothers. A small silver butane tank was placed at the end of a blue hose, away from the unit. Roper turned the tank's red valve, and Fuller Gibson struck a match to light the flame within the cylinder. Johnny Roper brought half a dozen long-handled branding irons from the pickup. He placed their stamp ends in the cylinder, where the hissing flame alternated between blue and orange.

Wes untied his dun horse and tightened the girth he had loosened before dinner. He swung into the saddle and took down his rope. "How's your chappin'?" he asked his grandson.

Jim Ed had not admitted to anything. "What chapping?"

"Then I reckon you'll be up to flankin' calves. Just watch you don't get a hoof in your mouth. They don't chew easy." He wrapped the end of his rope around the saddlehorn and tied a half hitch. "Pair up with somebody. Show them how quick a college boy can learn."

A girl's voice spoke behind Jim Ed. "I'll pair with him, Wes, and teach him how it's done." Glory B. Dawson held her jaw square, those large brown eyes laughing at him.

He said sharply, "Every time I turn around, you're digging your spurs into me. What do you think I am, a horse?"

She did not flinch from his resentful gaze. "Maybe next time you won't take it for granted that just because I'm a woman, I can't do anything but cook."

"I meant it for a compliment. I'll make it a point not to compliment you anymore."

"You smart-ass city dudes are always trying to show us country bumpkins our rightful place. Well, you're on my turf now. Maybe we can show *you* a few things."

He thought he would like her to show him a little humility for starters, but that was an unlikely prospect.

Jim Ed looked at the calves. He judged them to weigh considerably more than he did. "You really think you're going to wrestle those down?"

"*We're* going to do it, you and I. It's all timing and leverage. How are you on timing and leverage, pilgrim?"

"I haven't had any complaints from the girls."

Bill Roper was whetting a large pocketknife on a dark gray stone. He frowned at Glory B. "Your mother wouldn't hold with you wrestlin' calves. She wouldn't think it's ladylike."

"I didn't study to be a lady. I studied to be a rancher."

"She doesn't think much of that either, I've noticed."

Glory B. seemed a little reluctant about saying, "She's not here anyway. She went to . . . well, she's gone."

Roper blinked. "Oh," he said, and turned away.

Jim Ed caught something in Glory B.'s eyes—anger, perhaps, or hurt. She said, "But my grandmother'll be here, and it always pleases her to see me making a hand."

Roper asked, "She feelin' better?"

"Some. She said she'd be here."

"I'm glad to hear it," Roper said. He jiggled the irons in the butane heater, lifting one for a quick look. Satisfied, he said, "They're hot."

Wes Hendrix rode his horse slowly toward the bunched calves. They split apart at his approach. He picked a calf on the outside, moved in behind him and snaked a small loop down in front of the hind legs. The calf stepped into it, and Wes jerked up the slack. Holding the rope taut, he turned the horse and came out in a brisk trot, dragging the bewildered animal on its belly. When he stopped dragging, the calf struggled to get to its feet.

Glory B. said, "You grab the tail. I'll take the rope." She went down the opposite side of the rope from Jim Ed and gripped it with both hands a few inches from the calf's hind feet. "Now!" she shouted, and jerked hard. Uncertain, Jim Ed pulled the tail without much effect. The calf staggered but remained on its feet. Glory B. said, "Timing, pilgrim, timing! You've got to do it when I do. Now, pull!"

He yanked on the tail as she jerked the rope in the opposite direction. The calf's hind feet flipped into the air, toward Glory B. Its rump flopped over toward Jim Ed. He stepped back, but not quickly enough to keep the calf from striking him just below the knees and knocking him backward. He found himself suddenly seated in the soft sand, the struggling calf lying across his feet.

Glory B. said, "It's him that's supposed to be down, not you. Get up from there and grab his foreleg. And drop your knee on his neck so he can't get up." Uncomfortably aware that several men and boys were watching, Jim Ed pushed to his feet and grabbed at the flailing foreleg twice before he took a firm grip. The calf flung its head in fright. Jim Ed had difficulty in finding how to use his weight on its neck to hold it still. Glory B. ducked under the rope, gripped the kicking left hind leg and dropped to the ground on her hip pockets. She shoved the heel of her boot snugly against the calf's right leg to hold it out of action.

"See there," she said, "you use the calf's own weight and movement against him. Just like martial arts."

It did not surprise him that she knew about martial arts.

Wearing leather gloves to protect his hands, Fuller Gibson brought a hot branding iron and stamped a C Bar on the calf's left hip. The smoke had a yellowish tinge and burned fiercely at Jim Ed's nostrils. He saw that Glory B. was blinking and assumed it was stinging her eyes. It was reassuring to know she was not immune from *all* of life's inconveniences. A cowboy walked up with a large syringe in his hand and administered beer-colored vaccine under the animal's skin.

Bill Roper's sharp pocketknife deftly turned the bull calf into a steer. He said, "You'll have to pull his head up, Tater, so I can reach his right ear." One swipe of the blade left a swallowfork notch oozing a thin line of blood.

Roper's son Johnny came along with some thick black liquid in an old coffee can and dabbed it on the freshly-cut scrotum.

Glory B. said, "All right, pilgrim, you can let him up."

As Jim Ed released his hold, the calf scrambled free. Glory B. clung to its tail and let the calf's forward motion pull her to a stand. She said, "Now then, don't you ever let it be said that the cowboy life is not romantic."

Jim Ed saw the calf's blood smeared across his hand. He looked down at his legs and saw fresh green manure clinging to his jeans. "I wouldn't have missed it for the world," he replied.

Wes timed his heeling and dragging to keep two flanking crews busy. That was about the proper pace for the number of available irons and heating space in the butane burner. Jim Ed learned after the first three or four that throwing the calves was easy if he coordinated his move with Glory B.'s. He found himself enjoying the physical challenge of matching his weight and strength against that of the animals.

Bill Roper finished whittling on a calf. "Watch your granddaddy out there, Tater. You'll never see his like again."

Jim Ed did not understand. Roper explained, "He plays that rope like he plays a fiddle. Ain't many men got that knack anymore. I've seen him heel calves in a brandin' pen all afternoon and never miss more than one or two."

Jim Ed failed to see the significance. "Why not? Anybody had better be pretty good at what he does for a living."

"Pretty good?" Glory B. declared with a touch of indignation. "That old man is better than good. I wish I could rope half as well."

He started to ask her why a woman would want to rope at all and was glad on reconsideration that he had not put the question into words. She would probably have told him.

Not for some time did he see his grandfather miss a loop. But finally Wes missed once, twice and again. He slumped in the saddle, staring at the cattle and at the end of the rope lying on the ground with its loop drawn up small and empty. Bill Roper walked out to him. "Wes, you feelin' all right?"

Wes nodded. "Just a little tired all of a sudden."

Roper said, "Glory B.'s probably itchin' to heel a few. Why don't you let her spell you awhile?"

Glory B. did not wait for further invitation. She hurried into the adjacent corral for her horse. She tightened the girth, swung up and tied the rope securely against the horn. She looked to the big football player, who had been underemployed since the branding started. "Shorty, why don't you team up with the pilgrim yonder? We wouldn't want him to miss any of the glamour of the cowboy life."

Shorty! Jim Ed had never seen a nickname fall so far from the mark. The young man towered over him. He thought it fortunate that Shorty seemed benign. He would not want to have him for an enemy unless he had someone even bigger for a friend.

Jim Ed pointed his chin at Glory B. as she rode toward the calves. "Your girlfriend?"

"I hope so. With Glory B., it's hard to say."

"You've got my sympathy."

A big car drove up to the outside fence and stopped in the shade of a huge liveoak whose gnarled branches extended over into the corral like an umbrella. Some of the branded calves had taken refuge in their cool shade. An elderly woman took her time getting out from behind the wheel. She wore a cowboy-style felt hat. Its crown had little shape, and its brim was flat. It was for shade, not for appearance. Glory B. waved from the saddle. The woman returned the wave and leaned against the fence, her eyes warm with pride as she watched the girl. Wes Hendrix removed his hat and walked over to speak to the woman in a manner indicative of deep respect.

Shorty volunteered, "That's Glory B.'s grandmother, Lavinia Dawson. Miz Livvy, they call her. Her daddy was old Major Chatfield, who started this ranch."

The lady reflected a quiet dignity which evidently had not made the transition into the third generation. Jim Ed said, "Maybe she'll order Her Highness out of the branding pen."

Shorty shook his head. "It's always been understood that this ranch'll belong to Glory B. someday, if cheap cattle don't bankrupt it first. The old lady wants her to be prepared."

Jim Ed half hoped Glory B. would miss her first loop, but she caught a calf's hind feet and dragged him between Shorty and Jim Ed. She had chosen one of the largest calves still unbranded. "Grab him, pilgrim. Study long, study wrong!"

She had similar good fortune with several more throws, to Jim Ed's frustration. But finally she missed one. Jim Ed smiled. She rebuilt the loop and missed again. Jim Ed laughed aloud. She cast him a look of irritation and said, "Let's see how you laugh now, pilgrim." She roped a hefty calf around the neck instead of the heels, turned the horse and dragged the calf out. It jumped and bawled and kicked. She declared, "You've had it easy so far. Now throw *this* one, will you?"

Jim Ed looked at Shorty, but the football player grinned and backed away. "He's all yours."

Jim Ed sensed that the attention of everybody in the corral was centered on him. Most of the people probably hoped to see him catch one of those flailing hoofs in his mouth. He reached over the pitching, bellowing calf and tried to find a handhold. The calf's supple hide slipped free of his fingers. He caught a hoof against his shin, shooting pain all the way up his leg. He managed finally to get one arm around the calf's neck and one hand under the flank.

"You got him now," Shorty shouted. "It just takes brute strength and awkwardness."

Jim Ed had the awkwardness. He managed somehow to wrestle the animal to the ground. Dirt burned his eyes and scratched his throat, but he felt a glow of satisfaction for not having pulled away from the challenge.

The calf lay wrong, and Shorty helped him turn it over so the left side was up to receive the brand. Jim Ed heaved for breath while the branding iron and the knife did their work. Shorty smiled in silence. When they let the calf up, he said, "I'll show you a simpler way of doin' that. If she drags another one in here by the neck, you let me take him."

For the other crew Glory B. roped each calf by the heels so it was easier to handle. But each time Shorty's and Jim Ed's turn came, she purposely caught a calf around the neck. Shorty showed Jim Ed how to grab the animal while it was in the midst of a jump and use leverage to throw it on its side. It looked easy, the way Shorty did it. Jim Ed was not surprised when Shorty told him he had played fullback for the Big River Broncos.

Jim Ed knew by the way Glory B. swung the loop that she intended to hand him another bellowing, pawing, kicking present. She made a catch and jerked up the slack, then turned and came spurring, grinning wickedly.

The calf took a different view. The moment the noose drew tight around its neck it began jumping, bawling, running until it hit the end of the rope and was jerked back abruptly. Instead of letting itself be dragged, it set out in a run toward Glory B. The rope went slack, and the calf ran under the horse. Startled, the roan made a jump and tangled its feet in the trailing lariat. The calf hit the end again, bawling, doubling back. The horse stumbled and went down, slamming Glory B. to the ground.

Jim Ed realized with a cold shock that the rope had become tangled around her. Between the threshing horse and the frantic calf, that rope could crush her ribs, or even break her neck. Shorty yelled and started toward her, then tripped and fell. Other men came running, but Jim Ed was the nearest. He fished a knife from his pocket and opened the blade. The horse seemed about to get up. Jim Ed threw his weight against the roan and thrust the blade between the rope and Glory B.'s ribs. The rope parted. The calf ran back toward the others, kicking at the trailing length of lariat that stirred a thin line of dust.

The horse scrambled to its feet in a panic, its shoulder striking Jim Ed and knocking him rolling. He looked straight up at the big roan belly, the sharp hoofs striking soft ground on one side of him and then the other. Pain lanced his side, and most of the breath was knocked out of him. A hoof struck him a glancing blow across one shoulder as the horse tried to fight clear of him. Half blinded by dirt, Jim Ed was not sure which direction to crawl and get out of the way. He felt strong hands grab him, and strong arms pull him clear. Shorty Bigham, he realized. Glory B. was still in the saddle, fighting for control of the panicked roan.

As Jim Ed blinked away some of the dirt, he saw that most of the men had run to Glory B.'s aid. Only Shorty had rushed to help Jim Ed . . . Shorty and now Wes, who had been on the far side of the corral talking with Glory B.'s grandmother. Wes's face was drained pale.

"Tater, you hurt?"

"I'm all right," Jim Ed wheezed. It occurred to him that his hands were empty. "I lost . . . my knife . . ."

"The hell with the knife," Wes exclaimed, one hand on Jim Ed's shoulder as he looked him over carefully. Then Wes began to cough. He turned away, staggering back toward the corner. Lavinia Dawson was hurrying through a plank gate, her eyes wide.

Jim Ed continued to fight for breath. Shorty slapped his back with a violence that threatened to knock out more air than it might restore. When Jim Ed was breathing again, and he had cleared the dirt from his eyes, he turned to see what had become of Glory B. She was standing on the ground, patting her trembling horse on the neck and assuring her grandmother that she had never been in danger. But her face was pale, betraying the scare she had suffered.

Lavinia Dawson turned to Jim Ed. "Are you all right?"

"Fine," he managed, coughing. "Just fine."

Wes stood in the corner of the pen with his back turned. He held a tin cup so loosely that water spilled onto the ground without his seeming to notice. Bill Roper had gone to Wes's side and was talking quietly to him. Lavinia Dawson joined Roper.

Jim Ed's legs began to regain their strength. Moving toward Glory B., he said, "I'm glad you're not hurt."

For a moment her eyes were soft, and he thought she might thank him. But she held up the cut end of the lariat and demanded, "Pilgrim, do you know what a good rope costs?"

His anger rose above the aching of new bruises and the soreness from the morning's work. "More than gratitude, evidently," he responded, and turned away from her. He found his hat half buried in the sand. The roan horse had stepped on it. As he dusted it against his leg, the decorative green feathers floated off in six directions. His purple T-shirt was ripped all the way down the front. He had just as well throw it away. He muttered something under his breath and started toward his grandfather.

Glory B. called, "Pilgrim, wait."

He halted but did not turn around. She came up even with him and reached out as if to place her hand on his arm but stopped short of doing it. "Look, I . . ." Whatever she wanted to say, she could not bring it out. She finally managed, "I hope my horse didn't hurt you."

Jim Ed had expected more than that. "If he did me any good, I'll be glad to pay you for it."

He tried to straighten the battered hat. One feather clung, but it looked so forlorn that he pulled it loose and let it go. Glory B. said, "That's *some* improvement."

"A matter of opinion."

Bill Roper walked up, looking worriedly back over his shoulder. "Tater, Miz Livvy and I think you'd better take your grand-daddy home."

Jim Ed turned quickly. "What's the matter with him?"

"His face went plumb gray for a minute. He had to take a nitroglycerine pill."

"Nitroglycerine?" The significance hit him like the blow of a fist.

Roper's eyes were grave. "I reckon you didn't know he's got a heart condition."

Jim Ed's mouth felt as if it were still half full of dirt. "Nobody told me."

"Not many know about it." Roper's face twisted. He was plainly not used to giving unsolicited advice. "He may've given you the notion that he hasn't got much use for you. That's because he hasn't found much common ground between you yet. But his heart like to've quit on him when he seen you in trouble. You take care of him, Tater. He's a special old man."

Jim Ed nodded agreement. "I'll see if he'll go." He went to the patch of shade beneath the big liveoak, where his grandfather leaned against the fence beside Lavinia Dawson. Wes's face had regained most of its color, but he looked dead-tired. Jim Ed said, "Let's go home, Daddoo."

Wes was surprised, then pleased. "You ain't called me that since you was a little button."

"It just slipped out. I'll get our horses."

"Work ain't done here yet."

Bill Roper said, "You already heeled most of the calves. Why don't you go on home and lay down? We'll call for your help again another day."

Wes considered, glancing at Glory B. and her grandmother. "I'm doin' fine, but we gave Tater more exercise than *he's* used to. I'd better take him in so he can rest."

Bill Roper gave Jim Ed a wink that spoke of relief. "He looks like he needs it."

Jim Ed started for the gate. Glory B.'s grandmother caught his arm. Her face showed the lines of her age, but her eyes were the strong brown of her granddaughter's. "Young man, I want to thank you."

Jim Ed had never learned how to accept expressions of gratitude with grace. He pulled away. "I'd better get my grandfather home."

He led the two animals to the parked pickup and trailer. Wes stood in the shade of the barn while Shorty Bigham helped load the horses. He grunted his satisfaction when Jim Ed tied the reins on the right-hand side.

The foreman's handsome wife Hallie came out of the house, carrying a couple of bulging paper sacks. "Here's some leftovers."

Wes argued that such a gift was not necessary, but the protest was weak, more of form than of conviction. Hallie placed one sack in the pickup seat, the other on the floorboard. She declared, "I never did see a batch outfit where the men got anything fit to eat." She turned to Jim Ed. "Now, Tater, you see that everything cold goes in the refrigerator the minute you get home. Your old grandaddy'd probably let it spoil."

Jim Ed felt a warm rush of embarrassment over the easy familiarity. "Thank you, ma'am," he said, and cast a quick glance toward the corral, where Glory B. stood with her grandmother. She was not looking in his direction.

He was glad to get away.

He turned the pickup around and started out upon the graded road. Wes leaned heavily against the passenger corner, his hat cushioning his head. He looked older than seventy-seven. He closed his eyes, and Jim Ed thought he had gone to sleep. But the old man said, "I misjudged you, Tater. I wouldn't've imagined you had it in you."

Jim Ed could handle praise from his grandfather no better than he had handled gratitude from Glory B.'s grandmother. "Maybe I'd better take you into town and let a doctor look at you."

"He's *already* looked at me. He'd just tell me to take a pill, which I did, and to stay in my rockin' chair, which I won't. And he'd charge me thirty dollars. I'd rather spend it on whisky. Let's go home."

Jim Ed had seen the same expression in his father's face often enough to know that further argument would be like putting up his hands to stop the wind. "Whatever you say."

Wes was silent awhile. Finally he said, "Looks like your rock-and-roll T-shirt is totaled. Didn't do your little hat much good either."

"That ought to tickle you," Jim Ed suggested.

"I don't know. There's somethin' to be said for a man who goes his own way and don't just run with the pack." Wes reached down for the bottle on the floorboard, then changed his mind. He asked, "You hurtin' anywhere, Tater?"

"I'm hurting *everywhere,*" Jim Ed admitted.

"You'll hurt even worse tomorrow. But you done good today."

Chapter 4

Glory B. walked back to the branding pen when the last of the visiting help had loaded their horses into trailers and left dust hovering over the caliche road. The calves' ordeal was over. They had been turned into a large waterlot with the cows to pair up. They were quiet now, the young ones reunited with sympathetic matrons which stood patiently and let them take their nourishment from udders full of milk after a few hours' fast. Bill Roper and son Johnny had spread hay on the ground to help the cattle settle. That would at least partially offset their natural tendency to associate the pens with fright, pain and separation, an association which could make them difficult to corral next time.

Glory B. studied the ground, trying to remember just where the roan horse had gone down. Details were a blur to her. She touched her hand to her burning side, where the whipsaw action of the rope had left a deep and ugly welt.

Bill Roper had turned off the butane burner as soon as the last calf was branded. Now that the unit had cooled, he and the husky young Johnny were loading it and the branding irons into the back of Roper's dusty blue pickup. It made an ear-piercing metallic screech as he slid it across the pickup bed toward the steel "headache rack" that shielded the cab.

He asked, "What you lookin' for, Glory B.?"

She moved the scarred toe of her boot through the soft dirt. "The pilgrim's knife. He dropped it along here somewhere."

Roper and Johnny joined her in sifting through the sand. At length her toe struck something, and she reached down. "Got it," she said. The blade was still open.

Roper whistled softly. "Lucky some flanker didn't sit down on that. He'd've been marked for life."

Glory B. beat the knife against her leg to knock out sand. She put the end of it to her lips and blew. She tapped it against the palm of her hand a couple of times and folded the blade.

Roper said, "I'll be goin' over sometime tomorrow to look in on Wes. I'll take that if you'd like me to."

She started to hand it to him, then changed her mind. "Maybe I'll want to go with you. To see about Wes."

Roper nodded. "You sure you didn't get hurt none?"

"Just a little rope burn is all. It's nowhere close to the heart."

"That Tater saved your bacon."

"I didn't need him. Shorty would've gotten to me first if he hadn't stumbled."

"Seems to me like Shorty used to stumble a lot on the football field."

"Well, you'll remember that he stumbled the Big River Broncos into the first state championship they ever had."

Roper forfeited with a thin smile. "At least he's got a heart even bigger than his feet. Did you see him drag Tater out from under that horse?"

"I was kind of busy at the time."

"He could've got kicked himself, but he moved right in there and pulled that boy out of the way."

"That just backs up those people who call him a big dumb football player." But she felt a glow of pride in Shorty. "He never was one to worry much about consequences."

Roper turned to his son. "Johnny, you slip around yonder and open that waterlot gate so the cattle can go back out. Real easy now. We want them to leave in their own slow time."

Roper turned to finish loading the last of the branding paraphernalia into the bed of the pickup. He had worked on the C Bar as far back as Glory B.'s memory carried. He was one of those quietly efficient men who always did more than his job demanded or than its payscale justified, one of an anonymous army of capable cowhands and foremen without whom the ranching industry would never have survived into the twentieth century. Given the same level of responsibility in any other industry representing a similar financial investment, he would have been earning twice as much. Glory B. wished sometimes, when she allowed herself the leisure to think about it, that she could find a Bill Roper of her own age. When she was a high-school girl she had fantasized about something sad happening to Roper's wife Hallie, leaving Glory B. herself to fill the vacancy, reluctantly of course. She had put that childish thought behind her years ago. Even so, she considered Hallie Roper one of the most fortunate women she knew.

Bill had always been quick with a smile, but lately his joviality seemed sometimes forced. He probably would never tell her so, but Glory B. sensed that he brooded about the survival of the ranch. In terms of his job he had as much at stake as the three Dawson women who owned the place—Glory B., her mother and her grandmother. She wished she had a satisfactory answer, for herself as well as for him.

Johnny Roper worked his way slowly around the outside of the waterlot, cautiously avoiding any stirring of the cattle, and he returned the same way. One cow near the newly opened gate gave it a long and solemn consideration, then sauntered through it. Her calf trotted along behind her, its hide blistered but its belly full of warm milk. Other cows began to follow the example, all in a slow and deliberate walk. From the time of Glory B.'s great-grandfather Chatfield, the law on this ranch had been to handle cattle with gentleness and ease. Rodeo was for an arena in town.

Glory B. walked to the pickup with Johnny. "Good job," she said, and put a hand on his shoulder. He blushed. It was time, she decided, that she observe more formality with him. He had come to an age that he noticed girls.

"Bill," she said, "if you'll take Roanie in your trailer, I'll drive Gram home in her car. She looks tired."

Roper nodded and told Johnny to take the pickup to the long gooseneck trailer in which the horses had been brought to the camp for work. To Glory B. he said, "You ought to spend as much time with her as you can. She's not gettin' any younger."

Glory B. stared uncomfortably at Roper as he walked along after the pickup. He had reminded her of Lavinia Dawson's mortality. The lines were deepening in her grandmother's face, and brown eyes once bright were increasingly weary.

She walked toward the old house, set amid a cluster of massive liveoak trees already ancient when the first piece of lumber had been sawed here. She always enjoyed the look of the box-and-strip structure, a traditional pioneer style left over from her great-grandfather's time. The outer walls were of one-by-twelves nailed vertically upon a now-unseen two-by-four frame, with one-by-fours covering each join. Over the broad front porch at the top of the steps was a single piece of gingerbread molding, a whimsical jigsaw touch by some forgotten carpenter of eighty or so years ago, something business-minded Major Chatfield probably had not ordered and would not pay for. When Glory B. had been a girl, that one bit of hand-cut trim had fascinated her, for it was like an illustration out of *Hansel and Gretel.* It was a little warped now from age and exposure, but it gave the old place an elusive pioneer charm, something like her grandmother's big headquarters house where Glory B. had grown up.

She found Hallie busily wiping the last of the dinnerware, stacking on the table that which was to go back to headquarters and into the cabinet that which would stay here in Liveoak Camp. A strand of brown hair hung down over Hallie's face, a face Glory B. had always regarded as prettier than her own. Glory B. said, "It's been a long day, Hallie. I'll bet you and Bill'll be glad to get to bed tonight."

Hallie's eyes twinkled as with some secret thought which she did not share. She tilted her head as a way of pointing. "Your grandmother's resting in the bedroom."

There were two bedrooms, and Glory B. looked into the wrong one first. It was filled with small steel cots used by deer hunters who paid two dollars an acre each fall for the pleasure of trudging these rough hills and, if lucky, getting to shoot at a whitetail. Glory B. walked into the other bedroom, smaller but without the cots. She looked through a brass bedstead as old as the house itself. Her grandmother lay atop the spread, a sweater across her legs to protect their slow circulation against a cool breeze that lifted flower-print curtains away from the windowsill.

"We're finished, Gram. I'll drive if you're ready to go home."

Lavinia Dawson replied, "Ready enough. You suppose Hallie's still got any coffee left in the kitchen?"

Glory B. remembered the smell of coffee as she had come into the house. The coffee pot would be the last thing Hallie packed to take home, for Bill would probably want a cup of strength before he started the seven-mile drive over rough ranch roads. "I'll bring you one."

Hallie had heard and already had the coffee poured when Glory B. went into the kitchen. Lavinia Dawson cradled the cup in wrinkled hands and inhaled the aroma as if it were roses. It seemed to Glory B. that most elderly people she knew drew the breath of life itself from coffee. *She* would prefer a beer right now, but to say so might shock her grandmother into choking. Lavinia Dawson had no objection to seeing men drink beer, but for women she declared it unbecoming.

"You look wrung out, Gram. This old camp would make *anybody* tired. It looks tired itself."

Her grandmother gave her a long, slow smile. "You just don't have my memories of this place. When I was little we used to come over here from headquarters and spend days at a time while the men worked cattle. My mother cooked in that kitchen for the working crew. I slept in this very room. That is why I never let them throw this old bed out and put cots in here. As long as I live, I want this room to stay the same as it has always been." She pointed with her chin. "See those curtains? I made them and put them in here. I've been putting fresh curtains in this room since I was ten years old."

Glory B. remembered, for she had helped a couple of times.

Lavinia Dawson said, "I hate the thought that strangers will take over this ranch someday and tear down this old house. I hope it won't be done while I live."

"I won't let them, Gram. I'll stand outside with a shotgun if I have to."

"No you won't. A far better thing for you to do is to work and save this place for us . . . for you and your mother."

Glory B.'s voice hardened. "I'm not sure my mother wants it."

"Don't you be so hard on your mother, girl. She just dances to a little different tune than the rest of us."

"I wonder what tune she's dancing to tonight in San Antonio? With that man."

"She's a grown woman, living in that big house with nobody but two other women, you and me. You're old enough to understand that a grown woman needs things you and I can't give her. There's no reason she has to wear widow's black the rest of her life."

Stubbornly Glory B. said, "She'll never find another man like my daddy was."

Lavinia tenderly placed her hands against Glory B.'s cheeks. "Carr Dawson was my son long before he was your father. But it's been two years now. I've let go. You'll have to."

"I don't want to let go."

"But you must. If you want to honor his memory, the best way is to use that education you've been given. Bring in new ideas that can let us hold on to this ranch . . . *his* ranch."

Glory B. had doubts, but she did not want her grandmother to see them. "I'll do it, Gram. I'll do it if I have to bust a gut."

From his grandfather's weakened appearance, Jim Ed feared he might have to carry him into the house. By the time the pickup rattled across the cattleguard onto the homeplace, however, Wes was sitting up straight and watching the scenery go by. Two whitetail does bounded across the road and into the sheltering cedar, startling Jim Ed. The old man observed with animated eyes. He said, "I wish you'd take the road I showed you yesterday, up to the top of the hill."

Dubiously Jim Ed asked, "Don't you think I'd better get you home?"

"I *am* at home. Home is anyplace on this ranch." He pointed at the road. "Go on, take it."

Wes's jaw was set like one of the hill country's stony ridges. Jim Ed turned into the twin ruts of the rough pasture road and gripped the steering wheel so tightly that his knuckles went white. He knew he stood an excellent chance of dropping one wheel off into a hole and bringing the pickup to a jarring stop. "It'll be the same as it was yesterday," he remarked.

"I can look at it every day. It won't be this green but maybe one year out of five. A man lives the other four in hope and recollection."

"You've been here a long time. That's a lot of hope, and not many green years to recollect."

"An old man learns to be grateful for small favors."

Jim Ed felt qualms about pitting the vehicle against that big hill, pulling a trailer and two horses. Wes said firmly, "This old pickup could climb a water tower with a full load of stock salt. Gun it!"

The horses probably had their rumps flattened against the tailgate, Jim Ed thought, but he shifted into the lowest gear and pushed the gas pedal to the floorboard. The vehicle shuddered in reluctance, then managed the grade. Wes nodded his satisfaction. "When you're in charge, never let anything stop you . . . not an animal, not a machine and not a man. Show the feather and they'll eat you alive."

Jim Ed was halfway around the pickup to open the sprung door for his grandfather when Wes gave it a strong push and forced it wide with a grating protest of metal on metal. *Nothing will ever eat him alive,* he thought. Wes walked with stiffness the first few steps, working the kinks out of his legs. Then he moved more easily than Jim Ed, whose muscles ached from the day's punishment. In the face of his grandfather's strong showing, Jim Ed tried not to betray his own discomfort. He matched Wes step for step, though his legs resisted and his backside felt like raw beef.

On the rimrock, Wes stared down toward the river hidden by the heavy green foliage of tall pecan trees. His eyes smiled. "The *Indians* never seen this country with more grass on it."

Several sheep walked along a ridge, their tiny hoofs stirring a thin film of dust to mark their passage. Jim Ed said nothing about it, but Wes put in, "There's always stock trails and such that won't grass over. Still, we've come a long ways. We used to didn't know better, so we tried to take more than the land was able to give. The fifties drouth taught us what the limits are. You're seein' it now with its Sunday clothes on."

Jim Ed thought it looked more like Monday. He had little basis
for comparison except the countryside around Dallas and northward to Denton. By those standards, this rock-lined range was a
long way from prosperity.

Wes said, "I always dreaded the thought of dyin' durin' a
drouth and bein' buried in the middle of a dusty dry norther. I
always thought I'd like to be buried in the rain."

Jim Ed thought uneasily that his grandfather had not regained
all his color. "Hell of a thing to be talking about."

"Nothin'd suit that lake-promotion crowd better than for me to
cash in without givin' them a good fight."

"I can't believe they'd want to see you dead, just so they could
build a lake."

"I expect they'd take it as a sign that God loves fishermen and
water skiers better than old cowboys and goat herders." Wes
lifted his eyes to a dark cloud far to the west. "Comin' a rain over
yonder. Maybe it'll drift to us tonight."

"You don't really need one just yet."

"A calf or a rain are welcome anytime." Wes bent down and
broke off a small handful of grass stems. His voice was proud.
"Take a look at that, Tater."

Jim Ed did not know what he was supposed to see.

Wes said, "That's sideoats grama, growin' all the way up here
to the top of the hill. Used to not see it except in the bottoms, and
sometimes not there either." He pointed again. "See that big
whitetail buck at the edge of the liveoaks?"

Jim Ed blinked, surprised at his grandfather's sharp vision. The
buck had to be a quarter mile away, edging carefully out from the
protection of the timber to browse on some low-growing shrub.

Wes said, "That's Ol' Snort. I've got a bunch of hunters who
come from San Antonio every deer season. I tell them they can
have any other deer on the place, but they're to leave Ol' Snort
alone. There's people would pay a lot to hang that rack of antlers
in their trophy room."

"God knows you could use the money."

"Snort and me are buddies, sort of. He's part of this place."

"He'll die of old age one of these days."

"So will I. But till we do, we both belong where we're at." Wes's

eyes made Jim Ed turn away, uncomfortable. An edge of disappointment crept into Wes's voice. "Yesterday I brought you up
here, but you couldn't see nothin'. You still don't, do you?"

"I don't know what you *want* me to see."

"You'll see it, when you've been here long enough. I'll keep
bringin' you till you do." Wes turned toward the pickup.
"Enough of the pretty scenery. We got eggs to gather and a cow
to milk and horses to feed."

The sheepdog Pepper met them two hundred yards out from
the barn and raced alongside the pickup, barking with joy.

Jim Ed asked, "What does he do all day when you don't take
him with you?"

"I've caught him workin' the chickens, herdin' them up in a
bunch like sheep. Plays hell with egg production, but I don't need
that many eggs."

"You don't need a milk cow either. It'd be cheaper to buy the
little milk that you use."

Wes shrugged. "You *sound* like your daddy's son, always figurin'
the money first. The place wouldn't seem complete without a
milk cow. It'd mess up the whole pattern of the day. Milkin' starts
the day and ends it."

"Like the invocation and the benediction?"

"A man needs regular chores and a regular time to do them.
Otherwise he loses the order of his life. I think that's what kills so
many old farts who retire to town and sit on the porch. They just
go to waste there, rockin' and rustin'."

Jim Ed frowned as he pulled the pickup to a stop. "A little
rocking wouldn't hurt *you* right now. I'll do the chores."

Wes considered. "I'll let you do the heavy liftin'. But you don't
know how to milk a cow."

"I can learn."

"Later. Today it'd tire me more to teach you than to do it
myself."

Jim Ed unlatched the trailer's tailgate and let the horses move
backward to the ground. He led them together through the gate
which Wes opened. Wes reached for Yellowhammer's reins.

Jim Ed said, "I'll unsaddle him for you."

"A cowboy saddles and unsaddles his own horse. I ain't no invalid yet."

Wes patted the dog while he told Jim Ed how and what to feed the horses. That chore done, Jim Ed scattered milo maize on the ground in the chicken yard while the hens flocked and clucked and fought over the grains. Most would not stray far again. At dusk they would go into the henhouse to roost, Wes said.

Outside the milking pen, a reddish Jersey-cross cow bawled to her calf, penned up all day while she ventured into a horse pasture to graze. The calf responded. Wes said, "Ol' Red is as dependable as a pocketwatch. She always knows when it's milkin' time." He started toward the milk barn, but his steps were slow. He stopped and shrugged. "Aw, hell, I've got more milk in the icebox than we can use. Go let the calf in with her and feed her half a bucket of the milk-maker mix you'll find in the barn. The calf'll think it's his birthday."

Jim Ed stared with concern at his grandfather. *He's more tired than he thought he was.*

The dog, knowing Wes's routine, raced ahead to the milk pen, then turned with tail wagging, confused because Wes did not follow. Wes said, "Pepper, you'll have to drink it cold tonight."

The dog followed Jim Ed at a distrustful distance, watching for the old man to come. Jim Ed softly urged him to move closer, then rubbed him gently between the ears and under the throat. Pepper tentatively licked his hand, looking back as if fearing the old man might find fault.

Wes sat on the step in front of the big saddle and feed barn, watching the chickens scratch. He hollered, "When the calf quits suckin', turn the cow back out where she come from."

Jim Ed thought the cow's maternal instinct would make her reluctant to leave her calf, but when the feed was gone she seemed more than ready to quit the confines of the pen. *So much for motherly love,* he thought. The brindle bull calf butted at her udder one last time for good measure as she started toward the opened gate. Milky white slobber clinging to his chin, the calf accepted the separation. His filial attachment seemed dependent mostly upon the milk, and he had used that up.

Wes pushed away from the barn step, casting a practiced eye toward the raincloud still hanging off to the west.

Jim Ed fetched the leftovers Hallie Roper had placed in the pickup. Their bulk and weight sent pain through his sore arms, but if he said anything his grandfather would insist on carrying part of the load. Wes mounted the steps with more agility than Jim Ed was able to muster, his body aching in a dozen places. The dog stopped on the porch; the inside of the house was out of bounds. Wes held the door open for Jim Ed and talked affectionately to the black-and-white collie.

He doesn't need family, Jim Ed thought. *He's got friends here, and his dog and his horses. He doesn't need me.* He wished he were somewhere else, *anywhere* else, without a half-sick, crochety old man to worry about.

He emptied the sacks, setting aside food to warm for supper and putting the rest away. Hallie had sent enough to feed them several days. He turned on the oven to heat the beef and wished for his mother's microwave. Grandmother Maudie had never acquired one, and Wes probably would not know what it was for.

Wes poured a drink from a bottle in the pantry. Jim Ed frowned. "You think that's good for you?"

Wes's eyes narrowed. "Are you a doctor?"

"No, but I remember what happened to you this afternoon."

"Nothin' happened this afternoon. A bunch of people got excited over nothin', is all." He took a long sip out of his glass. "When *you* get to be seventy-seven, you can give me advice about my health." He took his glass into the living room and turned on the television news. He sat grumbling to himself about the latest problems in Washington and solutions that should be evident to any damnfool, even a professional politician. The news over and his glass empty, he started coffee on a butane burner. Jim Ed noted with silent disapproval that his grandfather did not wash the pot and drained off only part of the old grounds.

So long as he kept moving, Jim Ed managed to hold the growing soreness at bay. But when he sat at the table to eat, it fell upon him with a force that almost offset the appetite the outdoors work had given him. Even Wes's coffee tasted tolerable. It was strong enough either to cure any ailment or to kill on contact.

The old man ate in thoughtful silence, staring through the open window. When he finished, he rocked back his chair. He studied his big-knuckled hands. "All wrinkled, and spotted up like an Appaloosa horse. You wouldn't think that these hands used to wrestle steers in the arena, or grab a buckin' horse by the ears and bring him to a stop." He grimaced. "I just wisht I could roll back about fifty years and start over, knowin' everything I know now. Ain't no limit to what I could do with this place if I had that much time."

Jim Ed could honestly tell him, "I wish you could do that."

Wes shook his head. "I could, in a way. If I just had somebody young to pass on what I know . . . somebody that'd have fifty years to use what I could teach him, and what he could learn for hisself . . ."

Jim Ed looked away, knowing the direction the conversation was pointed. "When did you first start out to be a cowboy?"

"My old daddy carried me in front of him on the saddle before I was old enough to walk."

"That's the problem, then. I'm twenty-odd years too late already, even if I *wanted* to be a cowboy. I have neither the knack nor the interest."

"Don't sound to me like you've got much interest in *anything.*"

"There'll be something. I just haven't come across it yet."

"If you don't know what you're lookin' for, how'll you know when you find it?"

"That's the question I asked myself after four years of college. Four years wasted."

"They don't have to be wasted, no more than Bill Roper's boy wastes the time he spends learnin' to be a hand. It always looked to me like the most important thing a boy learns in school is *how* to learn. He has to keep learnin' as long as he lives, because the world keeps changin' on him as he goes along."

Jim Ed thought, *Like it's changed on you, and left you behind.*

Wes said, "I had a feelin' once that if I didn't like what was goin' on in the rest of the world I could just shut my gate. But the world kept climbin' the fence and comin' in. It taken one son away from me. In a way it taken the other one too."

He stared out the window again. "Now it's tryin' to take even this little old homeplace away from me. Acts like it's doin' me a favor by givin' me a chance to lay back and rest. But I ain't ready. When they carry me to the cemetery and put me down beside Maudie, I'll get rest enough."

The telephone rang. Wes jerked, seeming disoriented by the interruption. Jim Ed pushed away from the table and answered. It was Bill Roper, concerned about Wes's condition. Jim Ed said, "He swears he's all right, but he looks tired to me."

Wes trudged into the living room and reached for the phone, his face furrowed in reproach. "Hello! That you, Bill? Hell, there ain't nothin' wrong with me. Just ate a little too much dinner, is all . . . Tater? Aw, he's all right. Goin' to be awful sore, but I figured on workin' that off of him buildin' fence tomorrow. Naw, I don't need a day off. A good night's sleep and I'll beat you in a footrace. Come over and try me." He frowned at Jim Ed as if daring him to contradict. "Thanks for callin', but don't you lose no sleep over me. I'm a long ways from gone . . . All right. Goodbye."

He cradled the receiver, still frowning. "I feel fine, and don't you be tellin' anybody otherwise."

Jim Ed replied defensively, "He asked me, and I told him what I thought."

Wes studied him critically. "Your eyes show a little of your Uncle James Edward, but your mouth and your jaw are your daddy's. I hope we can get along in spite of that."

Wes stretched out in his big recliner chair and began to read the *Livestock Weekly* which Jim Ed had taken from the mailbox on their way home. He put his rancor behind him as easily as it had arisen. He talked about market prices for cattle and sheep, and how it was getting harder and harder for the rancher to stay. "When your daddy was young I could sell a dozen calves for enough to buy me a new pickup. Now I'd have to sell *thirty*. Every time prices get up to where the rancher and the farmer can make a livin', some people holler to Washington about the high cost of eatin'."

Jim Ed replied noncommittally, "I suppose," and continued drying dishes on a coarse cloth that once had been a salt sack. He had never given any consideration to livestock prices or costs of operation.

Wes said, "It used to be simple. When you sold somethin', you put the money in the bank. When you bought somethin', you taken it out. If you had more money at the end of the season than when you started, you'd had a good year. If you didn't have as much, you'd lost. Nowadays it's too damned complicated."

Jim Ed said, "That's how accountants like Dad make their living."

Wes grunted. "What kind of livin' is it when you don't produce somethin' real . . . somethin' you can eat or wear or ride in, or get under when it rains? Your daddy spends his life workin' with papers, and when he's done he hasn't produced a bite of food or as much as a cotton sock he can pull over his foot. It's like reachin' up and grabbin' a handful of air. You open your hand and it's empty."

Jim Ed forgot for a moment the dish towel and the wet plate in his hand. He walked into the doorway between the kitchen and the living room, dripping water on the floor. He studied his grandfather with surprise. "That's why I lost interest my last year in school. That's what I tried to tell Dad."

Wes lowered his chin and returned Jim Bob's stare over the reading glasses perched halfway down his nose. "Told him what?"

"Told him I didn't want to follow his footsteps and join him in the company. Told him I'd tried my best, but I couldn't find any substance in it."

"What did he say to that?"

"He said if I wanted substance I ought to look at his financial statement. I tried to tell him it's all paper. Our whole economy is built on paper. Take the paper away and it all collapses."

Wes nodded. "All that's solid is buildin's and machinery, people and the land. The rest is artificial, like a hot-house plant. Set it in the sunshine and it's gone." His face softened. "Seems me and you see alike. So what've we been arguin' about?"

Wes returned to his newspaper. Jim Ed finished the dishes and straightened up the kitchen. After a while he heard music from the living room. His grandfather stood beside a record player, a couple of albums in his hands. The music was old-time country fiddling. Wes's foot tapped time to a lively breakdown.

Wes said, "When I'm too tired to make music myself, it feels good to put Bob Wills on the Victrola."

Jim Ed had to smile. What his grandfather called a *Victrola* was a console stereo, another of Grandmother Maudie's purchases.

Wes turned back toward his recliner, the albums in his hand. "I don't reckon it's *your* kind of music," he said. "Next time we're in town, you buy some records *you* like."

Jim Ed shook his head. "My music would drive you to the barn. I won't be staying here that long anyway."

Wes blinked. "How long *will* you be stayin'? Your daddy never said."

Jim Ed shrugged. "We'll just have to see."

"Maybe long enough for me to educate you about music. Bet you didn't know me and your grandmother used to play for country dances in the old days . . . her on the guitar and me on the fiddle. James Edward taken after his mother on the guitar. Used to play with me sometimes. He was pretty good too . . ."

Wes's voice trailed off, and he stared toward the old picture on the mantle. His foot stopped tapping to the music. Quietly, painfully he said, "We had a polio epidemic in the fifties, along with a drouth. It hit mostly young people. We thought he'd be safe out here in the country, but that pasture fence wasn't high enough. He taken the bulbar type, and he was gone in five days."

Jim Ed nodded soberly. He had heard the story many times.

Wes sat in silence, staring at the mantle. The music played on, but his feet were still.

Jim Ed watched him uneasily, thinking he should try to get the old man's mind on something else. "I used to play the electric guitar in a little neighborhood combo. Even got paid for a few gigs, until my folks found out we were working in a beer joint."

He noted that Wes had begun tapping his foot again, and he was no longer looking toward the mantle. Jim Ed took that as a favorable sign. Listening, he tried to hear the music as his grandfather must be hearing it, but it was like trying to see the ranch through Wes's eyes. The gap between them was wide, their shared experience narrow. He picked up the San Angelo *Standard-Times* and sat down to read it, starting with sports.

He became aware after a time that the music had stopped again, but the old man did not move. He was not tapping his foot.

Asleep, Jim Ed thought. He watched a minute and saw no movement. Somewhere deep within, alarm began tingling. From where he sat, he could not tell if Wes was breathing. He pushed out of his chair and moved closer, alarm starting to build. From near enough to reach out and touch him, he watched his grandfather and saw no sign of breathing. Wes appeared still as death.

His heart, Jim Ed thought. His own was hammering. Hesitantly he reached out and touched Wes's arm, trying to remember just where to feel for a pulse.

Wes's eyes fluttered, then opened. He took a deep breath and looked around, startled. "Must've gone to sleep," he said. His eyes narrowed. "You all right, Tater? You don't look good. The day's knocks are startin' to fall in on you, ain't they?"

Jim Ed felt both foolish and immensely relieved. He would not have told Wes the truth for a thousand dollars. "I guess that's what it is. I think I'll go to bed."

"Tomorrow's Sunday . . . a day of rest. We'll sleep late."

Jim Ed stopped at the bedroom door and turned back for a last reassuring look. His grandfather was padding around in his sock feet, looking as if he had never known a sick day. "Good night."

"Good night, Tater. I promise I won't wake you up playin' the fiddle."

You'd just as well, Jim Ed thought. *I'll lie awake half the night anyway, wondering if you'll wake up in the morning.*

He had lain in bed perhaps half an hour, trying in vain to find a position that did not hurt. The telephone rang. He expected to hear his grandfather answer it, but when he counted four rings he decided Wes was already asleep. Jim Ed slipped from the bed and found the telephone in the living room's darkness. "Hello," he said softly.

"Jim Ed?"

He recognized his father's voice. "Yes, it's me."

"Then you got there all right. You ought to've called to let us know you made it." The tone was stern.

"Granddad would've called you if I hadn't." A little irritation crept into his voice at the thought of being checked up on. It was a family trait.

"The mood you were in when you left, I wasn't sure you might not decide to keep on going."

"The thought struck me. But I didn't have enough money to go very far." If he had had the money, he would be in Europe with David and Jack. That was to have been his graduation present.

"Are you getting along all right with your grandfather?"

"We're speaking."

"How does he act? Does he seem all right?"

Jim Ed hesitated, wondering if he should mention Wes's heart condition. "He acts like he thinks he's fifty-seven instead of seventy-seven. He has a mind of his own."

"Hell, I know that. Is he rational all the time?"

"Is *anybody?*"

His father's voice sharpened. "You know what I mean. Is he drinking a lot?"

Jim Ed frowned. "I wouldn't say it's a lot."

"But he *is* drinking."

"He's no teetotaler, but neither are you. Neither am I."

"Don't evade the issue. You know why I sent you there."

Jim Ed lowered his voice. "I told you before I left home . . . I don't want to be a spy."

"You're not spying. You're just watching out for him for his own good. If worst comes to worst and we have to challenge his competence in court, what you observe could be crucial."

Jim Ed said, "You'd better not count on it."

"That old place killed your grandmother. It'll kill him too. We'll make a home for him with us, or we can find a nice retirement home close by where some of us can look in on him."

That kind of company was the last thing Wes Hendrix would want, Jim Ed thought ruefully.

His father pressed, "Just remember that you were sent there with a job to do."

"I haven't forgotten," Jim Ed said grittily. "I've felt guilty every minute I've been around him."

"There's no need for guilt. He'll thank us someday."

"He won't. Not the last day he lives. Which won't be long if he has to move to the city."

"Tell him we all love him."

Jim Ed chewed his lip. "Damned poor way we have of showing it."

"What did you say?"

"Nothing. Just said good night."

"Good night." He heard a click as his father hung up. Hand shaking, Jim Ed placed the receiver back into its cradle. He walked to the front door and stood awhile listening to the night sounds. Wes had been right. There *was* life out there.

Chapter 5

The church was no more than a third full, though this was a beautiful Sunday morning that in Mayor Orville Levitt's view should have packed the pews and had latecomers standing in the rear. There had been a time, twenty or thirty years ago . . . But the congregation had gradually dwindled as farmers and ranchers moved off the land and away from Big River.

Levitt stared distractedly at one of the stained glass windows, a memorial to a Big River youth killed in World War II. The boy lay buried in the poplar-lined cemetery at the edge of town, but his family had long since moved away. Levitt hardly saw the window's colors, brilliant in morning's sunlight, for his mind wandered off on a twisting trail provoked by the sermon.

Brother McDaniel, so young he probably still wore the suit he had bought for graduation exercises from seminary school, read Proverbs 18:24: "A man that hath friends must shew himself friendly: and there is a friend that sticketh closer than a brother."

Levitt's memory reluctantly drifted back some fifty years to two young cowhands on the Chatfield ranch, sharing a delicious sense of danger as each in his turn climbed upon a snorting, pawing bronc for a few moments of wild exhilaration. Each tried to shine the brightest in reckless showmanship, yet depended upon and trusted the other to rescue him in event the ride ended in a wreck. He remembered times when, to administer the screwworm medicine that meant life or death to afflicted cattle in their charge, they would rope a full-grown animal that outweighed their horses, each man knowing the other would rush to his aid if luck turned sour. Out of such sharing had grown friendship of the Biblical mold, a bond Brother McDaniel was still too smooth-faced to understand, though he spoke of it. Now, as both men moved into the twilight of their lives, a shadow had fallen between them, and they were like strangers.

Levitt squeezed his hymnal so hard that the tendons on the back of his hand strained in bold relief against the brown-spotted skin. The book's spine cracked audibly.

His wife, Noreen, nudged him. Turning, he saw a mild reproach in her eyes, and he read on her lips a word spoken in silence: "Listen." He gave her a curt nod that she could take for whatever she wanted it to be. They had lived together so long that he often suspected she could read his mind and know the thoughts he left unspoken.

The minister said, "And we read in Psalms twenty-seven:ten: 'Thine own friend, and thy father's friend, forsake not.'"

The young minister's gaze lighted upon Levitt and remained, as if the Scripture were read for his benefit alone. Levitt cast a suspicious glance at Noreen. His rump prickled with impatience through the remainder of the sermon, and he was glad when the final hymn began. He felt a desperate need of warm noon sunshine and the air fresh with the scent of roses blossoming at the front of the church. His legs ached from years of standing behind the granite-topped counter in his drugstore, dispensing powders and pills, pain relief and placebos, wishing in vain for the wind in his face, the rocking gait of a pacing horse, the scent of new grass to drive away the haunting odor of antiseptics.

Spring. He should be out there with it, he thought. Spring offers a winter-weary world an annual chance for renewal. He wished it could rejuvenate people as well. He wished it could rejuvenate an old friendship, lost.

There had been a time, when they were younger, that he could have talked to Wes Hendrix and perhaps have brought him around to a different way of thinking. Levitt's mind had worked faster then, and he had been more facile with the language. Wes, for his part, had been more pliable. Now they were two old men brittle like the dried-out stalks of last year's corn, no longer able to bend, standing futilely against the winds of time that one day soon must break them both.

Noreen clung to Levitt's arm for support, and they blinked against a blinding sunlight as they haltingly descended the steps of a brick church a little shabby now but reminiscent of better days. Brother McDaniel and his slender bride of less than a year stood on the walk, she shining like a field of sunflowers, he shaking hands with each of his flock. Duty bade Levitt say, "It was a fine sermon, Preacher."

He was being charitable. As soon as Brother McDaniel learned to deliver a *good* sermon, he would move to a bigger church in a livelier town, as his predecessors had done for years.

The minister bore out his earlier suspicion. "As a matter of fact, Brother Levitt, the topic was suggested to me by someone near and dear to you. She thought it apropos."

The druggist cast a knowing eye toward Noreen, a short, plump little woman who had been a short, lithe young girl not unlike the minister's sparklingly pretty wife when he had sold his saddle for her sake most of fifty years ago.

Walking on, safely out of the minister's hearing, Noreen said, "The sermon made you think about Wes, didn't it?"

"I didn't need Brother McDaniel to remind me. Wes has already cost me a right smart of sleep."

"Wes, or your conscience?"

Noreen had been against the lake idea from the start. "It won't help the drugstore much," she had told him the day the subject had first been broached. "Unless you intend to start sellin' beer and fishbait."

He could not remember the last time he had won an argument with her. Usually he went ahead and did what he intended to, then told her about it later. But he wished she could see his viewpoint. He motioned with his hand. "Use your eyes, Noreen. Look down the street and remember what our town used to be. The only thing that can turn it around is outside dollars comin' in. That is what the lake can do for us."

"But at what a cost to Wes."

"When we first thought about the lake we didn't know it would cover up Wes's land. It was our intention to help people, not hurt anybody. But we've got to consider the good of the many and not the loss to one or two."

"Would you feel that way if the land to be taken was yours?"

"I'd like to believe I would. I *have* to believe I would."

There were days when he could hardly bring himself to go out the front door of his drugstore and face that long street with so many of its buildings empty, fronts boarded up or old plateglass windows broken out, looking like empty eyesockets in an ancient skull. He could remember Saturdays in times past when all the ranchers and farmers and cedar choppers came to town and hardly a parking space could be found from the courthouse square all the way out to the wool warehouse. Hardly anybody had been rich here then, unless one counted the Chatfields and the Dawsons, whose wealth was tied up mainly in land and live-stock. But most everybody seemed to get along somehow and, even if they had little money to spend, found a touch of luxury in simple things like the picture show, followed perhaps by a cream soda at Levitt's counter or a beer at Otto Schmidt's Stammtisch down the street.

Saturdays seemed to have gone out of style anymore. They had died, as this town was dying.

Noreen said, "I only know that Wes Hendrix is one of the best men who ever lived. That ranch was home to Maudie and him for forty years. You could at least wait until he's gone."

"The town may be gone before he is."

It was his and Noreen's custom after church to walk to the post office and pick up the mail so they could spend a quiet Sunday afternoon reading the newspapers from San Angelo and San Antonio. As they pulled away from the church crowd and crossed the asphalt pavement, its sun-warmed surface already reflecting summer heat up into his face, he heard the arrogant honking of a horn and knew instinctively it was meant for him. He deposited Noreen safely on the sidewalk—he now had to help her step up onto the curb—and he turned to see a black automobile with a badge painted on its door, lights mounted on its top. Instead of getting out and coming to Levitt, Sheriff Wally Vincent remained behind the wheel and motioned for Levitt to come to him. Levitt gave Noreen a regretful glance. "I'll be back in a minute."

Vincent had the air-conditioning running, but he rolled the window down as Levitt reached the car. "I talked to Matthew Jamison while ago. He says we're still on for tonight."

Levitt frowned and fidgeted. "I'd rather take a whippin' with a wet rope."

"It's time we settled this thing with that old fart."

Levitt flared. "That old fart is a friend of mine, Wally."

"That's why we want you to go with us. Maybe a friend can talk to him. And if a friend can't, then me and Matthew will. I'll pick you up about five. He's always home at suppertime."

"I don't want anything unpleasant, Wally."

"We're just goin' to tell him the facts of life. One contrary old man can't block the wheels of progress."

Vincent rolled up the window and drove away, leaving Levitt standing in the middle of the street, hunched a little, hands in his pockets. A vague sense of humiliation burned like an astringent. He was aware of Noreen watching him from the curb, making a judgment. He walked slowly toward her and stepped up off the street.

She said sternly, "He treats you like you were workin' for him. After all, you *are* the mayor of this town."

He gave the street a long, sweeping study. "Mayor of *this*? It's old and wornout and useless, like I am."

Defensively she declared, "Old you may be, but not wornout and useless. You'll be a better man the last day you live than Wally Vincent'll be on the best day he ever has."

Noreen was given to nagging at him sometimes, irritating him to distraction, but she never failed to stand up for him when criticism arose from outside.

She said, "I've told you for years, Wally's the wrong man to be wearin' that badge. He enjoys his authority too much. He should use it with a little regret. And you know he doesn't really care whether this town revives or not. He's just lookin' for a chance to get rich from that place of his."

"If it was only Wally, I'd say the hell with it. But it's the last good chance this town'll likely ever have."

"And what chance has Wes Hendrix got?"

Orville Levitt felt a sourness in his stomach. He was going to have to stop at the store and take something for it. "Dammit, Noreen, you don't make this any easier."

Jim Ed had tried lying on his back, on his stomach, on one side and then the other. He tried stretching out, and he tried pulling his knees up almost to his chin. Each position made him ache in a different way. He listened to the passage of a thunderstorm, to rain which trickled from the edge of the roof and lost itself in the softness of untrimmed bermudagrass along the dripline. Not until the wee hours of the morning did exhaustion finally drive him to sleep. It seemed only minutes before Wes flipped the wall switch and the ceiling light struck Jim Ed in the eyes with a piercing glare.

"Rise up, Tater," Wes said cheerfully. "The sun's already awake."

Jim Ed cut his eyes toward the open window. If there was any sunshine yet, it must have been on the other side of the house. "I thought we were going to sleep late."

"We did. It's six o'clock. Ol' Red's bawlin'. She don't know Sunday from Halloween."

Jim Ed tried to pull himself to a sitting position in bed. He groaned and dropped back. He lay a minute, staring up at the ceiling, then slid his feet out and let them touch the floor. He carefully manuevered his body from under the blanket.

Wes did not carry enough sympathy to be a burden. "The only cure for them sore muscles is to put them to work."

"I thought Sunday was a day of rest."

"Ain't nothin' more restful to the mind than some simple chore like buildin' fence. It's automatic, most of it, so your mind can run free; it can take you anywhere you want to go."

"The only place I want to go is back to bed."

"You'd be sore and stiff for a week. I've already put the coffee on. Don't you let it boil over." Wes walked out of the room with an easy step that made him seem twenty years younger than the old man who had trembled and turned white the day before. Jim Ed sat on the edge of the bed and listened to the slamming of the screen door, the clumping of boots across the porch and down the steps. Wes was humming again, like yesterday morning.

Once Jim Ed was moving about, the aching lessened. He swung his arms, and they limbered a bit. He felt a little heat and swelling where Glory B.'s horse had kicked his shoulder, but perhaps that, too, would pass. He managed to have breakfast ready by the time his grandfather returned from the milk pen.

Wes was pleased about the shower that had fallen in the night. "Almost half an inch. That'll keep the grass a-comin'."

Jim Ed said hopefully, "Maybe it's too wet for us to work on the fence."

"Naw. The rain won't hurt us a bit. Where we'll be diggin', it's mostly rock."

Sourly Jim Ed said, "That's good to hear."

Wes did not offer to let him drive the pickup, which was just as well. Jim Ed's stiffness and slow reactions might have put them into the ditch. The dog Pepper jumped into the pickup bed with the digging tools, barking at the chickens which ventured out of their enclosures to seek the day's offering of seeds and insects. The hens, busily clucking like back-fence gossips, paid the dog no mind.

Wes happily splashed through an occasional pothole of water in the two-rut road. His gaze would drift off across the pastures, and Jim Ed kept wondering nervously if he might miss the next bend. Wes pointed to a Hereford cow which Jim Ed thought looked the same as all the others. He described her ancestry back at least four generations. He was not sure anymore whether her great-grandmammy had been an old broken-horn cow or one with a brown spot of pigment around her right eye. It came to Jim Ed that the cows held almost the status of yard pets. When he spoke that thought, Wes nodded.

"That's about the only reason for keepin' the old hussies. They lose money with every bite of grass they take. Man has to keep sheep and goats to support his cows."

Jim Ed frowned, remembering the stern counseling session his father had given him before he had boarded the bus. Truman Hendrix said Wes had been borrowing against his land to keep his cow herd, hoping that by the grace of God and Safeway a favorable market would eventually return. Those cows had eaten up much of the ranch's declining value.

Jim Ed said to his grandfather, "Maybe that's one thing wrong with ranching. It's short on business principles and bogged down in sentiment." He realized he sounded like his accountant father, analyzing a client's capital venture hip-deep in the red.

"It always *was* that way," Wes replied. "For a hundred years back, it's lost money more often than it's turned a profit."

"Why do people stay if it doesn't make a living?"

"It ain't just a livin'. It's a way of life."

Wes had built cattleguards at the more often-used fence crossings in his pastures so he could drive through without stopping. Then he had negated their convenience by stringing wire gates across them because his nimble Angora goats learned to traverse the parallel steel rails. Jim Ed had to climb out and open a gate each time they came to a fence.

Wes said, "A goat has got as much mischief in him as a raccoon. He spends half his wakin' hours tryin' to figure out how to put asunder what man has joined together."

The new fenceline was marked by stakes set in the ground, starting high on a rocky ridge and continuing in an arrow-straight course down to an existing fence near the river. Where Wes had already made a start, posts stood like sentinels in formation for perhaps two hundred yards from their starting place against another fence. Beyond this beginning, recently cut cedar posts and stays lay piled at intervals, awaiting use.

Wes stopped the pickup near the first stake. He positioned himself squarely in the fenceline and sighted first along the row of posts already set, then down the row of stakes trailing off toward the river. "Look at that straight line," he said proudly. "Soil conservation boys surveyed it for me before talk ever started about that lake."

Jim Ed took stock of the posts already set, the many holes yet to be dug, the dozens of posts lying in wait. They represented a substantial investment not only of money but of time and labor. His eye kept being drawn toward the river. "They'll rip out all this when the dam comes in."

Wes's hands knotted. "They ain't built that dam. This fence says they ain't goin' to. Let's unload them tools."

Wes gave Jim Ed a pair of old leather gloves. "You'll need these, or your hands'll be like hamburger." He pulled up a stake and plunged a set of posthole diggers down over the small hole the stake's withdrawal had left. The steel clanged as it struck rocks just beneath the dark soil's thin surface. He spread the handles apart and lifted up about enough soil to fill a coffee cup. *Hardly an auspicious beginning,* Jim Ed thought. He watched his grandfather raise the diggers and drive them down as if he were trying to destroy that dam with his hands. Steel met stone with a noisy, quivering violence. Color arose in Wes's face.

Jim Ed reached for the diggers. "Maybe you've forgotten about yesterday, but I haven't."

His grandfather reluctantly relinquished his hold. Jim Ed made a strike with the diggers. They shuddered from the impact and sent shock rippling through his sore arms. He brought out but little dirt.

Wes picked up a long steel rod flattened into a wedge shape on one end. "I'm afraid you'll mostly have to use the crowbar."

Jim Ed plunged the bar down again and again, chipping away at the stones, kneeling periodically with a scarred and bent coffee can to scoop out the broken and powdered pieces. He measured progress in slow inches. Sometimes when he leaned on the bar to catch his breath, Wes would kneel with the can. The scraping sound was painfully discordant, akin to chalk scratching across a blackboard.

Jim Ed demanded, "How the hell deep is this rock?"

Wes poured out a canful of limestone dust and chips. "The smart boys say it's ten thousand feet, but we won't have to go that deep."

Though Jim Ed had no watch with him, he guessed he spent an hour chipping and hacking and cursing that hole before Wes declared it deep enough to hold the post against all challenges. Jim Ed dropped the heaviest end of a large cedar post into the rock-edged hole. It quivered and threw off dust as it struck the solid bottom. Wes backed off a couple of paces and sighted along the finished line. "Hold her straight up, Tater." He motioned.

"Ooch it a little more to yonderway." He came back and kicked the post at ground level to scoot its base an inch farther south, then walked off and sighted again.

Jim Ed wondered at his perfectionism. "Nobody'll see it."

"*I'll* see it." Wes began pushing dirt into the hole with his foot. When it had accumulated perhaps a foot deep along the bottom of the post, he fetched the crowbar and used its small end to tamp the dirt down solidly.

Jim Ed took over the filling and tamping. By the time he was done, the post felt set in concrete. He sighted along its top and saw that it was perfectly in line. He felt an unexpected glow of accomplishment.

Wes grunted in satisfaction. "This is your first fencepost. You might want to carve your initials in it."

Jim Ed looked down the slope at the long line of stakes waiting to be replaced. They seemed beyond counting. "It's the *last* post that'll deserve celebration." He wiped sweat from his forehead and pulled the little hat down. "You know it's all for nothing."

Wes did not acknowledge the comment. He picked up the diggers and marched toward the next stake. Jim Ed shook his head and carried the crowbar, wondering how a man's neck could get so stiff in just seventy-seven years.

After chipping until the next hole was a foot deep, Jim Ed paused. "Have you told my father about your heart trouble?"

Wes was sharply defensive. "I ain't got no heart trouble. And don't you be tellin' him."

"He's all the family you've got. He has a right to know."

Wes's eyes went severe. "Your daddy and me always get along best when we stay a ways apart. Don't you be tellin' him a bunch of foolishness and bringin' him out here for nothin'."

"I won't tell him, but *you* ought to."

Jim Ed made the rock sing with the strike of sharp steel. Wes watched him critically. "Seems like you're mad at me, and you're takin' it out on the crowbar."

Jim Ed did not stop. "I'm mad at both of you. You and Dad have got an old grudge between you—why, I don't know—and you've both put me in the middle."

Wes nodded. "That's why I place so much stock in friendship.

A feller's got no choice about who's in his family. He can pick his friends to suit himself."

Wes finally made a halt for lunch—*dinner*, he called it. He built a small fire inside a narrow circle of stones, then filled a coffee pot from a big can of water in the pickup and set it atop the stones. Jim Ed had not realized how hungry the work had made him. But Wes had been right about its taking the soreness out. He moved freely with little pain.

The coffee came to a boil about the time they finished eating the cold biscuits and cold bacon Wes had brought along. Wes poured it into two chipped-enamel cups and gave Jim Ed a piece of Hallie's chocolate cake to wash down with the black coffee. "How's this for a Sunday dinner?"

"My mother would say we ought to be in church."

Wes made a wide sweep with his hand. "Just look at that scenery, boy. Hell, we're *in* church!"

Wes did not call it quits until late afternoon. Jim Ed rubbed his arms. He could not remember that he had ever worked such a long, hard day. Hot, sweaty and grimy, he would not have expected to feel more exhilaration than exhaustion. Those cedar posts standing straight as Aggie cadets in formation . . . hardly a job that called for a college education. But he felt a curious sense of satisfaction.

Back at the headquarters, he fed the horses but kept looking across the corrals to a round concrete water-storage tank about thirty feet across and perhaps five feet deep. He made an attempt at milking the Jersey cow, but his hands were stiffening from the day's constant pounding. Despite the gloves he had worn, his palms were red and blistered. The cow kept glancing back distrustfully at him. As soon as she ate all the feed in her stanchion, she backed out of the stall. She would have knocked over the milk bucket if Jim Ed had not jerked it out of the way. Wes poured more feed for her and completed the milking.

Jim Ed turned the bull calf in to finish what was left. He said, "The water looks good in that tank. Any objections if I go in for a little swim?"

Wes shook his head. "It ain't our house water. James Edward and your daddy used to swim there."

Jim Ed fetched clean clothes from his room and laid them across an elevated pipe that carried windmill water into the tank. The dog Pepper watched with curiosity as Jim Ed stripped and climbed in. The water on top was warm from the sun, but a little deeper it was almost cold. Jim Ed shivered until he became used to it.

He was dimly aware that Pepper was barking, but in the cooling luxury of the water he paid little attention. He did not know a vehicle had driven up to the house until he heard two doors slam. Wiping water from his eyes, he recognized Bill Roper's blue pickup. The C Bar foreman walked up the steps to meet Wes, who had moved out onto the porch. Jim Ed assumed the other person to be Roper's son Johnny.

He did not recognize Glory B. Dawson until she was halfway to the tank. He glanced quickly toward his clothes but knew he did not have time to reach them.

Damn that girl. She's done it to me again.

Jim Ed flattened himself against the cement tank's inside wall. He would not put it past Glory B. to peer over the rim to see how clear the water was. He thought he knew what her first words would be as she stopped and stared unflinchingly into his eyes. He felt that she was laughing at him in some hidden place where he could not see.

"How's the water?" she asked.

In that, at least, she was predictable. He considered his reply, given with a thin edge of sarcasm. "Cool and wet. I don't suppose you'd want to come in and join me." He knew she would not. Or perhaps she would. With this girl, he could take nothing for granted.

"I don't have a bathing suit," she replied.

"Neither do I."

Mischief danced in her dark brown eyes. "Sounds tempting. But Bill and your granddad are old-fashioned. They might frown on such untraditional behavior."

Untraditional behavior. Big words for a girl from the cedarbrakes. "You wouldn't do it even if they weren't here."

"I might. But you'd jump out of that tank and run like a scalded dog."

Jim Ed remembered a warm night, a moonlit Dallas backyard swimming pool and a girl whose parents had flown to Houston for the weekend. "You might be wrong."

"I doubt it. But I suppose we'll never know, will we?"

"Come over sometime when nobody else is here."

She considered a moment, the mischief not yet played out. "I still believe you'd run."

Yesterday she had looked like a boy. Today her gender was not in doubt. She would never be a candidate for the Dallas Cowboys cheerleaders, he thought, but if he had encountered her in a suburban mall, without the memory of yesterday's goading, he might have been obliged to turn and look a second time. Her hair was brushed. Her blouse and bluejeans appeared fresh out of the washer, and snug enough to stimulate a young male imagination into full fancy. He suspected she wore them for his benefit, or perhaps his frustration.

He said, "I'm not kidding. I don't have any clothes on."

"Is that supposed to arouse me, or something?"

"I can't think of any other reason you'd come out here."

"Don't compliment yourself, pilgrim. You don't appeal to my prurient interests with your clothes on or clothes off."

"I'm glad to know you *have* prurient interests. At least there's hope for you."

"Don't get *your* hopes up. I don't see much for *you.*"

"You might, if I were to climb out of here right now. And I will if you don't go back to the house."

"Put up or shut up," she grinned, and stood her ground.

If it weren't for Wes and Roper he might, just to see what she would do. The girl in Dallas had slipped out of her bathing suit and let it sink to the bottom of the pool. But this one seemed more inclined to tease than to please.

He demanded, "What did you come here for, just to gig me some more?"

"Bill Roper and I were worried about your granddad."

"Bill Roper may have been, but you came over to see *me,*" he accused.

"Don't compliment yourself, pilgrim. I found your pocketknife, that's all. I brought it to you."

"You can lay it on my clothes as you leave, then I can get out of this tank."

"That's what I was going to do in the first place. I just wanted to see which one of us would blink first."

She moved away, skipping more than walking. He waited until she was well gone before he climbed out of the water and hurriedly put on the clean clothes without taking time to dry himself.

She was sitting on the porch steps and rubbing an appreciative Pepper beneath his chin when Jim Ed reached the house. She said, "I didn't look even once." She gave him time to acknowledge that minor courtesy, then added, "I doubt that I would've have seen much anyway."

Her faint tone of ridicule brought warmth to his face. "Do you get the best of *everybody,* or am I a special project?"

"You were yesterday. You reminded me of those self-appointed protectors of the urban faith that I ran into when I went off to college. They think a country girl is dumb as dirt . . . and just as easy to pick up. But since you're kin to Wes Hendrix I'm thinking about giving you a second chance."

"To do what?"

"I'll decide about that as we go along." She patted the step with the flat of her hand, an invitation for him to sit. He did, cautiously leaving space between them. The dog moved into the gap, inviting attention from either side.

Glory B. went silent for a time, petting the dog. She said, "I didn't thank you yesterday."

"You sure didn't."

"You must have known I meant to."

"I knew no such thing. I thought you were telling me in your own cute way to go to hell."

"If I'd meant to do that, I'd have left no doubt about it. I have trouble sometimes saying thanks. I never have trouble telling somebody to go to hell."

"I'll bet *that's* the godforsaken truth."

"I'm good at other things too, besides riding horses. Dancing, for instance. Do you dance?"

"I don't know if *you'd* call it dancing. It's probably not Big River's style."

"There's a place in town where a lot of us get together on Saturday nights. It's called the Blue Moon."

"Sounds like a joint where you could get a beer bottle broken over your head."

"You have something against beer?"

"No. As a matter of fact, I'm in favor of it."

"Then you might enjoy the Blue Moon. We haven't had a pilgrim killed there in two or three weeks. Come in some Saturday night. We might even teach you a new step."

His face wrinkled. "Like the Cotton-eyed Joe?"

"And maybe the Schottisch and Put Your Little Foot. We know *all* the new ones."

He sensed that she was still laughing at him, a little. "Your cedar choppers might not let a pilgrim like me in the door."

"They're broad-minded, most of them. But it wouldn't hurt if you'd leave that dinky hat at home."

"My hat goes where I go."

The dog looked up, suddenly alert. He quit the steps and trotted toward the road. It took a moment for the sound of an automobile to reach Jim Ed.

Wes and Roper walked out onto the porch as the car pulled into sight around a bend in the road. Wes squinted but grumbled that he could not make out whose it was.

Bill Roper said, "It's the sheriff's." He glanced questioningly at Wes, then at Jim Ed.

The car pulled to a stop, dust drifting up onto the porch despite last night's rain. Sheriff Wally Vincent crawled from behind the wheel to stretch his legs. Druggist Orville Levitt opened a back door.

Wes said, "They got Matthew Jamison with them. My banker. Probably come to twist the screw another turn."

Bill Roper said nervously, "Maybe I ought to stay, Wes. You might need a witness."

Wes shook his head. "Ain't the Chatfield-Dawson ranch already got enough trouble with the bank?"

Roper's mouth flattened grimly. "Matthew could call in a lot of notes on Miz Livvy if he taken the notion."

Wes said, "You and Glory B. go on along. I ain't fixin' to hit anybody. I wouldn't give Wally the satisfaction."

Bill Roper shook Wes's hand. "You take care of yourself, then. And Tater, you see that he does."

Glory B. took Wes's hand first, then Jim Ed's. "You remember what I said about Saturday, pilgrim." She followed Roper out to the pickup. They spoke to the new arrivals, who were hanging back, obviously waiting for them to leave.

Wes grunted. "What's Saturday?"

Jim Ed said, "Nothing. I wouldn't like it anyway."

The three men stood in awkward impatience beside the sheriff's black car until Bill Roper's pickup was on its way. The dog ran along in the dust almost to the road's first bend. Orville Levitt shifted his weight nervously from one foot to the other. The tall sheriff drew on a cigarette as if for sustenance. He kept his eyes diverted from Wes and Jim Ed on the porch.

Jim Ed glanced at his grandfather and marveled. *Afraid of him. One old man like that, and he's got them up a stump.*

Orville Levitt moved toward the steps, the other two falling in behind him. "Evenin', Wes," he offered with a forced joviality that fell flat. "Hope we haven't come at an inconvenient time."

Wes shook his head and forced a smile as weak as Levitt's. "If it wasn't you it'd be some other son of a bitch. I was fixin' to see what's in the icebox for supper. You-all et?" The invitation came from civility and not from the heart.

Levitt looked to his companions. "We're just here to talk."

The banker was the only one wearing a suit, though a loosened tie dangled forlornly over the druggist's rumpled white shirt. The sheriff wore the unofficial uniform of the smalltown Texas lawman: a spotless Stetson hat, Western-cut shirt and trousers. The shine on his shop-made boots was but little compromised by dust.

Wes said, "Well, then, you-all come on in the house."

It would have been cooler on the porch, but hospitality demanded more, even at the price of discomfort.

Wes asked Levitt, "How's Noreen?"

"All right. Gettin' around a little slow, but we're all doin' that, I suppose."

"Mighty good woman, Noreen."

The banker gave Jim Ed a quizzical look as if wondering whether he should offer his hand. Wes introduced his grandson. Levitt had a stronger handshake than the banker. The sheriff gave Jim Ed only a dark nod. Levitt made conversation by recalling Jim Ed having an ice cream cone in the drugstore when he was just a boy. "Things change," he added. "We don't have ice cream anymore."

Or much of a town either, Jim Ed thought.

Wes stopped by his own chair as if to stake his claim and motioned for the visitors to seat themselves. Jamison said, "Young man, we have business to discuss with your grandfather."

Wes cut in, "Whatever belongs to me will belong to Tater someday."

The banker shrugged and seated himself uncomfortably in a rocking chair that had been Grandmother Maudie's. "I suppose you know what has brought us here."

Wes stared at him until the banker looked away. "I could make a wild guess."

"We would like to save all of us as much time, money and unpleasantness as possible, Wes. I'm sure you know how much the people of Big River look forward to the new lake. I'm sure you understand how much this means to the community financially."

Wes said, "I've got no objection to them havin' a lake. I just don't want them to cover up my ranch with it."

"But the engineers have surveyed this river for miles in all directions. They say Wally's ranch is optimum for a damsite. Yours offers the best storage for the main body of water."

"They named at least two more places. Build in one of those."

The banker looked to the druggist. Levitt said, "But those are too far downstream to help Big River much. You know our town is sick. It needs a shot in the arm."

"So do all the towns downstream."

Vincent lighted another cigarette. "Let those towns watch out for themselves. We're tryin' to take care of what's ours."

Wes nodded. "So am I."

The banker gave the sheriff a cautioning glance. "Wes, I hear you've talked to Talcott and Pratt about representing you."

Wes fingered the pack of cigarettes in his shirt pocket, then dropped his hand. "Everybody says John Talcott is the best lawyer in two counties."

"He is certainly the most expensive."

Wes shrugged. "You pay cheap, you *get* cheap. I figured I'd hire somebody who can win."

"Where do you expect to find the money?"

"You ain't got a mortgage on *everything* I own, Matthew."

"It could be a long and costly fight, Wes, for everybody. And in the end you'll lose."

"With John Talcott? At the least I'd probably keep the thing tied up in court for years. Somebody downstream might go and build their own dam. That'd be the end of the fight."

Levitt's face was stressed. "It might be the end for a lot of us in Big River, too. You wouldn't want that, Wes."

"No, but why am *I* the one who's got to give up everything I've worked forty years to build? You-all seem to think it's all right if *I'm* squeezed out, so long as you can save what *you've* got."

The sheriff walked to the mantle and stared at the old picture of Wes riding the black bronc in a long-ago rodeo. "You won't be squeezed plumb out, Wes. You'll still have a strip of high ground up next to the pavement."

"A strip! What can a man do with that?"

"You could do a right smart of business. I'm figurin' on buildin' me a resort and boat ramps and such. There's a public out yonder cryin' for recreation. You could set up by the pavement and sell bait and groceries and stuff. And beer. You have any idea how much beer a fisherman can drink? Hell, you could make more money off of a beer license in a month than you can make off of cows the rest of your life. I'd be tickled to swap *my* old cows for a busload of tourists."

"You never had any more feelin' for cows than my son Truman did." Wes glanced at Jim Ed as if offering a silent apology. "I bought and paid for this ranch an inch at a time. Watered every foot of it with sweat, and a little blood, too. I raised my sons on it, and spent most of my married life here with Maudie. I ain't givin' that up just so you can build a boat ramp."

Matthew Jamison said, "We would move the house up onto the

high ground for you. Barn and everything, anywhere you choose."

Levitt put in, "You could just sit on the porch and enjoy the view out across the lake."

Jim Ed thought he knew the spot Wes would choose.

But Wes shook his head. "A man don't just live in a *house*. He lives everywhere his land is."

Levitt said, "We're not young men anymore, Wes. When a man is young he wants to ring every bell he can reach. When he gets old he does well to make one tinkle once in a while. Believe me, I know. You've earned your rest."

"I've earned the right to be left alone."

The banker argued, "The water district will give you more than the going market for your land. You could pay off all you owe and have enough left to be comfortable. You know how bad the ranch business has become. A year from now . . . two years . . . who knows what the land may still be worth? You might lose the ranch and have *nothing* left."

Wes stared silently past the visitors, toward the open door and beyond, out upon the land that was his life.

Jamison said, "I never could understand why ranchers get sentimental over a pile of rocks and cedar brush. You've got to look at them strictly from a business point of view. A ranch is just a factory, nothing more. Where others produce cars or refrigerators, a ranch produces beef and mutton, wool and mohair. That land out yonder is nothing more than a production floor, and the livestock is nothing more than the working machinery. They take the raw materials—the grass and weeds and the brush—and they convert them into the finished products. One cow, one piece of land, is about the same as any other. The only difference that matters is in how much they'll produce. Anything more than that is pure romanticism. This is the *real* world we're living in, Wes. We've had to outgrow romanticism."

Wes did not look at him.

The sheriff snapped his fingers. "That old picture just made me think of somethin' better than a bait stand. You could set up a ridin' stable, Wes. You've always loved horses. You could rent them for people to ride around the lake. And how many men alive today can say they rode old Midnight in his prime? You could make hay on that. People would come just to hear you tell those old rodeo stories."

Jim Ed watched his grandfather's face cloud. The old man stared first at the picture, then at the sheriff. His back became as straight as when he sat on a horse. He demanded, "Wally, did you ever read about Buffalo Bill?"

"Sure. Stuff like that was what made me want to be a peace officer."

"Buffalo Bill was a buffalo hunter and an Indian scout. A good one, too. But there come a time when they didn't need such things anymore. So he went into show business and made a mockery out of every real thing he'd done. He stretched the truth till even *he* didn't know what was fact and what was lie. I'd sooner slop hogs for a livin' than turn into somethin' like that, with people thinkin' I'm a puffed-up old windbag and laughin' behind my back."

He grimaced. "Sure, I rode Midnight. I was young. I needed to prove I was as good a man as anybody, and I did, by God. It wasn't no little thing. It wasn't somethin' to be made cheap by turnin' myself into a sideshow."

Vincent flushed, glancing at his two companions for support.

Levitt spread his fingers and stared at them. "We've been good friends a long time, Wes. It hurts me to see us fall out in our old age."

"It ain't the way I'd want it either. But it ain't like Big River had floods that put lives and property in danger; it never did. It ain't like Big River had to have drinkin' water; it's always had more than it needed. You-all just want the lake for a playground so tourists'll come and drop money on you.

"This old ranch is like a child to me, and you'd drown it. If the Lord had wanted a lake here he'd've slid a hill down into the river."

The silence was long and oppressive. Wes and his visitors avoided looking at one another. At length the sheriff declared disgustedly, "Well, it's all been said, ain't it?" He surveyed his two companions in anger. "Old man, all I can say is, you'd better watch yourself when you come to *my* town."

Orville Levitt snapped, "Wally! Shut up!"

Vincent eyed Levitt with surprise.

Banker Jamison pushed to his feet, leaving Grandmother Maudie's old chair rocking. "I am sorry it has come to this, Wes, but I have to tell you: Our institution can no longer extend credit for a losing operation that has no future."

Wes said quietly, "You made a lot of money off of me over the years, Matthew. The interest I've paid you probably built the west wing of that bank."

"These are changing times. We have to look to the highest economic use. We ride the ship or we are left drowning in its wake."

Jamison and the sheriff moved to the front door. Orville Levitt hung back. Pain was in his eyes. "You've said *no* tonight, Wes, and we'll talk about it no further now. But maybe tomorrow, or the next day or the next, you'll see things in a different light. Give me a call if you decide to talk. Any time, day or night."

Wes started to put his hand forward but stopped himself. "Don't you be settin' up waitin', Orv. You need your rest."

Levitt paused in the doorway. "I have a mental picture, Wes, of you and me sittin' in a boat together with our feet propped up and lines in the water. We're both old enough that all we ought to do is go fishin'."

"Never had time to learn how," Wes responded quietly.

"That's the pity. You could have time now. So long, Wes."

"So long, Orv. You watch out for yourself, and Noreen."

Wes stood inside the screen door and watched the men drive away. Presently Jim Ed heard the pantry door open and close. Wes walked out onto the porch, carrying a water glass half filled with raw whisky. He slumped into a hide-bottomed chair.

Jim Ed looked darkly at the glass but said nothing. Wes responded grumpily to the look. "Got to drown out the noise of them damned motorboats."

Wes sipped the whisky until he had put away half of it. "You hungry?"

"Some," Jim Ed admitted.

"Well, you go on in and rustle up somethin' for yourself. I've lost my appetite." He stared into the glass.

Jim Ed hesitated, feeling he should not leave his grandfather alone in this dark mood but knowing nothing he could do to help. He poured off what was left of the morning's coal-black coffee and, following Wes's example, retained part of the grounds. He added fresh makings by guess and by gosh, then put water in the pot and set it on a butane burner. Rummaging in the refrigerator, he decided on the easiest course, making a sandwich of Hallie's leftover steak.

He hoped the smell of coffee would draw Wes into the house, but it did not. He turned off the burner, added cold water to settle the grounds and poured two cups. He carried them out onto the porch. Wes had emptied the glass. Jim Ed said, "Here, maybe some coffee'll make you feel better."

Wes's eyes narrowed at the first sip. Jim Ed realized he had fallen short as a coffee maker. How could he make decent coffee with old grounds and a pot that probably hadn't been scrubbed clean since Grandmother Maudie had died?

Wes said, "It ain't too bad, Tater. You just got to learn that it don't take a lot of water to make good coffee."

"Coffee costs money. Water's free."

"You've never had to carry it in a bucket a hundred yards to the house." Wes's eyes promised a smile, but it never came to fruition. He sipped awhile, then handed Jim Ed the half-empty cup. "You know where I keep that bourbon bottle. How about puttin' a good snort in this for me?"

"You've already had a good snort."

Wes frowned. Jim Ed decided that a man who had managed to make it to seventy-seven ought to be capable of deciding for himself what was going to kill him. He went to the kitchen and poured two jiggers into the cup, then added enough coffee to finish filling it.

Wes sipped carefully, and his eyes showed pleasure. "I declare, you'll learn how to make coffee yet."

"Now, don't you think you ought to eat some supper?"

"It don't take much grub for an old man. It goes to tallow anyway."

Jim Ed doubted his grandfather had ever carried a pound of tallow in his life. "It takes fuel to keep the engine running."

"My engine's all right." Wes motioned with the cup. "Just needs a jump-start now and then."

Jim Ed looked down the road. The dust from the sheriff's automobile had long since settled. "They'll keep coming back. They'll hire however many lawyers it takes."

"But I've already got the best one."

Jim Ed remembered what his father had said about Wes borrowing against his land until he stood a chance to lose it. "You once had this place paid out free and clear, didn't you?"

Wes nodded grimly. "There was a time I didn't have to borrow even for operatin' expenses. There was a time this little ranch fed us good and raised two boys. We never drove a Cadillac or taken no trips to Europe, but we had all we needed. Now it won't even support one dried-up old fart like me."

His gaze was still on the road. "Strange, the way life changes things on you. That time I rode Ol' Midnight, they taken my picture. My name was in the papers. People went out of their way to shake my hand and talk to me. I was a hero for a while, and people liked to brag that they knew me. Now all that's gone; it don't mean a damned thing anymore. I'm just an old man standin' in everybody's way."

Wes pulled a handkerchief from his pocket to blow his nose. A crumpled paper fluttered to the porch floor. Jim Ed stooped to pick it up. "Something you need to keep?"

Wes unfolded it, his gnarled hands shaking. "Auction receipt for them two calves I hauled to town. Been intendin' to put it in my files." He finished his coffee, then pushed stiffly to his feet and went into the house, wobbling a little. He walked to a bookshelf and dropped the receipt into a cardboard shoe box.

Jim Ed's mouth fell open. "*That* is your file?"

"I ain't no bookkeeper. There's a lady in town who figures my income tax. She sorts it all out once a year."

Jim Ed stared at the box. "I don't believe this."

"What's wrong with it?"

"Everything. If Dad knew . . ."

"I don't see it's any of his concern. He never cared about this ranch."

"But accounting has been his life. If he saw how you keep your records, he'd have a fit."

Wes regarded him with a fleeting belligerence. "You're a college boy. I suppose you think you could do better?"

"*Anybody* could do better than throw the receipts into a shoe box."

"Have at it, then; I don't care. See if you learned a damned thing besides how to quit school." Wes carried his empty coffee cup to the pantry.

Jim Ed would not have considered the task had Wes not flung it at him as a challenge. Gritting his teeth, he carried the shoe box to the kitchen table and began taking receipts and miscellaneous papers out of it. Some were crumpled like the one Wes had dropped from his pocket. Some were torn in two and incomplete. Others had been scribbled on with little regard for their original purpose. It appeared a hopeless undertaking. He contemplated dumping them all back into the box and admitting defeat. That would suit the old man to a T. But Wes and Truman were not the only stubborn men in the Hendrix family. He began sorting, first setting the monthly bank statements to one side, then trying to separate auction sales records from receipts for goods bought. He found to his dismay that Wes had put a little of everything into the box, from grocery slips to feed bills.

Laboriously he separated them into stacks of like kind until they half covered the table. The sugar bowl sat atop the livestock auction records to keep the breeze from taking them off onto the floor. A salt shaker held down the feed bills. A coffee cup rested shakily on a miscellaneous lot of receipts for items ranging from a new tire to half a load of fenceposts. Jim Ed spent a goodly part of an hour trying to decide into what category to place various pieces out of an assortment of papers that defied classification. Finally he said, "You'll have to tell me what these were for."

Sipping at a cup which held bourbon instead of coffee, Wes stared in disbelief at the chaos of papers in all colors, sizes and stages of disintegration. He examined several that Jim Ed handed him. He handed one back. "Damned if I know." He held another at arm's length, then closer to his face as if unable to read it.

"This one might be for some scours medicine I had to buy for the calves. I can't remember."

"If you don't remember, how can you know which ones you can deduct for business and which ones you can't?"

Wes shrugged again. "I leave that up to the lady who fixes my income tax. Way it's been the last few years, there's more expense than income anyway." He pointed toward another shoe box in the bookshelf. "You ain't through yet."

Jim Ed groaned.

As he worked down through the second box he found beneath the receipts and other papers a miscellany of photographs. Some were fairly recent color prints which his mother had sent to Wes and Grandmother Maudie of Jim Ed and his parents, of their home in Dallas. Others were older black-and-whites of Jim Ed as a boy. Grandmother Maudie had taken them with a box camera on her visits to Dallas. He came across a couple of himself as a small boy, sitting on a horse while Wes held him in the saddle. The recollection was painful. He recognized other pictures as being of his father and a lad who had to be his uncle. James Edward was the proper cowboy in every one. Truman Hendrix always looked as if he were wearing someone else's clothes.

Toward the bottom of the box he found pictures so old they were brittle, browning a bit. He recognized Grandmother Maudie as a young woman, and Wes as a young man in the prime of health and energy, usually sitting on a horse. A few photos had him riding broncs or roping calves or goats.

Jim Ed came finally upon a picture of Wes as a young cowboy of twenty or so, standing with his arm around a beautiful girl. Jim Ed assumed her to be Grandmother Maudie until he compared the photo to others. This girl was more slender than his grandmother had been in even her earliest pictures. She had eyes that would have melted stone, Jim Ed thought, and a smile that lighted her face like sunrise. He was drawn by a magnetism that fifty-odd years had not dimmed. His curiosity was aroused beyond endurance. He carried the photograph to Wes, who sat with the coffee cup dangled carelessly from one finger.

"Who is this?" he asked.

Wes took the picture in a shaky hand and seemed to have

difficulty focusing his gaze. A gradual smile lightened the deep creases in his face. "A girl I knew once, before I met your grandmother."

"Who was she?"

"That was a long time ago. What do you care for?"

"Just curious. She must have been a knockout in her time."

"Most beautiful girl I ever seen."

"Did you have a *thing* going with her?"

Wes's smile fell away. "A thing?" Resentment leaped into his eyes. "That's the way with you kids nowadays, you all think in just one direction. You don't hold anything sacred."

"Didn't you ever . . . even once?"

Wes's voice was stern. "There was honor in them days. A boy didn't crawl into bed with a girl ever time his britches got to feelin' tight. We respected one another."

"I didn't mean to upset you. But she was so good-looking, I couldn't help but wonder . . . You know how it is."

"I'm afraid I do."

"How come you didn't marry her?"

Wes stared across the room at nothing in particular. His voice softened. "I wasn't nothin' but a wild cowboy with rodeoin' on my mind. Her folks said she should save herself for somebody who'd amount to somethin'."

Jim Ed felt a surge of indignation. "They had a hell of a nerve."

"They was right! They was protectin' their daughter." Wes seemed to drift off into memory and was gone awhile. "She was ready to run off with me and get married in spite of her folks. I was the one who stopped it, before it was too late. I knew I could never give her what she'd been used to."

"What became of her?"

"She married a good, hard-working man that had prospects. I found your grandmother, who'd never had much and and didn't ask for anything except for me to love her."

Jim Ed took the picture from his grandfather's shaking hand. "Did my grandmother know?"

"I never lied to her or kept no secrets."

"Any regrets, then, that you didn't marry the other girl?"

Wes pondered. "Some things, a man never forgets. But regrets? No, when I tally it all up, I reckon not." He gave Jim Ed a thoughtful study. "If I'd married that girl, *you* wouldn't be here."

"Maybe you'd have a grandson who didn't disappoint you."

Wes made no answer. He lost himself in his memories. Gradually he dozed off. Jim Ed's gaze touched on the old photograph of Wes Hendrix riding Midnight.

He thought he knew what Wes had carried with him into the saddle that day . . . what he had set out to prove, and to whom.

Chapter 6

Few men aroused a sense of awe in Sheriff Wally Vincent, but attorney John Talcott did. The man was old and bent and wizened, so it was not a sense of physical threat that prevented Vincent from looking Talcott in the eye for more than a moment. Rather, it was a feeling of powerlessness. Too many times, Vincent's considerable physical strength and legal authority had fallen into ashes against the man's sharp courtroom wit and his familiarity with obscure corners of the written law.

Walking down the courthouse steps, Vincent met Talcott coming up. The attorney spoke civilly enough. "Afternoon, Wally." Not *Sheriff*, not even *Mister Vincent*, but the condescending familiarity of *Wally*. Vincent nodded without speaking and yielded room by moving a little farther toward the handrail. He paused to let his gaze follow the old man through the tall, heavy door and into the dark cavern of the long hall.

Probably working on Wes Hendrix's case, Vincent thought sourly. *Trying to cheat us out of that lake we need so bad.*

He tapped his foot impatiently and frowned while a jail trusty he had detailed to mow the courthouse lawn wiped bird droppings from the official black automobile's hood and top. The trusty was known as Big River's friendly neighborhood burglar, though the only thing he had ever burgled was a liquor store. He took a couple of swipes at the dust on the door and stepped aside to reveal the sheriff's badge painted there two feet high in silver and black.

"How's that, Cap?" he asked. "Clean enough?"

"It'll do for now. Better get back on that mower. And don't you leave a bunch of clippin's on the sidewalk this time, do you hear me?"

"I hear you, Cap." The man saluted like a soldier.

As Vincent opened the car door and started to climb in, he looked up at the dark green foliage of a giant liveoak tree already ancient when the two-story limestone courthouse had been built in 1903. There was no practical way to keep birds from lighting in the branches, and the town's meddlesome clubwomen wouldn't hear of mutilating the venerable tree by trimming it back from his parking space. His own wife Faye was among the ringleaders, aided and abetted by Orville Levitt's wife Noreen. Now *there* was a woman who could make Jesus Christ use God's name in vain, he thought. It took a court order, almost, just to tip the tree's branches when they began to invade the street and become a traffic hazard.

Legend, revered here like a story out of the Bible, told about one of the county's pioneers taking refuge behind that massive trunk after Indians shot his horse from under him. When construction began on the courthouse years later and the builders wanted to cut down the tree, the gray-bearded old settler had stood them off with his rifle, declaring that the tree had once saved his life, and he would die to defend the tree.

It was probably another damned lie like the story about the Indian couple jumping off Lover's Leap. But a man didn't win votes debunking old stories that people wanted to believe. Especially when tourists stopped to read the historical marker and then tarried long enough to leave a little money in some of the business houses around the courthouse square.

He slammed the door and turned on his radio so the dispatcher could reach him in case of emergency. The likeliest emergency he could foresee was that the trusty might slip off to the Stammtisch for a couple of beers. Or it was getting about time for Fuller Gibson's monthly complaint that somebody was stealing cattle from him again. Gibson saw cow thieves behind every cedar bush.

Vincent backed into the street, then paused to make sure the trusty was working. Satisfied, he eased the automobile into motion and made a slow circle of the courthouse square. The old pensioners of the whittle-and-spit club had their domino table and chairs set up on the grass by the east entrance and were playing Forty-two, the only game they seemed to know. The perennial competition started with the rising grass in the spring and lasted until first frost, interrupted only by meals, darkness, rainfall and funerals. Players changed through the years as nature's relentless toll removed old members and brought others into the fold, but the game had found immortality.

Vincent's intended destination was Lacy's café, which stood by itself a couple of blocks out on the highway toward the auction ring. He noted with displeasure the two cars parked in front. He went on by, for his visit should be paid when no eavesdropping customers were in the place. It was midafternoon, and respectable men should be at work, he thought. Some people couldn't find time to get their jobs properly done but could always *make* time to drink coffee. Well, *his* office employees didn't get away with it. They did a day's work for a day's pay.

While he waited for the customers to leave, he decided on a drive through Little Mexico. It never hurt to look things over. Those people down there always nodded pleasantly, and some even smiled at him, but a man never could see past their eyes and tell for sure what they were thinking. It used to be that a sheriff could just invade Mexican Town once in a while, knock a few heads together and keep things quiet. That was the way old Dad Eustis used to do it—knock down the first man who looked crossways at him and drag him off to jail. It worked equally well on Mexicans and cedar choppers and cowboys celebrating the end of the month. Nobody messed around with old Dad Eustis.

But that had been in the golden days before the Miranda decision. Times had changed. The Mexicans voted nowadays, and there were so damned many of them! Looked to him like they were going to take Texas back, and they weren't going to need Santa Anna's army. They were going to win in bed, outbreeding the gringos.

He saw a middle-aged Hispanic man and his teenage son lifting a black, greasy engine out of an old dumptruck, using a winchline and a ginpole on another truck very little younger. Vincent stopped to watch, thinking the Mexican community would lose one of its political leaders if that line should break. Rolando Zuniga influenced a lot of votes in this part of town.

He waited until the two swung the engine over onto a workbench beneath the shade of a liveoak, then he got out of the car and walked toward them. The teenager regarded the sheriff with misgiving that bordered on hostility, but the elder Zuniga flashed a smile with teeth unbelievably white. So far as Vincent knew, they were all his.

"Howdy, *amigo,*" Vincent said, forcing a smile in return. "You-all need any help?"

Zuniga reached for a soiled cloth to wipe his hands. "Sheriff, you want to buy a truck cheap?"

He extended a hand to which a considerable amount of grease still clung. Vincent gritted his teeth and accepted the handshake, feeling the gum on his fingers. "No, you'll be needin' that truck one of these days. When they get the lake project goin' and I start my fishin' lodge, I'll be wantin' some dirt work done."

He would probably use a general contractor for most of it, but it never hurt to spread a little work around among the voters, especially if their name was Zuniga.

Zuniga said, "We will be ready. When we finish the overhaul on this truck, it will run like a new one. Pity, Sheriff, we cannot overhaul our old wives as well."

"Damned shame," Vincent agreed, considering the wish well stated. Faye could certainly use some rejuvenation. "If you need any help on the heavy liftin', I can send a trusty over."

"No need, Sheriff. I have my sons, and their motors do not need an overhaul. My grandchildren prove that."

"Well, then, take care." Vincent nodded with a studied pleasantness and turned back toward his car. It was all he could do to keep from taking out his handkerchief and rubbing at the grease, but that must wait until he was out of sight.

One of these days they could have the damned sheriff's job. Once he got that resort running smoothly, he wouldn't need a county paycheck. He wouldn't need to pretend he liked Mexicans and niggers and babies anymore. They could all go kiss his ass.

He made a couple more blocks but saw nothing that needed his attention. Whatever devilry they pulled down here in Little Mexico, they usually waited until dark. He U-turned on the caliche-packed street—few were asphalt-paved in this part of town—and returned to Lacy's café. The town was too small and its business too sluggish to attract any of the national fast-food chains or franchises, except for a Dairy Queen. Almost any Texas town large enough to have a post office had a Dairy Queen. Old Grandma Lacy worked hard to compete.

He was relieved to see no cars parked in front. He got out and pushed close to the front window, trying to see through the reflections. A tiny turkey bell tinkled as he opened the door. A pretty waitress stood behind the short counter, wrapping knives, forks and spoons in paper napkins for the evening's supper trade.

"Come in, Sheriff," said Stella Tenney. When she smiled, it was as if somebody had turned on another light. "Coffee?"

"I'd like that," he replied soberly, looking around the small, table-crowded room, smelling cold grease from the noon cooking. The customers had all gone. "Anybody in the kitchen?"

"No, honey. My grandma's gone home to rest a little before the supper run starts."

"Good. I've got somethin' private to talk to you about."

She slumped a little, her smile quickly faded. "If it's another lie that my ex-husband has told you . . ."

Vincent shook his head. "I haven't heard from Hobart. This is about somebody who stands a good chance of *becomin'* an ex-husband." He went silent until she brought him the coffee. He spooned sugar into it but no cream, then stared at the young woman while he stirred. She was still a little short of thirty. She would look hardly twenty if she wore less makeup, he thought. She used a bright red lipstick that reminded him of the style popular when he was a boy in the 1940s. Her blouse was a size too little, probably on purpose, and unbuttoned almost halfway down. How her ex-husband had walked away and left all that Vincent could never understand.

He sipped the coffee without taking his eyes from her. Her

nervousness built until her hands trembled. This silent waiting was a technique he had used on many a prisoner to break him down. At last she pleaded, "Well, Sheriff, tell me."

He set the cup back into the saucer with a clatter. "Addie Wilkins was in to see me this mornin'. She had a good deal to say about you and her husband."

Stella Tenney's face reddened. "Me and Leroy are just good friends, is all."

"That's what Addie says. *Real* good friends. She says Leroy's seldom home anymore, even to sleep."

"Maybe if she took better care of him he'd stay home. But I don't see it's any of the law's business who I'm friends with."

"That's the same thing I told Addie. But she said it *would* be the law's business if she came over here one day and put a bullet between those mascaraed eyes. Her words, not mine."

The young woman's blue-green eyes grew larger. "You think she'd really do a thing like that?"

"You wouldn't think so, just to look at her. But I remember when that Hitchner kid shot three men who'd been messin' with his sister. And him a choirboy, too. So you never can tell."

Stella stared at the floor, her hands still shaking a little. Vincent could usually take a detached attitude in cases like this, but he found himself caught up in a strong urge to reach across the counter. He squeezed the coffee cup to keep his hands occupied and away from what they *wanted* to do.

She said, "I like Leroy. He's been good to me when I needed somebody to *be* good to me."

From the gossip Vincent had heard, Stella liked just about everybody, so long as they were male, and Leroy was by no means the only man in town who had been good to her. Many of the town's clubwomen had marked Stella down in their books as a menace to domestic tranquility. Even before Addie, a couple of them had demanded to know when the sheriff was going to start enforcing the laws against prostitution in this county. But so far as he knew, Stella had asked nobody anything for whatever favors she chose to grant. And if a man decided to give her a bracelet or a set of earrings or some such out of his own free will and Christian generosity, that was not a matter for the law.

It was no secret that the café's popularity had little to do with old Grandma Lacy's kitchen. Stella's ripe looks and the unspoken suggestion of secret sin would have kept a crowd in this place if Grandma cooked nothing but ham hocks and grits. Vincent could sympathize with Leroy Wilkins, for his own wife was given to spells of winter chill, even in the summertime.

He said, "You're a handsome woman, Stella. There's a-plenty of eligible men in this town. You don't need Leroy."

She came around the counter and sat down on a stool beside him. He thought he could feel her warmth, but he decided it was his own, rising. She said, "I know a lot of folks don't think much of me, Sheriff honey, but they don't understand. I like havin' men around me. I don't mean to steal some other woman's husband, but he wouldn't come to me if there wasn't somethin' lackin' at home, now would he? That ain't my fault."

The temptation of such a woman could *make* something go wrong at home, he thought. He stared at the third button on her snug blouse and wished either to close it or to open the rest of them. He took a stronger grip on the coffee cup.

"I'm not a preacher," he said. "I'm just a public servant, tryin' to keep the peace."

Jim Ed Hendrix had never heard of stomachworms. Over breakfast, his grandfather told him more than he would have cared to learn.

Wes said, "It's the sheep you got to worry most about." He smeared butter and molasses together on his plate and wiped them up with a sourdough biscuit. "Especially the lambs. You see, in a good wet year like we've got now, that little bitty worm climbs way out on the end of a blade of grass and waits for a sheep to come along and swaller it. The worm makes itself to home in the gut, like a summer boarder with all the hash he can eat, and when it's full it lays its eggs. Them eggs drop out on the ground in the sheep pills and start the whole she-bang all over again. That's why we got to gather and drench the sheep, to kill the stomachworms before they draw the whole bunch down like a gutted snowbird."

Jim Ed thought about the bay horse named Rowdy, and he dreaded. "Have we got to gather those sheep on horseback?"

"They ain't exactly housepets that we can whistle up. Of *course* we got to go out on horseback. But we'll have help. Ol' Pepper'll do most of the work."

"He won't ride that horse for me."

Wes grinned. "You can't let a dog have *all* the enjoyment."

Jim Ed walked to the corrals while Wes opened the chicken-pen gate to let the hens out for the day's foraging. He leaned upon the fence from the outside and stared balefully at the calm-looking Rowdy, which stood head-to-rump with Wes's dun, Yellowhammer. Rowdy gave the appearance of having been ridden regularly to Sunday school. Jim Ed could not be sure whether or not the horse was looking at him. Horses' eyes were set into the sides of the head, and they could seem to be looking in two directions at the same time. In the eye that faced him, Jim Ed saw no evil.

Wes's voice came from behind. "You tryin' to hypnotize him?"

"I would if I knew the words. I can't speak horse."

"You will if you stay here long enough."

Wes walked into the saddleroom and carried out a pair of bridles. Talking softly, he approached Rowdy first. The bay horse gave him a wary study and took half a step backward as Wes casually raised his hand toward the animal's nose. "Whoa, son. Behave yourself now." He touched the nose, let his hand move slowly up the other side of the horse's head, then slipped the bridle reins around Rowdy's neck. "You bridle him, Tater. Time you and him understood one another."

"I think we already do."

Rowdy held still as Jim Ed slipped the bits between his teeth, then pulled the bridle up over his ears. He almost gave the impression of enjoying it. "I can read your mind," Jim Ed said. "You're looking forward to throwing me off again." He saddled the bay while Wes caught, bridled and saddled the dun. Pepper stood outside the corral, tag wagging vigorously. Jim Ed wondered if a touch of the sadist might lurk behind that friendly demeanor.

Wes did not have to tell Jim Ed to lead the bay around the corral a few minutes and soften him up; he remembered that lesson from Saturday morning at the C Bar. When he thought he had led him enough, he asked, "Anything special I ought to do?"

Wes nodded. "Get on him where the ground is soft."

Jim Ed tried to remember the instruction Wes had given him about how to mount a horse that was not entirely to be trusted. With his left hand he gripped the reins and the mane a little forward of the saddle, and his right hand went to the horn. He raised his left foot to the stirrup and gave himself a springing boost with his right foot as he swung up, leaning forward to help offset any sudden movement.

"That's pretty good, Tater," Wes said with approval.

Rowdy disagreed. Before Jim Ed got his right foot safely settled in the stirrup, the horse lunged forward, then jumped straight up. The second move was unnecessary, for Jim Ed was already lost. He felt himself go out of balance, slipping forward over the bay's neck. He grabbed a handful of mane as the horse came down and gave him a solid jolt that lifted him out of the saddle. He kept sliding forward, holding the bay around the neck as weight and momentum carried him over the left side. He slammed his nose hard against the horse's neck and got a mouthful of mane on his way down. Still hanging on, he managed to land more or less on his feet, then went to his knees in the soft dirt. The bay tore away from him, ran a short distance and stopped, turning its head to look back at him.

Wes observed, "That was some improvement over the last time. I believe you're startin' to catch on."

"I'm tickled," Jim Ed said with irony. He was surprised that he had not lost his breath, and that the only thing which hurt was his nose. He raised his hand to it, expecting blood but finding none. His Tom Landry hat lay on the ground.

Wes said, "Ol' horse is gettin' to like you, I think. He didn't damage you none."

"I'm sure glad he's on my side," Jim Ed responded, walking toward the bay, half hoping he might jump the fence and run away. But the horse stood and watched him calmly as a spectator at a chess match. In a way it *was* a chess match, Jim Ed thought.

"That's the way, Tater," Wes encouraged. "Get right back on him so he'll know he ain't run a bluff on you."

Jim Ed knew no better way of mounting than he had used the first time, so he did the same thing again. The bay trotted gently around the pen, responding easily as Jim Ed tugged the reins in one direction, then the other. The dog had remained on the other side of the fence until the horse had finished pitching. Now he slithered under and came up beside Wes to watch Jim Ed and the bay. Jim Ed took that as a favorable sign. Wes stiffly mounted his dun and rode up beside Jim Ed. They circled the corral together.

Wes's voice was warm with approval. "A lot of boys wouldn't've got back on him. I'm not sure your daddy would've at your age."

"I didn't know I had any choice."

"A man's got a choice about everything in this life, except leavin' it."

Riding out into the pasture, Wes whistled unnecessarily for Pepper to come along. The dog was trotting along beside him, joyous at going.

The pasture was fenced smaller than the one Jim Ed had ridden on the C Bars. Its liveoaks and cedar brush limited visibility, and he wondered how Wes ever managed to work it by himself. Before they had gone far, Wes pointed to the fence, lying on their left. "You keep goin' in the direction we've started, and stay in sight of that fence. I'll move a little more toward the middle. Any sheep you come across, throw them in my direction. Me and Pepper'll push them a little farther to the center. When we get to the far end, we'll come back down the other side and drive everything toward the house."

Jim Ed remained dubious, remembering how many hands had helped gather the C Bar cattle. Wes moved away at an angle, pushing the dun horse to a slow trot. Jim Ed rode as he had been instructed and kept a watch on Rowdy's ears. A horse often telegraphed what he was about to do by the way his ears moved. If he suddenly laid them back, Jim Ed was prepared to grab the saddlehorn and anything else that seemed solid. But Rowdy was the picture of patience and understanding. His ears, pointing forward, indicated sheep before Jim Ed could even see them.

The first set, a dozen or so ewes with large lambs at their sides, edged away from Jim Ed's approach. Fortunately they were moving in the proper direction, toward Wes, so Jim Ed gave a whoop and helped their resolution to get away from him. He saw the black-and-white Border Collie coming on the run, making a long swing around the sheep, then moving in behind them. Where they had merely trotted from Jim Ed, they ran from the dog. Two hundred yards away, Wes was shouting instructions. Pepper seemed to understand, for he first dropped to his belly to let the sheep calm down, then closed in to start them moving again, slower. Presently Jim Ed saw the dog dart out once more, a little forward and to the left, and come out of a clump of brush with another small cluster of sheep. He pushed them toward Wes, as he had done with the others. Jim Ed began to understand how his grandfather had managed most of the time in the absence of outside help. That dog was worth at least two men on horseback, and more if they were of Jim Ed's caliber.

He came in a little while to the back fence and followed it to the point where his grandfather and Pepper waited. Wes asked, "How's Ol' Rowdy treatin' you?"

"He hasn't made a false move."

"He'll be eatin' out of your hand pretty soon."

"And take half my fingers off."

Wes leaned forward to pat the bay horse on the neck. "A man learns to appreciate a good friend and accept his faults because the friendship is worth it. A good honest horse ought to be forgiven one or two little flaws in his character."

He touched spurs gently to his dun and rode along the fence. On the other side of the net wire ran a graded county road, serving other ranches as an access to the paved highway. In a bit Wes stopped abruptly, mumbling an oath. The remains of a deer hung by the legs from the top of the fence.

"How did that happen?" Jim Ed asked.

Wes grunted. "Watch a deer jump sometime. Often as not, he gathers his hind legs up under his belly. If he don't lift himself high enough, those legs go between the two top wires and hang him up. This one was probably runnin' from a car."

The dead deer seemed to put Wes into a dark mood for a while. Shortly he came upon a couple of sheets of discarded newspaper that had blown across the fence and lodged against the base of a cedar tree. Wes scowled and dismounted, grabbing up the news-paper. He wadded the two sheets, then began looking around for a place to put them. He saw none.

Jim Ed swung to the ground and lifted a large flat rock by one end. Wes gave him a surprised glance, then shoved the paper underneath, where worms wiggled in agitated response to the sunlight's invasion of their dark, damp home. Jim Ed eased the rock back into place.

Wes seemed almost embarrassed. Defensively he said, "I don't understand why some people have to trash up the land."

Jim Ed responded, "I don't either."

Wes turned away, but not before Jim Ed saw pleasure in his eyes.

After they had ridden a short distance, Wes stopped again. He said, "You go on till you reach the corner, then start back toward the house. Me and Pepper'll be throwin' sheep to you. Just let them trail along the fence as slow as they want to go, short of stoppin' altogether."

Sheep bleated somewhere in the cedar. Pepper cocked his head in that direction and seemed about to go into a frenzy. Jim Ed had never seen anyone so happy in his work, unless it might be Wes.

He found there was nothing complicated or strenuous about gathering the sheep. Wes and Pepper kept pushing little bunches toward him, and he would ease them along to the others plod-ding down the fence. Sheep being gregarious animals, they seemed eager to join their kind in a bleating, dust-raising mass. The lambs were of various sizes, the smaller ones tending to become farthest separated from their mothers and dropping back to the rear. Once he had listened awhile, Jim Ed found the din not unpleasant. He wondered how a mother and her young could distinguish each other's bleating amid such a mixture, but now and again he would see a ewe drop back and quickly make an anxious reunion with her lamb, doing a great deal of bleating. Almost immediately the lamb would begin punching at her ud-der. The larger lambs had to drop to their knees.

The sheep stopped just short of the corral gate. The bunch knotted up while those in the lead resisted entry. The dog moved in at Wes's command, and two ewes trotted briskly through the opening. The others followed as the dog pulled back and gave them room. Dust boiled up in their wake. Jim Ed dismounted to close the gate behind them before they had time to change their minds and make a dash back for the pasture. Wes rode to an interior gate which he opened to a smaller pen, shaped like a funnel, pinching down at one end to a long, narrow alleyway hardly wide enough for more than two animals to move abreast. He motioned for Jim Ed to push the sheep into it. Pepper helped by running and barking, finally jumping up onto the woolly backs of the tightly packed animals, forcing them to fill the alley, its fences no taller than the sheep.

Jim Ed coughed at the dust, but his grandfather seemed to thrive on it. Wes stood staring at the sheep, his gaze running slowly over those pinched into the narrow alley and the others jammed into the crowding pen. "They're doin' good this spring," he said with pleasure. "Close to a hundred percent lamb crop, and it looks like these ewes are goin' to raise them all."

Jim Ed still wondered. His grandfather had always called himself a cowboy, and somehow that image did not reconcile with this old man standing here proudly surveying these bleating sheep. It certainly did not square with that browning old photograph of the young rodeo star making a ride on an outlaw bronc named Midnight.

He commented, "I can't say that they're very pretty."

Wes replied, "They would be if they was yours, and lambs was sellin' for seventy cents a pound." Wes began leading his dun horse toward the barn. He said, "I hated sheep at first, but they growed on me. I decided they can't be all bad if they make you more money than cattle. Besides, an old cow'll sometimes try to kill you. So will a horse. An old ewe may be dumber than dirt, but you don't find any malice in her.

"Anyway, sheep can be good for the land if you don't graze them too heavy. They eat a lot of weeds and brush and give the grass a better chance to grow. In a wet spring you'll sometimes see broomweeds take over the moisture and crowd out most of the grass on ranches that don't run sheep. But sheep eat broomweeds when they're young and tender, and they'll hold them down. A good sheep ranch, run right, is apt to be in better shape than most straight cow outfits. The Lord put everything on this earth for a purpose."

Jim Ed smiled. "Even Dallas?"

"It's not meant for man to understand the Lord's thinkin'."

Jim Ed had not even a vague idea what his grandfather meant when he spoke of drenching sheep. He fancied that they might be run into a dipping vat or sprayed somehow. Wes tied his horse near the barn, then motioned for Jim Ed to help him carry some things to the windmill. There the old man poured white powder from a packet into a large plastic jug, filled the jug with water and stirred it until the powder went into suspension.

"Maudie used to help me do this," he said. "Since she's been gone I've had to do for myself." He led Jim Ed back to the sheep-crowded alley. "You climb over into there and catch the sheep for me one at a time. Hold their heads up. I'll handle the drenchin' gun."

Jim Ed quickly saw what the narrow alley was for. The sheep were too tightly packed to present much resistance. He found it easiest to straddle them and hold them still with the pressure of his legs while he used both hands to force their mouths open. The drench gun had for its barrel a long, thin tube which Wes pushed down each animal's throat, squeezing out a dose of the worm-killing solution. As he withdrew the tube, Wes used a square piece of colored chalk to make a mark down the animal's nose. That, Jim Ed realized, was to prevent giving any of them a repeat dose, although Wes assured him that a double dose would do more harm to his wallet than to the sheep.

Wes worked slowly and methodically, using a patience Jim Ed would have doubted that he had. In rough hands, the steel tube of the drenching gun could do injury to an animal, but Wes's hands were gentle to the task. By the time the last sheep had been drenched and chalk-marked, Jim Ed's shirt was streaked with sweat and clinging to his back. He looked up at the windmill, its fan turning very slowly, and wished he could feel even a little of that cooling breeze.

Wes wiped a sleeve across his forehead. "Fixin' to turn hot. I'm glad we finished early, before it got bad."

Jim Ed pulled at the shirt. It drew right back against his skin like a mustard plaster. "We're through workin' sheep for the day?"

Wes nodded. "Sheep always suffer when you handle them too much in the heat. Ol' Pepper don't work as good, either."

Jim Ed said, "That suits me. I could use a little shade."

"It's not you I was thinkin' about; it's the stock. Me and you, we'll go work on that fence after dinner."

Jim Ed suppressed a groan. For a minute he had thought the old man might be softening up.

Wes sent him to open the pasture gate so the sheep could drift back out, ewes and lambs pairing in their own good time. When Wes began unsaddling the dun, Jim Ed took the silent cue and did the same for the bay Rowdy. There were other pastures and other sheep, but they would not be worked today. He squinted up toward the noonday sun, not yet at its midsummer peak of heat but carrying an uncomfortable authority already. He wondered if Wes was serious about building fence.

They ate, then Wes announced that he intended to take a nap and suggested that Jim Ed do the same. Not used to it, Jim Ed lay on his bed and tried consciously to coax sleep. It was a long time in coming to him, so that he had just dropped off when Wes's heavy boots tromped across the floor and awakened him.

Wes said, "I'll bet you feel better now, Tater. A short nap is good for the soul. Come on, we got fence to build."

Jim Ed was disabused of any lingering notion that the old man might be developing a soft spot.

The first couple of holes were a bit easier to dig, and he thought perhaps Wes had been right about the struggle being less difficult as they worked their way down the slope toward their goal at the river. The third hole seemed to be of solid rock from the first inch of surface all the way to the bottom. Once the sweat broke free, however, he found the work not so taxing as before. The soft breeze against his soaking shirt cooled his skin. He paused to rest at intervals, watching Pepper worrying his way down through the timber along the river, trying to flush out something that would run from him. Jim Ed remarked that he had not seen Old Snort.

Wes said, "We'll probably see him if we stay to the cool of the evenin'. Deer shade up through the heat of the day."

Jim Ed wiped his face. "That shows their intelligence."

"Deer don't have note payments to make, or taxes to pay. Are you allergic to sweat?"

"Not when there's good reason for it."

"There's reason. This is Ol' Snort's stompin' ground, him and a lot of other wildlife too. If Big River was to build that lake they're a-wantin', he'd be out of a home."

"He'd just move up away from the waterline."

"And overcrowd other land that's already got about all the deer it can support. Reduce the habitat and you reduce the wildlife; it's as simple as that."

Wes's determined eyes told Jim Ed that the subject had been carried as far as it needed to go for now. If his father wanted Wes convinced, he had better send someone more persuasive, or come himself. He got on his knees and scooped out chipped rock with the small, bent coffee can.

Wes turned and surveyed the fenceposts already solidly in place. He grunted his approval. "You ain't doin' too bad."

Jim Ed found that after he had reached a certain level of discomfort from the heat, it became no worse. He even took pleasure each time Wes measured the depth of a new hole and declared it sufficient. He found satisfaction in completing a piece of work and knowing he had given it an honest effort. Each time he and Wes set a post permanently in a hole, he took fresh stock in the results of his labor, a lengthening fenceline, a river less distant than when he had started.

He had heard somebody—perhaps Wes, perhaps his father— say that work was sometimes its own reward. He was not yet totally convinced, but he would no longer reject the premise out of hand.

They labored until the sun was nearing the tops of the tall pecan trees on the river. The last post set, the tools loaded into the pickup and Pepper whistled up from his latest raid in the timber, Wes leaned against the vehicle's grill and stared down the slope. "I can see somethin' stirrin' at the edge of that liveoak motte. Watch, and I think you'll see Ol' Snort pretty soon."

Jim Ed sat on the ground, his arms folded across his knees. Surely enough, in a few minutes he could see the big buck advance cautiously from the cover of the foliage, pausing frequently to look around. Pepper tensed, preparing to bark, and Wes bade him be quiet. Shortly the buck worked his way down to the water, two does trailing closely behind him.

Wes said, "Tell me somethin' in the city that does the heart half as much good, and I'll eat that citified hat of yours."

Jim Ed admitted, "The hat is safe."

Supper was mostly the noon meal warmed over, except that Wes made new coffee. Jim Ed sipped it and found he was slowly beginning to tolerate Wes's bull-stout brew. Even so, the first time he got the chance to do it without Wes watching him, he was going to scrub that evil pot.

Wes went through the newspaper he had picked up from the mailbox, then turned on the television but found nothing to his liking. He took his fiddle out of the case and walked onto the porch. He sat in a hide-bottomed rocking chair and plucked the strings, tuning the fiddle by ear.

Jim Ed picked up the discarded newspaper and went through the headlines, finding little of interest. He listened to his grandfather on the porch, warming up to the instrument, playing a slow tune. Jim Ed put down the newspaper and stood leaning on the doorjamb, letting the tune play through his mind. It was something old-fashioned, something a world apart from the music that stirred his pulse and his feet. Yet he would admit that it had a pleasant melody, even a rhythm, if one too restrained for his personal taste.

He thought of the guitar hanging on the wall of his room, the one James Edward was said to have played before Jim Ed was born. Without consciously willing it, he found himself going to the room and lifting the guitar down from its place. It evidently had not been played in years, or even dusted. He rubbed his sleeve over it and plucked the strings. As Wes had done, he tuned it by ear the best he could. He had learned on one not dissimilar.

He listened to his grandfather's music and tried to pick up the chords that would meld with it. About the time he thought he had the hang of it, Wes brought that tune to a close and started another. Jim Ed concentrated on it, got the rhythm, then stepped out onto the porch.

Wes's eyes widened in surprise, and he almost dropped the melody. His mouth curved into a smile, and he quickened the tempo. Jim Ed matched him, even though the guitar and the fiddle were not quite in tune with one another, and his feeling for his grandfather's music was not all it should have been. The old man played one song after another, and Jim Ed brought up the accompaniment by ear, the best he knew how. It was much different from his little combo in Dallas.

Wes tried one particularly fast tune but slurred the notes and shook his head, easing the fiddle down into his lap. He flexed his fingers and said, "Stiffened up on me. I can't play the fast ones anymore like me and Maudie used to."

"You do fine," Jim Ed told him. "I'm afraid I don't know much about your music."

"You do fine," Wes said. The old man's eyes glistened, and he looked away. "First time I've had anybody play along with me since your grandmother began to fail. A fiddle's all right, but it oughtn't to stand alone, any more than a *man* ought to."

Wes softly played a few bars that Jim Ed vaguely recognized. The old man stopped to tell him, "This is the Kelly Waltz. It was a particular favorite of your grandmother's. I don't think we ever played together but what she asked for this one."

He started over. Jim Ed struggled a minute, finding the rhythm and the chords. He was soon caught up in the melody. He remembered he had heard his grandmother hum it many times. He watched his grandfather's eyes, misting as they stared off into the darkness. He suspected the music carried the old man back to a remembered time that was young and bright, a time when his fingers did not lag stiffly on the strings, when the guitar and the fiddle were finely tuned one to the other. Jim Ed could only imagine how it must have been, and he wished he could know.

You just keep on playing, old man, he thought. *I'll stay up with you the best I can.*

Chapter 7

Glory B. Dawson kept a firm grip on the hackamore rein in case the pony might decide to drop its head and pitch. It was only green-broke and still likely to yield to outbursts of independence. She reined the young horse in a wide circle around the corral, the hoofs stirring a fine white dust. "He's got a nice, smooth gait," she shouted to ranch foreman Bill Roper, his husky form hunched on the plank fence beside his son Johnny.

"I thought you'd like him," Roper replied. "Fuller Gibson paid Juan Sanchez for the breakin', but the pony humped up the first time Fuller got on him. He'd be tickled to make a trade."

Glory B.'s grandmother walked slowly toward the corral, her face shaded by a flat-brimmed old cowboy hat that seemed a mismatch with the housedress she wore. Lavinia Dawson took each step carefully, as if it brought pain. Glory B. kept the sorrel in a long trot through a couple more circles around the corral, then brought him to a stop where her grandmother leaned against the outside of the fence. Lavinia had a reputation as a good judge of horses. "Reckon we ought to trade for him, Gram?"

Lavinia Dawson smiled. "Law, girl, *I* won't be riding him. *You're* the one who's got to be satisfied."

"I can't ride old Roanie *all* the time." She looked back at Roper. "Do you think he'll work? There's no place on this ranch these days for anything that won't pull its weight."

Roper shrugged. "Juan says he already watches a cow."

She reached down to pat the pony on its neck. Startled at the unaccustomed touch, it jumped. Her rump bumped against the cantle of the saddle. She was in no danger of losing her seat, however. She had learned to ride a horse almost as early as she had learned to walk. She asked, "What've we got that we could afford to swap? Money's too tight to be buying him."

Roper said, "We have an old oat-thief or two that I'd like us to get shed of. They're the kind Fuller likes best, slow and gentle."

Glory B. reached down again, easier this time, to pet the sorrel bronc. Its skin rippled at the touch, but the horse did not jump. "Does he have a name?"

"Fuller didn't say so. Call him what you want to."

Glory B. warmed to a thought. "He's skittish, but he can be gentled. I think I'll call him Pilgrim."

Roper threatened to smile. "After anybody I'd know?"

She did not reply. "How about opening the gate for me, Johnny, so I can let him run a little?"

Lavinia Dawson warned, "You watch out now. You never know what a green-broke animal'll do."

"He's just another pilgrim who hasn't learned yet what's good for him. But I'll bet I can teach him."

Roper grinned. "You *are* talkin' about the horse?"

"What else?" She pulled the bronc's head around as the gate opened, and she touched her heels gently to his sides. She wore no spurs; they could cause unnecessary trouble with a young horse like this. As she rode out the gate and into the open pasture, she glanced up toward the big two-story, bay-windowed frame house her great-grandfather had built when her grandmother had been but a girl. A woman stood on the broad porch, arms folded, her stiff stance expressing a disapproval evident even at fifty yards.

Well, Mother, Glory B. thought, *I don't approve of everything you do, either.*

She slackened the rein. The bronc moved quickly into a long lope, an easy, rocking movement that Glory B. found pleasant. A startled jackrabbit bolted from behind a cedar bush. Glory B. tightened her grip on the rein, expecting the pony to shy to one side or the other. It did not. *Pretty level-headed for a pilgrim. You're liable to work out just fine.*

She turned him one way and then another, testing his response to the rein. It was fair enough, considering the relatively short time Sanchez had trained him. It would be a lot better before the summer was up. At length she reined him around and headed him back, holding him to a slow trot. Most horses under saddle liked going toward the barn, for that usually meant release, and perhaps even feed. They were easily spoiled by letting them run in that direction, like chronic clock-watchers on a salary.

"Wouldn't want to teach a pilgrim any bad habits," she said. "Most of them have already got their share."

She glanced up toward the big house. Her mother still watched, her arms folded. Glory B. anticipated the lecture. It had been delivered so many times that it had fallen into a set pattern, like an aging teacher's lessons or a politician's patented speech. Glory B.'s father had wanted a son; her mother had wanted a daughter. Both had been disappointed. Her grandmother had accepted Glory B. as she was, guiding her subtly with a loose rein as Glory B. intended to do with this pliable bronc.

She rode back into the corral and swung to the ground, stepping away quickly in case the horse might try to paw her. Experience had taught her that hope was pleasant, but safety lay in expecting the worst.

Johnny Roper's voice was excited. "How does he ride?"

She extended the rein toward him. "Take him out and try him for yourself." She suspected Johnny had been hoping she would reject the pony so he might have a chance at it. The bronc would need to be ridden regularly and hard to work down the rough edges. That would be Johnny's pleasure and privilege when Glory B. was too busy. Like Glory B., he had been a good rider before he had learned to spell *horse.*

She looked toward her grandmother. "You're smiling awfully pretty this morning, Gram. Feeling better?"

Lavinia Dawson's eyes hinted at mild rebuke. "What do you mean, *better?* There's been nothing wrong with me."

It was useless to remind her grandmother that she had eaten almost nothing the day before and had been unable to retain even that little. The lingering aftereffects showed as faint blue pockets beneath Lavinia Dawson's brown eyes. The old lady had shrugged off Glory B.'s recent suggestion that she travel to San Angelo or San Antonio for a thorough physical checkup. Her reply was one Glory B. would have expected from Wes Hendrix: "All a doctor ever does for me is to drain my purse."

Probably just her age, Glory B. reasoned. *I hope fifty years from now that I can be half the woman she is.* She put her arm around her grandmother as they watched Johnny ride into the pasture and repeat Glory B.'s reining exercises.

She said, "That's going to make a good horse, Gram."

Lavinia observed, "I'm glad you like him. But there's a lot more to running a ranch than riding a horse."

"That's the part I like best."

"It used to be one of the requirements of ranch life. Now it's getting to be one of the luxuries. The time you spend studying the market and keeping books is what really counts. Ranches make it or lose it in the office."

"That's why I went to school, Gram, to learn that part. But I have to tell you: I don't enjoy it. I'd much rather be out here in the open."

"I know. Your grandfather hated to see the sun go down. That meant he had to go to the house. Your father, God rest him, was a lot the same way. That's one reason this ranch is in a financial squeeze. He hated bookwork. He hated going to the bank. He hated keeping performance records on his cows. He never would learn to hedge the calves; he just accepted what the market would give him the day he got ready to sell."

"I don't enjoy those things either."

"Three generations of men on this ranch thought they weren't working unless they were on horseback or doing something with a pick and shovel. The harder they sweated and the tireder they got, the more they felt justified. They didn't know how to just sit and figure and think. That didn't satisfy their Puritan conscience. They thought sitting at a desk was idle, and being idle was an abomination in the sight of the Lord."

"They could've always hired bookkeepers."

Lavinia shook her head. "They could've hired cowboys

cheaper and done the bookkeeping themselves. They'd have known more about their business. They could've paid dependable men like Bill Roper to take care of the routine work so they would be free to do the planning and the bookkeeping. That's where salvation lies for us, if it's anywhere."

Glory B. looked at her grandmother as if she had just stepped on her favorite toy and broken it. "Something deep down tells me you're right. But it's a far cry from the good old days."

"I've lived for seventy-five years, and I've never seen *the good old days*. They were always some other time." Lavinia Dawson stepped away from the fence. "Would you walk with me back to the house? I'm afraid I need to sit down awhile."

Glory B. frowned. It was not like Gram to tire from so small a thing as walking to the barn. She took her grandmother's arm. "Mother's been standing on the porch and glaring at me. I'd just as well go listen to the lecture and get it over with."

"I won't always be here, girl. The day will come when you two have nobody except each other."

"Ever since I can remember, she's been trying to make me over into what she thinks I ought to be. She doesn't ask what I want to be."

"And you? Do you accept her as *she* is?"

Glory B. pinched her lips together. "I don't like her running after that jackleg lawyer from San Antonio, if that's what you mean. He's not half the man my father was."

"He's a *different* man than your father was. That doesn't mean he's a lesser man. I gather that in his field he's a person of some importance."

"Not to me he isn't."

Glory B. had been supporting some of her grandmother's weight, but now the old lady seemed suddenly short of patience. She exerted her independence and pulled away. "Girl, I learned a long time ago not to try to change people once they are set in their ways. Even if you can, everybody ends up miserable. Take them as they are or leave them be."

Lavinia paused at the flowerbed beside the steps that led up onto the broad porch. Her mood softened as she looked at a fading remnant of bluebonnets. A month ago the bed had been full of them. She said with a touch of wonder, "You seldom see them stay in bloom this late. Every day there are fewer of them. I wonder how much longer these will hang on."

"It's been a wet year," Glory B. observed. "I guess they just enjoy being alive."

"But one day we'll look and the last of them will be gone," Lavinia said wistfully. "Like the people we love. Turn away a little while, and when you look back, some of them are gone. Think on that before you fuss about your mother."

Only as they ascended to the porch did Lavinia allow her granddaughter to help her again. When they cleared the steps, she pulled free. "Life is difficult enough," she said, "without trying to live someone else's in addition to your own."

Part of the porch floor had been rebuilt twice over the years because of its exposure to weather and wear, but the gingerboard trim remained the same as in old photographs Glory B. had seen of her grandmother as a small girl, dressed in her Sunday best and seated on the steps. Oval glass in a hand-carved front door had turned slightly blue during the long years, but it had otherwise survived into the fourth generation of Chatfields and Dawsons, unchanged and unbroken. The sense of continuity had long been among the ranch's strongest assets. Now a different era, new and unprecedented challenges, threatened to devalue that continuity and perhaps even end it.

Entering the large parlor was, in some respects, like stepping back seventy or eighty years to the time of Major Chatfield. Glory B.'s mother had wanted to modernize it, but she had consistently been outvoted on any major changes by Glory B.'s father and grandmother. There had been compromises, mostly in the kitchen. The house was much better lighted than in the major's time. In the parlor stood a console television, and out back a black steel-mesh satellite dish discreetly placed behind an old washhouse so it was out of sight. But the parlor chandelier was original. The wallpaper was of a flowered pattern probably little different from the one Lavinia Dawson's mother had chosen before the carpenters finished. Wooden beading lined many inside walls and suggested an age long gone. The house, Glory B.'s city-born mother said, was an anachronism, a tombstone recalling a frontier time more properly lived down than lived up to. But to Glory B. that past and its traditions were an anchor to which she had clung during many a threatening storm. Her grandmother, the trustee of that tradition, had always held the lantern and guided her through the darkness to warm, dry shelter. She had long felt more in common with her grandmother than with her mother.

Madeline Dawson stood at the doorway that led into the cavernous downstairs hall. She took a long draw on a cigarette. "Gloria Beth, I want to speak to you." Her voice was firm.

Glory B.'s response was just as cool. "I'm here, Mother."

"You had a telephone call awhile ago from that truck driver."

"By *that truck driver* I suppose you mean Shorty Bigham?"

"I did not promise him you would return his call."

"But I will. I suppose he was at his father's garage?"

"I did not ask. I hoped you would not."

"He's my friend, one of my best friends. Of course I'll call him back."

Glory B.'s mother left the doorway but stopped two full paces from her daughter. They had become used to keeping at least that much distance. Looking at her mother, Glory B. saw some reflection of herself, but it was like a reflection in a mirror, flat and cold and unreachable. Madeline Dawson had been a beautiful woman once, and Glory B. supposed she still was, in the eyes of men. But Glory B. could see only the barrier raised by an old and basic conflict that seemed only to worsen with the years. It had started the first time Madeline Dawson had handed her daughter a pair of black patent dress shoes and Glory B. had reached for boots instead.

Madeline said, "He'll be a truck driver all his life."

"Some of the best people I know are truck drivers."

"Surely in four years at college you could have found friends who aspire to a better future. One purpose of education is to acquire more sophistication in your taste."

Madeline Dawson had come from an old Galveston shipping family which traditionally trained its women to be ornamental so they might marry well. A pleasant smile, an ease with polite conversation and an ability to wear fashionable clothes were of more consequence than skill in the kitchen. She had been brought up to be a *quality lady*, which meant she could not screw in a lightbulb for herself. Unfortunately, her family had fallen on hard times as Galveston declined. They salvaged little more than a name, warm memories and attachment to a dream of someday recovering lost glory. On dark days when Glory B. allowed herself to wallow in suspicions, she wondered if her mother might have perceived that return to glory in her marriage to Carr Dawson, scion of an old West Texas ranching family. If so, she must have been sadly disappointed, for life in this rugged hill country was as alien to that of Galveston as if they had been two nations, two separate cultures.

Glory B. said caustically, "When I first went off to school I met some of the sophisticated college men you're always touting me onto. As a whole, I find truck drivers more honest."

"Every group has its predators."

"But they're easier to spot among cowboys and truck drivers. They haven't learned to cover it up with prep-school bullshit."

Her mother flinched at the language.

A thought struck Glory B., and she smiled perversely. "I *have* met a university man here. He might suit you better than Shorty Bigham."

"Almost anyone would."

Glory B. could visualize her mother going into shock at the sight of Jim Ed Hendrix with his garish rock-music T-shirt. "Maybe I'll invite him over one of these days."

She glanced at her grandmother. Lavinia Dawson shook her head and retreated toward her bedroom.

Glory B. wondered sometimes if the old house was big enough to hold three Dawson women of three different generations and three often-contrasting ways of thinking.

Wes Hendrix jerked the needle from the calf's neck and raised up, his rough old hand holding the vaccination syringe high so the sunlight would show him he had emptied it. "That'll either cure him or kill him," he declared, stepping back from the squeeze chute that had held the young animal immobile. "You can let him out."

Jim Ed pulled a long steel lever hot from the sun. The heavy collar that had gripped the calf's neck parted with a loud clanking noise. The animal stared a moment in fright, then lunged forward, kicking at the chute as it broke clear. The sun struck silver on a thin stream of mucus trailing from the calf's nose.

Wes pointed his chin at the squeeze chute, its green paint chipped and worn and stained by the blood of countless cattle which had suffered through treatment of one sort or another in its loveless embrace. "One of the best inventions the rancher ever had, that and the pickup. That chute takes the place of a roper and a flankin' crew. If a man has to, he can do the whole job by himself."

A little of the mucus had landed on Jim Ed's sleeve. Rubbing it, he said with a touch of irony, "Are you sure all these modern inventions haven't taken the romance out?"

Wes grinned. "The romance went out of *me* years ago." He glanced upward toward the noonday sun. "Gettin' on to dinnertime. We'd better go see what we can whomp up to eat."

Jim Ed offered no objection.

Wes said, "Speakin' of romance, this is Saturday, ain't it? I've worked the butt off of you all week."

"I haven't complained."

"Tell you the truth, I thought you'd be hollerin' to go back to Dallas by now, what with me workin' you so hard and Ol' Rowdy pitchin' with you every time you get on him."

"He hasn't managed to throw me off in the last three days."

"You're learnin'. But if you was really to want to go, I'd set you up to a bus ticket."

Jim Ed looked at the ground. "You want to get rid of me?"

"No. But I don't want to hold you if you'd rather go. You've lasted longer than I expected, and probably longer than your daddy figured too, I'll bet."

"It's longer than *I* expected," Jim Ed admitted. "But I'm getting used to the place." There was more that he could not tell his grandfather. It was better to stay here than to go home and face the music for not finishing the duty his father had imposed upon him.

The calf's mother stood on the far side of a fence, bawling. Jim

Ed swung the gate open, and the two ran to each other. The cow sniffed the calf to make sure it was her own. The calf immediately rammed at her udder.

Wes nodded in satisfaction. "It's when they get too sick to suck that you really got to worry. He'll be all right."

As they entered the house Wes said, "While I fix us a bite, why don't you go and take yourself a shower? I'd like you to run to town before the stores close this afternoon."

"What for?"

"Big River ain't pleasant for me these days. I got a prescription that needs refillin'. Besides, Maudie's old car needs to be driven every once in a while to keep the battery up and the motor runnin'. Thought you might like to go to the picture show or somethin'."

"The Big River picture show closed down a long time ago."

Wes seemed surprised. "I'd forgot. Last time I went was to see John Wayne."

"That's the last time a lot of people went."

Jim Ed took the shower as suggested and washed his head. When he walked into the kitchen Wes said, "Dinner's nearly ready. Why don't you fix us some iced tea?"

He noticed that his grandfather seemed to be looking around him rather than at him during the meal. While Jim Ed gathered the dishes and put them into a sinkful of hot, soapy water, Wes left the kitchen. That gave Jim Ed a chance he had waited for. He emptied the coffee pot, submersed it and gave it a thorough scrubbing with a steel brush.

Wes was back presently, carrying an old leather wallet, hand-tooled like his saddle. "I told you when you come that I couldn't pay you no wages, but you've done a right smart more work than I expected."

"I didn't ask for anything."

"Give an old man a chance to keep his conscience clean." Wes placed several bills on the drainboard. "Here's a list of groceries we'll need. I trade at the Red and White." He reached into the cabinet for a small, empty bottle. "This is the prescription. Take it to Orville Levitt's drugstore."

"I thought you fell out with him."

"He's got the only drugstore left in town."

Jim Ed finished washing the dishes and stacking them in a draining tray. He dried the utensils and placed them in the drawer where they belonged, then hung up the salt sack that he used as a towel. "Anything else?"

"No. Stay as long as you want to, and have a good time."

"Where would I have a good time in Big River?"

Wes looked away. "There's a place called the Blue Moon that a lot of the young folks go to. You might run into somebody you know."

"I don't know anybody in Big River."

Wes blurted, "Glory B.'ll be there," then caught himself.

Jim Ed demanded suspiciously, "When did she tell you that?"

Wes busied himself drying dishes with a cotton cloth. "This mornin', on the phone. She called to ask me how I was gettin' along. Just happened to mention the Blue Moon, and I just happened to remember, is all."

"Just happened to." Jim Ed sniffed. "She's probably got some kind of a trap set for me."

"She's a good girl, that Glory B."

"And Rowdy's a good horse. He just tries to break my neck."

Wes noticed the coffee pot for the first time, left upside down to drain. Crestfallen, he turned it over and looked inside. "What have you done?"

"Just scrubbed that old pot. It didn't look like you ever had."

Wes was as dismayed as if Jim Ed had just shot his horse. *"Scrubbed* it? Ruined it, you mean. God, boy, don't you know you never scrub a coffee pot? It takes months to get the flavor right again. I'd just about as well throw it away."

Wes was still mourning the violation of the pot when Jim Ed left, chagrined.

Grandmother Maudie's gravy-colored Ford was eight years old. It was evident that Wes seldom drove it, for the engine was sluggish, trailing dark smoke the first mile or so. Jim Ed turned around once, fearing it was about to stall out. If he had to walk back to the house he did not want the distance to be overly taxing.

But the engine settled into an even rhythm, and the smoke stopped. He decided the car would safely make the trip to town.

He drove up and down the main street a couple of times, trying to remember Big River as it had been during his few boyhood visits. He had paid scant attention the day Wes had picked him up from the bus stop at Levitt's. Now that it appeared likely he was going to spend a while with Wes, it would not hurt to know where everything was.

Probably a third of the business buildings stood empty and dark. He noted the theater which Wes had forgotten was closed. Its sagging marquee still carried half the letters from the title of the last picture exhibited, and a faded color poster from the movie slumped inside a wooden frame, the glass cover still in place though cracked all the way down. If this had been Dallas, he thought, youngsters would have smashed that glass with a rock long ago. They must not have much imagination in Big River.

The gasoline gauge showed less than a quarter of a tank, so he pulled in at a service station. The proprietor sat in a tilted-back wooden chair, its scarred old legs reinforced by heavy wire. He leaned forward to bring the chair's front legs down hard upon the concrete driveway as Jim Ed drove up to a full-service pump. He scowled and leaned back against the wall when Jim Ed went on to another pump marked "self-service." The price difference was fourteen cents a gallon. If the car needed ten gallons to fill its tank, that was $1.40 for checking the oil and perhaps a half-assed job of windshield wiping with a greasy squeegee. Jim Ed was not too young to remember when stations did that for free.

He could feel the proprietor's gaze burning him while he raised the hood and checked the oil for himself. The man stood only when Jim Ed dug out his wallet, and then with reluctance. He took the money without gratitude, his attention focused on Jim Ed's hat.

Jim Ed asked, "What do people do around here for excitement?"

The stationkeeper counted out Jim Ed's change. "Well, *you* might find some excitement out at the ropin' arena." He pointed his chin toward the highway. "A bunch of the boys are runnin' calves this afternoon."

"Why do you think I would find any excitement in that?"

"There's a couple of them boys get a kick out of whittlin' you city fellers down to size."

Jim Ed saw a small fly-specked placard that had probably been thumb-tacked to the wall for twenty years. It said, "If you like our service, tell your friends. If you don't, tell us."

He said sarcastically, "Thanks for the service. Any extra charge for the information?"

The proprietor shook his head. "It's on the house."

Jim Ed drove back down the street, his stomach souring. He was rapidly losing interest in Big River. He parked in front of Levitt's drugstore, avoiding the yellow-painted strip of curb reserved for buses. He put Wes's empty medicine bottle in his pocket and walked into the store. The first thing he noticed was a musty smell that reminded him of neighborhood stores he knew in older sections of Dallas, their furnishings harking back to the 1930s. A marble-topped soda counter remained from an olden time, though it was stacked high with racks of miscellaneous merchandise, from fingernail polish and lipsticks to support hose and corn plasters. It had been years since anyone had sat on the revolving stools to be served a fountain Coke or a banana split.

A woman's voice said, "May I help you, young man?" The voice was not unfriendly, exactly, but strictly business.

Jim Ed had a hard time finding her among the accumulated clutter of forty or fifty years. She was a short, plump, gray little woman he guessed to be in her seventies.

"I've got a prescription here to be refilled."

"My husband is the pharmacist, and he's out for a few minutes. But give me the number. I'll type up a new label so you won't have to wait too long."

He handed her the bottle. Surprise brightened her face. "This is for Wes Hendrix!" She studied Jim Ed with new interest. "You'd be his grandson from Dallas. I've heard about you."

"Yes ma'am," he said noncommittally. He supposed a lot of people had heard about him. They didn't see many specimens like him around here.

"Lands sakes," she went on, "I can't say you look much like Wes." She moved closer and peered so intently into his face that

Jim Ed backed away and bumped into a counter. She said, "Then again, you *do* look a little like Wes did, first time I ever knew him. That was way back yonder. Somethin' about your eyes, I think. Yes, that's what it is, the eyes, and the shape of the nose. Wes was a right handsome man when he was young. Turned many a girl's head. I'll bet you do too, don't you?"

Jim Ed glanced uneasily toward the door. "I'll come back after a while and pick up the medicine."

"No, you wait. Let me look at you." She was smiling, and Jim Ed had a feeling that as she stared unabashedly at him she was seeing somebody else. "Yes, you do remind me of Wes, the way he used to be. I knew Wes even before I knew Orville, my husband. He cut quite a figure in those days, Wes did. Rodeo rider, and all that. He could have had his pick among the girls in Big River."

She moved around into better light. Jim Ed remembered the old photograph he had found of his grandfather and a beautiful young girl who was not Grandmother Maudie. She had married someone else, Wes had said, someone who had prospects. A drugstore in those days would have looked a lot more promising than a proficiency at riding broncs.

He asked, "Did you know him well, back then?"

She kept smiling. "Well enough."

So much for *that* little mystery, he thought.

Noreen Levitt said, "Orville and me, we've argued a lot about that new lake. I'm on your granddaddy's side. I reserve the woman's sacred right to disagree with her husband, guaranteed by the constitution and the bill of rights."

"He'd be tickled to know."

He heard footsteps at the front door. Against the glare from the plateglass window he recognized Orville Levitt, moving at a slow and deliberate pace. Levitt blinked, seeing Jim Ed.

Noreen Levitt said needlessly, "This is Wes Hendrix's grandson."

"I know," Levitt replied, hesitantly extending his hand.

Jim Ed responded with an uneasy reserve, remembering the tension between his grandfather and Levitt.

"How *is* Wes?" Levitt asked.

"Fair enough. Just needs a refill on some medicine."

Noreen Levitt held up the new label she had typed on an ancient Underwood. Levitt disappeared for a minute behind stacks of boxes and bottles. When he reappeared he was placing a fresh bottle into a small white paper bag. "Wes's been much too long usin' this up," he said. "If you have any influence over him, I wish you'd see that he takes his medicine when he's supposed to. It's for his own good."

Everybody's telling him what he ought to do for his own good, Jim Ed thought, *just the way they do me.* But he sensed from the druggist's eyes that the concern was real.

"I'll try. He doesn't listen very well."

Levitt shrugged and rang up the sale on an old mechanical cash register. "Tell me somethin' I didn't already know."

Jim Ed was nearly out the door when Levitt called him. The elderly druggist walked up slowly, his brow creased. "You've got to understand, son. Wes and me, we punched cattle together before I went off to pharmacy school. For most of fifty years I counted him as my best friend. It hurts to come to a partin' of the ways. But I've got to consider the good of the whole community. That doesn't mean I don't still love and respect your grandfather. I do. I just wish I knew how to tell him that. I wish *you* could tell him."

Jim Ed nodded. "I wish I could too."

Outside, he looked at his watch and decided it was much too early for supper. He had not yet spotted the honkytonk known as the Blue Moon, so he decided to look for it. Driving out the main street, he saw a sign heralding Lacy's café. In the window, blinking red letters declared "Beer" in brilliant neon. Suddenly a week's deep thirst took his full attention. He made a left-hand turn and parked beside a black automobile. A tiny bell tinkled as he pushed the door open and was hit in the face by a cool blast from an evaporative air conditioner. "Come in," said a pleasant young voice. "Find a seat anywhere."

He stopped in midstride, caught by surprise. Sheriff Wally Vincent slouched at a small table, nursing a half-empty coffee cup. Beside him stood a waitress whose full-blown figure was probably in violation of some Big River ordinance on morality. The sheriff gave Jim Ed a hard stare, but the waitress's smile was a whole Welcome Wagon. "What'll it be, honey?"

For a moment Jim Ed was hard put to reply. He was too involved just in looking at her. "Whatever you have on draft."

"It'll have to be bottle or metal, honey. Civilization hasn't got to Big River yet."

He ordered Coors in a bottle and sat down several tables away from the sheriff, the only other customer. She brought it, along with a chilled glass. "Shut your eyes while you pour it, honey, and you can pretend it's draft. Haven't seen you in here before, have I?"

"I'm new in town."

"I'd've remembered. What's your name?"

He told her. She said, "Mine's Stella. Stella Tenney." She glanced toward the sheriff, who still glared at Jim Ed. "Now, honey, don't you mind Wally Vincent. He looks mean, but he's just a pussycat underneath. Ain't you, Wally honey?"

The sheriff pushed away from his table and walked to Jim Ed. He pointed his thumb at the beer bottle. "You better not overdo them suds. We don't tolerate drunk drivers here." The bell over the door rang goodbye to him as he walked out.

The waitress watched him leave. "Wally's never been anywhere but Big River in his whole put-together. He doesn't know there's life anywhere else. But I lived in Houston three years, when I was married. I knew lots of people there that these Big River folks would never understand."

Even if Jim Ed could have thought of something appropriate to say, she would not have given him the chance. "I *was* married, but I'm not anymore. Are *you* married? No, I can tell you're not. You don't look married."

He was about to ask her what married people looked like, but she told him before he could get the words out. "Married people always look browbeaten and bored. I looked that way when I was married to Hobart. I decided to get out of that trap before I got to lookin' like all these dowdy old married women around this town. Variety, that's the thing. Variety keeps you young. You wouldn't think I was twenty-seven, would you? Fellow the other day asked me when I was goin' to graduate from high school. Said he'd've asked me out, but he was afraid I was under age. I told him I was twenty-two. You know, he was on his way to San Antonio on a business trip, but he stayed here to take me dancin'. He never did know but what I was just twenty-two."

Jim Ed poured what was left of the beer into his glass. "Speaking of dancing, do you know a place called the Blue Moon?"

Her smile widened. "Sure, honey, it's farther out on the highway." She tilted her head to indicate direction and in doing so thrust her breasts toward him. He tried to look away but could not. He gripped the cold glass tightly.

She said, "I was thinkin' about goin' out there tonight myself, after we close up. But I haven't got a date. I hate to go alone. Makes a girl look too available, you know what I mean?"

He said, "I just wondered where it is. Somebody happened to be talking about the place, that's all."

Her smile narrowed but did not lose hope. "It's kind of countrified, honey, nothin' like they got in Houston. But people in Big River don't ask for much. Maybe if you happen to drop by there tonight we'll see each other."

"Maybe." He finished his beer and took a long, lingering look at that lush figure. He decided he would spend some time in the Blue Moon whether Glory B. Dawson showed up or not.

He drove out the highway, coming upon a roping arena. It seemed to him that no Texas town was too small to have a roping arena where the local cowboy types on horseback could chase hell out of long-legged, flop-eared Brahman calves. A horseman spurred the length of the arena, futilely swinging a rope over his head while a calf outran his horse. A dozen or so other men sat on horses or stood on the ground in the arena, watching. Jim Ed drove on past the livestock auction and found the Blue Moon. It appeared to be an old World War II surplus army barracks, set down and repainted to match its name. Now it was sun-faded to a weak baby-blue. From outside he could see little else that had been done to it. It was probably the kind of place that, if live musicians ever performed there, kept chickenwire in front of the stage to protect them from flying bottles and glasses.

He turned back, slowing as he approached the roping arena, knowing he had time to kill before supper. He had about as much interest in calf roping as in the care and feeding of the Tibetan yak, but on impulse he pulled in at the steel-pipe gate and parked near the bullwire fence of the arena. He watched a roper on a black horse make a run and miss his calf. He recognized Shorty Bigham, who had dragged Jim Ed out from under Glory B. Dawson's frightened roan horse that day in the branding pen. Shorty rode slowly back toward the chutes, undergoing good-natured abuse from his friends along the fence.

Jim Ed stood beside the car as two young horsemen drove a dozen Brahman calves from a catch pen at the far end of the arena back to the front end for another round of roping. Shorty Bigham was among several riders who moved out to help put the calves through a gate. Jim Ed walked around the back side of the arena, past the nervous calves in the catch pens, toward an opening he could see near a small set of bleacher benches four tiers high. A couple of dozen spectators hunched there, their enthusiasm well contained.

Shorty saw him and waved, pulling his black horse around. "Howdy, Tater. How'd you like to come rope one?"

Jim Ed shook his head. "I'd make a fool of myself."

"No worse than *I* been doin'." Shorty leaned from the saddle to shake hands across the arena fence. "Sure 'nuff, want to try?"

"Every shoemaker to his own last. I get in *enough* trouble punching keys on a computer."

Shorty made a motion toward the bleachers. "Glory B.'s settin' over yonder with her grandmother. Why don't you go keep them company till I rope another calf—or rope *at* him?"

Jim Ed squinted. If Glory B. would dress like a girl, he might have noticed her before. She looked as if she had been roping calves too, her clothes baggy and worn, her face shaded by the same battered old hat she had been wearing the day they had worked cattle. She was about as much like Stella Tenney in the café as a burro was like a racehorse. He suspected she had been watching him since he had left the car.

He saw Sheriff Wally Vincent farther down the arena fence on another set of bleacher seats. Vincent fastened upon him the same glare he had exhibited in the café. Jim Ed wondered if the lawman ever changed expressions.

He tipped his hat to Glory B.'s grandmother. "How are you, today, Mrs. Dawson?"

The old lady gave him a gracious smile. "I'm fine. And your grandfather?"

"Tough as a boot."

Glory B. inched away from her grandmother and motioned for Jim Ed to sit on the bench between them. "Hey, Hendrix, you've had about the highest honor anybody can bestow in the ranch country. I've named a colt after you."

"You've saddled a poor colt with the name Tater?"

"No. *Pilgrim.*"

"I thought you were going to drop that *pilgrim* business."

"I couldn't help it. He has so many of your characteristics . . ."

"He must be a prize."

"He will be when I'm through training him."

Jim Ed heard a sound from Lavinia Dawson and turned, but the old lady was studiously watching Shorty back his black horse into the narrow roper's "box." A cowboy fastened a barrier string in front of Shorty, not to be released until the calf crossed a line dragged in the dirt by someone's bootheel. The chute gate flew open, and the calf raced out. The barrier string snapped. The black horse burst from the box.

Glory B. shouted, "Go get him, Shorty!" Shorty swung a small loop and cast it toward the calf. It sailed over one floppy ear, then dropped to the ground, empty. The black horse stopped abruptly, as it had been trained to do. Shorty remained in the saddle, drawing up the spilled rope and rebuilding its coils.

Glory B. shook her head. "Shorty can't drop a rope and make it hit the ground."

"Do you judge everybody by how good a cowboy he is?"

"If I did, that'd sure put you at the bottom of the list."

"I never claimed to be anything except what I am."

"And what *are* you, pilgrim?"

"I'm still trying to find out."

He noticed two burly young men talking to the sheriff and wondered if Vincent was giving them his cold show of authority. He watched a couple more ropers, then became aware that the two men were standing in front of him, giving him a Wally Vincent stare. They looked like the kind who would throw beer bottles in the Blue Moon. One said, "Hey, you, you drove through the gate without payin'."

Jim Ed blinked. "I didn't see anybody there to pay."

"You could've asked around."

Glory B.'s voice was tight. "Pay no attention, Hendrix. This is just a country arena. Nobody pays at the gate."

The man turned sarcastically to Glory B. "You fixin' to start a dude ranch, Glory B.?"

She said stiffly, "Go away, Milo Potter."

The other man said, "That sure is a pretty hat he's got on, Milo. Looks like it ought to fit me just right."

Milo leaned forward and grabbed the hat from Jim Ed's head. "Then try it, Marvin."

The one named Marvin put it on, then pulled it off. He took out a pocketknife. "It's too small, but I can fix that."

Jim Ed heard Lavinia Dawson groan in apprehension. The rise of slow anger brought him to his feet. He grabbed at his hat and missed. Glory B. clutched his arm, but he pulled free and clenched his fists. The men's size told him they might be able to do whatever they wanted to. But he could make them bleed for their fun.

He stepped down from the bleacher seat and grabbed his hat from Marvin's hand. He said, "Unless you think you need an audience, let's go out yonder." He pointed toward the parking area.

"Lead out," said Milo. "We'll be right behind you."

Glory B. and her grandmother were both standing up. Jim Ed turned apologetically to the old lady. "I'm sorry, Mrs. Dawson."

Glory B. declared angrily, "Milo Potter, I'll get you!"

Jim Ed walked out toward a cluster of cars and pickups. He said, "You'd better know before we start: I don't fight clean."

Milo grinned. "Neither do we."

Jim Ed turned. Milo crouched, putting up his fists and taking a stance that looked like old pictures of John L. Sullivan. Jim Ed feinted, then kicked him in the groin. Milo dropped to his knees and bent over in moaning agony.

The one called Marvin declared, "That wasn't fair."

"Told you."

Marvin put up his fists and began to hop from side to side. "Come on! Come on at me!"

Jim Ed stood and waited for him to get through with the histrionics.

Marvin declared, "I'm fixin' to tie you into a granny knot. I'll knock a fart out of you that would heat the schoolhouse all winter."

A shadow fell across Jim Ed. From the corner of his eye he sensed a horseman moving up beside him. Shorty Bigham's voice spoke sternly, "Now, Beetlebrain, before you go too far, you'd better know that this feller is a friend of mine."

Marvin quit hopping but kept his fists up. His face turned redder. "Who you callin' Beetlebrain?"

"Everybody calls you Beetlebrain."

"Not to my face, they don't."

"I'm lookin' at your face, and I'm callin' you Beetlebrain."

Jim Ed glanced up at Shorty. On that black horse, from the ground, he looked as big as a barn. From where Marvin stood, he must look like a barn about to fall on somebody.

Marvin protested, "Look what he done to Milo."

Milo sat on the ground, still bent over and looking green.

Shorty drawled, "On him it looks good."

Marvin said, "I can't let him get away with that. I'm fixin' to trim his wick."

Shorty placed both hands on his saddlehorn, one atop the other. They looked like cured hams. "Well, then, you go ahead and do what you have to. But when you get through whippin' him, me and you are goin' to have us a little discussion." He stepped down from the saddle. He stood half a head taller than Jim Ed.

Jim Ed said, "Thanks, Shorty, but I can handle him. I've got a black belt in karate." It was a lie.

Marvin backed off a step, then another, confused, apprehensive. "Now, Shorty, I didn't know he was a friend of yours. That puts a whole different complexion on everything." Cautiously he eased over to Milo and helped him to his feet. "We didn't mean no harm. You know we never would really hurt anybody. Just hoorawin' the dude a little, is all. If we'd known he was a friend of yours . . ."

"You know now."

The two men moved away, Milo still bent over and dragging his feet. Marvin kept looking back.

Jim Ed said finally, "Hell of a Welcome Wagon you people have got here."

"Ain't it? The Potter boys are like a pair of barkin' dogs. Run from them and they'll chew you up. Run *at* them and they'll trip over one another gettin' away."

"I appreciate it, but you didn't have to put yourself out. I believe I could have handled them."

"I reckon. I just hated to see you get your knuckles all bruised up."

Sheriff Wally Vincent strode toward them, his face clouded up for rain. "What's the trouble here?"

Shorty looked around innocently. "Trouble? Only trouble I've had is in missin' calves all afternoon. We seen old Milo stumble over his own feet, and we come to help him up, didn't we, Tater?"

Jim Ed nodded.

The sheriff looked frustrated. He stepped up close, his nose about a cigar's length from Jim Ed's face. His eyes crackled. "I told you before, we don't need no big-city smart-asses comin' in here and causin' trouble."

Jim Ed did not reply.

Vincent said, "You watch your step, boy, or your old granddaddy'll be havin' to come in here and bail you out of jail." He turned and walked briskly to his car. He slammed the door and raised a cloud of dust as he pulled away, the motor racing.

Shorty stepped backward and studied Jim Ed's face intently. "I do wish you'd do somethin' about that hat if you figure on stayin' around here long. It makes it all-fired strenuous, bein' your friend."

Jim Ed felt a smile, slowly and painfully born. "I'm sorry to be a burden to you . . . friend."

Glory B. gave her grandmother her arm and walked her to the big car Jim Ed had seen that day at the branding pen. She came then to Jim Ed, her eyes troubled. "I'm sorry about the Potter boys. I think Wally Vincent put them up to it."

Jim Ed grunted. That thought had not occurred to him. But another did. "He's not really after me. He's after my grandfather."

Glory B. said, "You learn fast, pilgrim. I hope my pony does as well." She turned to Shorty. "Thanks. I knew I could count on you."

Shorty shrugged. "No sweat. But I don't think Tater really needed me. He was handlin' them fine."

"He would've wound up in Wally Vincent's jailhouse." Her gaze went back to Jim Ed. It was soft and approving. "I've got to take Gram home. I'll be coming back to town tonight. Any chance you might be at the Blue Moon?"

He said, "I hadn't even thought about it."

"Well, *think* about it." She turned and walked to her grandmother's car.

Jim Ed said, "She sent you to rescue me, didn't she?"

"I never did like them Potter brothers anyway. In grade school I used to have to clean their plow about once a month."

Jim Ed had caught up on any curiosity he might have had about calf roping. He drove back toward town, passing the café. Wally Vincent's official car was parked in front of it again. Jim Ed had considered eating supper there tonight and warming his libido on the sight of that luscious waitress, but he decided he would settle for steak fingers at the Dairy Queen.

He passed a dry-goods store that displayed Western wear in its plate-glass window. The door was still open. The courthouse clock told him it was a quarter to six.

He made a U-turn and parked across the street from the shop. He took a long look at his hat, lying on the seat beside him.

Aw, what the hell? he thought. *When in Rome* . . . He climbed out of the car and walked across the street into the store.

"I'd like to try one of those cowboy hats," he told the clerk. "Size seven-and-a-quarter."

Chapter 8

Glory B. held her head beneath the steaming spray of hot water to wash the shampoo from her hair, then tempered the control slightly to reduce the temperature. She stood beneath the shower, running her hands over her shoulders and down her body to rinse away the slickness of the soap and whatever lingered of the arena dust. She luxuriated in the warm stimulation of the water driving against her face. Then, knowing the cost of the butane gas that heated it, she turned off the shower. She squeezed water from her hair and pushed it in rivulets down her shoulders and her breasts before she pulled back the plastic curtain.

Towel pinned around her, she sat on the edge of her bed, holding the hot-air dryer close to her hair. The sound of a voice caused her to lower the dryer and glance up at a tall mirror on her dresser. She saw the reflection of her mother, standing in the doorway and watching her, smoking what little was left of a cigarette. Glory B. had seen her light one just before she came upstairs to shower. This had to be another.

"Are you decent?" Madeline Dawson asked.

"I suppose," Glory B. replied. She tugged the towel upward, for it had sagged. She felt a touch of annoyance. Her mother seldom came into Glory B.'s room anymore except to advise or criticize, and this usually led either to argument or a chilled silence.

Madeline took short, quick steps to Glory B.'s bathroom and dropped the remnant of cigarette into the commode, where it died with a hiss. "Don't you keep an ashtray in here *anywhere?*"

Glory B. frowned at the thin veil of smoke which had trailed her mother. "I don't need one." Her voice took on an accusatory tone. "Those things will be the death of you someday." Glory B. laid down the dryer and began to brush her hair.

Madeline walked to the window. "I suppose you're going to *that place* again?"

"You went there, didn't you, in the old days with Daddy?"

"Only until I convinced him there were better places to go."

"Not in Big River there aren't."

Madeline had not made up her face today, and the few wrinkles appeared deeper than usual. She cut her gaze nervously from the door to the window and back to Glory B. Her hands trembled a little. She dug into a pocket of her slacks and brought out a cigarette pack. She held it a moment as if surprised to see it in her hand. "I just finished one of those, didn't I?"

Glory B. stopped brushing. "Mother, are you all right?"

The question caught Madeline off guard. She stared at her daughter as if she did not quite comprehend. "I don't know. I guess so."

Glory B. wondered if her mother might have been drinking. She did that occasionally, a refuge from loneliness, but seldom before nightfall. Madeline seated herself on the bed, nearer to Glory B. than she had been in some time. She fumbled with the package but did not take out another cigarette.

While her mother watched in brooding silence, Glory B. brushed her hair, then walked to her closet. She sought out a Western-cut blouse and a pair of jeans, spreading them on the bed. Madeline said nothing, but Glory B. read the opinion in her eyes. She considered a moment, went back to the closet and lifted out a black dress.

Her mother's eyes widened in surprise.

Defensively Glory B. said, "I just decided I need a change."

"I would agree, but I'm curious about this sudden decision. You *are* going with that truck driver, aren't you?"

"Shorty said he'd pick me up about eight-thirty."

Madeline shifted her gaze to Glory B.'s telephone, as if waiting for it to ring. "You said something about a university man. I don't suppose *he* will be at that place tonight?"

Glory B. turned her face away. "I don't know. It's his business where he goes."

Madeline watched Glory B. pull the dress over her head and arose to help her zip it up the back. "As I remember, I bought you this for your high school graduation dance. You've filled out since then. It's snug at the top."

"Anything wrong with that?"

"It depends upon the object of the game, and the players."

"I haven't decided the object of the game . . . yet."

"Then you'd better be careful, or the decision may be forced on you before you're ready."

The telephone rang. Madeline gasped as if caught off guard, though Glory B. suspected this was what she had been waiting for. Madeline grabbed the receiver and said anxiously, "Hello. Hello."

Glory B. went back to brushing her hair, a little uncomfortable about listening to her mother's side of a private conversation. She wished Madeline had taken the call in her own room.

Madeline said, "You're home now? . . . A good bit later than you expected, isn't it? . . . Oh. Well, at least you're back, that's the main thing. Did everything go as you wanted it to? . . . That's fine. Yes, I wish we could have been together this weekend. I've missed you . . . Next week perhaps? . . ." She listened a long time, smiling. "I'll be waiting . . . Love you too. Good night."

She gently placed the receiver back on the cradle and for a long moment held her hand there as if in a caress. When she turned, her face was radiant. Her hands no longer trembled.

Glory B. said needlessly, "I suppose that was *him?*"

"He had to fly to Oklahoma City for a deposition. It took much longer than he expected. I'm always nervous until I know he has gotten home all right."

"He's a grown man. Daddy used to make a lot of trips, but you never worried over *him* like this."

Madeline's face lost its glow. "Then one day he got in his car to make a simple little run over to Big River, and he never reached there." She paused. "I didn't even kiss him goodbye."

Glory B. was touched to see her mother blink away the threat of tears. "So now you worry that something like that might happen to Adam?"

"We never can know what the day will bring."

Glory B. kept brushing, but she watched her mother in the mirror and began to understand something she had not seen before. "It's really serious between you two, isn't it?"

"Are you surprised?"

Glory B. considered. "I guess I am. I thought it was just sex, and nothing else."

Madeline shook her head. "You still have a lot to learn about life. *And* about sex, I hope."

Glory B. decided any direct answer might tend to incriminate her. "I just never could see you with anybody except Daddy. I've felt like Adam was crowding in where he didn't belong."

"He won't take your father's place, but he's made a place of his own. Life goes forward, with us or without us."

"You'll have to give me time. The notion of you with somebody else takes getting used to."

"But you *will* get used to it. You may even grow fond of Adam, when you let yourself get to know him."

"I'll try. He's made *you* happy. That's one big point in his favor."

Madeline said, "I'd be happier still if you and I could find a common meeting ground."

Glory B. shrugged. "I guess it was just in my nature to take after Daddy's side of the family."

"You've always been something of a mystery to *my* family."

"We're even. They've always been a mystery to *me*. They're city people. They've always seemed detached from reality somehow."

"What do you consider reality?"

"The land, and what grows from it. Your family is pavement. All I understand is grass."

Madeline said wistfully, "And I don't understand that at all."

Shorty Bigham might not be graceful in his movements or sophisticated in his speech, but he was always punctual. If he said he would be there at eight-thirty, he showed up at eight-twenty-nine. He was driving a shiny new red "doolie" pickup for which he made heavy monthly payments out of the bull-hauler wages his father paid him for driving livestock trucks up and down the hill-country backroads. Glory B. thought that pickup needed dual wheels on the rear like a boar hog needed teats, but they were the fashion for ranch-country youths who had come along a couple of generations too late to be full time horseback cowboys of the old tradition. Doolie pickups and snuff-can circles worn in the hip pockets. Shorty stood just inside the front door, crushing the broad brim of a Western hat in his hands. He nodded assent to a kindly but one-sided conversation from Lavinia Dawson, who sat looking tired in a soft reclining chair. He cast uneasy glances toward Glory B.'s mother, for she was being unusually hospitable to him.

His jaw dropped as Glory B. walked down the stairs in the black dress, parading herself a little. "My God!" he exclaimed, then glanced sheepishly at Lavinia Dawson. "Excuse me, Mrs. Dawson." His eyes went to Madeline. "And you too, Mrs. Dawson."

Glory B. did a little whirl at the landing, letting the skirt flare. "Think anybody'll notice?"

"It may touch off a riot," Shorty declared.

"Just a small one, for my ego," she said. "I wouldn't want to see anybody hurt . . . real bad."

Lavinia Dawson arose carefully from her chair to kiss Glory B. on the cheek. Glory B. puzzled at the weariness in her grandmother's eyes. Lavinia had hardly left the house all day; she had no reason to look so tired. Lavinia smiled. "You-all have a good time now." She took Shorty's hand, and he shook it as if she were a cowboy. "I know you'll bring her home safely."

"I'm a careful driver, Mrs. Dawson, else my daddy wouldn't trust me on the road with his high-priced trucks."

Madeline Dawson observed quietly, "All the danger doesn't come when you're driving."

Shorty kept looking flustered, staring at Glory B.'s dress. He even opened the pickup door for her, something he seldom thought to do. Usually he treated her like one of the boys.

On the way to Big River the dress became something of a

hazard. The pickup drifted as Shorty kept looking away from the road to Glory B. "I can't remember the last time I ever saw you with a dress on." His face colored. "You know what I mean. It's not your birthday or somethin', is it?"

"No. I just felt like a change."

"Boy howdy, you sure made one! I didn't know you could look so damned good." He clenched his fist and made a punching motion at his own chin. "I didn't say that right either."

Pleased, Glory B. replied, "You said it just fine." She placed her hand on his leg and gave a gentle squeeze.

Shorty grinned. "I can't wait to see their faces. With a little advance promotion, half the town would buy tickets." The grin subsided. "There's just one hitch about tonight. I got to leave town at five in the mornin' and drive down to Rocksprings for a load of goats."

She smiled. "I'll see that you're home before five."

"It'll need to be a lot earlier than that." He shrugged. "Oh well, I couldn't sleep anyway, thinkin' about how you look in that dress."

He drove in silence, glancing often at her. After a time she perceived trouble in his eyes. He said, "I been wonderin'. Is Tater goin' to be there?"

"He didn't say, one way or the other."

"The dress is for him, ain't it?"

She flushed. "Of course not." But she knew he had seen through her. For all his football-player size and strength, Shorty had intuition like a woman.

She asked, "If that were the truth, Shorty, would you really mind so much?"

He was a minute in answering. "Sure, I'd mind. But I suppose I'd get over it. I've got over it before."

She tightened her fingers on his leg. "I don't even know if I like him or not. It's probably just gratitude because he cut me loose from that rope. If I liked him, why would I start needling him every time I see him?"

"Because one side of you says you don't *want* to like him. It's tryin' to convince the other side. And not doin' much good at it, the way it looks to me."

"I can't think of anything I have in common with him."

"There must be *something.*"

"Well, one thing. He reminds me of somebody I detest."

"Maybe you don't detest that guy as much as you want to. Maybe that's why you can't figure out how to feel about Tater."

Glory B. glanced quickly at Shorty, but he held his eyes to the road. She made no response; she could not.

Shorty shrugged. "I hate to be takin' up for my competition, but I feel like there's more to Tater than meets the eye. He didn't really need my help against them Potter brothers. He was doin' all right."

"Sure. He was fighting dirty."

"That's the only way to fight the Potters. I used to do it about once a month when we was kids. Dirty was all they knew."

"Anyway, you backed him up because I asked you to. Thanks."

She leaned to Shorty and kissed him, and nearly put the pickup into the ditch. "You're a friend, Shorty."

It took him a moment to regain control and get the vehicle lined out straight. "But *only* a friend. That's the best it's ever goin' to be, ain't it?"

"My *best* friend. If I live to be as old as my grandmother, I'll never have a better one."

Jim Ed stood outside the front door of the Blue Moon, steeling himself for disappointment. The longer he looked at the peeling exterior, the less he expected inside. As he entered, his first impression was that somebody had forgotten to pay the light bill. His eyes slowly accustomed themselves to the dim environment, and he decided the owners were simply trying to make sure the light bill was the least of their expenses.

The loud clatter of billiard balls drew his attention to a pair of pool tables at the far side of the room. One table was idle, but two young men who looked like cowboys occupied the other while their jean-clad womenfolk stood against the wall, watching. Jim Ed assumed they were girlfriends because no wife would make such a concentrated effort to fake interest in the game.

The floor was of well-worn and somewhat splintered pine except the dance-floor section, which he assumed had been worn so badly that it had had to be replaced. That part was oak. One couple stood in the center of it, holding hands, while another couple hovered over a gaudily lighted and winking jukebox. The young man ran his finger down its long list of selections. At length he put a coin into the slot and punched the buttons. Jim Ed expected the machine to play Western honkytonk music, but it started blaring a screaming-guitar rock instead.

He had not expected such good taste.

He turned toward the bar. It was the best-lighted part of the place, especially at the cash register. He suspected from the bar's obvious age that enough beer had passed over it to have put the river into full flood and drown the unwary from here to the Gulf of Mexico. The bored-looking bartender appeared old enough to have served all of it himself. A waitress at the end of the bar gave Jim Ed a look of absolute indifference and took a long drag on a cigarette. In the dim light she passed for forty. He suspected that in better light she would do well to look fifty-five. Her dress was much too low-cut for what little she had to conceal. He thought a high-buttoned collar would be an improvement.

Jim Ed seated himself on a stool. The man at the bar gave the waitress a chance to take his order, and when she did not he said, "Name it. If we ain't got it, you don't need it."

Jim Ed ordered a Lone Star on draft and got a long-neck bottle instead. The man did not offer him a cold glass. Drinking straight out of a long-neck was supposed to be some kind of a macho trip. The music shattered, the high-pitched guitar sound too much for the narrow limitations of the jukebox.

Jim Ed remarked, "That's not the music I thought I'd hear."

The proprietor wiped the bar with a rag that had probably been clean last Tuesday. "It ain't? I never pay it no mind. The only music I listen to is the bells on that cash register." He gave Jim Ed a quick study. "New here, ain't you?"

"I'm from Dallas."

The bartender pondered. "I've known some good people from Dallas. Some real horses' asses, too. You got a name, or you just answer to 'Hey you!'?"

"I'm Jim Ed Hendrix."

The man's interest picked up. "Kin to Ol' Wes?"

"Grandson."

"Scrappy old dickens, that Wes. I try to keep out of politics myself. Business I'm in, I sell to all sides and always agree with whoever's buyin'. Personally, I'd like to see the lake get built. It'd sure be good for my trade. But I hate to see things get tough for that old man. He really figurin' on givin' them a fight?"

"Says he is."

The barman shrugged. "Oldtimers say Wes was a great bronc stomper in his day. I'm afraid this bronc is fixin' to throw him. You ain't a bronc rider, are you?"

"Not hardly."

"You don't look like the type. Studyin' your sunburnt face I'd say you've got an indoor job with the government, and you ain't used to a lot of fresh air and sunshine."

"The last half is right."

"Well, if you ain't got a job with the government, you probably *wish* you did. I wish *I* did. No sweat, no heavy liftin', no puttin' up with drunks. Just kiss the right asses, put in your hours and go home with money in your pocket."

The two couples left the dance floor as the music ended. The waitress sauntered to their table, the cigarette dangling from her lower lip. Jim Ed was compelled to watch her, trying to remember when he had last seen such a monument to apathy.

The barman said, "If you're in here lookin' for a pickup, you're liable to be disappointed. They mostly come in pairs. And don't get any notions about Mabel. She's old enough to be your mother. In fact, she's *several* old boys' mother, and most of them are bigger than you."

Jim Ed promised to try to bear up under his disappointment.

The bartender's face brightened as he looked toward the door. "Here comes my best meal ticket," he said.

Jim Ed turned. The waitress Stella Tenney walked in, wearing a dress that would do credit to a fire engine. A step behind her came an apprehensive-looking man who appeared to be in his late thirties. His gaze searched over the small crowd with some urgency. Jim Ed suspected he was hoping no one knew him.

Stella walked directly to the bar and spoke to the man behind it. "Good evenin', Jake honey. How's it goin'?"

"A little slow so far, but I expect it'll pick up."

"Well, when Mabel gets back up here you tell her I want my usual. This here is my friend John. John Smith, from Abilene. Tell Jake what you want to drink, honey."

The man who answered to Smith asked for bourbon and branch. Stella turned her gaze to Jim Ed. "Don't I know you? Sure, you had a beer in my place today." She could not remember Jim Ed's name but gave him no opportunity to tell her. She introduced him to her date, who was not consumed by curiosity. Jim Ed noted a white circle around the third finger of the man's left hand. He probably had the wedding ring in his wallet.

She said, "John's in auto parts. I'll bet that's an interestin' line of work. I always did like cars." She patted the flustered man on the cheek and turned back to Jim Ed. "You come on over to our table and sit with us, why don't you?"

Jim Ed could read supplication in Smith's eyes. He shook his head. "Thanks, but two's company. Three's overpopulation." Smith's eyes said *thanks*.

"Well, honey, anyway you can come and ask me for a dance later on, can't you?"

"I'll do that," he promised.

He watched the wiggle in her walk as she made her way to a table beside the dance floor.

The barman chuckled. "It's a good night for business when Stella comes in. They try hard to get her drunk, but the joke's on them. They don't have to."

Jim Ed sipped his beer slowly, for he had no wish to get drunk. He kept watching Stella and her date. Dancing, the salesman did everything except make love to her on the floor. Between dances, her date put away far more bourbon than she did. If he was trying to get Stella drunk, he was going about it in a peculiar way. Jim Ed suspected he was trying to keep his courage up for the task ahead.

Each time the door opened, Jim Ed turned to look. He was repeatedly disappointed until at last Shorty Bigham appeared with a pretty girl on his arm. Jim Ed was let down at first, for he had expected to see Glory B. He looked again as they approached the bar, and he almost slipped from the stool. This *was* Glory B.

Their eyes met and locked. She stopped in place. Shorty kept walking and inadvertently jerked her out of balance. Jim Ed already felt out of balance. He managed a grin at Shorty. "I thought you were going to bring that girl with the patched britches, the sassy one."

Shorty replied, "It's as much a surprise to me as to you. They had to run fingerprints on her before I was sure."

Glory B. was plainly trying to suppress a pleased smile. Jim Ed's stare began at the top of her head and worked downward. He would not have imagined her to look this feminine, even in a dress. He waved three dollar bills at the barman. "Whatever they want, Jake, and another one for me."

Jake slid three longnecks halfway down the bar. "Catch." He offered no glasses.

Glory B. asked, "Have you got us a table, pilgrim?"

"Us?" He looked at Shorty. "This world goes in pairs, not in threes."

Shorty shrugged. "It won't be just three anyway. When they see Glory B. in a dress, there'll be a crowd around us all night."

She said, "The circus doesn't come to town very often." Glory B. led the way to a vacant table adjacent to the dance floor.

Stella Tenney stared at her with honest admiration when malice might have been easier. "It isn't fair, honey. So many girls haven't got a man at all, and you've got two."

Glory B. glanced at the man known as Smith, who was having trouble focusing his eyes. "You do all right, Stella."

Stella looked at her companion. His chin was beginning to droop. "Sometimes. I don't know about tonight." She shrugged and turned to Jim Ed. "I see now why you waited. But you *will* ask me for a dance after a while, won't you?"

"Sure I will." He doubted Smith would be able to drag his feet across the floor much longer.

Jim Ed held back, for Glory B. was Shorty's date, but when Shorty neglected to pull out a chair for her, Jim Ed did it.

She smiled. "A gentleman. There is no end to surprises."

Shorty looked chagrined. "She puts on a dress and her whole personality changes. Usually she pulls out a chair for *me.*"

Despite Shorty's assurances, Jim Ed felt awkward about the threesome. He stood, leaning on a chair. "I think as soon as I've finished my beer I'd best be getting back out to the ranch. My grandfather will probably have a day's work lined up for me again tomorrow."

Shorty nodded toward the empty chair with a sudden impatience. "Aw, sit down, Tater. You'll be with us whether you stay here or not."

Jim Ed saw no logic in that remark, nor was he sure of Shorty's mood in speaking it, but he seated himself. Shorty poked his beer bottle at him. "Cheers."

Jim Ed clinked bottles with him and made a sort of salute in Glory B.'s direction. "Skol."

The jukebox had gone hungry for several minutes, but somebody fed it again. Another rock piece started. Glory B. began tapping her fingers on the table, following the beat. Shorty gave her an apologetic look. "I can't dance to *that.*"

Glory B. turned to Jim Ed. "You can, can't you, pilgrim?"

He took that for an invitation, but he looked at Shorty before he moved. Shorty nodded. "Go ahead. I'll just sit here and sulk till they play somethin' by George Strait."

Jim Ed led her out onto the floor. The beat was lively and loud and gave them no chance to talk. It allowed Jim Ed an opportunity to observe Glory B. in motion, however, to watch that black skirt lift and flare, to see trim legs heretofore hidden behind denim.

"You ought to burn them," he said, half shouting to be heard above the music.

"Burn what?" she shouted back.

"Every pair of blue jeans you've got. And every damned old workshirt."

The music finished. Jim Ed took her by the arm, enjoying a momentary tingle as Glory B. leaned against him. He would rather have stayed out here with her, but he felt an obligation to Shorty. When they returned to the table, Shorty was at the jukebox, punching buttons.

Jim Ed said, "*Now* he'll get fiddles."

"You have something against fiddles?"

"My grandfather plays one."

"I know. I've heard him and your grandmother play together, years ago. They were really something."

He said with regret, "I never got to hear them."

"You should've spent more time out here. You've missed a lot."

"Couldn't help it." He decided she would not care to hear about the strain between his father and grandfather; she would not understand. It was unlikely such things happened in her family.

Her bright brown eyes stared, to his growing discomfort. She squeezed his hand, then quickly let go, a look of surprise in her eyes. She seemed almost relieved when Shorty returned to the table.

Shorty grinned. "We won't have to listen to that screechin' rock for a while. I put two dollars in there for George Strait and Merle Haggard." He waited for the music to start, then wiggled his finger at Glory B. She followed him out to the floor. Jim Ed sat watching them and found his foot tapping to the rhythm. He had not listened to much country and western music. It had never seemed appropriate to most places he had been. He found it not unpleasant, here in its natural element.

A woman's voice spoke behind him. "Pilgrim?" Stella Tenney stood there, looking uncomfortable. "I heard Glory B. call you that. I forgot what you told me your name is."

He stood up. "Jim Ed." He glanced back at her table. The man known as Smith sat with shoulders slumped, head tilted forward. His eyes were open, but it was obvious he was not seeing much.

"Dance with me, Jim Ed? Please?"

He took her in his arms, and she laid her cheek to his. She pressed herself against him as snugly as she could and still manage to dance. Her body warmth and the soft scent of her perfume were a heady challenge to his resistance. At another time he would have left here with her and not looked back. She hummed softly to the music.

Smith tipped over his glass and let it roll onto the floor at his feet. Stella said with irony, "I can sure pick them sometimes."

Smith made no move to retrieve the glass. Jim Ed asked, "An old friend?"

"Yeah. One I just met about suppertime. He was cold sober then. I may need somebody to take me home."

Jim Ed glanced across the dance floor at Glory B. She was watching him. He said, "I don't know, Stella. I may be tied up."

Stella followed his glance. "She's a good girl, that Glory B. She's one woman in Big River who doesn't treat me like Typhoid Mary. I guess it's because I've never been any threat to her. Until now, anyway."

"She's not my girl, she's Shorty's."

"You'd better look again."

Though Glory B. was dancing with Shorty, her eyes were on Jim Ed.

Stella pulled away a little. "I don't think you'd better dance with me anymore. That's a girl I wouldn't want to hurt."

"She's got no claim on me, or me on her. Every time we meet, she skins a little hide off of me."

"She's tryin' to tell you somethin', honey."

"She has an odd way of doing it."

"Listen with your eyes, not your ears. You'll get the message." The music ended. Jim Ed escorted Stella back to her table. The waitress Mabel had brought Smith another drink. His gaze was fixed on the glass. He did not even look up.

Jim Ed said, "Sorry about your date."

"I'll live. I don't know about *him.*"

Jim Ed sat alone while Shorty and Glory B. danced out all the music Shorty had paid for. Finally they came back to the table. As Shorty had predicted, friends of his and Glory B.'s flocked around, laughing, exchanging gossip, commenting on how pretty Glory B.'s dress was. Jim Ed sat at the edge of the crowd, not really a part of it, and felt like a spare tire gone flat. He half considered taking Stella home.

Gradually the crowd began to pull away to dance or drink or shoot pool, and Jim Ed, Shorty and Glory B. were left alone. Shorty talked about trucks and horses and calf roping until Jim Ed had about all of that entertainment he could stand. He dug a handful of coins from his pocket and gave them to Shorty. "I know you're tired of that rock music. Why don't you go find us something you like?"

Glory B. smiled knowingly as Shorty made his way around the dancers toward the jukebox. "Don't get the notion you can fool Shorty. He knows when you're trying to get rid of him."

"I didn't think it was that obvious."

"Everything you do is obvious, pilgrim. So come on, let's dance some more."

The first of Shorty's tunes began, a slow and sad melody, faintly familiar. Jim Ed took Glory B. to the dance floor. She turned into his arms, dropping her head to his shoulder much as Stella had done. The perfume was different, but the warmth between them was stronger. They did not talk at first; they seemed simply to melt together, and that was enough. The melody kept pushing itself into his consciousness, however, until he remembered where he had last heard it.

"What is that song?" he asked her.

"*Faded Love,*" she replied quietly. "Every old fiddler in the world knows that one."

"My grandfather sure does." It was the melody that had awakened Jim Ed the night he had arrived at the ranch, a melody that had haunted him ever since. "The way he played it, I think it was about the saddest music I ever heard."

"It's for hearing when you're sad, or when you're very happy. Which are you, pilgrim?"

The music ended, but he stood there and held her, and she clung to him. He became aware of Shorty watching them from the table, doing a poor job of hiding his hurt. "I don't know," he said. "I'm not sure which I *ought* to be."

A couple of Glory B.'s girlfriends were waiting when Jim Ed took her back to the table. Clad in jeans, they made thin jokes about her dress, then invited her to go with them to powder her nose. She seemed to consider declining, but she said to Jim Ed and Shorty, "Don't you-all go away." She followed the girls.

Jim Ed tried to avoid meeting Shorty's eyes. "Why is it that women have to have a convoy to go to the powder room?"

Shorty said, "I don't know. Just always been that way." Something in his voice compelled Jim Ed to look at him. He saw anger in Shorty's face, and hurt, and resignation.

Jim Ed struggled for the right thing to say. He suspected there *was* no right thing. "Look, Shorty, I didn't come here to monopolize your girlfriend. I'll leave."

Shorty's voice was strained. "She's my friend, but she's not my girl. She's not *anybody's* girl, unless she's yours."

Jim Ed wanted to deny it, but there had been something in the way Glory B. had held on to him that could not *be* denied. "I like you, Shorty. I wouldn't do anything on purpose to hurt you."

Shorty said, "I know that. But it happens, and it does hurt." He took a long drink from his beer bottle. "I've had strong feelin's for Glory B. ever since we were in grade school together, but I guess I always knew there wouldn't nothin' come of it. We were too much like brother and sister.

"It's like my daddy told me about workin' real hard for one of these big ranches, hopin' to climb to the top. He said cowpunchers like us can only go up so far; we'll never make it all the way. When one of these big companies needs somebody new at the top, they never reach down and bring up one of their own. They go to Texas A&M or someplace and bring in some outside feller.

"It's like that with Glory B. I've always been around, too much around. It's not her fault or mine or yours. It's just the way things are."

He shook the bottle, looked at the clock over the bar, then finished his beer. "I don't want to be mad at you, Tater, but I guess I am, a little. Best thing is for me to get out of here before I get any madder. Would you take Glory B. home?"

Jim Ed pushed to his feet. "You don't have to leave, Shorty. I will."

"No, you stay. I may not be the smartest old boy ever raised in Big River, but I know how the land lays. Just tell Glory B. I got some goats to haul tomorrow, and I decided to go on home and get some rest."

Jim Ed felt he should not give up the argument quite so easily, badly as he wanted to. "She'll think I ran you off."

"If I didn't want to be run off, you couldn't do it. She'll know that. Good night, Tater." Shorty turned and took a couple of steps, then came back, his eyes narrowed. "One thing: you treat her right. Hurt that girl and I'll bend a bumper jack over your head."

Jim Ed awkwardly extended his hand. Shorty either overlooked it or chose not to see it. He was quickly gone. Jim Ed stood and looked at the door, not knowing which feeling ran strongest, guilt or gratification.

Glory B. was momentarily surprised, as he thought she might be, but not as disappointed as he expected. She said, "He *did* tell me he had to get up early and make a trip."

"It looks like you're stuck with me for the rest of the evening."

She took his hand. "I'll just have to try and make do."

They danced again. He got to wishing for more slow, easy country and western music so he would have an excuse to hold her closely and let Glory B. rest her head on his shoulder, and feel her warmth and softness against him.

He noticed that Stella Tenney's date had his head on the table and appeared to be asleep. Stella was dancing with anybody who asked her, including some schoolboy-looking youths probably in this place on false IDs, or no IDs at all. After a time a tall figure appeared in the doorway. Sheriff Wally Vincent paused there, giving the room a lawman's practiced grim and searching gaze that seemed to lay a chill over the place. The younger boys disappeared as if by magic, probably hiding out in the restroom until Vincent was gone. Vincent passed over Jim Ed once without paying him any notice, then cut his eyes back as recognition came. Vincent saw that Jim Ed was with Glory B., and he gave her a quick, tentative smile. It was politically advantageous to stay on the good side of the Chatfield-Dawson ranch.

He proceeded to Stella Tenney's table, where Smith had lost all interest in entertainment and appeared to have cashed in his chips for the night. Vincent bent close to Stella's ear. He smiled and talked in low tones drowned out by music from the jukebox. She nodded to whatever he said. Vincent motioned to one of the young men nearby. Together they lifted Smith from his chair and got his arms over their shoulders so they could carry him out the door. Stella followed with the man's hat and coat.

"Well," Jim Ed said, "at least somebody'll take her home."

Glory B. frowned. "When Wally Vincent smiles he reminds me of a boy fixing to pull the legs off of a grasshopper."

"I'm grateful to John Smith, anyway. He gave the sheriff something to do, so he left *me* alone."

"You stay out of his way. There's nothing as scary as a man who gives you a handsome smile just before he hurts you."

They danced the rest of the evening, seldom sitting at the table for more than a few minutes, for he did not want her out of his arms, and she seemed loath to leave them. The lights went out once, and he seized the opportunity to kiss her while they stood in darkness, the music suddenly gone. He found her eager, and their lips were still pressed together when the lights returned. She flushed, looking around quickly. She laughed in a husky voice when she realized they were not the only couple who had taken the same advantage of the moment and had been caught by the lights.

"I think we had better sit down awhile," she said, her breath short.

"Or else leave," he suggested.

"Not yet. We'll just sit."

Hands clasped across the table, they talked of weather and wars, of dreams and disappointments. At length she asked, "What do you find to do out there all day on that little place of your grandfather's?"

"I don't find anything; *he* does. You'd be surprised how many jobs he can turn up to keep my hands from being idle." He told her of the fence-building project, of drenching sheep, of searching for and doctoring sick animals.

"Nights, I've been working on his financial records and trying to set up a good, simple bookkeeping system for him. You wouldn't believe how little attention he's ever paid to it."

Her eyebrows arched. "What do you know about bookkeeping?"

"I'm a business administration major, or was. My dad wanted me to become an accountant, like he is."

"But do you know anything about setting up ranch records?"

"A ranch is a business, or ought to be. The principles are the same whether it's a goat farm or a hardware store."

She sat in thoughtful silence, staring past him. "You said you *were* a business major. Have you quit?"

"I flunked my final semester. I don't see any point in going back to finish. I want to do something more interesting with my life than spend it adding up figures."

"If you're all that tired of it, you must hate doing your grandfather's books."

He was a little surprised by his own answer. "Once I got into them, I've kind of enjoyed it. A challenge, I guess."

"Maybe it's the difference between working in classroom theory and working on something real."

"Maybe."

The lights flashed on and off. Glory B. said, "That's Jake's way of telling us he's about to close up. One more dance and we've got to leave."

Jim Ed looked at the clock. He wondered how all that time had gone by without his noticing it. He took Glory B. in his arms, and they danced slower even than the music called for. They were still standing in the center of the dance floor, in each other's arms, when Jake pulled the plug on the jukebox and its colored lights winked their final flicker.

Jim Ed opened the door of Grandmother Maudie's old Ford and held it for Glory B. When he seated himself behind the steering wheel, she slid up close beside him. He did not know the way to the Chatfield-Dawson headquarters. She gave him directions, then sat silently, leaning against him and clinging to his arm.

Finally she said, "If you enjoy working on Wes's records, you would *love* working on ours. They'd be ten times as big a challenge."

"I probably wouldn't know where to start."

"You could start anywhere. They're a mess. We'd even pay you for your time."

He suspected this was a ploy to get to see him again, a ploy with which he had no argument beyond his not yet having gained full competence in accounting. "It takes time to work up a set of books."

"You've got the summer, haven't you? Come back over tomorrow . . ." She held her watch up close to her face. ". . . this afternoon. I can show you a little of the ranch, and some of the books."

"I'm afraid my grandfather will want me to 'go to church' with him. His idea of church is being out on that new fenceline, punching postholes into the rock."

"Ask him. Or I can call and ask him if you're afraid to."

He took affront, a little. "I'm not afraid. I just don't like to stir him up when it's not necessary. He has a crusty edge to him when he doesn't get his way."

"It seems to run in the family. Okay, then, *you* ask him."

"I will."

The headlights picked up a high stone arch with a C Bar brand in its center. The tires rumbled over a cattleguard. Glory B. leaned her head against Jim Ed's shoulder. He felt his blood warming, his heartbeat quickening. He took his right hand from the wheel and touched her leg. She made no move to push it away. He slowed the car gradually and pulled to a stop. As he turned toward her, she put her arms around him and sought his mouth with hers. They pressed together until they had to pause for breath. Her face was warm, almost hot, against his cheek. He moved his hand gently along her leg, then up her side. He could feel the rapid beating of her heart as he dropped his head and pressed his lips against the soft bulge at the top of the dress. His hand moved to her breast and felt for buttons but found none.

She whispered, "The back. It zips."

He found the zipper and slipped it down, then moved his hand inside her dress. He felt her tremble to his touch and arch her body toward him. Then, as if she had felt an electric shock, she suddenly stiffened and pulled away.

"No," she said, her voice hardly more than a whisper. "Not now."

He swallowed, his breath short, his heart thumping. She pulled farther away.

"I don't understand," he said. "I thought you wanted to."

"If we don't stop now, we won't stop at all."

"But why should we stop?"

"I'm not ready. I can't tell you why. I'm just not ready."

Frustration colored his voice. "I guess I was wrong. I felt like we needed each other."

"Pilgrim, I don't *need* anybody."

He pulled away from her, half in anger, half in disappointment. He leaned to the window for breath and saw a cow standing in the moonlight, watching impassively. He said, "Damn!" and the cow jerked away in fright at his voice, running a few steps before stopping to look again.

He sat and simmered in silence for a minute or two, trying to regain control. He said, "I don't know what I did . . ."

"It's not just what *you* did. It's what others have done too. I thought this time might be different. You'd better take me on home."

Flustered, she struggled with the zipper. It crossed his mind that if he took her back into his arms and kissed her, he might rekindle whatever she had so suddenly lost. But he did not try.

They rode in silence the rest of the way. She stayed on her side of the seat. He knew the largest house would be hers, so he pulled up in front of it. He did not cut the motor. He sat a moment, stewing, then got out, went around the car and opened the door for her. He managed to say, "I enjoyed the evening, Glory B. Whatever went wrong, I'm sorry for. I suppose this means your invitation is off."

She stared hard at him. "Are you really any good at accounting, or do you just talk a good game?"

Defensively he declared, "I was pretty damned good at it until the last semester."

"All right," she said. "You're hired. I take Gram to church, and we get home for dinner about one o'clock. I'll be looking for you to eat with us."

He stood first on one foot, then the other. "Glory B., I wonder if I'll ever figure you out."

"Don't try. Just accept me as I am." She took his hand. "What happened a while ago wasn't your fault; it was mine. I got carried away and let it go too far."

"If we keep seeing each other, aren't you afraid you may get carried away again sometime?"

"If I do, it'll be my idea, and I'll let you know." She brushed his lips with a quick kiss. "Don't forget. One o'clock."

He wouldn't forget. He wouldn't sleep, remembering.

The dog Pepper met him, appearing in the headlights fifty yards out from the house. Jim Ed put the car in the old garage and closed the swinging wooden doors as quietly as he could, hoping not to awaken his grandfather. The effort was wasted. From the front porch he heard the quiet sound of a fiddle. Wes was playing something more cheerful than *Faded Love*.

Walking up the steps, he saw the old man sitting in a chair leaned back against the wall. Wes asked, "Have a good time?"

"It was okay. What're you doing up this late?"

"Couldn't sleep. Funny how quick I've got used to you bein' here. I laid there with my eyes wide open, knowin' you was gone." He leaned forward. "Let's see you." As Jim Ed moved closer, he said, "Well, I'll be damned. You got you a new hat."

"I didn't throw the other one away."

"Good. I was about to get used to it. At least it showed you go your own way and don't foller after the sheep. Did you see Glory B.?"

"I saw her. In fact, I just got through taking her home."

He could see Wes grin, even in the near darkness beneath the porch roof. Wes said, "I had a feelin' in my bones that you two would get along if you tried hard enough."

There was no way Jim Ed could have told him what had happened. An old man wouldn't understand. He said, "She wants me to spend the afternoon with her. I hope that's all right."

The grin came back, wider than before. "I wouldn't have it no other way. You'd better go hit the soogans, or you won't be fit company for a sheep, much less a girl like Glory B."

As Jim Ed undressed, he could hear Wes playing a jolly fiddle tune out on the porch.

Chapter 9

C Bar foreman Bill Roper stood on a long, narrow wooden platform beside a welded-steel cattle-working chute, watching his son Johnny and Jim Ed Hendrix shout and wave their arms at a dozen or so Hereford cows which circled stubbornly and raised dust in a small crowding pen. Glory B. Dawson waited on the outside with a long piece of rusted pipe in her hands where the crowding pen narrowed to funnel shape and provided an entry into the chute for unsuspecting cattle. These cows, however, had been through the chute before and remembered that it meant bad news. They were the day's remnants, crafty holdouts which had resisted every previous penning and now were concentrated in a final rebellious bunch. They kept going around and around in the small enclosure, refusing entry. Roper grinned as he watched Jim Ed jump in front of them, making noises meant to turn them back into the proper direction. The cows were not buying.

Old Wes Hendrix slouched at the chute's open end, his rough hands gripping an iron bar that controlled the headgate. He held the gate open to provide a deceptive view of daylight and freedom that might lure a cow into making a run down the chute. He would jerk the bar and slam the gate before she reached it, trapping her and those which might follow her into the false promise of escape. But Jim Ed and Johnny had yet to get these wise hussies to take the chute. Glory B., standing impatiently at her station outside, shouted advice and counsel that went unheard in the wind and confusion and the anxious bawling of cows and calves separated from one another.

Wes turned loose of the bar and flexed his hands as if they were going to sleep. His sharp old eyes cut toward his grandson, working feverishly in the crowding pen. "Bill, you reckon Tater'll ever make a hand?" The question carried but faint hope.

"He shows a lot of want-to," Roper replied. He could say that with honesty and not have to bring up the point that Jim Ed was starting late. In Roper's observation, not many who waited until maturity to begin ever fully mastered the cowboy trade. Top hands were almost always those who had grown up on horseback and learned at the sides of fathers, uncles or brothers from the time they were big enough to sit in a saddle alone. Working with horses and cattle carried too many subtleties and nuances almost impossible to articulate or teach; a boy or girl learned them easier than an adult, and more by instinct and observation than by conscious instruction. It took years.

Wes grunted, "I'm glad he ain't bein' paid by the hour." But the old man's face betrayed pride in Jim Ed's making an honest effort, if a hopelessly inexperienced one.

Roper said, "He's come a long ways this summer. How long has he been with you now, six weeks?"

Wes shook his head. "Five. But with Glory B., is more like it. I get a day or two of labor out of him, then she hauls him over here to work on the C Bar accounts, or off to a range field day or a cow symposium someplace. She's tryin' to educate him into bein' a rancher, looks like. But one day he'll go back to Dallas, and all her effort'll be for nothin'. He ain't really all that interested in cows."

Roper smiled. "But he's mighty interested in Glory B."

Wes frowned. "If he's makin' a nuisance of himself around here, I want you to tell him so."

"No," Roper assured him. "He's been earnin' whatever Miz Livvy's been payin' him. She says Tater's gone a long ways toward settin' up a new set of books for the outfit. I tell you, Wes, he's got me spendin' more time writin' reports than I spend on *real* work. I record the hours I put in and what I work at, the miles I drive the pickup and the part of the operation I drive them for. Says he's got the whole ranch divided up into *profit centers.* If we had any of *them*, this outfit wouldn't be in so much trouble with the bank."

Wes nodded. "He's done the same thing with me. He uses words I never even heard of. Imagine, a button from Dallas that don't know whether cows sleep in caves or roost in trees, and he's tryin' to teach me about the ranchin' business."

Roper said, "Maybe we better pay attention to him. Miz Livvy seems to think Tater's on the right track."

Wes smiled, lightening the burden of his years. "Well, if Livvy's pleased, I reckon I'm pleased too."

It always pleasured Roper to see Wes smile. Wes had long been a father figure to him. Roper's own cowboy father had died young, crushed beneath a fallen horse, leaving his son to finish growing up under the watchful and demanding tutelage of such men as Wes and the late Tol Dawson, Miz Livvy's husband. Roper acknowledged a debt he could repay only by living up to examples set by that hardworking generation of cow people.

His eye was caught by a movement near the big house. Lavinia Dawson and Roper's wife Hallie were walking down toward the pens to watch the finishing-up of the work. Lavinia clung to Hallie's arm for support. Wes's gaze followed Roper's, and he frowned. "Livvy's walkin' awful slow."

Roper said, before he thought, "I'll be walkin' slow too, when I get to her age." He realized too late that Wes was no younger.

The creases deepened in Wes's face as he watched the elderly woman. "It's hell to get old."

Roper watched his wife. A puff of wind picked up her skirt, and she reached quickly to push it down. He supposed there must be something wrong with him. Even after being married to her so many years, a quick glimpse of her still-trim legs could wrest his mind away from everything else. With that woman snug in his arms, he thought, a man could overlook an earthquake. He wondered sometimes if Wes Hendrix in his earlier years had ever been so fortunate as to feel that way about Maudie, or even some other woman. He hoped so. It was too good a thing for one man to monopolize.

He forced his attention back to the crowding pen, in time to see Jim Ed jump in front of a cow, trying to turn her. She knocked him halfway across the pen. Arms flailing, he went down on his back. Roper heard Wes groan, partly from anxiety and partly from exasperation.

Johnny ran to help. Glory B. climbed the fence and was halfway down into the crowding pen when Jim Ed waved them both off and pushed to his feet without aid. Roper could see that he was not hurt. Glory B.'s words were lost in the wind, but from her manner he suspected they were not complimentary.

Wes grumped, "I'm glad he's good with an addin' machine, because in half the summer he ain't learned his way around a cow pen."

The cow which had struck Jim Ed wearied of the circling and started down the chute in a hard run toward the false daylight ahead. She snorted a challenge as she ran. The other cows followed her in single file through the narrow passage. Wes jerked down on the bar, and the steel headgate slammed shut with a loud clank. The lead cow ran headlong into the ungiving barrier, which shuddered under the impact. She quickly tried to back up. But at the far end of the chute Glory B. shoved the iron pipe in front of two posts as a barrier just behind the rearmost cow. The chute was too narrow for the cows to turn. They were trapped.

Roper filled a syringe from a small bottle of clear liquid. "Wes, I'm not crazy about all the new things they come at us with, but I've got nothin' against technology that makes things easier. One shot of this new stuff and we don't have to dip or drench or spray or nothin'. Just give them the needle and turn them aloose."

He administered to the first cow, which threshed and reared and bawled in protest. He walked back to the second and the third and so on to the end of the chute. For the cows, resistance was futile, and the injection was so quickly given that they had time to do nothing more than flinch.

Johnny and Jim Ed climbed out from the empty pen and walked up to watch. Roper nodded, and Wes lifted the bar, opening the headgate. The first cow snorted and made a leap for freedom. She belligerently horned her way through cattle which stood outside in the main pen, already treated. She did not stop her aggression until she reached the comparative safety of a corner, buffered from the humans by other animals. The remaining cows moved out of the chute in single file, almost sheepishly, as if humiliated by having been outwitted. Roper studied the first cow so he would know her the next time he saw her. When her calf was weaned this fall, she would make a one-way trip to town. Wild cows had been a welcome challenge to a cowboy spirit in his youth, but now he had no patience with them; they spoiled the rest. "Johnny, I wisht you'd open the outside gate and let them find their way back out where they came from."

It sounded like a polite request, but for his son it was an order. Johnny took care to circle well around the cows and not make them run from him. Wildness was not to be encouraged, at least not where his father could see.

Lavinia Dawson beckoned Jim Ed to the fence where she and Hallie stood on the outside. She asked him about his injuries. He assured her there were none except to his dignity. Wes walked over to Lavinia and Hallie and took off his hat in the deferential manner of his generation. It was a gesture Roper always intended to emulate but sometimes forgot. Wes never forgot because he did not have to remember; it was ingrained in his nature. He inquired about Livvy's health. She told him she had not felt better in a long time. The look in Hallie Roper's eyes said otherwise. So did the fatigue in Lavinia's face. There had been a time, not so long ago, when she would have been in the midst of the work, as Glory B. was now.

Roper said to Wes, "I'm obliged to you and Tater for comin' to help. Let's go up to the house for some coffee."

"Thanks, Bill," Wes replied, "but me and Tater are close to finishin' that fence. I thought we might get some wire strung before dark."

Glory B. dusted her old Levis with her floppy hat. She looked disappointed. "Wes, I was kind of hoping you wouldn't need him the rest of the afternoon. There's still part of the ranch I haven't had time to show him yet."

Wes said, "No time? You been bringin' him over here every other day for a month."

"But we've kept him busy working on the books."

Roper watched with amusement as the old man wilted under the quiet coaxing of Glory B.'s eyes. Those eyes could either melt a stone or burn a hole through it, depending upon her intentions. That ability to manipulate men was one thing she had inherited from her Galveston mother.

Wes said, "I wouldn't've thought there's a rabbit track on this place that he hasn't seen by now. But you-all go ahead. We'll work on the fence tomorrow."

Glory B. smiled. "Thanks, Wes. I'll see that he gets home." Jim Ed had missed the conversation, talking with Lavinia. Glory B. shouted, "Come on, pilgrim. First one to the pickup gets to drive." She started running. Jim Ed looked to his grandfather for confirmation, then followed in a trot, grabbing the top rail of the fence and vaulting over to overcome some of the lead she had taken. Roper winced, imagining the pain if he had tried that.

Lavinia Dawson chuckled. "I guess he *wasn't* hurt much."

Johnny walked up, then turned to watch Glory B. jump into the driver's seat of a pickup just ahead of Jim Ed. Jim Ed went around to the other side and crawled in. Johnny seemed bemused. "Dad," he asked, "you reckon Glory B. and Tater are goin' to get married?"

"Son, they're just a couple of kids yet."

"How old were you and Mama?"

Roper looked at Hallie. "Older'n them."

Johnny arched an eyebrow and started counting on his fingers.

Roper added, "As old, anyway. You oughtn't to be askin' about things that're none of your business."

Wes stared after the pickup as it pulled away. "You don't reckon . . ."

"No," Roper said quickly. "They're both too smart to rush into somethin' like that. Why, me and Hallie knew each other for four-five years before we jumped over the broomstick." He gave Johnny a reproachful gaze. "Long's you're not goin' to build fence, Wes, you'd just as well have that coffee."

Wes nodded. "I'd be obliged. I ain't been able to make a decent cup of coffee since Tater scrubbed out my pot."

Hallie said, "It's already made. I'll be with you as soon as I walk Miz Livvy home."

Hallie took Lavinia's arm. Lavinia leaned to her for support.

Wes gave Roper a dark and questioning glance. Roper could only shrug as they followed a few paces behind the women.

Wes watched the dust settle behind Glory B.'s pickup, winding across a pasture road and out of sight amid the big liveoak trees. He remarked, "Wouldn't it be a caution, though? She's all cowgirl, and he's all city. They ain't got a thing in common, hardly."

Roper did not speak his thought, for Lavinia Dawson might hear and be embarrassed: *It doesn't take but one thing.*

The men followed Lavinia and Hallie up to the front of the big house. Livvy paused at her flowerbed. "I thought they'd all be gone, but there's still two bluebonnets left. Did you ever see them stay on so late, Wes?"

Wes admitted, "I never did pay all that much attention to flowers. But it does seem unusual. I suppose the house protects them."

Livvy said, "They look lonesome, all by themselves."

Hallie helped Lavinia up the steps and across the porch. Roper noticed that Wes's gaze followed until they had disappeared through the door. Wes's voice was pinched. "She's failin', Bill."

Roper nodded sadly. "She won't admit there's anything wrong with her. It's a damned shame, seein' her now and rememberin' the way she used to be."

He hated to acknowledge the aging of people like Lavinia and Wes. Not only did it give him a foreboding of a future without them, but it was a reminder of his own mortality, a reminder that his little aches and pains, now but a nuisance, would take on major proportions in years to come.

He started walking toward his house but stopped when he realized Wes was not keeping pace. Wes stood alone, staring off toward a dark green cluster of liveoaks, and beyond toward the limestone hills. He rubbed fingers across his eyes.

Roper asked, "Wes, you all right?"

Wes seemed a little startled at his voice. "Yeah, sure. Must've got some dirt in my eyes down at the pens."

The house the Ropers used had been built in the 1930s and in many ways showed its age. But it was roomy and solid. Roper thought it was better than any he could likely ever buy for himself and Hallie. He woke up in the middle of the night, sometimes, grieving over having to leave this ranch if it were not somehow to be saved.

He and Wes and Johnny walked through the high-ceiling living room to the big kitchen, which also served as dining room. While Roper rustled around in the kitchen cabinet for cups, Johnny took a can of Coke from the refrigerator, shook it a couple of times and pushed in the tab. The drink spewed across the floor. Johnny looked guiltily at his father and rushed to wipe up the mess with a dishrag.

Wes mused, "My boys used to do that. James Edward especially. Provoked Maudie half to tears. She'd tell me it was my job to punish him. I'd take him out to the barn for a talkin'-to, but I never could take a strap to him. Always been glad I didn't."

Johnny looked hopefully at his father, as if urging him to take Wes's thinly disguised advice to heart. Roper said, "As long as your mother didn't see it . . ."

A voice came from the door. "See what?" Hallie stood there, head cocked questioningly to one side.

Roper said, "Nothin'. He's already taken care of it."

Wes asked her, "What do you think is the matter with Livvy?"

Hallie's face was grim. "She claims she's only tired, but she's hurting. She says her doctor just gave her some pills and told her to rest. But she doesn't know how. She's never rested in her life." Hallie's voice became accusatory. "That trait seems to run in your generation."

Wes shook his head. "In our day we always had to scratch for everything. Even as big as this ranch was, Livvy never had no silver spoon."

Hallie poured three cups of coffee. "You know, Wes, you ought to be taking better care of *your*self. This stuff isn't good for your heart."

"If I was to give up everything that ain't good for me, I'd dry up like an old locoweed cow and die of starvation. I'd rather go thisaway." He sipped the coffee, his eyes narrowed. His voice went tight. "Sometimes, the way the good things are fadin', it don't seem like there's much left to stay for."

Jim Ed was glad Glory B. had beaten him to the pickup and was doing the driving, for he could look at her and not worry about the bumps and turns in the ranch road. He wanted to reach over and touch her, but he did not know how she would receive the move. Trying to predict her moods toward him was as frustrating as trying to predict changeable Texas weather. Times, she seemed to want him close, but not too close. Other times, she would be distant, but not too distant. The weeks he had been coming to the C Bar to work on the ranch records had been by turns exhilarating and dispiriting. She played a game whose rules he had not been able to discern.

At least the C Bar pay had been good.

"Where are we going?" he asked, though it made no difference to him.

"Around. Just around."

He had seen cowgirls at rodeos, carrying flags and running barrels a-horseback. They were always clothed as if they had just shopped out a Western-wear store. Glory B. usually looked as if she had just *swept* out one. Except for her face and those dark brown eyes, she bore little resemblance to the dressed-up girl he had been taking to the Blue Moon the last several Saturday nights. He said, "You don't look much like the romance of the Old West."

"If you want the romantic West," she said, "go to the movies. Out here you take it like it comes, and it comes like this most of the time. Did you ever see a movie hero dirty his hands pulling a baby calf out of a heifer too young to give birth without help?"

"Can't say that I ever did."

"Not much romance in it except for the bull, and he's never around for that end of the business."

He laughed. "If you're still trying to bring a blush to *these* cheeks, you'll have to try a lot harder. Nothing you say catches me off guard anymore."

She gave him a long study, so long that he feared she might let the pickup run off the twin-rut road and into a ditch or a liveoak tree. But she seemed to know these C Bar ranch roads as Wes Hendrix knew his. "If I didn't think you were worth salvaging, I wouldn't try."

"Salvaging? That makes me sound like a sunken ship."

"I'm talking about turning you from a city slicker into a cow man. Considering the short time you've been at it, you haven't done too badly. I'd say there's hope."

"But what's the point? You know as well as I do that they're going to turn my grandfather's ranch into a fisherman's paradise. I'll be going back to Dallas and taking him with me."

"If you believe that, why do you help him build that fence? It's a lot of hard, brutal work to be doing for nothing."

"He's making a statement. If I didn't help him, it'd be the same as helping *them.*"

"You've put a lot of sweat into that fence."

"And blood. We've set those posts like they were in concrete. At least we'll have the satisfaction of knowing they'll have to work just as hard pulling them up from there."

She smiled her approval. "You may not realize it, but there's a lot of Wes Hendrix in you. You could do worse than pattern after him."

"I don't see you modeling much after your grandmother. She's gentle and quiet, and I'll bet she's never poked a cow with a piece of steel pipe."

"Wrong, pilgrim. She used to ride horseback and work cattle like a hired man. She wasn't raised to be a hot-house flower like . . ." Glory B. broke off.

Jim Ed said, "Like us city folks?"

"Like my mother, is what I was about to say."

Jim Ed puzzled. "I thought you and your mother got along."

"We didn't used to. I finally realized she can't help it. Her people bent the twig, and that's the way it grew. They thought the main thing a woman was born for was to get herself a man to take care of her and then obey his every whim. They believed there was something wrong with a woman who wanted to take care of herself."

"Like you?"

"Sure, like me. For years I used to wonder what would ever become of my mother if she was left on her own. And I found out. She was helpless after my father died. I swore I'd never let myself get a foot caught in that trap." She gave him a questioning glance. "I've never heard you talk about *your* folks."

He shrugged. "There's nothing much to tell. My grandfather doesn't get along with my father, and my father doesn't get along with me."

"Maybe you just don't understand each other."

"I think we understand each other much too well. I guess nobody gets born into a perfect family."

She nodded but said nothing more for a while. She pulled off onto a rough road that led to a wide valley, where the layered limestone hills drew apart. "I don't want you to think this ranch has stayed stuck in the mud for eighty years just because our books aren't up to snuff. We've contributed our bit to science." She pulled up, after a time, at an aluminum gate set in a straight stretch of netwire fence. She cut the engine and opened her door.

Jim Ed unlatched the gate and held it for her to walk through. She motioned with her hand. "They call this Glory B.'s brush pile."

He saw only a flat stretch of pasture, much like the one they had just driven through except that most of the standing brush appeared dead, and the grass was taller without its competition. She said proudly, "I did this in my sophomore year. This is my *squirt, squat and count* project."

He had no idea what she was talking about, and told her so.

She said, "I did a brush control experiment here. Took a dozen or so different sprays and set up a series of treatment strips. Walked through here with a knapsack sprayer and squirted every bush, or dropped a pelleted herbicide on it. Every so often I go back through to count the dead ones and the live ones. I can tell you what worked and what didn't. Earned six semester hours credit for the effort, too."

She seemed to be waiting for a compliment, so he gave her one, though he was not sure he grasped the significance.

She said, "My great-grandfather and my grandfather over-stocked this land. They didn't intend to; they just didn't know its limits. It's up to our generation to try and bring it back as far as we can. If we don't, it'll pass over to somebody who will." Her voice went stern. "I'll be damned if I'll see this place go to anybody except me and mine!"

Noting the set of her jaw, he commented, "I wouldn't want to be the one who tried to take it away from you."

"That's why we've had you to working on the ranch accounts, so nobody'll get the chance. I hope you didn't think we invited you just because we like your looks."

He would have admitted, if anyone had asked him, that he was not sure *why* Glory B. brought him over here. Times, her eyes told him she wanted him to make love to her. But when he made a move that she might take for a serious pass, she would back away and start talking about cattle or horses, sheep or feed. The closest he ever got to her was while dancing at the Blue Moon.

At least she no longer snapped at him the way she used to.

She drove to a windmill that stood near the head of a draw and got out of the pickup beside the weather-darkened rock wall of a water tank six feet high. She placed her hands upon the rim of the tank and jumped, trying to see over it. She did not bring herself quite high enough.

"We had to re-leather the windmill," she said. "I want to see if the tank has filled up yet."

Jim Ed did as she had done, his extra height carrying him all the way up. He braced himself with his hands and looked over the top. Water lapped within a couple of inches of the rim. He started to tell her, but she had walked around the tank and started to climb upon an old wooden ladder. As she placed her weight upon the third rung, it broke. Jim Ed ran, but he was too far away to catch her. She landed on her back, both legs uphill against the ladder. Her floppy hat went rolling. She spoke a few words he could not imagine her grandmother ever using, and she tried to push herself up.

Trembling a little from the scare, Jim Ed grasped her shoulders. "Wait. Move easy and make sure you didn't break a leg or something."

Carefully she moved her right leg, then her left. He watched her eyes for sign of pain. All he saw was a flash of self-anger. She said brittlely, "I've climbed that damned ladder a hundred times."

"Maybe you *do* need somebody to take care of you. Let me help you up." Putting his arm around her, he carefully brought her to her feet. She fell against him as her shaky legs gave way. He grabbed her. Their eyes met and held. Her lips parted to speak, but a strong want forced him to press his mouth against hers, choking off whatever she had been about to say. She made a surprised sound in her throat, then brought her arms up around him. She pulled back for breath and stared with widened eyes.

He declared with a hint of challenge, "If you're waiting for me to apologize, forget it. That's just something that's needed doing for a long time now."

"Then do it right," she retorted, and brought her arm up around his neck, pulling his head down. She pushed her mouth against his and held fast until he felt his lungs begin to ache. It was he who reluctantly had to pull away.

Breathing heavily, he protested, "You'd smother a man to death."

"But he'd be buried with a smile on his face." Her own face was flushed a little. She drew back to arm's length but continued to hold to his hands. Her gaze never left his eyes. "You say that tank is full of water?"

"Near to running over."

"Then there's no need for us to stay here any longer."

"I don't suppose so." He did not move for a minute, nor did Glory B. Finally she turned, still holding one of his hands, not letting go until they were at the vehicle. She drove in silence, studiously keeping her eyes to the road. At length she said, "I want to show you the prettiest spot on the ranch." She pulled off onto a dim trace that wound around a tall hill and then went into a climb that challenged the lowest gear. The grade was even steeper than the one up which his grandfather periodically forced his pickup so he could look off down toward the river. She stopped where the faint trail played out, a little below the top of the hill. She pulled the handbrake and sat there, staring speculatively at him for a minute before she opened the door and climbed out.

He had to scramble to catch up with her as she climbed the last forty or fifty feet to the hilltop. She turned and made a sweeping motion with her hand. "When you've got your head deep in the record books, I want you to remember this view. This is what the whole thing is about."

Jim Ed could see for what he guessed must be twenty, perhaps thirty miles across row after row of flat-topped limestone hills, each row bluer than the one in front of it as he gazed toward the lowering sun. The canyon immediately before him was ragged and deep, cedar trees spotted upon its sides, heavy liveoak timber a solid green along the dry creek at the bottom of it. This was a broader view even than the one his grandfather had shown him, except that from here the river was more distant.

She said, "I've been saving this until I thought you were ready to appreciate it. What do you think?"

He was not sure what she wanted him to think, but he remembered with regret his grandfather's disappointment at his bland first reaction to that other hilltop. "It's the biggest thing I ever saw," he said, and meant it.

She placed her arm around his waist. She said, "My grandmother first showed me this place when I was just three or four years old. I thought it was the whole world. She said it was, almost. It was all the world *she* ever wanted. She said it was something she could share without giving up any of it."

He admitted, "It belongs in a picturebook."

"It belongs just where it is. You can't shrink it to fit into a camera. But I've always carried it in my head, and drawn on it for comfort when I've been away from here and homesick." Her arm tightened around him. "I'm going to keep it. Whatever it takes, Jim Ed, I'm not letting this get away from me."

He could not remember that she had called him Jim Ed before; it had always been *pilgrim*, or Hendrix, or at best *Tater*. He sensed that she had brought him up here as a test of some sort. He sensed also that he had passed. They stood a long time, arms around one another, the hilltop wind sweet and cool in their faces, a contrast to the summer warmth of the valley below. She turned, at last, into his arms. She kissed him, then started down the hill toward the pickup.

She said, after a time, "You slacked off in school because you were bored with it. Do the ranch books bore you?"

He would have to admit that he had been surprised. As with his grandfather's records, he had found his interest sparked once he started on the C Bar accounts. It was different somehow, working on records that represented something real, something he could see, people he knew. It was not like the impersonal tedium of classroom exercises. He said, "I like it fine."

"Good, because I don't intend to let you stop."

He did not recognize Liveoak Camp at first because they came into it from a pasture road instead of from the highway as he had done that day with Wes. But he knew the windmill when he saw it, and remembered the comfort its cool water and Bill Roper's talcum powder had given him at a time of desperate need. He remembered the picket and lumber corrals, the old box-and-strip house and his grandfather's genuine regret that he once had loved this place, then left it.

Glory B. stopped the pickup in front of the house. She sat there, staring through the windshield. At length he asked, "Are we going to stay or go or what?"

She turned to look at him. Her eyes were severe. "There's something I feel you ought to know . . . something I haven't told my mother and couldn't tell my grandmother in a hundred years."

"Sounds terrible."

"Maybe. It depends on how you look at it. The first year I went off to school, there was this man. I was just a freshman, green from the country. He was a senior from Dallas, big-city sophisticated, and he had this fancy van rigged up like an RV."

Jim Ed thought he could guess the rest of the story. "You don't have to tell me. It's none of my business."

"But I want you to know. I thought I was in love with him. I thought I needed him. It took me a long time to realize he was just using me. Even after I knew, I couldn't do anything about it. I'd promise myself I wouldn't see him anymore, but the next thing I knew I was in the back of that van again. I felt dirty and used and cheap, but I couldn't quit. I *didn't* quit. He quit *me.* He left town the day after graduation, and that was the last I ever saw or heard of him."

She paused, and he sensed that she was waiting for his reaction.

He said, "You don't think you're the first girl that ever happened to, do you? These days it happens to a lot of them. Most of them, maybe."

"You don't mind?"

"I've got no reason to blame you for anything. I'm not exactly an amateur myself."

She studied him, her eyes asking if he meant what he said.

He told her, "Maybe now I understand why you took such a disliking to me right off. I was him all over again."

"I was afraid you might be," she admitted. She pulled the door handle. "Let's go in. We can fix coffee in the kitchen."

She waited for him at the steps and took his hand. She looked up at the surviving gingerbread trim. "I guess an old house like this can't be pretty to most people, but it's like a bit of family history still alive. My great-grandfather built it. My grandmother still loves to come over here and remember."

She led him into the kitchen. She pointed to a corner where a bare table stood. "Right there is where I first saw you."

He nodded. "You nearly bit my head off."

"You made a typical male chauvinist remark. You had it coming to you."

"All I said was that the doughnuts were good. I wish we had some now. They'd go with the coffee."

She slipped her hands beneath his arms. She looked him squarely in the eyes, then stood on tiptoe and kissed him. "Do you really want that coffee?"

"It was *you* who suggested it."

"Well, *I* don't want any coffee. Not now." She drew his head down and pushed herself against him, pressing him to the wall, pulling his arm around her waist and holding it there. She kissed him hungrily as she had kissed him at the windmill, holding until he felt his lungs would burst. When she drew back for a breath, her face was flushed. He hugged her and placed his cheek against hers and found it fevered.

She took his arm and led him into a small bedroom. She left him to walk to the windows and raise them. A breeze lifted the flowered curtains. She looked a minute toward the distant hills. When she turned, she had unbuttoned her shirt. She pulled it free of the waistband and let it slip from her arms. She placed both hands upon Jim Ed's face. They felt like fire.

"I told you once that I didn't need you. Maybe I still don't. But I *want* you, Jim Ed Hendrix."

It was the final strand in the last section of the fence. Jim Ed had drawn it taut with a "come-along," and Wes was using a pair of heavy wirepinchers to make the wraps that would hold it. They both looked up toward the droning of a small single-engine plane, circling overhead. It had already made one pass at low altitude, as if somebody were trying to see what the old man and the young one were up to.

Jim Ed suggested, "Maybe they're studying their lake site."

Wes declared, "It ain't their lake site, not by a damn sight!" He finished the wrapping and wiped his sleeve across his sweaty face. "You can ease off now. All that's left is to steeple it down to the posts and wire up to the stays."

Jim Ed backed away, lifting his hat to shade his eyes from the late-afternoon sun while he studied the circling plane. Whatever they were up to, he saw nothing he could do about it. He took a look down the long line of new fence. It was arrow-straight, net wire on the bottom, two strands of barbed wire at the top, catching and reflecting the sun. "The first day we came up here, I wouldn't have bet on ever getting it finished."

Wes contemplated the fence with quiet satisfaction. "There's no limit to what a man can do once he makes up his mind he ain't allergic to sweat." He did not tarry long at self-congratulation. He pitched the come-along into the bed of the pickup, where it made enough clatter to wake Pepper and bring him out from his nap beneath the vehicle. The dog wagged his tail, expecting to go home. But Wes took two hammers and a sack of steeples out of the pickup. "Let's be gettin' after it. The sooner done, the sooner we celebrate."

"Celebrate?"

"I thought we'd drive into town and have supper at Old Grandma Lacy's café. She makes a good chicken-fried steak. Might want to wash it down with a beer or two while we look at her granddaughter Stella. You've seen Stella, ain't you?"

"I've seen her. None of that sounds good for your heart. Especially looking at Stella."

"The best thing for my heart is gettin' this fence finished. I hope some of the lake crowd *is* in that plane. They can look at this job and know I ain't fixin' to give up."

Jim Ed grimaced, his gaze following the plane. They wouldn't fight Wes out here at this fence. This ranch was *his* turf. They would fight him in the courtroom. That was theirs.

He saw a fleeting doubt cross his grandfather's face as he watched the plane disappear. Wes could handle anything that came at him on his land. He had handled bad horses and wild cattle, had weathered drouth and down markets. But a courtroom fight was as alien to him as Jim Ed's bookkeeping methods had been. Wes said, "A man can't do everything himself. I know I can't shear a sheep. When shearin' time comes, I hire Ol' Esteban Rodriguez and his crew. When my pickup needs workin' on, I take it to Whitey's garage. For this fight, I hired John Talcott, the best lawyer in town."

Jim Ed held a U-shaped steeple in place around a barbed wire and tried to hammer it into the hard cedar post. One side bit in, but the other resisted so that the steeple bent over. He pulled it out and started again with a fresh steeple. The impact lifted dust from the post's dry bark. He had to stop and sneeze. When he finished and stepped back, Pepper came to sniff at the fallen, bent steeple, then left his signature at the bottom of the post.

Wes said, "He marks his territory, and I mark mine. They ain't fixin' to run either one of us off." Wes hammered a steeple with an effort that bordered on violence. He moved down to another post, taking out his anger on hammer and steeples. For a time he and Jim Ed leapfrogged past one another until they reached the point they had finished the day before. They started back the way they had come, using pinchers to twist short pieces of galvanized wire around the stays that supported the fence in the broad spaces between the posts. Jim Ed kept watching his grandfather's face for any dangerous degree of fatigue. The old man must be dog-tired, but his determination to finish kept the adrenalin pumping. Jim Ed stood back and let Wes have the satisfaction of tying the last stay. Wes stepped away from the fence, his hands on his hips, and declared, "They'll play hell takin' *that* down."

Jim Ed nodded, but he could say nothing in support. He heard the faraway drone of the airplane engine.

Wes said, "Well, let's load up. I can already taste that steak."

Jim Ed made a point to do all the heavier lifting, putting the tools into the pickup, and the extra roll of barbed wire. Finished, he saw Wes leaning on a fencepost, absorbed in watching something down toward the river. Wes pointed. "Ol' Snort. He's in the edge of that brush yonder. He'll be comin' out directly."

Jim Ed marveled sometimes over the way the old man's eyes could pick up something that his own much younger eyes had missed. He had to stare at a fixed point and wait for movement to show him where the buck deer was. After a lengthy wait he saw a patch of grayish-brown as the animal edged cautiously out of the timber's dense cover. The rack of antlers blended with the low branches of the liveoaks and the native pecan trees. Snort moved forward a few feet at a time, stopping to jerk his head from one side to the other, alert for any threat.

Pepper came to full attention, spotting the deer. Wes mumbled, "Pepper, you hold still." The dog sat, unwillingly.

The deer moved farther out into the open, finally dropping his head to pick up a mouthful of grass, then raising it quickly to continue his vigil while he chewed. A pair of does moved from the brush but remained behind him as if for protection.

Wes smiled. The anxiety, the fatigue were gone from his face. Observing that deer, he was at peace. Jim Ed could not bring himself to watch old Snort; he was compelled to watch his grandfather instead, and to enjoy the contentment in the old man's eyes.

He became suddenly conscious of an engine's roar. He saw the plane flying back low over the trees that lined the river. He saw the buck go into a panic and race toward the fence. Not used to its being there, he ran into it and bounced back, going to the ground. He jumped to his feet and started again. Jim Ed heard his grandfather's voice, taut with anxiety. "High, Snort. Jump high!"

The buck leaped, bringing its hind legs up under its belly. It did not leap high enough. The hind legs slipped between the two barbed wires at the top of the fence. The deer crashed down on the other side, its legs entangled.

Wes wheezed, "My God!" and hobbled toward the pickup as fast as his legs would carry him. He did not give Jim Ed time to get around to the other side. Jim Ed grabbed onto the tailgate and jumped up into the bed with the tools and wire. The dog made a running leap and joined him as Wes stepped on the accelerator and bounced down the fenceline. Jim Ed took hold of the welded headache rack and hung on.

Dust swirled around the pickup as Wes braked to a quick stop. The buck threshed in agony. At a glance Jim Ed knew both of its hind legs had been broken by the momentum of the leap, and now the sharp barbs lacerated them as the animal struggled helplessly against the unyielding grip of the wires.

Wes got out and stared, his jaw sagging. Jim Ed climbed down and joined him, listening to the buck's thin bleats of pain and bewilderment. Tears tracked through the dust on Wes's leathered cheeks. His voice was so quiet Jim Ed could barely hear him. "Tater, I wisht you'd go fetch my rifle."

Jim Ed got the .30-.30 Wes always carried on the pickup's window rack. He levered a cartridge into the chamber. "You want me to do it?"

Wes shook his head. "Ol' Snort's my friend. I'll do it."

Jim Ed looked away as his grandfather brought the rifle to his shoulder. The explosion echoed back from the hills. It was followed by the drone of the engine as the plane circled around, still low. Wes looked up, and Jim Ed saw him lift the rifle as if to bring it back to his shoulder.

"Daddoo," he said, "don't."

Wes shook his head. "Wouldn't help much, would it? They'd have me for sure then." He handed Jim Ed the smoking rifle and walked toward the still form of the deer. Jim Ed got an iron bar from the vehicle and shoved it between the two top wires of the fence, twisting them to free the animal's legs. The deer's body slumped to the ground on the other side of the fence in a small pool of blood.

Wes stared. His voice was strained. "I never once thought

about a thing like this happenin'. I built the fence to *save* this place, not to kill anything."

Jim Ed could not help staring at those big antlers and thinking how much some city hunter would have paid Wes for a chance to take that trophy home. He felt ashamed; that was an accountant for you, thinking about the money. He placed his hand on his grandfather's thin shoulder. "You don't want to just leave him here for the buzzards."

"We'll drag him off out yonder to that clear spot where there's no grass to catch fire. We'll pile dead brush over him and burn him."

Later, watching the gray smoke billow up, Jim Ed listened for the plane but no longer heard it. His grandfather was looking back toward the fence. "You believe in signs, Tater?"

"I believe in signs that say 'Sharp curve ahead,' or 'Watch for fallen rock.'"

"I'm talkin' about omens, like good luck ahead, or bad luck."

"I wouldn't know how to read those."

"I'm readin' one now . . . Ol' Snort and that fence. He was a wild thing, used to bein' free. A wild thing dies when you coop him up. The way *I'd* die if they tried to put me in a nursin' home or some such, like they do so many old men. I'd rather somebody'd shoot me, like I done for Ol' Snort."

He turned back toward the pickup. Morosely he said, "I hope you didn't have your heart set on that chicken-fried steak. I've kind of lost my appetite."

Chapter 10

Stunned, Glory B. stood at the front door and stared through its antique oval glass at the man sitting in the black Cadillac on the graveled driveway. She turned back to her mother. "You're married?" she exclaimed.

Madeline raised her left hand. The wedding ring's stone was large, but her eyes shone even brighter. They made her look ten years younger. "Yesterday, in San Antonio. We decided to do it in a low profile. The only witnesses were a law partner and his wife. They were the ones who introduced us."

Hurt made its way into Glory B.'s voice. "You could have invited Gram and me." She glanced up the stairs, where Lavinia Dawson had lain in her bedroom most of the day, not feeling well enough even to come down for meals.

"I wasn't sure how either of you might feel about it," Madeline said. "Your grandmother because I am her son's widow and you because you could never see another man in your father's place. As I told you before, darling, Adam is not taking your father's place. No one could. But he has made a place of his own."

Glory B.'s hands were shoved deeply into the pockets of her jeans. "I can't say I didn't see it coming, sort of." She looked up the stairs again. "How did *she* take it?"

"She kissed me and wished me well. She said she didn't know why I had waited so long."

"Why did you?"

"You, mostly. Before, you would have hit the roof. But here of late you've seemed happier than I've seen you since your father died. It's that Jim Ed Hendrix, I suppose."

"I suppose." Glory B. looked away lest her eyes betray a lot more. Her mother would have been shocked if she'd known how many times Glory B. had been to Liveoak Camp with Jim Ed in the last few weeks. But she was not ashamed. It was not the same as that affair in school had been.

The man had gotten out of the car. He leaned against the open door, nervously smoking a cigarette. He wore a business suit that even from here Glory B. could see had been made to order for him; it had not been bought off a store's rack.

Glory B. said, "I won't bite him. You should invite him in."

"I will. I don't want him to leave here feeling that he's caused a rift between you and me; he doesn't deserve a guilt trip like that. But first I want to explain to you how it is with me."

"You don't have to explain anything. You're a grown woman, and I think I am."

"But I want to. You know I loved your father. Otherwise I could not have stayed here so long. I tried, but I never really fitted in with this life. I never contributed much to the ranch. After your father died, the only thing which held me here was you. I knew you would be miserable anywhere else, and I couldn't have gone without taking you."

Glory B. twisted her hands and felt ashamed. She had never considered that Madeline might have been making a sacrifice on her behalf. She wondered if she had ever really known her mother, if she had ever really *tried* to know her.

Madeline said, "Now you don't need me anymore, at least not as you once did. You can make your own way, and do it better without my being here as a drag on you. I've been a constant worry to your grandmother too."

Glory B. protested that it was not so, but she knew her mother and grandmother had little in common except a family name that both had acquired through marriage. When they had not been able to see alike, it had usually been her mother who had given in, and Lavinia who had had to suffer the guilt of winning.

Madeline said, "There was a void in my life after I lost your father. Now Adam makes me feel fulfilled again."

Glory B. hesitantly placed a hand on her mother's arm. "I understand."

"No, you don't really, and you never will because you're stronger and more independent-minded than I could ever be. I can't get along without someone to lean on. You could get along without anyone, if you had to. I am not at all sure I envy you that." She walked to the door. "I am going to call Adam in now. I hope you'll make him understand that there are no hard feelings."

"There aren't."

She had seen Adam Lattingham before, through an angry veil of resentment. Now she could see him as a man who looked amazingly like her father, strong and tall and well-featured. He seemed a man who could hold his own in a courtroom, but at the moment he was apprehensive and vulnerable in the face of a new stepdaughter's judgment. He stood just inside the door, hands nervously clasped in front of him.

Glory B. gave him a quiet study. "I can't call you Dad, and it would seem childish to call you Uncle."

"My friends just call me Adam."

"I'm your friend, Adam," Glory B. said. She took two long strides and hugged him.

He was a moment getting past the surprise and responding with an embrace that almost squeezed the breath out of her. He said with relief, "I've been up against judges that made me nervous, but none I ever dreaded quite so much as you, young lady."

"You just keep my mother happy and you'll have nothing to dread from me."

He looked toward Madeline. His eyes had the same buoyant shine as hers. "I intend to do my best."

After the goodbyes, Glory B. stood in the open door and watched the black car as long as it was in sight on the packed-caliche road toward town. She was left with an unsettling ambiguity, a pleasure in her mother's happiness, compromised by a feeling that a door had closed on a part of her past and would never open again.

She walked up the stairs and paused in the open doorway of her grandmother's room. Lavinia Dawson lay on the bed. She wore a dress but had her shoes off. A sweater lay spread across her legs, a tribute to failing blood circulation. Her eyes were open and fixed sternly upon Glory B. She said, "I heard the car. Are they gone?"

"They're gone."

Severely she said, "I hope you didn't let your mother leave here with any bad feelings between you."

"No. I hugged her. I hugged them both. They left happy."

A thin smile came to her grandmother's face. "I'm glad. I thought about getting up and going down to be sure, but I decided you're a woman now. I shouldn't have to point out your responsibilities."

Glory B. moved closer to her grandmother's bed. "But what about you, Gram? Dad was your son. It's got to make you feel awkward, seeing her married now to a stranger."

"The past can be like a crutch sometimes, when you're in need of comfort to get you through a long, dark night. But it's no substitute for the daylight. When you open your eyes you're back in the present, and you have to live in it. You should always remember your father and honor him, but you can't expect your mother to spend the rest of her life in mourning. She's still a young woman, by my standards if not by yours. Do you understand?"

"I think so. I'm trying, anyway."

"You've always taken pride in doing for yourself—too much pride sometimes. Your mother tried to mold you to her pattern but never could. She had to let you go your own way. Now you have to let *her* go."

"I will. I guess I just did."

"That's my girl." Lavinia beckoned for Glory B. to lean over and kiss her, and raised up to meet her halfway. The old lady suddenly gasped and fell back, both hands going to her stomach. Glory B. thought she went two shades paler.

"Gram, what is it?"

Lavinia was a moment in answering. Her eyelids were tightly closed, her face twisted. When she opened her eyes, tears glistened. She took in a long, slow breath, then expelled it. Her hands pressed against her stomach. "I think you'd better get me to town."

Trembling, Glory B. reached for the telephone directory. She fumbled with the pages until she found the one which listed the doctor's number, then accidentally let the book flip shut. Tears blurred her eyes; she knew she would be unable to read the number anyway. She quickly dialed the Roper house. "Hallie? Something's the matter with Gram. I've got to get her to town. Is Bill around?"

Hallie's voice reflected Glory B.'s alarm. "No, he and Johnny are out working some young horses. Hang on. I'll be right there."

"Call the doctor first, please. Tell him we're coming."

"I will. You keep hold of yourself. Don't panic."

Almost before Glory B. could help her grandmother up from the bed and into her shoes, Hallie was rushing up the stairs, taking the steps two at a time. She paused only for a quick glance at Lavinia's face, gone almost gray, and put an arm around her. "Miz Livvy, you just hold tight." She helped Glory B. support Lavinia down the stairs, through the hallway and out to the drive. She took Glory B.'s keys and hurried to the garage.

Lavinia leaned heavily on Glory B. Even so, she turned to survey her flowerbed. "It's gone," she said sadly. "It's gone."

"What's gone, Gram?"

"The last bluebonnet."

"Bluebonnet?" Under the strain Glory B. could not comprehend what her grandmother was talking about.

Lavinia said, "There was still one left here yesterday, way past its season. I guess its time just came. Like mine."

"Don't talk that way, Gram. The doctor will fix you up."

"He can't take twenty years off of my life. He can't take back a day of it, any more than I could put blossoms back on the bluebonnets."

Hallie drove up, jumped out and opened the car's rear door. She helped put Lavinia into the back seat. "I'll drive," she told Glory B. "You sit with your grandmother."

"You're a friend, Hallie."

Hallie blinked back tears as she studied the slumped form of

Lavinia Dawson, the jaw set hard in defiance of pain. "*She* is the friend," she said.

They pulled away from the house in a shower of gravel. Half a mile up the road they came upon Bill Roper and Johnny. Johnny was exercising Glory B.'s colt. Hallie slowed but did not stop. "Hospital!" she shouted at her husband, and drove on. Glory B. looked back through the rear window and the dust. She saw Bill put his horse into a run toward the house. Johnny struggled to catch up.

Big River's small hospital had become a clinic. Once it had kept two doctors busy, but now there was only one, and when long hospitalization was needed he usually sent his patients to San Angelo or Kerrville or San Antonio. Glory B. sat with Hallie in the waiting room while the doctor examined Lavinia behind closed doors. Glory B. drummed her fingers on her knees, pulled her knuckles, got up and looked out the window a dozen times. Hallie stared absently into a motorcycle magazine, old and crinkled and torn. Glory B. knew Hallie had as much interest in motorcycles as in deep-sea diving.

Bill Roper and Johnny arrived presently. Roper looked to Hallie, asking with his eyes. She answered silently with a slight shrug. Glory B. had long marveled at the easy way Bill and Hallie had of communicating without words, almost as if thoughts moved from one mind to the other. She envied them that closeness. Bill squeezed Glory B.'s shoulder, then sat down beside Hallie and placed his arm around her. She leaned to him. No one had spoken.

Johnny stood with hat in his hand, a little frightened. Lavinia Dawson had always been a fact of his life, as steady and dependable as the passage of his days, and as close as his own two grandmothers. Glory B. motioned for him to sit beside her. She hugged him, and he gave her none of his shy resistance.

Glory B. had looked at the wall clock a hundred times before the doctor came out. He walked straight to Glory B. His face was grave, telling most of it before he spoke. "I've called the hospital in San Angelo. They'll have a room waiting for your grandmother as soon as you can get her there."

Glory B. stood up quickly. "Do you know what's wrong?"

"I think so, but I'd rather leave the diagnosis for someone more specialized than I." His face creased. "This didn't just start today. She's been hurting for some time, hasn't she?"

Glory B. nodded. "She wouldn't tell us anything."

"I wish she had, a lot sooner. But that's their way, most of those hardy oldtimers. They won't quit until they fall and can't get up."

As never before in her life, Glory B. felt the stab of real fear. She saw it reflected in the eyes of Hallie and Bill.

Hallie said, "We'll go with you."

Glory B. shook her head. "There's no telling how long this may take. Right now we need you-all more at the ranch." She moved toward a pay telephone in the corner. "I'll call Jim Ed."

Wes and Jim Ed were waiting in Wes's old green pickup out on the highway. Glory B. pulled over to the shoulder, glancing at her grandmother in the backseat. Lavinia appeared half asleep. The doctor had given her something to ease the pain. Glory B. stepped out of the car, and Jim Ed put his arms around her. She leaned to him for comfort, and cried a little. Wes hobbled across the highway and bent to peer anxiously through the rear window at Lavinia. When he straightened, he looked back down the road instead of at Glory B. and Jim Ed. What he had seen had shaken him. He said huskily, "You-all better go."

Jim Ed pulled from Glory B.'s arms and opened the back door. "You stay with your grandmother. I'll drive."

Wes hugged Glory B. "If I can do anything . . ." There was nothing he could do, but it was a thing people said. The gesture was futile, the compassion genuine. Glory B. saw a deep sadness in Wes Hendrix's eyes.

She looked back as they drove away. Wes was still standing beside his pickup the last she saw of him.

True to the doctor's word, the staff in the San Angelo hospital's emergency room was expecting them. Lavinia Dawson stared forlornly at her granddaughter while a nurse checked pulse and blood pressure. Glory B. barely had time to give Lavinia a kiss before they wheeled her away. Glory B. watched a pair of white doors swing open, then close behind her grandmother, hiding her from view.

Almost always, she had known what to do next in any situation

she confronted. Seldom had she doubted her ability to stand up
and master a challenge. Here, staring at the sterile and empty
whiteness of those tall doors, she was helpless. She felt as if the
ground were caving away beneath her feet. Too many doors had
closed in front of her today, shutting her off first from her
mother, now from her grandmother.

Jim Ed had written down the number of the room assigned to
Lavinia. Putting his arm around Glory B., he took her there, and
she clung to him in numbed silence through the two long hours
before Lavinia was at last wheeled into the room and gently
placed on the bed, drugged into sleep.

A nurse said, "They'll run full tests tomorrow. She'll sleep until
morning. I think you young people had as well go somewhere and
do the same thing."

Glory B. bent to study her grandmother's face. It was pale and
peaceful and betrayed no pain. She turned back to Jim Ed.

He said, "Come on, then. There's nothing more you can do for
her tonight."

She leaned against him in the car until he pulled up to a motel a
few blocks from the hospital. He said, "I'll go see if I can get us
some rooms."

She clasped his hand. "Not rooms . . . just room. Stay with
me tonight, Jim Ed." She put her head against his shoulder. "I
need you!"

The next day was long and devoid of news. Jim Ed watched
with helpless sympathy as Glory B. sat numb and silent through
the hours that Lavinia was out of the room. Once he took her
outside, against her protests, walking with her to the Concho
River for fresh air and exercise. They lunched in the hospital
cafeteria, where Glory B. picked at her plate and left most of the
food uneaten. Early in the afternoon, hoping the history might
divert her attention for a while, he took her to old Fort Concho, a
well-preserved frontier post that had been home to the Indian-
fighting cavalry a century and more ago. They walked through
the museum and among the old stone buildings, but always Glory
B.'s gaze went back in the direction of the hospital.

Sitting in the empty room, they talked from time to time,

though Glory B.'s conversation rambled; her mind was not on it. Every sound in the corridor brought her to attention. Footsteps that seemed to be approaching the door would bring her eyes wide open in expectation, then leave her disappointed as they passed on by.

Orderlies brought Lavinia into the room at midafternoon. She was awake but sedated. The orderlies professed to know nothing, though Glory B. questioned them with all the insistence of a Texas Ranger. The nurse who came to check Lavinia's pulse said all she knew was on the chart. That was confined to pulse rate, temperature and medication administered.

It was near suppertime when a doctor came, making his rounds. He was infuriatingly evasive. He used long words Jim Ed had never heard in accounting courses. When he left, the only information he had imparted was that Lavinia would be taken to surgery at seven in the morning.

Lavinia patted Glory B.'s trembling hand. Jim Ed wondered if the trembling came from anger, fatigue or fear. Lavinia had said little since her return from the tests. Now she admonished, "Don't you be fretting so, girl. There's nothing any of us can do now except leave it up to the Lord and the doctor."

"That's not good enough, Gram. I've always been able to do *something*."

"You're grown now. It's time you learn that you can't always carry the whole load on your own shoulders. There are occasions when you just have to stand back and wait while someone else does something." Lavinia's gaze went to Jim Ed. "Has she eaten anything today?"

"Very little."

"She'll be a patient in here with me, first thing you know. I want you to take her somewhere for supper. Don't let her up from the table till she's eaten it all."

Jim Ed tried to smile, but it wasn't in him. "I'll see to it."

Lavinia said, "They'll be giving me something in a little while to make me sleep, so there's no use in you-all coming back here tonight. Jim Ed, I want you to see that she goes to bed early."

"I will."

Glory B. kissed her grandmother and walked to the door. She

looked back with regret, not wanting to leave. Lavinia waved her on. "Go now. You need your rest, and I need mine."

Jim Ed held the door for Glory B. Lavinia crooked her finger. "Jim Ed, I want to speak to you for a minute."

Jim Ed's eyes met Glory B.'s. Hers held a question but no answers. She went on out into the corridor. He walked back to the bed. Lavinia reached for his hand. He gave it nervously.

The old lady's brown eyes were amazingly strong, he thought, for the pain she had endured, and the medication. She gave him a moment's intense study. "Now, don't get the idea that I am criticizing you. I sense that you've been *making* love with Glory B. It shows all over both of you. But do you *love* her?"

He felt heat come to his face, and he stammered. "Yes. Yes, ma'am, I do."

Lavinia's hand tightened on his with a strength he had not anticipated. She said, "Glory B.'s never talked to me about it, but I know she's been hurt in the past. She's tried to build up a wall high enough that nothing can reach her. But no wall is that high. I know, because I built one myself. She needs help."

"I'll do whatever I can."

"Be patient, then. Be gentle, and be *there*."

Jim Ed tried to be optimistic with Glory B., but long before the doctor came out to report to them about the operation, he had a strong premonition that the prognosis would be dark. He kept a protective arm around Glory B. He felt her stiffen as the impact hit her. She clasped her hands tightly, the knuckles going white, but she held her head high and did not take her eyes from the doctor. She kept her composure with pride and dignity until they were back in Lavinia's room, the door closed. Her grandmother was still in recovery, so they had the room to themselves. She fell into Jim Ed's waiting arms. He held her in a grim silence and made no attempt to interfere while she cried herself out.

Lavinia Dawson was conscious when orderlies and a nurse wheeled her in. Glory B. summoned strength to smile and put on a show of humor for her grandmother. "We had about decided you up and ran off with the doctor. He's handsome enough."

Jim Ed was at a loss for anything intelligent to say. "That's what we thought, all right."

Lavinia's voice was weak, but her will had not flagged. "You don't have to pretend. He's told me."

Glory B. laid her cheek against her grandmother's. She cried, "Oh, Gram!"

Lavinia raised her hand and gently ran her fingers through Glory B.'s hair. "There now, it comes to all of us sometime. I'd like to stay awhile longer and spoil all your babies, but I can't, so that's that. The Lord let me spoil *you*. I couldn't have asked for better."

"Gram, I don't know how I'd ever get along without you. There are so many things I need to know."

"I've taught you as much as I could. The rest, you'll have to learn the way I did. I only wish I could've held out until the ranch was secure for you. My father left me a going concern. I'm leaving you a mess."

Glory B. cried, "I don't care about that. I just care about you."

Lavinia held her while Jim Ed stood in awkward silence. He decided at length to go out into the corridor and leave them their privacy. As he reached the door, Lavinia called, "Jim Ed. Wait." He turned back.

She said, "I don't want your grandfather to hear about this from someone besides family. I want *you* to tell him, the gentlest way you know how."

Jim Ed's jaw went slack. He wanted to ask why, but no sound came.

Lavinia said, "You don't know about your grandfather and me, do you? Not many do, anymore. I knew Wes Hendrix long before he ever met your grandmother, and before I ever met Tol Dawson. He was a cowboy for my father, over at Liveoak Camp. We were in love with each other once, or thought we were. We would have been married if he hadn't been strong enough to recognize the mistake we were about to make and call it off."

Jim Ed caught his breath. "*You* were the one. The one in the old picture."

"Old picture?"

"He has an old picture of him with a girl. I just thought . . . ."

He caught himself before he blurted that he had assumed the girl in the picture was Noreen Levitt.

Lavinia sighed. "You mean he kept that picture, all these years?" A smile slowly came across her face, and she stared up at the ceiling in silence. He knew it was not the ceiling she saw, but old memories carefully stored away, safe from the hazards of time. She said, "I was hurt for a while, deeply hurt. But in time I came to see that he was right. I met Tol Dawson, and he met Maudie. That was the way things were meant to be.

"We've been friends for all these years, good friends. But I never forgot the way it was with us once. I suppose Wes never forgot either, or he wouldn't still have the picture."

Glory B. said with wonder, "Gram, I never knew. I never even suspected."

"It was better that way, at least until you were old enough to understand. I have no regrets over the way things turned out. If Wes hadn't stopped us before we went too far, I would never have married your grandfather. Your father would never have been born, and neither would you." She looked first at Glory B., then at Jim Ed. "I guess it's fitting that another generation finds what we had, and what we lost."

Jim Ed worried all the way home about the manner in which he might break the news to Wes. He found his anxiety had not been necessary. Wes met him at the front steps after Bill Roper let him out of the pickup. Bill had offered to stay awhile, but Jim Ed had told him to go on; Bill had his own sorrows to deal with. One look at Wes's solemn face told Jim Ed that his grandfather had already guessed.

Wes said, "She's not goin' to make it, is she?"

Jim Ed's throat suddenly went so tight that he could not speak. He simply shook his head.

Wes nodded dully and turned away, staring out across the pasture. He made no sound except to clear his throat. In a while he asked, "How long?"

Jim Ed found his voice, a hollow one. "It's hard to predict. They just sewed her up. They found the cancer too far gone to be operable."

Wes still faced away from him. His gnarled hands opened and closed. "I figured I'd be the first one, with this bum ticker and all. But the last couple of times I seen her, I knew. It showed in her eyes."

The eyes. Jim Ed remembered, suddenly. It had been the eyes that had struck him most about the girl in that old picture. He walked into the house and went to the cardboard box where he had left the collection of old photographs. He riffled through them until he found it. He turned it so that it caught the light. He realized why he had not recognized those eyes when he had looked at the picture before; he had barely known Glory B. then.

Now he could see a little of Lavinia Dawson, the Lavinia Dawson he knew. But the eyes . . . they were the eyes of Glory B.

Wes hobbled in and looked at the picture. Quietly he said, "No reason you shouldn't know now. That is Livvy."

"She told us."

Wes blinked. "She did? All of it?"

Jim Ed shrugged. "I don't know about *all* of it. I don't know how much there was to tell."

Sternly Wes said, "I want you to know that there wasn't nothin' casual about it, or cheap like so many today. We just kind of fell into it. She would come over to Liveoak Camp when we was workin', and then she got to comin' when we *wasn't* workin'. One thing sort of led to another. We was just two kids who didn't know much about the world. We just knew the way we felt. We knew we was supposed to feel ashamed, but we didn't. We just loved one another, and nothin' else mattered. Not for a while, anyway."

"You were the one who broke it up. Why?"

"I'd left the ranch and gone to rodeoin' for a livin', and makin' damned poor money at it. I got to thinkin' about how different she was raised. All I'd ever done was work for cowboy wages or foller the rodeos. As far as I could see ahead, that was all I'd ever do. It was poor pickin's for a well-raised woman like her. Ol' Major Chatfield told her, but she wouldn't listen to him. Finally *I* had to tell her, and she had to listen. Love feels fine in the bedroom, but it don't hold up well in an empty kitchen.

"I grieved awhile when she married Tol Dawson, but I could

see the right in it, too. Then I met your grandmother, and I knew I'd made no mistake."

"Hasn't it been kind of awkward, you-all living so close together all these years?"

"Not really. We'd both found somethin' we wanted. Wasn't no reason to dwell on old times."

He turned away, clearing his throat again. Jim Ed watched him with concern. "But it hurts to see old things go, doesn't it?"

Wes slumped into his recliner. "When you get to my age that's about all you've got left, is old times and memories." His voice took on almost an angry edge. "There damned sure ain't much *future* out there." He stared across the room at the mantle, where so many old photographs stood. "You know why I've fought them so hard on this lake thing? It's the land, sure, because I love this place. But it's more than just the land; it's the memories that are tied up in it. This place keeps the memories alive.

"If I was to leave here and go live in the city the way your daddy wants me to, I'm afraid the memories would fade. They'd be like trees with their roots cut off; they'd dry up and die. So would I. I need the land. That's where all my roots are."

Jim Ed wished he could give Wes some kind of assurance, but he had none. One day they would come with their bulldozers. It might be a week, a month, a year . . . but they would come.

Wes said, "I had a call from my lawyer. Talcott says he's set up a conference of some kind. Wants me to meet him at his office tomorrow mornin'."

"How did he sound?"

"You never can tell with lawyers. They're like poker players; it's part of their game to make you guess what they're thinkin'. It keeps you on your left foot all the time."

Jim Ed could honestly say, "I hope he has good news," though he strongly suspected otherwise.

Wes said, "With a horse or a cow or a sheep, I can pretty well tell what they're fixin' to do. But I never had much truck with lawyers."

Jim Ed started to place the picture back in the box. Wes beckoned him. "I wisht you'd bring that here." He reached over to a small end table for his reading glasses. "If you don't mind, I'll let you do the milkin' and the feedin' this evenin'. I'm kind of down in my back."

"Sure," Jim Ed said.

As he walked out the door with the milk bucket, he looked back. His grandfather was studying the old picture. Later, when he had fed the horses and was walking toward the house with the bucket half full of milk, he heard music. It was not the television or the record player. It was Wes Hendix's old fiddle. The melody was the same slow, sad piece Jim Ed remembered hearing the night he first arrived.

Faded Love.

A catch came to his throat again. He walked back to the barn and sat on the step. He patted Pepper on the head and gave his grandfather time to play out his grief alone.

Chapter 11

For the third time since opening his drugstore at eight-thirty, Orville Levitt walked to the plateglass window and looked out upon the quiet street. His thin rump prickled with anxiety, and he rubbed a hand over his face. He found it sweaty, though the morning's heat was only beginning to rise. His wife Noreen was counting cosmetics, jotting notes on a pad. She arched an eyebrow. "You look as nervous as a politician at the Pearly Gates. What're you watchin' for, anyway?"

"Got a meetin' over in John Talcott's office at nine-thirty. Official business. Just lookin' for somebody who's supposed to be there and hopin' he shows up in time."

"Somebody I'd know?"

"Yep," he said, offering her no further information. She gave him a look of silent rebuke and went back to counting face powders and creams. She had never taken kindly to being left out of things, whether of a personal or a municipal nature, and sometimes he had to remind her that being a mayor's wife did not make her a member of the council. She might as well have been granted a vote. At one time or another she had presided over every important woman's club in town. These were a political force overlooked only at an elected official's peril.

Outside the store, Sheriff Wally Vincent stopped a moment, his gaze sweeping up and down the street, taking in the scant traffic. Levitt, watching through the big glass, read an impatient oath on

Vincent's lips as the lawman turned to the door. Vincent's gaze was fixed on Levitt's usual place at the pharmacy counter toward the rear. He jerked in surprise as he became aware that the druggist stood beside him, near enough to touch. He demanded, "Seen anything of him yet?"

"He's still got twenty minutes. It's a long ways from Dallas."

Noreen demanded, "Who is it that has you two comin' unraveled?"

Vincent blurted, "Truman Hendrix. He's supposed to be here and help us talk sense to his old daddy this mornin'."

Levitt gave the sheriff a frown. On certain matters it did not pay to volunteer too much information to Noreen. She would find out in due course anyway, through mysterious sources of her own, but sometimes if he could delay the information long enough, she did not have a chance to do anything about it.

She said sternly, "So you'll have the son become an accessory to you-all takin' that old man's ranch away."

Levitt had been through this argument with her a dozen times or more, and he did not want to get his stomach tied in a knot this morning even before the confrontation with Wes. He said, "You know it's for the good of the whole community."

"Sure," she replied sarcastically. "I know that's why Wally's so interested in it."

Vincent's face twitched, but he attempted no reply. Few people ever got the last word in an argument with Noreen Levitt.

Noreen's mouth went into a brittle little smile that always meant she was about to stick a barb into someone. "While you're waitin' for Truman, would you like some coffee, Wally?"

"I don't believe I'd care for any, thanks."

"Just thought you might. I hear you've been drinkin' an awful lot of coffee lately."

For a moment Vincent appeared puzzled, then his face reddened. He stalked out the door.

Levitt's stomach churned. This was fixing to be one hell of a morning. He walked back to his wife and demanded, "Now, what did you have to go and say a thing like that for?"

Her eyes were the image of innocence. "I just offered him some coffee."

"No, you offered him a needle, and twisted it off in him."

"Well, everybody knows he's been spendin' more time over at Old Grandma Lacy's café than in his office. And everybody knows it isn't Old Grandma Lacy's coffee he's interested in."

"You're hintin' about Stella Tenney. Wally Vincent's not the only man who likes to go and exercise his eyes lookin' at her. I've dropped in over there myself from time to time."

"At your age, all you can do is look. But Wally's got all the instincts of an alleycat. I wish you didn't have to have anything to do with him."

Levitt had no quarrel with that wish; it crossed his mind every time he found himself in the sheriff's company. But he said curtly, "If a lot of women in this town spent more time takin' care of their homes and families, they wouldn't have time to make up so damned much idle gossip."

"There's nothin' idle about *this* gossip," she said, "and not much idle about Stella Tenney, either."

Levitt grumbled, "There's one thing good about Stella Tenney livin' here."

"What could that be?" Noreen wanted to know.

"So long as the gossips are talkin' about *her,* they're leavin' somebody else alone. At least when she gets to our age she'll have somethin' to remember."

Noreen grinned wickedly. "What makes you think *I* don't?"

Levitt knew that was a bluff. At least, he *thought* it was a bluff. He gave her a long study while she continued with her inventory. Well, hell, even if it wasn't, that had been too long ago to bother him now. *Today* was enough to worry about.

The clock showed twenty-five minutes after nine when a gray Buick pulled up just beyond the space reserved for the bus. Truman Hendrix got out and exercised both legs a minute. His gray business suit, usually neat, was badly rumpled. It was plain that he had been behind the steering wheel for some time. His furrowed face bore some superficial resemblance to his father's but had the pale color of a man who spends most of his day indoors. Levitt reflected that it never seemed right for Truman to be middle-aged. He still wanted to remember him as a schoolboy, coming in for an ice cream cone or a frosted Coke, often with his brother James Edward. Even as a boy, Truman had always looked as if he were working on his first ulcer. By contrast, James Edward never seemed to spend three minutes worrying about anything. That the Lord had chosen to take life from a boy who enjoyed it so, Levitt had never understood.

Truman's face showed that he dreaded the morning as much or more than Levitt did. He glanced toward the drugstore with obvious misgivings, then walked slowly in that direction.

Levitt met him at the door. "Good mornin', Truman. It's almost time."

Apologetically Wes Hendrix's accountant son reached forward to shake hands. "It's a long way here from Dallas. I left after office hours yesterday and stopped for the night in Brownwood. To tell you the truth, I didn't sleep much."

"Neither did I," Levitt admitted. "It's not a pleasant business."

"But it has to be done."

"I take it you haven't seen your daddy yet."

Truman shook his head. "I thought it would be best for me to stay out of sight until the rest of you have talked to him. If he knew I was here he would smell a rat and wouldn't even come in."

Noreen broke in. "Well, *I* smell a rat. You-all are just goin' to gang up and overpower him, is that it?"

Levitt and Truman glanced at one another uneasily. Levitt wished he knew how to shut her up, but he had been trying that for close to fifty years. He could only hope that she would not chance to see Wes this morning before the rest of them did.

Truman said, "It's for his own good, Noreen. He's too old to be trying to run that place by himself. We'll find him dead out there one of these days, fallen off of his horse and lying in the middle of a pasture."

Noreen replied, "Seems to me like that's just the way he'd want it."

Wally Vincent came back, standing in the doorway, his gaze searching for Truman. "Seen your car. I was wonderin' if you was ever goin' to get here."

Truman stiffened a little. He and Vincent had known each other as boys. James Edward had skinned his knuckles on

Vincent's chin a couple of times. Truman had always simply turned his back. He said defensively, "Dallas is a long way."

"Not any too far to suit me. The sooner you get that old man away from here, the better I'll like it."

Noreen interjected, "Guilty conscience, Wally?"

Vincent tried to ignore her. But she would not be ignored. She declared, "We always try to hate people we set out to rob. Kind of makes it easier on our conscience."

Levitt could see anger working the cords in Vincent's neck, though the sheriff restrained himself from making any reply. Levitt said, "Aren't you about through with your inventory, Noreen?"

She crumpled the note pad in one hand. "In other words, mind my own business."

Truman hastily declared, "We didn't say that, Noreen. But we're thinking of the community, and of my father's welfare too, even if he doesn't know it." He turned to Levitt. "I must say I'm a little surprised that John Talcott finally came around to agreeing with us."

Levitt shrugged. "He saw he couldn't win. And he saw in the long run that it would be to Wes's benefit."

Noreen's voice retained its bite. "I'm glad I won't have to be there to see Wes's face when he realizes what you-all are fixin' to do to him."

Truman said, "He'll be grateful to us someday."

She sniffed. "When pigs fly."

Jim Ed saw the gray Buick parked near the Levitt drugstore and was momentarily startled. *It can't be,* he told himself. There were probably half a dozen gray Buicks in Big River just like his father's. He asked his grandfather, "Now, where is John Talcott's office?"

Wes raised his hand and pointed. "That's it yonder, on the next corner. Used to be a dry-goods store there. Town got too small for the store, but it's got more lawyers than it ever had."

The date on the building's square top said 1926, but the windows and the brick veneer that went up to awning level and stopped were of much more recent vintage. Whoever had planned the remodeling must have assumed that no one would look higher than that, Jim Ed thought. He pulled his grandmother Maudie's Ford in against the curb. He said, "You don't want me in there, do you?"

Wes frowned. "You got somethin' better to do?"

Across the street at a service station, Jim Ed could see Shorty Bigham's red doolie pickup raised up high on a grease rack. He thought he saw Shorty standing to one side, supervising the draining of the crankcase. "I haven't seen Shorty in a long time," he said. "I'd kind of like to talk to him." *Apologize to him* was more like it.

Wes said, "You been workin' on my books. John might raise some question you can answer, like how I'm goin' to pay him."

That, Jim Ed thought, *would* be a good question.

He gave Shorty Bigham a final regretful glance. If Shorty saw him, he gave no sign. John Talcott greeted Wes at the door. The attorney, about Wes's age, was not smiling. Jim Ed took that for an unfavorable sign. Talcott said evenly, "I'm glad you could come in, Wes. Maybe we can get this matter all cleared up today."

"It'd be a relief," Wes acknowledged, but his eyes mirrored an uneasiness like Jim Ed's.

Talcott looked at Jim Ed. "If you'd like to come back after a while, say an hour . . ."

Wes said, "I'd like Tater to stay. Anything I got'll be his, eventually."

Jim Ed discerned that Talcott had rather not have him, but the attorney deferred to Wes. "As you will. Come on back to the conference room then." He led the way past a middle-aged secretary who seemed to be working very hard at appearing busy and not looking up from her typewriter. Wes stopped in surprise in the doorway and glanced questioningly at Talcott. Jim Ed tried to see past him. He recognized Orville Levitt, Sheriff Wally Vincent and the banker Matthew Jamison.

Talcott said, "Wes, everybody here is your friend, whether you realize it at this moment or not. I've been in conference with them off and on for several days."

Stiffly Wes said, "I've had conferences with them too. They all know where I stand."

Talcott motioned toward two empty chairs. "Make yourself comfortable, Wes." He made no offer to Jim Ed, who suspected he was trying to rush the obligatory amenities and get the unpleasant business finished as quickly as possible. The attorney said, "Wes, I have studied the case thoroughly and have come to the reluctant conclusion that you cannot win. Your only course is to make the best settlement possible and bow out with grace."

Jim Ed watched his grandfather's face turn to stone.

Talcott said, "I have negotiated what I believe is better than a just compensation for your land. It is more than the appraised value by fully thirty percent, enough to pay what Matthew says you owe the bank and leave you a most generous retirement fund. That, together with the proceeds from the sale of your livestock and equipment, would set you up with more comfort than you have ever enjoyed in your life. And I'd say you've earned it." He pushed a thick contract across to Wes. "As your attorney, I have made the best possible deal for you, I think. I would strongly urge that you accept."

The nervous Jamison put in, "One more thing he did not mention, Wes: you will not be out any attorney fees. The water district will pay Mr. Talcott."

Wes's eyes narrowed, and his chin jutted stubbornly as he gave the lawyer a look of contempt. "I believe you already did." He cut his gaze back to Orville Levitt. "I suppose you had a hand in this, Orv?"

Levitt nodded uncertainly. "I wouldn't go along with it until they agreed to give you a healthy bonus for the land. I know how much it means to you."

"You don't." Wes's voice was near breaking. "You couldn't." He started pushing to his feet. "If you-all want my land, you're goin' to have to send *him* out to shoot me and *carry* me off." He pointed his chin toward Wally Vincent.

Jim Ed heard a commode flush behind a door in a corner of the room. The door opened, and Jim Ed caught a sharp breath. Wes froze, half out of his chair. "Truman!"

Truman Hendrix moved forward hesitantly, his hand extended. "Papa." Surprised, Wes was a moment in accepting the handshake. Truman then held out his hand to Jim Ed. "Hello, son."

Jim Ed took it. The best he could say was a weak, "Dad?" He wished he were back at the university.

Wes recovered first. His voice reflected hurt. "I suppose you're in on this with them, son?"

"Nobody's *in on* anything, Papa. It isn't like that. The town needs the lake. And you need off of that damned cedar pile before it kills you the way it killed my mother."

"Your mother was happy livin' on that cedar pile. She might've died years sooner, cooped up in a house in town."

"You heard what John said, Papa. You'll come out of this with more cash money than you've ever had your hands on. You can buy anything you want."

"What I want, I've already got. I just want to leave things the way they are. I wish everybody else could." He gave Orville Levitt another glance, more of pain than of anger.

Truman went on, "Things have changed for everybody else, Papa, and for the worse. The lake offers other people a chance to save things that are as important to them as that old ranch is to you. Once you're gone from it, you won't miss it half as much as you think. You'll have a chance to rest for the first time in your life, to sleep half the morning if you take the notion. You'll have all the time in the world. I want you to sign the papers, Papa."

Wes turned slowly to Jim Ed. "What do *you* say, Tater?"

Jim Ed tried to speak, but his throat seemed to close tight.

Truman said, "James Edward has nothing to say here, Papa. But he *would* have, if the case were to go to court."

Wes's eyes cut so hard that Jim Ed could not meet them. He looked at the floor. "Dad . . ." he pleaded.

Truman said, "I sent him here this summer to help you, Papa. But I also told him to keep watch on your physical condition and your mental condition, to serve as a witness if need be."

Wes's voice cut like his eyes. "To spy on me, is that right, Tater?"

Jim Ed struggled to find voice. "It's not like it sounds. He sent me here for that, but I haven't done it. I haven't told him a thing that would hurt you."

Wes seemed not to hear him. "I should've known. I should've put you back on the bus the day you first come." He raised his hand as if to strike, and Jim Ed stiffened, waiting for a blow that did not come. Wes pushed his chair back and stalked out of the room with a stride that belied his age.

Anger gave Jim Ed voice. He turned on his father. "Why didn't you just shoot him? It wouldn't have hurt him half as much. I hope to hell you're satisfied!" He ran out after his grandfather. "Daddoo! Wait!"

Wes stood on the street in front of Maudie's car, digging in his pockets.

Jim Ed called, "Wait. I've got to talk to you."

Wes's eyes still cut. "The keys," he said, raising his right hand with the palm up. "The car keys."

Jim Ed handed him the keys. "Daddoo, I want to explain."

Wes walked around the car and slid into the driver's seat. Jim Ed grabbed at the handle on the passenger side and found it locked. Wes started the engine, then sped away from the curb, leaving Jim Ed choking on dust the tires raised from the gutter. He wanted to cry out but realized it was no use.

He heard a door slam at the service station across the street. Shorty Bigham had just climbed into his big pickup. Jim Ed shouted, "Shorty!" and waved a hand to catch his attention. He ran across the street, dodging around a moving cattle truck that nearly choked him with its exhaust and the smell trailing it.

"Shorty," he exclaimed, "I need a favor."

Shorty frowned. "I already let you take Glory B. Ain't that favor enough?"

"You just saw my grandfather pull away. I've got to catch him."

"Didn't look to me like he much wanted you to."

"But I've got things to explain to him."

Shorty studied him a moment, then jerked his head. "Get in."

Shorty made a quick U-turn and started off in the direction Wes had taken. "I suppose he was headed back to the ranch?"

"It's the only place he has to go."

Shorty gunned the pickup into a speed well above the legal limit. "If Wally Vincent catches me, there'll be hell to pay."

"He's in Talcott's office," Jim Ed assured him.

Shorty whipped out onto the highway. A quarter mile ahead was Grandmother Maudie's gravy-colored car, doing perhaps seventy miles an hour. Shorty said, "You better take a deep hold on your hat." He gunned the pickup even harder. "What'd you do to make the old man so mad?"

"I hurt him. I didn't mean to, but I hurt him."

Shorty grunted. "Can't say that surprises me none. You've got a habit of hurtin' people that try to be kind to you, seems to me like." He leaned toward the steering wheel. "I ain't seen Glory B. in a while. How is she?"

"She was fine till her grandmother took sick."

Shorty nodded soberly. "I heard about Miz Livvy. She's a grand old lady."

They were rapidly gaining on the old car. Jim Ed said, "Shorty, I've felt real bad about you and Glory B. It never was my intention to hurt you."

Shorty did not take his eyes from the road. "Hell, I never figured you did. Things just happen, that's all. Deep down, I always knew I was like a brother to her, and nothin' else. I knew somebody'd come along someday and she'd go off with him. I just hoped he wouldn't be a son of a bitch."

"I never thought I was. Not till a little while ago, anyway." His gaze was on the old car ahead. "Are we friends?"

Shorty shrugged. "If you don't mind me gettin' mad enough at you once in a while to kick your butt. Like now, for instance. What did you do to hurt Ol' Wes?"

Jim Ed explained, as best he could.

Shorty said, "But why did you agree in the first place? You could've told your daddy *no.*"

Jim Ed told him about flunking out of the university. His father, furious, had demanded that he come down to his grandfather's ranch for the summer and get his head together, and in the process keep an eye on the old man's behavior. "You don't know what *mad* is till you've seen it in the eyes of a Hendrix. I was afraid he'd break a blood vessel if I didn't give in."

"I guess I can relate to that. I remember the time I stove in the fender on my daddy's best truck." Shorty pulled the pickup just behind Maudie's Ford and waited for an oncoming truck to go by, then pulled out to pass. He pressed the horn to get Wes's attention. As Shorty pulled abreast of Wes, Jim Ed motioned for his grandfather to pull over. Shorty went on around him, then drove off onto the shoulder and stopped. Wes passed him and kept going.

Shorty said, "You *did* make him mad." He drove back upon the highway and pulled up beside Wes again. He stayed even with him while Jim Ed pleaded with his grandfather to stop. Finally, seeing a car coming in the opposite direction, Wes cut the wheel to the right and drew over onto the shoulder. Shorty quickly dropped behind him and stopped the pickup.

Wes got out of the car, his face flushed. "You damned kids tryin' to get yourselves killed?"

Jim Ed said, "We're trying to get you to listen to me."

Wes would not look at him. "Well, I'm listenin'."

Jim Ed realized he was talking too rapidly, but he had to get it said. He explained the reason he had agreed to come to Big River. "I was in trouble with my dad. At the time it didn't look as if I had much choice. And I'll be honest with you: I did intend to keep tabs on you. But as soon as I got here I changed my mind. I haven't seen anything that I thought would help them, and I wouldn't have told them if I did."

Wes gave him a quick look before cutting his gaze back to Shorty's clean and shiny pickup. "Not even that new fence?"

"That fence is a sign you're stubborn, not crazy."

"Some'd say it's the same thing with a senile old man."

"Anybody who calls you senile has got me to fight."

Shorty put in, "And he can give it to them, too. I'll bet he never told you about them Potter brothers."

"No, but I heard, just the same." Wes frowned at Shorty. "Seems to me like he took away somethin' you thought you had a claim to."

Shorty grunted. "He's a city boy. You got to make allowances for ignorance."

Wes turned back to Jim Ed. "Then I reckon I can make allowances too." He jerked his head toward the car. "You take the wheel."

Starting around to the other side, Wes paused to tell Shorty, "You know, boy, you drive that thing a way too fast."

Shorty smiled. "Yes sir. So I've been told."

Jim Ed reached out his hand, and Shorty took it. "Thanks, friend."

Shorty shrugged. "Just don't you ever hurt her."

Jim Ed assumed his grandfather wanted him to drive on to the ranch, and the old man told him no differently. They pulled across the cattleguard. Wes motioned. "The hill."

Jim Ed put the car up the hard grade, fearing its low-slung oil pan might drag a high center. When he stopped, Wes got out without speaking and started on ahead of him to the top, afoot. Jim Ed set the handbrake and followed.

Wes walked a little farther than usual, all the way to the edge of a rimrock. Jim Ed sensed that his grandfather had rather be alone, so he hung back, watching from a distance. Wes must have stood for ten minutes, silently surveying the valley, the river, the cedared hills. When he turned, he looked ten years older. His eyes were dull with defeat. He passed Jim Ed without looking at him and walked back down, moving slower than when he had climbed up. He got in the car and hunched down in the seat.

"Home?" Jim Ed asked.

Wes only nodded, looking at his boots.

The old man did not speak until they pulled up in the yard. He got out, stared a moment at the house, then said, "I wisht you'd run down to the milk pen and turn the calf out where it can find its mammy. I'm goin' to scatter a little feed for the horses and the chickens." He looked back up the road. "They'll be comin' out here directly to carry on the conversation where it left off. I don't want to be around."

He turned away as if to discourage any questions, and Jim Ed asked none. He asked nothing until they climbed back into the car, a couple of days' clothes stuffed into a small suitcase. Jim Ed put the key in the ignition and started the motor. "Where to?"

Wes pointed with his chin. "Out the back way. Otherwise we're liable to meet them comin' in."

Jim Ed drove across a couple of pastures and reached a graded county road that cut into the San Angelo highway several miles farther on. He stopped at the edge of the pavement. "Now where to?"

Wes motioned him to turn left. Jim Ed complied, moving out onto the highway and setting the cruise control to keep the speed almost legal. "San Angelo?" he asked.

Wes nodded. "I want to look in on Livvy."

He said almost nothing during the two hours it took for them to reach San Angelo. They pulled in at a quick-stop for a hamburger, and even then the only thing Wes said was, "Be sure and have them put mustard on it instead of that damned mayonnaise." Part of the hamburger still uneaten, he got up and walked to the door, turning and asking with his eyes if Jim Ed planned to spend the day there.

Jim Ed took him into the hospital, up the elevator and down the hall to Lavinia Dawson's room. He knocked quietly, then gently pushed the door open to look inside. Lavinia smiled in recognition, and Glory B. almost shouted. "Jim Ed!"

Jim Ed said, "Miz Livvy, I brought somebody."

Tears came to Lavinia's eyes. She raised her hands for Wes to take. No words passed between them. Glory B. came around the bed, took Jim Ed by the arm and led him out of the room. In the hallway she kissed him. "Thank you. She needed that."

"So did he," Jim Ed replied.

Glory B. led him to a waiting area near the nurses' station and sat down beside him. He told her what had happened.

She said solemnly, "So now the floor's been taken out from under him. What's he going to do?"

"I don't know. Try to find another lawyer, perhaps. What about your grandmother?"

Glory B. stared at the floor. "They'll be sending her home in a few days. Home to die." She blinked away tears. "Kind of like Wes, except that he won't even have a home to go to."

Wes came out of Lavinia's room, finally, his head down. He walked past Glory B. and Jim Ed, halting at a window which faced out upon the city. He stood with his back turned. He blew his nose, wiped his eyes and turned. "I expect we'd better go, Tater. Livvy needs her rest."

Glory B. put her arms around Wes. "I've done a lot of praying for her. I'll add you to the prayers."

Wes hugged her. "If I ever had a granddaughter, I'd want her to be you."

Glory B. glanced back at Jim Ed. "Who knows? Maybe things'll work out."

Jim Ed unlocked the car door for Wes and held it while his grandfather crawled in. As he settled in on the driver's side and put the key in the ignition switch he asked, "Where now? Back home?"

"And run into that bunch, settin' there waitin' like a flock of vultures?" Wes pondered. "I've had it in mind for a right smart while to go back and visit the place where I come from. Ain't seen my daddy's old homeplace in thirty years."

That was all the explanation he offered, and Jim Ed asked him nothing more except directions. He wondered if Wes might be toying with the idea of going back to live out his days where he had grown up.

They drove the rest of the afternoon. Wes slumped in the seat most of the time, uncommunicative, as if he had mentally shut himself off in a room alone. Jim Ed suspected he was listening with his mind to the distant echoes of a long-ago time. About all he said was, "We'd better stay all night in Lubbock. The old town may not even have a tourist court anymore."

Sleeping in a separate room in the ranchhouse, Jim Ed had not been especially aware that the old man snored so loudly. He lay awake half the night, or so it seemed, listening. And just as at the ranch, Wes was up shortly after five, stomping his boots across the floor. Jim Ed protested sleepily to the light shining in his eyes. "You haven't even got a cow to milk."

"That's no reason for sloth. It's an easy thing for a man to allow himself to fall into lazy habits."

Jim Ed was not familiar with Lubbock, and it took him a while to find a restaurant open. He refused to let Wes rush him through breakfast, though Wes fidgeted as dawn's first light began to spread across the city. Jim Ed had no intention of driving unfamiliar highways in the dark of early morning. Wes complained about the biscuits, which obviously had come out of a can, but the summer had brought Jim Ed around to Wes's view that the worst kind of biscuit was better than the best toasted lightbread. He took his time and drank enough coffee to give his kidneys a thorough flushing.

When they put the fading lights of Lubbock behind them, the sun came up into the fullness of a late-summer morning. In contrast to the previous afternoon, Wes sat up straight. He talked about landmarks they passed. He began to tell about events of his boyhood on the little ranch that his father owned but lost in the cattle depression that followed World War I. He talked of boyhood friends, cowboys all, who had played with him and ridden with him, sharing their grub, their money, their hopes and their dreams.

Wes pointed to a road. "Up yonder a ways lived the best calf roper ever I seen for somebody who was not a contest hand. Ol' Red Weaver was his name. He could throw off to the right-hand or the left, didn't make him no difference. I seen him in a brandin' pen one day heel somethin' better than three hundred calves and not miss a loop, hardly."

Jim Ed remembered Bill Roper telling virtually the same story about Wes.

Wes said, "I've often wondered whatever become of Red. He's probably still around here someplace. He never would take a job that carried him far from home. And Ol' Grover Cleveland Ransome, there was another top hand for you, maybe the best! Could ride just about anything that wore leather—horse, mule or bull. He tried Ol' Midnight twice. I think that was about the only bronc he never did manage to ride sooner or later."

"But you did."

"Just lucky." Wes pondered. "Well, luck was part of it, but I *was* pretty good in them days, if I do say so. Not a worn-out old fart like now, that's for damned sure."

Wes pointed again. "This ol' country's pretty flat, but you can see a little rise over yonder if you look real hard. Just beyond it is where Ol' Snort Yarnell lived out his last days. Taught me a lot, Ol' Snort did. He was a leftover from the open-range times, wilder'n a peach-orchard boar, even when he was as old as I am now. Claimed he was born on the Chisholm Trail and suckled by a Longhorn cow. I always kind of believed it."

The farther they went, the nearer Wes moved to the edge of his seat. He braced his arms against the dashboard and leaned forward as if he were trying to get there ahead of the car. Excitement rose in his voice. "Right yonder. Right yonder is where we turn. My old daddy built a nice entrance gate there."

Jim Ed slowed and turned in. There was a cattleguard made of old secondhand pipe, and it had an oil company sign on it, with a lease name and number. Off to one side lay a small pile of rubble that Jim Ed realized had probably been Wes's father's entrance gate.

Wes blinked, and sadness came into his voice. "Papa and us worked awful hard gettin' that gate to lookin' nice."

The road was packed with caliche for the easier passage of oilfield equipment trucks. At intervals, abandoned oilwell locations lay like scars on the grassland, their pads sterile of vegetation because of the deep caliche and the oil spillage. Concrete foundations stood like tombstones to mark the death of dreams. Rusted pipe and twisted piles of heavy cable lay scattered like the battlefield relics of a lost war.

Wes grumbled, "Wasn't none of that trash here in my time."

He commented about how the mesquite and other brush had taken over, crowding out much of the grass. He recalled that this had been mostly open prairie. "When I was a button, chuckwagon cooks had to hunt like hell even to find firewood. Movin' camp, they'd go two miles out of their way to pick up dead mesquite and throw it into a cowhide tied under the wagonbed. Just look at this mess now, would you?"

He cautioned Jim Ed to slow down. "The headquarters is just around this next curve. See the windmill yonder, in the brush?"

Jim Ed slowed and made the bend. He heard his grandfather groan. He saw no house, no barns, nothing but a fallen-down set of old wooden pens. The only sign of use was a steel-towered Aermotor windmill, pumping water into an old round concrete tank. The skeleton of a wooden tower lay on the ground nearby, rotted into almost total collapse.

Wes said softly, "Many's the time I helped Papa pull the rods out of that old mill. It was him built the tank." He got out and walked around it. He brushed away an accumulation of dirt and uncovered an old inscription drawn long ago into the wet concrete of the wide rim: "Wesley Hendrix, Apr. 29, '17." He smiled thinly. "I was sittin' on a horse when I done that, a little ol' paint horse we called Patch. Papa raised hell when he found it, but the concrete was done set up."

He walked over the old ground, pausing often to look around. He spent longest at a rotting set of short cedar posts set in the form of a rectangle. Half angrily he said, "I don't know why they had to tear the house down. It was a good one. The well water was always gyppy. My mama had her cistern right yonder for drinkin' water." The only remnant of the cistern was the outer concrete wall. The hole had long since been filled, probably to keep a horse or cow from falling into it.

Wes walked back to the tank, finally, and leaned over to catch a little windmill water in his hands from the end of the pipe. He tasted it cautiously and made a face. "The water sure ain't improved any. Even tastes a little like oil now. Contaminated from all them damned oil wells."

He walked to the car, turning back for a final look. Sadness was in his face, but anger was stronger. "Damn them!" he declared. "Damn them for what they done to a good country!"

He spoke not a word as they drove back out the way they had come in, and as they moved on down the highway. He sat up straight again when a silver municipal water tower showed on the horizon. "Well," he said, "we'll see if they've torn down the town as well."

Jim Ed's first harsh impression was that if they had not, they should have. Compared to this, Big River was a model of architectural splendor. An abandoned oil-field equipment facility scarred the roadside just inside the city limits sign, its rust-stained sheet-metal building slumped, the windows broken out. Obsolete machinery on either side of it was crusted by old oil and grease and dirt. A sagging cyclone fence was a trap for dried tumbleweeds and scrap paper carried by the winds.

Wes hunched in the seat, his face twisting as he looked. "It wasn't no San Antonio or Lubbock," he said thinly, "but it was a right clean little ol' town when we lived here."

Jim Ed saw one motel, old enough that it still had carports. Its sign offered kitchenettes, another giveaway as to its age. He saw no indication that it accepted either MasterCard or Visa, or perhaps they did not accept *it.* He said, "I'm glad we spent the night in Lubbock."

Wes only grunted. He pointed to a two-story frame building that appeared to have been abandoned for twenty years. "That was the mercantile and grocery," he recalled. "Biggest store in thirty-forty miles."

The only active business houses Jim Ed could see along the main street were a quick-stop grocery with gas pumps out in front, a couple of major-company service stations in buildings that looked almost as old as Wes, and a small restaurant that displayed the word *Beer* in bigger letters than the word *Eats.*

Wes said, "Let's pull in at the café. We'll have us some coffee and make some inquiry."

The place still had the original old pressed-metal ceiling and beaded lumber to better than waist height along the walls. The waitress was a middle-aged woman, twenty pounds plumper even than Noreen Levitt. She got up from a table and put down a newspaper she had been reading. Without saying a word, she gave the clear impression that she would rather have been in Amarillo.

"Coffee," Wes said in a tired voice. "And a piece of pie to help sweeten my stomach."

"Ain't got no pie," she said, not volunteering any information about whatever they *might* have.

"Well then, a doughnut or a sweetroll."

"Ain't got none of them neither. Route man ain't been through town yet today." Her tone implied he should have known.

"Well then," Wes said, momentarily defeated, "I'll just put a little sugar in my coffee and make do."

"You want cream too?" she demanded, implying that it was going to be a certain amount of trouble for her.

Wes shook his head. Jim Ed could see color rising in his face. "No cream. Just bring the coffee the way it was born."

She turned to Jim Ed. "What about you, Sonny Boy?"

"Same as him. Only bring the cream." He didn't really want it, but he decided the challenge might do her good.

She delivered the coffee, then sat down at a table and resumed her occupation with the newspaper. Wes sipped at the coffee. He could drink it much hotter than Jim Ed. Jim Ed knew by his grandfather's expression that it was every bit as bad as he had expected it to be.

Wes said to the waitress, "I used to live here."

"Is that right?" she said, avoiding any show of interest.

"I was wonderin' if you might know any of the people that were here in my time. Would Ol' Red Weaver still be around?"

She shook her head. "Don't believe I ever heard of him."

"What about Grover Cleveland Ransome? You sure ought to know him if he's still livin'."

"I only been here two years."

Wes called off several more names and got the same response, except that her voice was becoming more and more irritated. Finally she got up, dropped the newspaper on the table and said, "Phipps is out in the kitchen. Maybe he knows them." She disappeared out back. In a minute or two a tall, sallow-looking man in a once-white apron showed up. "What can I do for you?"

Wes began asking him about the same people. Each name drew a shake of the cook's balding head until Wes mentioned Grover Cleveland Ransome. "Say," he said, "I believe that's the old man who lives with the Netters. Her daddy, I think he is. She hollers at him like he was one of her kids, though. I'm glad *I* ain't her daddy, or her anything else."

Wes asked directions. The cook told him to turn right at the next corner and stop at the Good Times Package Store. "Bruce Netter has got the only whisky joint left in town. He can tell you if that's the right man."

Wes's hands began to tremble with excitement. "Ol' Grover. Damn, but it'll be good to see him after all these years." He got up from the table, leaving half of his coffee in the cup. "Come on, Tater."

The liquor store was easy to find. The proprietor, who looked sixty or so, was only slightly disappointed when Wes turned out not to be a paying customer. "Grover? Sure, he's my daddy-in-law, all right. Good old man, after his fashion, but he's a pain in the ass sometimes, know what I'm sayin'? Always livin' in the old days and tellin' what all he done then. Can't even zip up his own britches now, hardly."

He said the old man lived in a small shotgun shack that had been moved in and set down beside the larger one where Netter and his wife lived. "We tried livin' in the same house with him, but the old man was up at all hours of the night, stompin' around, coughin', spittin', goin' to the john. It's hell to get old, and more hell to live with somebody that is."

The directions were easy to follow; the town was not large enough to get anybody lost for more than a few minutes. The Netters' house was covered with stucco, the steel netting showing through in spots where the plaster had fallen loose. The little house beside it was a relic of oil-field boom days, narrow, no hallway, just a straight shot from front room to bedroom to kitchen in the back, hence the term *shotgun*.

Wes glanced at Jim Ed, then frowned at the old house. "Ain't much for show, is it?" He walked toward the tiny porch, only to be stopped by a gaunt, mean-eyed woman who stepped out of the stucco house and demanded, "You lookin' for somebody?"

Wes replied, "Grover Ransome. I was told he lives here."

The voice was sharp. "What do you want with him?"

"We're old friends. I just come to see him."

She approached, arms folded defiantly. "Every time anybody comes to see him, he gets all stirred up and crazy, and it takes us a week to jar him back out of the past. I wish people would leave him alone."

Wes turned his eyes from her, toward the shotgun shack. "I sure don't mean no harm. But me and Grover used to ride together. I ain't seen him in years."

She gave him a critical study and clearly was not impressed. "Well, go ahead then, but don't you be stayin' too long. I don't want him all stirred up." She strode back to the other house and slammed the screen door.

Wes watched darkly until she was out of sight, then climbed the steps and drummed his knuckles against the screen door. "Grover! Grover, you home?"

Jim Ed heard loud sound from inside, evidently a television set blaring a game show. Wes tugged at the screen, but it was hooked. He rattled it with some violence. "Grover! Somebody's come."

The volume went down on the broadcast, and Jim Ed heard a shuffling sound as the old man came to the door, dragging one foot a little. It was plain that he had suffered a stroke at some time. His feet were in old houseshoes, the toe cut out of one. He stared vacantly at Wes. "Who's there?" he queried suspiciously, raising his hand toward the hook but not touching it until he was sure he was safe.

Jim Ed heard joy in his grandfather's voice. "It's me, Wes Hendrix. Don't you remember me, Grover?"

The old man inside the screen stared in confusion for a long moment, mumbling the name. "Wes? Wes who?" Finally recognition came, and he flipped the hook out of its place. "Wes Hendrix! I'd of swore and be damned that you was dead."

Wes pulled the screen open and gripped the old man's hand with enthusiasm. Grover winced. His joints were swollen from arthritis. Wes asked, "What made you think I was dead?"

"Everybody else is, pretty near. You-all come on in. Who's that you got with you?"

Wes introduced Jim Ed, who took care to be gentle with Grover's hand. He looked around the little room as the old cowboy dragged back across the floor to turn off the television. It was an ancient black-and-white set, probably a castoff from his daughter and son-in-law. The volume was better than the picture. The old man's rocking chair had pillows in the seat and back, covering upholstery frayed from age. The walls were hidden by faded photographs that must have dated back fifty or sixty years, the best Jim Ed could judge. Most appeared to have been made at rodeos and on ranches. An old saddle lay in a corner, dusty and dry, badly in need of oiling. A rope and bridle lay across it as if ready for immediate use, but the rope was so old and limp that it hung like a drape. Spurs dangled from a hook on the wall, the leathers dried and brittle. All these things were relics of a disappeared past. The place was an unkempt, neglected museum, or perhaps even a mausoleum for the living, Jim Ed thought.

It had an old-man smell, a little like Wes's house, a vaguely unpleasant mix of liniment and talcum powder and rubbing alcohol, and some miscellaneous medical odors he could not identify.

Grover said, "Wes, I wouldn't've knowed you, hardly. You've gone and got old. You don't ride horseback no more, do you?"

Wes assured him that he did, as much as he could, but of course he no longer broke broncs. "We broke some good ones in our day, didn't we?" He turned to Jim Ed. "Did I tell you, Ol' Grover here was about as good a bronc rider as ever I knew?"

"Not as good as you," Grover argued. That led to thirty minutes of reminiscences about horses, from some misbegotten ranch mounts all the way to Midnight himself. The two old men relived the day Wes had ridden the famous bronc. Grover cackled, "A lot of sad money changed hands that day, I'll tell you, button. All the *smart* money was bettin' on the horse. I never did tell you, Wes, but I lost ten dollars on you myself."

Wes seemed surprised, and perhaps a little aggrieved, even after all this time. "The hell you say." He pondered sadly. "That's all been a long time ago, and hardly anybody is still livin' that remembers. It don't mean much to anybody now what we done in them days. We're just useless old codgers standin' in the middle of the road while everybody else is tryin' to pass."

The conversation turned to other cowboys of their mutual acquaintance and age. Wes asked, "Do you ever see Ol' Red Weaver anymore?"

Grover shook his head. "I was a pallbearer for Ol' Red. Been seven-eight years now. Died of emphysema, just flat choked himself to death. Always was hell to smoke, remember?"

Wes shook his head. "I don't know why I never heard. Live too far away, I reckon. What about Ol' Dan Holliday? Dan Howdy-do, we used to call him."

"Killed in a car wreck, must've been fifteen years ago. Drunk, they said. Got to drinkin' pretty bad when the arthritis fixed him to where he couldn't ride no more. Shame. He was a good hand in them days. We was all good hands."

Wes mused, "A man had to be good at what he done or he

couldn't hold a job. Ain't like today, when a ranch'll hire anybody that can stay on an old plowhorse without fallin' off."

"The truth," Grover agreed. "The mortal truth. You remember Ol' Brewster Downing?"

"Sure. He was another good hand. Taught me more than just about anybody I ever knew except Snort Yarnell and Ol' Major Chatfield. The way I heard it, Ol' Brewster finally got him a little ranch around here, didn't he?"

"Sure did. Nice little outfit, only he didn't have nothin' but the surface rights. Oil companies finally just about cut his place to pieces and ruined all his water. Ol' Brewster's in a nursin' home down in Lubbock. Daughter taken me over there a year or so ago. She had business in Lubbock anyway."

Wes said, "I'd like to see him."

"No you wouldn't." Grover's eyes took on a haunted look, a vague dread. "He just lays there with his eyes wide open and don't see nothin'. He don't know nobody, not even his own kids. They have a diaper on him, just like a baby. God, I'd sooner die than get in that shape."

Jim Ed looked away, half afraid the old man might be able to read his thought: *You're not a long way from it.*

Wes looked away, too. Jim Ed guessed the same thought had crossed his mind.

Somehow, after that, Grover seemed to lose himself. The conversation began to wander, touching on stories from twenty years ago, forty, fifty, stories that trailed off into nothing or got entangled with one another. Wes glanced at Jim Ed once or twice, a deep pity in his gray eyes. Clearly, Grover had slipped back in time. He began talking about rodeos he was planning to ride in, roundups he intended to work, a horse he was breaking that would make the world sit up and take notice.

In a little while Jim Ed heard a loud knock at the door. A woman stood on the porch. "Papa!" she called with some impatience. "Didn't you hear me call you? It's time you came on over and had your dinner. I'm not going to warm it up for you. You come get it now or dammit, you'll eat it cold!"

Jim Ed saw fear leap into Grover's eyes. Fear in the man Wes said might be the best bronc rider and all-around cowboy he had ever known. Grover reluctantly ventured out from the warm safety of the past to the emptiness and threat of the present. "I'll be right there, hon," he answered, pushing himself up painfully from his chair. "Wes, I got to go."

As he moved into the light, Jim Ed saw a bruise on his cheekbone. "Comin', hon," Grover called. He turned at the door. "I'll be back directly. You be here, Wes?"

Wes shook his head. He blinked a few times, his hand knotted into a fist. "No, Grover. Me and Tater, we got to be gettin' on. It was sure good to see you again. Sure good."

He stood on the porch with Jim Ed, watching the lanky old man drag himself across to the larger house and, holding to a handrail, painfully pull his legs up the steps. As he entered the house, Jim Ed could hear a woman's angry voice berating him.

He turned back to Wes, but Wes would not look at him. Jim Ed said, "Anywhere else you'd like to go?"

Wes considered. "That whisky store."

Jim Ed thought Wes might give Bruce Netter a stern talking-to, but all he did was buy a fifth of bourbon. He pitched it into the seat of the car and stood a moment, letting his gaze sweep the rude streets of what had once been his hometown. He took something from his pocket and hurled it far out into a weedy vacant lot, then climbed into the car.

"Let's go home," he said in a bitter voice. He twisted the cap from the bottle and raised it to his lips. He did not put the cap back into place.

Chapter 12

Although the sun was almost down, the summer evening's heat remained heavy and oppressive, radiating back from the concrete sidewalk to burn Sheriff Wally Vincent's face. It aggravated a sour humor which had kept his stomach teetering on the verge of rebellion for most of two days. He wished for a breeze to cool the sweat which stuck his shirt to his back, but any that might be moving down the valley was blunted by the tightly huddled buildings along Big River's main street. Once the lake became reality and he finished building the boat docks and resort he planned at the ranch, Vincent would gladly relinquish the Sheriff's office—it was just a wage job anyway—sell his house in town and leave this place for those who didn't know better or couldn't afford to live somewhere else. His wife Faye recoiled at any discussion of moving back to the country—she had grown up there and enjoyed town much better—but she would go whether she liked it or not. That was the way things were run in the Vincent family.

Though Orville Levitt usually closed his drugstore at six o'clock, Vincent could see him puttering around in the back. Suspicious, he placed his face against the plate-glass window and shielded it with one hand to reduce the reflections. He would not put it past Levitt to have heard something about Wes Hendrix and to have kept the information to himself. Vincent was well aware that Levitt did not approve of him. The feeling was reciprocated.

This town needed young and vital leadership, not a mayor so old that he was probably his own pharmacy's best customer, just trying to keep himself alive. There was no telling what progress this community could make if it were not held back by old mosshorns like Wes Hendrix and Orville Levitt, and by nosy, gossiping old women like Noreen. It could become a busy tourist attraction trading on its new lake, its hunting, its hill-country mystique like Kerrville or Fredericksburg or Bandera, and raking in all that money from well-heeled visitors trying to escape for a few days from the stress and congestion of Houston or San Antonio or Austin. Matthew Jamison's bank might enjoy some six-figure local accounts for a change and not be eternally hostage to the roller-coaster ups and downs that bedeviled the cattle market. If there was a worse investment in the world than a damned slobbering old cow, he could not imagine what it might be. His Hereford-loving father-in-law would turn over in his grave if he knew the plans Vincent was hatching for that rockpile of a ranch the old man had nursed and babied for forty years.

People had dug around in these hills with pick and shovel for a century and more, looking for Jim Bowie's legendary lost silver mine. The whole story was probably just another outrageous Texas tale made up by some drunken liar in an age when great liars were legion. But let them watch Wally Vincent. He was fixing to show them where the *real* gold was.

He tested the door but found it locked. He grasped the handle and gave the door a sound rattling. Orville Levitt took his own good time about coming to the front and opening up. His expression was downcast. "Come in, Wally."

"Thought you went home a long time ago."

"Did, but I came back to restock some shelves. Atmosphere around the house is kind of frosty anyway."

Vincent frowned. "That's what you get for lettin' Noreen have the upper hand. Tell her that by God you're the boss."

Levitt's voice was dry. "Like you, Wally?"

"Damned right, like me. My wife don't give *me* no sass."

Vincent's disposition was not improved by the skepticism in Levitt's eyes. He demanded, "You heard anything out of Wes?"

Levitt shook his head. "Truman's been stayin' at the place since yesterday. Promised he'd call if Wes came home. Nobody seems to have any idea where he might've gone."

"Well, we know he went to the ranch first. I found that out from the Bigham kid." He gritted his teeth. He suspected he could have learned a lot more if that boy's big truck-driving daddy hadn't been standing there the whole time, hovering around his son like a protecting angel. If Vincent could have gotten that kid off alone . . .

He demanded, "You think John Talcott's been levelin' with us that he don't know nothin'? He *is* Wes's lawyer."

"*Was.* You saw the way Wes looked at him. John feels real bad. He did what he thought was best for Wes. So did Truman. That's more than *we've* done. We've just thought about what was best for Big River, and us."

"Anything wrong with that? A man's got to watch out for himself, because there sure ain't nobody else goin' to." He could not understand the pain in Levitt's face. Once a man made up his mind to something, he ought never to look back. He said firmly, "If you hear anything, don't you just sit on it. You come and find me."

He gave Levitt no more of his time, turning abruptly and walking back out into the street. He saw Bill Roper drive by in a pickup with the C Bar brand painted on its door. Knowing how thick Roper and Wes Hendrix had always been, Vincent had driven out to the C Bar headquarters yesterday and put the ranch foreman through a proper grilling. Roper hadn't told him a damned thing. What was worse, he had let him know in the most combative terms that if he *had* known anything, he would not have told it. That C Bar outfit was so big it had always done just about as it pleased, but things were fixing to change. Old Lady Dawson was dying, the way Vincent had heard it. The place was fixing to fall into the hands of a schoolgirl whose youth and inexperience would probably finish pushing it into bankruptcy. Four generations of ownership by one old-fashioned, bull-stubborn family was just about enough.

He almost regretted that he wouldn't be needing the sheriff's job much longer. Nothing would suit him better than a chance, the first time an occasion arose, to let the C Bar bunch feel the full authority of the law without having to consider their financial and political influence. That Bill Roper, in particular, would look real good sitting there with his face pressed between the bars and no Old Lady Dawson to come to town raising hell about it.

Vincent found nothing on the courthouse square to hold his attention further. He got in his black county automobile and drove to Lacy's café. Just one car sat in front; most of the supper crowd had already gone. The bell tinkled over the door as he pushed it open. A teenage Hispanic boy and girl were finishing hamburgers at a table in the corner.

Stella Tenney came out of the kitchen, responding to the bell. Her mouth dropped open at sight of Vincent. She glanced quickly at the teenagers and forced a courteous formality. "Good evenin', Sheriff. What can I do for you?"

He winked. "You *know* what you can do for me."

Eyes narrowed, she pointed her chin toward the two youngsters. Vincent thought the pair were so wrapped up in each other that they would not notice if the place caught afire. He could understand the feeling, for Stella had that effect on *him*. Staring hungrily at her, he wondered how he had ever considered his wife pretty twenty-odd years ago. He supposed his notion of beauty had been considerably influenced by the size of her father's ranch.

She asked, "Menu, or just coffee?"

"Coffee'll do for now. Later, maybe more . . . a whole lot more. Been three nights now since me and you entertained one another." He took a table where he could watch the street through the big window. She leaned near as she set the coffee in front of him. Her perfume and the warmth he felt from her body were like gasoline tossed on a fire already threatening to flare out of control.

She no longer addressed him as *honey*, the way she did most folks. Sometimes he could not tell whether she was really drawn to him or was simply too fearful to put up resistance. In the long run it didn't matter. Results were what counted.

"Grandma's still in the kitchen," she warned.

"Old woman can't hear thunder." But he said no more, and he restrained an impulse to run his hand up and down her thigh.

Presently the gray-haired, slightly stooped woman came to the kitchen doorway. She gave the sheriff a look that said she had never voted for him and never would. She told her granddaughter, "Looks like we're about through, girl. You'll lock up?"

"Sure, Grandma. You go on home and get your rest now. See you tomorrow."

Vincent glowered at the two teenagers, who had long since finished their hamburgers and now dallied, feeding each other French fries one at a time. Mexicans! There had been a time they would not have been allowed to eat in here like white folks. That's what the country got for letting everybody vote, he thought. A man couldn't say anything anymore, but nobody could stop him from thinking what he felt like.

After what seemed half an hour, the pair downed the last swallows of their Cokes and got up to leave. The boy paid Stella at the register, his eyes never leaving the girl. He placed his change on the table as a tip without counting it. The two left the café arm in arm and got into the only vehicle left in front other than the sheriff's.

Vincent remarked, "There's a couple that can't hardly wait for dark." He ran his hand up the front of Stella's blouse.

She commented, "Seems to me like *you* can't either." She drew back a step. He reached for her again, and she moved farther. She said, "There's a time and a place for everything. This ain't either one."

"I'll be along later. Leave your back door unlocked."

Her brow creased. "You know, you ain't near as sneaky as you think you are. There's rumors goin' around about you and me."

"Who gives a damn about gossip?"

"I think your wife does, for one."

"All I have to do is tell her there's nothin' to it. She believes what I tell her."

"She was in here yesterday. Sat at that table right over yonder and drank two cups of coffee and looked daggers at me the whole time. She knows."

"I'll handle her. As for the others, I don't give a damn."

Her voice took on a testiness he recognized; he had heard it often enough from his wife. She said, "Well, maybe *I* give a damn. I want to protect my reputation, even if you don't."

"*Your* reputation? Hell, you *are* livin' up to your reputation. Except you've never asked for money."

Her face went scarlet. She picked up his half-empty cup of still-hot coffee and dashed it in his face. Sputtering, he grabbed her arm and pushed quickly to his feet. He brought back his hand to strike her but caught himself in time. He let her go, picked up a paper napkin and wiped off as much of the coffee as he could. Brittlely he said, "I'll be around tonight and collect for that."

"You'll find my door locked."

"It'd better not be. You'll be buyin' yourself a new door. Or a bus ticket out of town."

Her eyes widened in fear. "You wouldn't."

"Wouldn't I? I'd cinch the votes from seventy-five percent of the women in this town if I was to bust you for vagrancy. So you think about that, Stella. You think real hard."

She stepped back, well out of his reach. "You're a real brass-plated son of a bitch, Wally Vincent. And you're buildin' yourself up for a fall."

"Who's goin' to throw me? You?" He opened the door and turned to give her his most menacing stare. "Tonight, Stella."

He walked out to his car and stood beside it a moment, his gaze taking in the street. He saw a familiar Ford of 1970s vintage and watched as it passed, heading toward the center of town. A grim smile crept across his face.

"Ask," he said, "and ye shall receive." He got into his car and followed.

Jim Ed thought it would have been better to have driven directly to the ranch. More than anything, his grandfather needed to go to bed. Wes had put away almost the whole bottle of whisky on the long drive home. He was slumped in the seat, talking incoherently to himself. Every once in a while his voice would rise in anger but not in clarity. Jim Ed was seldom sure whom he was railing at. He could only nod in agreement, and compassion. In his grandfather's place he would probably have drunk too much too. A lot of ground had been cut from under Wes the last few days.

The needle on the gasoline gauge was dangerously near the empty mark, so Jim Ed had thought it expedient to come by town and fill the tank. He would not want to walk part of the way home, supporting an old man who probably could not walk at all.

Passing Orville Levitt's store, he saw Levitt at the door, locking up. The old man looked more slump-shouldered than usual, carrying a weight that was not entirely of age. Levitt turned in time to see the car. Recognition was instantaneous, and he waved both hands. Jim Ed grumbled softly. The last thing Wes needed now was a renewal of yesterday's confrontation.

The rearview mirror showed Levitt following in a hobbling gait as near a trot as he could muster. Jim Ed looked at the gasoline gauge again and knew he had no choice. He pulled in at a service station on the corner past the drugstore. Stepping out of the car, he looked back in resignation. Perhaps when Levitt saw Wes's condition he would recognize that it was futile to argue now. Jim Ed saw no reason for argument anyway. They had Wes by the short hair.

A schoolboy station attendant began filling the tank. Orville Levitt was almost out of breath when he reached the car and bent to look in at Wes. He glanced up with misgivings. "Is he all right?"

"No," Jim Ed replied curtly. "He's drunk. I should think you'd know why."

"You shouldn't have let him. You know the condition of his heart."

"And you should know my grandfather well enough to realize that whatever he decides to do, he'll do it or bust a gut trying."

"God yes, how well I know."

Wes raised his head and looked up at Levitt but seemed not to recognize him. Or perhaps he just didn't give a damn anymore.

Levitt said, "You need to get him home and put him to bed. Maybe I ought to go with you."

Jim Ed tried to keep his voice civil. "You're part of his problem. I think the best thing you can do is keep out of his sight."

Levitt nodded sadly. "I guess you're right. I just wish there'd been some better way . . .."

He turned toward the sound of a big engine. Sheriff Vincent's car pulled in against the curb. The tall, blocky lawman climbed out, making a cold smile that touched Jim Ed with a chill.

"Well," Vincent said in a voice heavy with irony, "the prodigal decided to come home."

Levitt took a defensive stance beside Wes's door. "This is not the time, Wally."

"No? I don't know any better time to march him over to Talcott's office and make him sign them papers."

Levitt argued, "Talcott's closed. We can do it another day."

"I can phone him and get him down here." Vincent pushed past Levitt and grasped the door handle. "Come on out, Wes."

Jim Ed walked quickly around the car. "You leave him alone."

Vincent's eyes went half shut, but Jim Ed could still see the threat in them. "You talkin' to me, boy?"

"He's not in any shape right now. You can wait a day or two."

Vincent pulled the door open and leaned in. "He's drunk. By God, he's drunk." He shook Wes's shoulder. "Get out of the car, old man." He grasped Wes's arm and started pulling him.

Jim Ed's face went to flame. He grabbed the sheriff and tried to force him away from his grandfather. "I said leave him alone!"

Wally Vincent responded with a shout, bringing up a massive fist that Jim Ed hardly saw. It was as if a horse had kicked him in the face. He stumbled off the curb and sprawled on his back. Lights flashed and wheeled crazily in concert with a roaring pain in his head.

He lay a moment, aware that Vincent had pulled Wes from the car. The old man staggered. Orville Levitt attempted angrily to interfere, but Vincent pushed him aside. Wes came out of his stupor. He cried, "Tater," and tried to reach his grandson. Vincent yanked him back. Wes struggled, and Vincent slapped him. "Old man, you're under arrest."

Wes doubled over, clutching at his chest. He made a cry that brought Jim Ed swaying to his feet in alarm. Wes would have fallen had Vincent not held him. Vincent dragged him toward the black car with the badge painted on the door. "Drunk and disorderly," he declared. "I've got a cell just waitin' for a useless old fart like you. Time you get out, you'll be beggin' to sign that paper."

Jim Ed cried, "He's not just drunk. He's sick."

Orville Levitt regained his composure, and his determination. "Wally! He's havin' a heart attack!"

Vincent paid little attention. "He's just drunk."

A black rage overtook Jim Ed. He threw his arms around Vincent, trying to wrestle the big man loose from Wes. Vincent stumbled and went to one knee, then came up, trying to drive the knee into Jim Ed's groin. Jim Ed slammed the sheriff against the black car. Vincent reached for the pistol at his hip, then dropped it in the gutter as Jim Ed's fist struck him full in the face. Jim Ed gave him another fist in the stomach.

Out of the corner of his eye he saw Wes sinking toward the sidewalk, Orville Levitt easing him down so his head did not strike the concrete. Wes's hands convulsed against his chest.

Jim Ed grabbed up the pistol. It was his intention to pitch it across the street where Vincent could not handily reach it, but once his hands were on it, he seemed unable to turn it loose. "Damn you," he cried, "you'll let him alone!"

Vincent's nose was bleeding, as was Jim Ed's own. He saw blood spotting his shirt, and his knuckles were torn. Blood on his hands made the pistol grip sticky.

Vincent stared at the weapon, his eyes betraying a momentary fear. "Now, boy, you just lay that thing down."

The anxiety in Levitt's voice was like ice laid against Jim Ed's spine.

"Wes!" the druggist cried. "You hang on!" Desperately he went through Wes's pockets. "Where are they?" he shouted. "Where are they?"

Jim Ed trembled. "Where's what?"

"His heart pills. He's always carried them in his pocket."

Jim Ed felt confused, panic rising rapidly. "I don't know. They ought to be there." Suddenly he remembered. His grandfather had reached into his pocket just before they had left his hometown. He had hurled something into the weeds.

"My God! He threw them away!" He let his arm drop, the

pistol's muzzle pointing to the sidewalk. Wally Vincent was upon him in one stride, wrenching the pistol from him, striking him across the side of the head with it. Jim Ed sprawled again, on his stomach.

He heard Levitt declare, "Wally! Wes is dyin'!"

Vincent stood swaying, catching his breath, his face crimson. He was oblivious to the crowd rapidly gathering around. He holstered his pistol and started toward Wes. "Like hell he is. I'm takin' him to jail!"

Levitt lunged at the sheriff, grabbing both his arms. At that moment he was not just another wearied old man; he was the cowboy he had been fifty years ago, strong and forceful and driven by a righteous anger. "Listen to me, you bone-headed son of a bitch! If you let him die, I'll file charges on you for manslaughter!" Only then did Vincent seem to become aware of the spectators gathering. He hesitated, and Levitt gave him no chance to resume the initiative. He took charge.

"Tater! I hope Wally left you in shape to drive." He did not give Jim Ed time to answer. He looked to the boy who had filled the tank. "Help me put Wes in the car!"

A bystander lifted Jim Ed to his feet, and he slid behind the wheel. Levitt crawled into the backseat after Wes. Vigorously rubbing Wes's arms, he said urgently, "Whip back to the drugstore. He's got to have a heart pill." Jim Ed made a tire-squealing U-turn and pulled into the bus space at the drugstore's curb. He massaged his grandfather's arms while Levitt hurried into the store. The druggist was back almost at once and placed a pill in Wes's mouth.

"Now," he ordered, "to the doctor. Hurry!"

Jim Ed made another U-turn and sped up the street, past the sheriff, past the bystanders still gathered in front of the service station. An elderly woman was shaking her finger in Wally Vincent's face.

Someone evidently had telephoned the doctor, for he was standing out front with a nurse and an orderly, waiting to rush Wes inside. Jim Ed could only follow in their excited wake, his heart hammering. The vision was blurred in his right eye. He put his hand to his face. He felt heat and swelling and the gumminess of warm blood.

He tried to follow Wes and Levitt and the doctor, but a nurse stopped him at swinging double doors. "You'd best wait here, young man. We'll advise you as soon as we know anything."

He dropped down upon a couch, his burning eyes closed, his face in his trembling hands. His stomach churned, and he felt that it would empty itself at any moment. He could not remember the last time he had been in church, but it felt right to pray a little, under his breath.

He became conscious of the front door opening, heavy footsteps crossing the floor. He knew before he opened his eyes that Wally Vincent stood before him, towering like a hunter animal about to fall upon its prey.

Vincent said, "You comin' easy, or have I got to put the cuffs on you?"

Jim Ed stammered. He could not bring out an answer.

Vincent grabbed one of Jim Ed's wrists, then the other, clamping handcuffs over them. "You comin' now, or have I got to cold-cock you?"

Jim Ed pleaded, "At least wait till I know about my grandfather."

"We ain't waitin' for nothin'." Vincent's eyes had the look of a hawk. "I got enough now to send you off to work for the state for two or three years, boy. Resistin' a lawful command, attackin' an officer of the law, attempted murder . . ."

Jim Ed's ears roared. "Attempted murder?"

"You taken my pistol and tried to shoot me with it."

"I didn't try to shoot you."

"You held it on me. I got plenty of witnesses. Time you get out of jail, boy, that old granddaddy of yours'll have a beard plumb down to his feet." He took hold of the short chain between the cuffs and yanked hard. "Come on!"

Jim Ed tried to turn, to see if somebody would not come out from behind those double doors and help him, or at least tell him something. But Vincent dragged him outside, pitched him into the backseat of the black car and sped off to the jail. For the first time in years, Jim Ed bowed his head and cried.

The jail was probably eighty years old, but a state law required that it and others like it be kept to an ever-tightening set of standards. The cell had a toilet and washbasin. Jim Ed was able to wash the blood from his swollen face, though the effort seared the lacerated skin. His right eye, almost closed, throbbed with a vengeance. He sat hunched on the hard mattress in a black and smothering despair.

He listened for footsteps that might mean news, but the jail was as quiet as a church. So far as he could tell, it housed but one other inmate, in another cell. The man appeared to be a wetback, probably on storage here for safekeeping until the Immigration Service could pick him up and deport him to Mexico. The man spoke a few words to him in Spanish, but Jim Ed's command of that language was slight. Effort at communication was soon abandoned. Jim Ed sat in a brooding silence, remembering the agonized look upon his grandfather's face as he had sunk to the sidewalk.

"God," he whispered, "please watch over him."

The cell gradually darkened as night came on, and it remained dark until someone flipped a switch that lighted a dim bulb on the ceiling between the barred cells. Jim Ed gave up and stretched out upon the mattress, but he did not sleep. He kept seeing his grandfather, hearing his voice, sharing the old man's desperation.

He became aware, finally, of a key rattling in the outer bullpen door. He raised up, trying to focus his vision. The right eye was swollen shut. Wally Vincent approached his cell.

"Rise and shine, boy!" The anger was gone from Vincent's voice. He sounded almost happy. He sought out a key from a large ring and unlocked the cell door. "Come on out of there."

Jim Ed pushed shakily to his feet. He found his ribs hurting and tried to remember when the sheriff had struck him there. "My grandfather," he said. "What about my grandfather?" He held his breath.

"The old bastard is too mean to kill," Vincent said. "He's already settin' up and takin' nourishment."

Jim Ed let the breath go. "Thank God." He grasped one of the bars for support.

Vincent tapped his foot impatiently. "If you ain't comin' out, I'll shut the door again and let you spend the night."

Jim Ed straightened a little. "I've been bailed out?"

Vincent said, "I've decided to be generous. There ain't goin' to be no charges after all."

Suspicion burned like poison. "How come?"

"When your granddaddy came around, we had us a little talk. We made us a little deal."

Jim Ed suddenly knew what the deal had been. His stomach burned. "You blackmailed him!"

"Go throwin' that word around and you could find yourself back in here so quick it'd make your head spin."

"It's spinning now," Jim Ed said disgustedly. "You had him beat anyway, if you'd just been patient."

"Patience is for old people. I never did like to stand around and wait. If you're comin', come on. If you're not, you can share this place with Pablo tonight."

As Jim Ed walked outside, he saw Orville Levitt and Bill Roper waiting, their shadows long in the light of the street lamp overhead. Both stepped forward to meet him. Roper bent and peered closely at Jim Ed's face. His voice quivered with anger. "Orv, we've got to do somethin' about that."

"The doctor'll fix him up."

"That ain't what I mean. It's time we see to it that Wally Vincent is retired for good from the county payroll."

Levitt said bitterly, "That won't bother him much, now that he's got what he wants."

Jim Ed demanded, "What about my grandfather?"

Levitt said, "He'll be all right. We got that pill down him in time, you and me."

"Not me," Jim Ed said. "*You* saved his life."

Levitt shrugged. "He saved mine a time or two, back in our cowpunchin' days. Come on, he wants to see you."

Roper took them to the doctor's clinic in the C Bar pickup. The doctor met them in the lobby. He studied Jim Ed's face with dismay. "Your grandfather needs to sleep now, but he won't until he sees you. Don't stay long. When you come out, I'll do something about your face."

Jim Ed was surprised to find his father sitting in a chair beside Wes's bed. Truman arose quickly. Like everyone else, he examined Jim Ed's face and muttered about Wally Vincent.

Wes's cheeks were drained and his eyes were dull, but he did not look half so bad as Jim Ed had expected. Wes said in a thin voice, "Wally don't miss a chance, does he?"

Jim Ed cried, "You shouldn't have done it. You shouldn't have given up to him on my account."

Wes had the hopeless look of a man who had surrendered without condition. "I'd lost anyhow. Maybe Ol' Snort was an omen. I knowed for sure in John Talcott's office. It was just a question of time." He reached out a hand, and Jim Ed took it. "I'd've done anything to get you out of that jail. No tellin' what Wally'd've done to you if I'd left you in there."

"You've signed the papers?"

"I will tomorrow. I gave my word."

Truman said, "Papa has agreed to come to Dallas and live with us as soon as he's put his affairs in order."

Jim Ed could see dread rise in his grandfather's eyes. He declared, "Dallas isn't for you."

Wes said painfully, "I don't see that I got a choice. I've played out my last hand, looks like."

Tears burned Jim Ed's left eye. They could not make it past the swelling in the other. *Six months,* he thought. *He won't live six months.*

When the doctor had finished cleaning and painting and patching his face, Jim Ed reluctantly climbed into his father's automobile, and the two started toward the ranch. Jim Ed stared morosely at the lighted dashboard. "You know he never even liked to *visit* Dallas. He'll hate *living* there."

"He'll get used to it. Once he puts that damned old ranch behind him, he'll realize he's a lot better off."

"You can't cut an old tree off from its roots and transplant it. It'll die."

"Lots of old people have had to leave the land and move to the city, especially these last few hard years. They learn. Your grandfather is tougher than you give him credit for."

Jim Ed kept remembering the despair in Wes's eyes. "Tough

enough to will himself to die. You know he threw his heart pills away?"

"Orville told me. But that'll all pass, once he's acclimated to a new way of life. An easier way."

A dependent way, Jim Ed thought. He saw old Grover Cleveland Ransome in his mind's eye, and he shuddered. "I hated this country when I first came here, but it grew on me, like *he* grew on me. I know what it means to him. I think I even understand why. But *you* don't. You always hated it."

Truman kept his eyes on the narrow arc of ranch road illuminated by the headlights. He stopped for a cow and calf that had bedded down on the flat caliche surface. The cow moved quickly, but the calf stood and stared in confusion at the headlights until Truman honked the horn. He said, "I ought to have been born in the city. I never did fit here. In Papa's sight I couldn't do anything right when it came to cattle and horses. Even sheep wouldn't pay any attention to me.

"James Edward was the cowboy. He could do anything he set his mind to. Everything *I* tried turned into a wreck. Papa always held James Edward up as an example to remind me of my short-comings. I just couldn't be the hand *he* was. I wasn't born that way. I just counted the years it was going to take me to go out on that highway and never come back.

"But I owe Papa. He drove me into finding a trade, and making myself a professional at what I did. He never would stand for anything less. It's probably a good thing that I never was a good cowboy. If I had been, I'd probably still be on one of these old ranches working for house, groceries and six hundred dollars a month. Some of us are born to be one thing and some another. We can't change that."

Jim Ed said bitterly, "We both know what Wes Hendrix was born to. And now they've taken it away from him."

He slept little, reliving over and over the nightmare that the previous day had been. Truman had made an appointment to meet John Talcott at the clinic at nine-thirty and carry the papers in for Wes to sign. Talcott's secretary was there to notarize the event, witnessed by Orville Levitt and the doctor.

Jim Ed thought Wes's color was better, though defeat remained a sickness in the old gray eyes. Wes said nothing more than was necessary to answer questions. After signing with a shaking hand, he turned toward the wall.

Levitt's face was as sad as Wes's. "I'm sorry, Wes. I wouldn't've had it this way atall."

Wes said in a strained voice, "If you-all don't mind, I'm awful tired."

Jim Ed stayed a moment after the others left the room. He squeezed Wes's hand. "I'm sorry too."

"Don't be blamin' yourself. It'd've happened the same without you. Like I told you once, it ain't just the land; it's the memories tied to it. Maybe keepin' the memories alive costs more than we can afford to pay. You seen the way it was with Ol' Grover. The past is fine to visit, but it could be a prison if you was to let yourself get trapped there like he is. Now go along, boy, and let me rest."

Jim Ed walked out into the clinic lobby, where the others talked quietly among themselves. He realized someone was missing. "Where's Wally Vincent? Why isn't he here to crow?"

Orville Levitt glanced at John Talcott and smiled thinly. "Wally's *eatin'* crow today, I think. Seems that lake won't be doin' him much good after all."

Talcott nodded. "Faye Vincent was waiting when I opened my office this morning. She wanted me to start divorce proceedings. It seems she caught Wally after midnight in a bed not his own."

Jim Ed thought he knew. "Stella Tenney."

Talcott nodded. "Odd thing. Faye had received an anonymous telephone call that her husband would be going to Stella's. She took Noreen Levitt for a witness. They sat in her car and watched him go in the back door. They waited a little while, then walked into the bedroom and switched on the lights. The evidence was beyond challenge."

Levitt's smile broadened. "Noreen said the sight was too scandalous to talk about, but she kept me up all the rest of the night, talkin' about it."

Jim Ed said, "Wonder know who telephoned the tip?"

Talcott replied, "It was a young woman's voice. Faye said she would swear the woman sounded like Stella herself, but of course that doesn't make sense."

Levitt looked toward the double doors. "At least Wally won't profit from your grandfather's sacrifice. By inheritance the ranch belongs to Faye, not to Wally. And he'll play hell winnin' another election. That ought to be some satisfaction to Wes."

"It's some to me," Jim Ed said, rubbing his hand gently across his sore and swollen face. "But my grandfather has still lost."

Glory B. and Hallie Roper brought Lavinia Dawson home to the big house at C Bar headquarters two days later. Glory B. telephoned Jim Ed. "When're you taking Wes home to the ranch?"

"This afternoon. The doctor says it's safe."

"Could you bring him by here on the way? Gram wants to see him. And I want to see *you.*"

"I don't think you want to see me right now," he told her. "I look terrible."

"We heard. Come anyway. You might find it worth your while."

He puzzled for a long time over how she meant that.

Truman was dubious, but Wes and Jim Ed overruled him. Jim Ed put his father's Buick through the decorative arch and onto the road to the C Bar headquarters. Truman was full of admonitions as he opened the car door for Wes. "Now, Papa, you walk slowly. Jim Ed and I will help you up those steps. You don't want to exert yourself."

Wes shook off his son's assistance. "I've walked on my own two feet ever since I was a yearlin'!"

Jim Ed helped him anyway, when they reached the steps. Glory B. met them on the porch and threw her arms around Jim Ed. Truman stared. No one had prepared him for that. Glory B. moved back a step to regard Jim Ed's face with misgivings. "That *is* going to heal, isn't it? That's not a face I'd want to look at for the rest of my life."

Hallie Roper held the screen door open and welcomed Wes with glad words and a light kiss on the cheek. Bill Roper waited in the parlor, his big hand outstretched to Wes. "You gave us a bad scare," he said. He took the opposite side from Jim Ed. Between them, they supported Wes up the stairs despite his protest that he could travel for himself.

At the top, Glory B. took Wes's arm. "Gram is waiting to see you." She escorted him into her grandmother's bedroom. Hallie Roper raised her hand, signaling Jim Ed and Truman and Bill to wait a little. In a moment Glory B. was back in the hallway. She said, "They'll be more at ease if we leave them alone a few minutes."

Jim Ed noted that his father betrayed no surprise. He must have known, all these years.

After a time, Wes opened the door. "Livvy wants everybody to come in."

Livvy Dawson's face was drawn and pale, but her eyes showed that a strong will for life still lingered. Whatever was coming, she was meeting it head-on, without a whimper. She grasped Jim Ed's hand and, like everybody else, had something to say about the deplorable condition of his face.

She shifted her attention back to Jim Ed's grandfather. "Wes, I've had a lot of time with nothing to do except think. It saddens me that you've signed away your ranch."

Wes shrugged darkly. "I didn't have no choice."

"I hear they're paying a good price for it."

"Some things, money can't make up for."

"It can make up for a lot if you put it in the right place. You know the financial shape *this* ranch is in, I suppose."

Wes frowned. "I've never pried."

Lavinia looked at Glory B., and love warmed her eyes. "I've had a good life. I have but one real regret in leaving it. I regret that I can't pass my father's ranch on to Glory B. in as strong a shape it was left to me."

Glory B. gently placed her hand on her grandmother's pale forehead. "Gram . . . it doesn't matter."

"It *does* matter, a lot." Lavinia's gaze went back to Wes. "Old friend, you could help me."

"How? I can't even help myself."

"The money you'll get for your ranch wouldn't pay off what we owe, but it would give Glory B. a firmer foundation to build from."

"You want to borrow it?" Wes swallowed. "It's yours."

"Not borrow it." Lavinia reached for his hand. "We've had a lot in common over the years, Wes. One thing, we've both loved that old Liveoak Camp."

Wes could only nod.

She said, "I'll sell it to you, Wes. It won't be the same as *your* place, but maybe it'll serve."

Wes's jaw dropped. "You'd sell me Liveoak Camp?"

"For Glory B.'s sake, so she can save the rest."

Truman cried, "Papa, no . . ."

Wes's gray eyes began to come alive. "Liveoak Camp." He spoke the words reverently, as he had the first day Jim Ed had come. "But it was your daddy's place. It'd be a pity to let it go out of your family."

Lavinia turned to Glory B. and Jim Ed, whose arms were around one another. "I have a feeling it won't be far out of the family."

Truman argued, "But, Papa, you'd just be trading one old wornout ranch for another. You're not in condition to take care of a place like that by yourself anymore."

Lavinia put in, "Bill and Hallie have been looking for an investment of their own to go along with their work here. If you took Bill in as a partner on the livestock, Wes, you'd have all the help you need."

Wes trembled with rising excitement, enough so that Jim Ed was glad Orville Levitt had given him a new bottle of pills to carry in his pocket. Wes's gaze went to Bill Roper. "It could be a poor investment. You know the shape the cow business is in."

Roper said eagerly, "It'll get better. I laid awake all last night, hopin' you'd say yes."

Hallie took her husband's arm. "When *he* doesn't sleep, *I* don't sleep. Please let us do it, Wes."

Wes walked away and stared out the window. He wiped a hand across his eyes before he let anyone see his face. He turned back to Truman. "Son, much obliged, but I don't believe I'll be needin' your spare bedroom after all."

Truman argued, "Papa, you'll die out there one of these days!"

Wes nodded. "I couldn't pick a better place to do it." Leaning over Lavinia, he grasped both of her hands and kissed them. "Livvy, you're a blessed woman."

"I'm a *business*woman. I know a good deal when I see it, that's all." Her eyes were soft, shining in the memory of long ago. "I'm tired now. If you-all don't mind, I'll rest awhile."

Hallie Roper walked to the windows and pulled the shades to darken the room. Then she went out with her husband and with Truman, who was still shaking his head. Glory B. and Jim Ed paused at the door to look back. Wes lingered by Lavinia's bedside. He was holding her hands.

Glory B. led Jim Ed to a window at the end of the hall. Through it, he could see the limestone hills stretching to the west, one after another after another, turning blue as the sun lowered behind them. Glory B. said, "Times change. People come and people go, but those old hills stay the same. However mixed up or troubled I may get, I can look at them and recover my perspective. They're timeless."

Jim Ed had not thought of them as an emotional anchor. "I suppose."

"My great-grandfather Chatfield would have cussed anybody who accused him of being a romantic. But I like to think he put this house just where it is so his family would always be able to draw strength from this view. Four generations of us have stood here and looked out this window."

"You won't be the last," he said.

"Damned right I won't. I made an ironclad promise to Gram that there'll be other generations here after me."

"You'll need help to get those other generations started."

"Do you have anyone in mind?"

"I've got a wasted semester to make up. After that, I'll apply for the job if you can find some use around here for an inexperienced business manager."

She leaned to him, clutching his arm as she stared out the window. "Stick with me, pilgrim, and you'll *get* the experience."